Rozalia Alone

Rozalia Alone

Rosita Fanto

Rosita Fanto

ALSO BY ROSITA FANTO
PRESAGE
THE OSCAR WILDE PLAYING CARDS
WITH RICHARD ELLMANN
ULYSSES A VAUDEVILLE
THE JAMES JOYCE CARDS
HOPE—MOODS—
ESCAPE—MOODS—
JOKER'S JOY
LADY OF THE CARDS

Copyright © 2010 by Rosita Fanto.

Library of Congress Control Number:		2010901937
ISBN:	Hardcover	978-1-4500-4247-5
	Softcover	978-1-4500-4246-8
	Ebook	978-1-4500-4248-2

This is a work of fiction. Names, characters, places and incidents either are the product of the author's imagination or are used fictitiously, and any resemblance to any actual persons, living or dead, events, or locales is entirely coincidental.

This book was printed in the United States of America.

To order additional copies of this book, contact:
Xlibris Corporation
1-888-795-4274
www.Xlibris.com
Orders@Xlibris.com
75405

For my Brother Alfredo

When William Faulkner accepted the Nobel Prize in 1950, he said, in part: "I believe that man will not merely endure, he will prevail. He is immortal, not because he alone among creatures has an inexhaustible voice, but because he has a soul, a spirit capable of compassion, sacrifice and endurance."

BOOK I

I

I speak seven languages fluently with the wrong accent in each one of them. I am frequently asked, why seven languages? But it could not be any other way. I was born in a town on the Delta of the Danube in a Central European country. How far could I go with just one language? Frontiers are only a few hours away. Another language, another mentality, another temperament, another climate, geographically and politically speaking.

After nine months of meditation in mother's womb, I am bored. Nothing is going on. No sonography. No e-mail. No fax. No mobile phone. No TV. No PC. I cannot wait another forty years to have it all, and I decide that it is time for me to enter the outside world. To emphasize my rebellion and my utter dislike for set rules, I slalom out of the maternal pouch backward, and the midwife in attendance exclaims, "IT is almost here! Give IT another push! IT doesn't show its head! Good God, such a darling little arse!" But IT, undecided, makes a stop. Let them wait. Do they expect a boy or a girl? Shivering between in and out, I finally emerge. I don't give the normal baby cry . . . I save my breath, and cry without making a sound. There is so much yelling and shrieking going on anyway. Towels, hot water, and so on. All that slimy slippery blood and then, "Oh! It's only a girl." When she sees me, mother

says, "Oh no!" A nurse wipes mother's forehead and combs
her hair. I guess she's right. Babies are only digestive tubes.
Mother takes another look at me. "God, she's ugly! How odd
she looks. Where did she get that black hair? Can you see how
she winks with both eyes? Her face is terribly red. I can't stand
it! Get her away from me!" She bursts into tears.

It is understandable that, after such a long labor and a most
antagonistic first encounter, and with the disappointment that
I am of the wrong sex, I am not my mother's sweetie pie. Not
experienced enough to play it safe and be androgynous, I am
ready to give up on my parents when a man with a slight odor
of tobacco takes me in his arms, presses me gently against
his face, kisses my forehead, laughs, and dances around and
around, holding me close to his heart. He sings, "You are my
love. You are my first. You are my only one!" It is Father. It is
five thirty in the morning. And he already fills in the forms for
the life insurance policy. Such a huge amount.

By ten o'clock, people arrive. The room is full of flowers.
Roses. Exhausted, mother leans against large, clean, lacy
pillows. The white linen sheets smell of fresh laundry. I am
wrapped in a dry warm cloth. A soft light plays on the silk
blanket that covers my pretty little cot next to the big bed.
Refreshments are served to Mother's family, to Father's family.
Mother is the youngest of six children, an orphan. My Aunt
Josephine, her sister, recently ordained a Catholic nun after
her fiancé, a doctor, died or abandoned her, leans over me,
kisses my hand, makes the sign of the cross, and mumbles a
prayer. Another sister, Giselle, is there, staring at me. She has
traveled five hours to be next to her beautiful little sister, my
mother, Anca, who at twenty-four has just had her first child.
Unfortunately only a girl. Father's family is also on hand. Two
sisters, Tony and Hany. One brother, Carol. One grandfather,
Avram. No grandmother shows up. They both died long ago,
one from diabetes, the other from cancer. The name of the

maternal grandma was Marie Rose. The name of the paternal grandma was Roza. So instead of IT, I am named Rozalia.

There is plenty of confusion. Father, whose name is Dan, is Jewish. In certain Central European countries Jews are not citizens. They only have the right to have an identity card stamped by the local police. In 1919, at twenty-five, father applied for his citizenship according to the new law issued that year by which someone of mosaic religion could then become a citizen of Romania. Mother comes from a Christian family of Greek-Orthodox landowners. When both her parents died, her tutor—trustee-executor, a very conservative honest man, sold the land and invested the proceeds in solid, secure bonds of the Russian Empire. In 1918, with the communist revolution and the New Soviet regime, the bonds became worthless. The Soviets did not recognize the Czarist, capitalistic Russian debt. The bonds can only be used as wallpaper. Fortunately, by now, the trustee-guardian's wards have finished their education and are of age. They are also very good-looking. The girls are even ravishingly beautiful, with the exception of Matilda who is slightly cross-eyed and looks like a dachshund. However, she is well taken care of, married for years to a good man who sold the bonds from his wife's dowry way before the collapse in Russia and successfully invested the proceeds in real estate. Anca, my mother—the youngest, the prettiest, and the liveliest—married father, who at twenty-seven is already making a very good living in his store. Jews can't own land or be gentlemen farmers. They can only pursue a profession or have a commercial activity.

II

Schwester ("sister" in German) Elizabeth, my nurse, smells of detergent. She is a big woman with smiling blue eyes. When she sings German lullabies with an Austrian accent, she tickles me so that I can smile at her too. Sometimes she takes me in her arms to show me the newborn piglets in our backyard. One is bigger than the rest, very pink, and it makes high-tech musical noises. I name the piggy Tannenbaum. I am told it will have a red apple in its mouth for Christmas.

When Schwester Elizabeth takes me out in my pram, she wears a long navy blue scarf on her head, with a thin white border nipped at her neck and a navy blue cape over her white uniform. Once a week she leaves me for a couple of hours at the convent, where my Aunt Josephine is called Sister Marie Josephe. I am very impressed by my aunt's attire. A long black veil over a kind of white hood frames her scrubbed face. Only her hands emerge from the large, loose, long-to-the-floor black gown she wears. Like Schwester Elizabeth, she is also called Sister, in French, *Ma Soeur*. She has many sisters who dress like her. Some are called Mother. One is called Mother Superior. Soeur Marie Josephe talks to me only in French. She has brown eyes, a turned-up nose, and full lips. I recognize her because she does not lower her head all the time like the other nuns do. Usually she takes me into the parlor and speaks to me in a very low voice. She always sits in the same tall chair under a copy of Leonardo da Vinci's painting *Last Supper*.

One day, while I am peacefully resting on her knees, she pulls out from under her many layers of long skirts a package wrapped in white tissue paper tied with a pink silk ribbon and lays it on the table next to her. Holding me over her shoulder, she goes to the door, closing it without a sound. Then she draws the curtains over the window that faces the internal court. She starts to undress me. Her rosary beads and the cross dangle to and fro. I am greatly amused by the novelty of this game. I "Bla, Bla, Goo, Goo," a few times to show my joy. I put the rosary in my mouth and suck on it wildly. I am about to go for the cross, hoping for a sweeter flavor, when Aunt Josephine, Sister Marie Josephe, opens the parcel. Out comes a white dress with rows and rows of white lace and a matching bonnet. She slips the long camisole over my head, on top of which comes the long lacy embroidered dress. After fitting the bonnet on my head, she ties the bow under my chin. Then, she draws the curtains apart and looks at me.

"Pride is a sin. But you are a princess!" she says. "Rozalia, my darling, shh, quiet!" And she covers me with a blanket.

For the first time I see her lowering her head while she carries me in her arms across the inner court toward the chapel. The door is slightly ajar. We enter. The chapel is cold, heated only by candlelight. A priest is there, as if he has been waiting for us.

Father Christoforu wears a shorter white lacy overall to cover his black frock. He takes us to a tall gray basin half-filled with water. Aunt Josephine sticks her finger in it.

"It's freezing," she says. "Please, Father, have the Holy Water heated a bit."

She removes my bonnet. Father Christoforu interrupts his prayer. His eyes roll up to Virgin Mary who looks down at us from her niche.

"It's Holy Water, my child, how can it hurt anyone?"

"But, Father, if she catches a cold, I am in trouble."

"Don't you have any faith in God Almighty?'

"I do, Father, and I know that to argue with a priest is a sacrilege." She clutches me to her bosom. "But if you can't have the Holy Water heated, the girl's soul is in danger because she'll never be baptized."

So the priest nods to the altar boy, who goes behind a door and returns with heated Holy Water that is twice blessed. Again, Aunt Josephine sticks her finger in the baptismal font and blows a couple of times on the container before the priest pours it on my head. It feels nice.

Now Aunt Josephine, Soeur Marie Josephe, is my godmother. This is our big secret. My christening day is an even bigger secret.

*   *   *

I am almost four years old. By now I have a brother, Odo, two years old. I am in the garden under the oak tree next to the swing. I push him on the swing high up to the sky. He is laughing. He has a dimple on each side in his pink cheeks, blue eyes, curly gold hair. He has father's coloring. He is mother's sweetheart. When Schwester Elizabeth takes us out, people on the street stop to look at Odo and say what a beautiful child he is. I am usually ignored. Besides Father, Aunt Josephine, and Schwester Elizabeth, who are leaving us in another month, nobody pays much attention to what I am doing.

I look like Aunt Josephine, says mother, her mouth turned down. Mother looks like no one. She is a beauty in her own right. Mother comes home from shopping. She carries two stuffed animals. She shouts at me to stop pushing Odo so high on the swing. She gives Odo a teddy bear and me a monkey. She says I wear her out and that the monkey looks just like

me. I am not upset. I think of Tannenbaum, the pink piggy.
He's gone. He's been gone for three years. Now behind the
tree is a wired enclosure with five hens and a cock. We know
we are not allowed to go in there. Every morning, Odo and
I stand on the other side of the wired fence and are given a
freshly laid egg pierced at both ends. From the slightly larger
hole we suck out the white and the yoke of the warm raw
egg. It is supposed to make us strong. We also eat toasted
bread smeared with bone marrow, for our teeth. We rinse
our hair with chamomile or vinegar. If we have a pimple on
our eye, fresh hot urine on a pad should heal it. And it does.
There are other remedies for all sorts of accidents. Everybody
knows about them.

When we go on picnics and we smell hay and cow dung,
we hand our cups to the peasant who milks the cow. The
milk jets straight from the udder into our cups. Odo drinks it,
licking the white mustache on his mouth. I hate to drink this
warm buttery white liquid which is supposed to be good for
me. I take a small sip, turn my back on the cow, and spit it
out. Sometimes I am seen and then I never hear the end of
it, about hungry children and how ungrateful I am. And as
if that's not enough, how I'll have no teeth when I grow up.
No teeth will grow back when I lose mine, even if I put them
under the pillow at night.

III

Once in a while Ilona, the Hungarian servant, has a black eye. She says that Janos, her husband, beats her on Saturday nights when he comes home from the *carciuma* (the pub). Grownups are funny. Not ha-ha but peculiar. I hear Mother say that Aunt Josephine is wacky. But she never has a black eye or a bruise on her lips and she is such fun.

We sit at the kitchen table. I hear Ilona telling Schwester Elisabeth about the neighbor being so dumb that she must have been conceived by a candle instead of the normal way. I ask what is normal. Schwester laughs, and then takes a spoonful of chocolate cake. As she swallows the last bit, she puts her glasses on her forehead and, shaking her head, says there is also a possibility that the neighbor has been masturbating since childhood. She adds that a lot of masturbating makes people dumb. I immediately ask what is masturbating. Schwester answers that it is to play with yourself. "Doing what?" I ask. She puts a slice of the chocolate cake on my plate, clears her throat, *hum hm hm*. "Touching one's *pipi*," she replies. I think for a few minutes, looking at the chocolate cake. I am not going to eat it until I clear up the mystery. I am puzzled because everybody's *pipi* is different. "Odo's *pipi* is different from my cousin Nicu's *pipi*. They are both boys. Why?" I ask. Schwester Elisabeth answers, lowering her voice, "Odo's is circumcised." I ask more questions about circumcision. Then I am told to go to my room, to bed, for a nap. I climb into bed, slide under the sheet, and think very hard. I am confused. How can I try circumcision on myself? It seems complicated. Maybe I can try to masturbate. So I put a small pillow way up between my legs and pretend I am riding a donkey. I move and move. My eyes are tightly shut. I see myself dancing on tiptoe with the satin ballet shoes Aunt Josephine gave me for Christmas. I whirl around on my toes until I am up in the air. With my arms, I swim toward the sky. A very happy feeling takes hold of me. I move faster and faster. My heart is pounding wildly. *Boum boum boum.* I am all sweat. Now I lie quietly, waiting to turn into an idiot. But I only feel nice and pleased with myself and a little hungry. I keep my eyes closed and wait some more. Nothing. Maybe nothing happens right away. Maybe it takes some time. I must try again. I am so looking forward to becoming an idiot.

When I open my eyes, father is sitting on a chair next to my bed and, with a towel, he wipes my forehead. He takes me in his arms, holds my hand, and says, "You charmer, you definitely are my little girl. We'd better take your clothes off and change into something pretty." He helps me undress, shakes talc on me, and hands me the blue dress. I am dry and feel happy to be with Father. Whenever he comes home from work, he pays attention to me, his little girl, and he talks to me like to a grown-up. No baby talk.

Odo is asleep in his bed. The bed has bars, and I am not allowed to put them down when he's asleep. He is on the other side of the room and has lots of stuffed animals sitting on shelves. And now that Schwester Elizabeth is leaving, I will take care of him. Though he is my only brother, he is my favorite because nobody has dimples like his. He always hugs me, and at night, when he wakes up and starts singing, I let him sleep in my bed.

Father takes my hand and we walk to the sitting room. The fire is ablaze. The mantelpiece is covered with framed pictures of family members. I like the one of mother and father on their wedding day. They are all dressed up and look funny and stiff. We sit down on the burgundy velvet settee. Father lights a cigarette and blows a few smoke rings. I follow the smoke until it disappears. It's what we call our voyage to the stars. He says it's impossible to touch a star, but it's important to try and reach it. He strokes my head and tells me we will be moving into a new house in Bucharest, the capital, where the schools are better. I will have a room of my own, and Odo will have his. We will have a garden. Ilona and her husband Janos are also coming. I am pleased. Ilona will be doing the housework. I was worried about who would take the carpets and the mattresses outdoors and beat them. Janos will take care of the garden and make deliveries. I ask about the store, and Father tells me he will have a larger one. He will be selling yards and yards of fabric, and in a few years I can go with him to the store and help him do the bookkeeping. I say I like books and I can hardly wait to be with father all day long.

IV

In Bucharest, I have spent only one week at boarding school with the nuns of Notre Dame de Sion, and I catch scarlet fever. The nursing is not great so I end up with rheumatic fever and I have to be careful for the rest of my life. Heart and joints. Aunt Josephine hugs me, telling me I am as important to her as Jesus is, or maybe just right after him, and she gets angry with the nuns. She says that if I am not a very strong child it's because the nuns made me take my bath dressed in a long nightgown—my body should never be seen naked, not even by myself. She mumbles that a child with fever can take a bath without staying in a wet gown while waiting to get into dry clothes. She also blames the nuns for waking me up at dawn, sick as I was, to prepare the host which, at communion, the priest places on my tongue. I am told to swallow the blood and body of Jesus. Sometimes it gets stuck to the roof of my mouth, and I keep asking how the body of Jesus can be in a wafer I made with my own hands that same morning? I ask a lot of questions.

After my scarlet fever, I don't go to school anymore, instead I have private lessons at home. So I can be sick all the time and pass exams at the end of each year. I keep skipping grades and soon I am seeing only girls older than myself.

It's September and I am nine years old. The air is mild, the sun slants through the yellow reddish leaves on the tree in front of my window. Aunt Josephine has long ago left the order. Now she lives not too far away from us in a three-room walk-up apartment. The walls of every room, including the bathroom and the kitchen, are covered with books. There are many dictionaries on unexpected subjects. She tells me that her time is spent reading, studying, translating books and articles when she is not giving private lessons in French, English, German, Italian. Also Piano, Philosophy, Science. When I come to see her and she is working with a student, I sit on a chair by the door and listen enraptured until the lesson is finished. Then she makes tea in a samovar and puts a silver spoon in a glass with a silver handle, so that the glass does not break when she pours the boiling tea. Two lumps of sugar and a thin slice of lemon. She puts a slice of my favorite home-baked cake on a plate with tiny hand-painted flowers. Now I am ready to start the journey into the mind's wonderland. It's impossible to be bored while she piles so many gifts in the drawers of my brain. "Open up and let knowledge creep in," she tells me. "A whole library to carry with you forever." She doesn't play stupid games with me like other grown-ups do. Aunt Josephine talks to me like no one else does.

"There are many roads to choose from," she tells me. "You, Rozalia, will have to decide which one to take." Her hand lingers on my head as she looks me in the eye and lowers her voice. "Beware, my child, of ready-made ideas. Check things out on your own." Then she puts a spoonful of rose-petal sherbet in a glass of water next to an open book by Schopenhauer. I lick the sherbet off the spoon while she talks about pessimism and then explains Nietzsche in German. She does not neglect Goethe either.

By the time I am eleven, I am deeply involved in French literature with Corneille, Racine, Moliere, even Lamartine, Rimbaud, and Verlaine's poetry. She reads Homer with me, the "Iliad" and the "Odyssey." Somewhere in between we read Shakespeare's plays and Marlowe. She wants me to learn Ancient Greek and Latin. But I am not particularly keen on dead languages and grammar. I don't mind Latin, but Ancient Greek is too dead for me. "Greek makes me think of rattling skeletons," I tell Aunt Josephine. So we read Plato's Republic in English. She does not neglect science, either. Whenever we have to interrupt our talks because of a student waiting for his lesson in the other room, she leaves me with Scientific Dictionaries, instructing me to look things up and try to work out solutions to problems.

There are days when Aunt Josephine just sits with me and we laugh. We eat and laugh about anything that comes into our minds. We stuff ourselves with cakes and sandwiches and do not care anymore about Schopenhauer and the likes of him.

Once a week, in the afternoon, Father takes a box at the Opera. Odo and I sit in front of Mother and Father. I look forward to those afternoons. My head is turned in such a way that I can see both the stage and Father's face. His lips move to every word in the libretto. His hands accompany the beat of the music. The arias in *La bohème, Tosca, La traviata,* and *Madame Butterfly* make his eyes water.\

Mother sometimes sends us to the movies with Ilona, who sits between Odo and myself. Today we are watching *Tarzan.* The big tiger is running after Tarzan, ready to jump on him. I get very excited and frightened; I really want to stop that tiger. I squeeze a finger and squeeze some more. As soon as Tarzan escapes from the tiger I feel the finger is now longer and the skin on the finger I am squeezing is very smooth. When the lights are turned on, the man sitting next to me has slipped his raincoat over my hand. He asks if I have been very frightened. I don't understand what he is talking about. We get up to leave and we slowly walk out of the movie house. The man rushes past us. He is wearing his raincoat and his fly is wide open. His *pipi* is big and sticking out. I ask Ilona to look at him. I want to know what this is. She tells me it is some dreadful disease some men have. It's like a stiff neck one can't get rid off.

We return home and I tell Mother about the man with the terrible disease. From there on, when we go to the movies, I sit between Odo and Ilona.

There are especially happy moments when, after dinner, Father talks to me by the fire. Odo reads his comic book, lying on the carpet. Mother, reclining on the sofa, lights another cigarette, then turns the remains of the thick Turkish coffee in her cup upside down and tells us what the future has in store. Before the evening is over, Father winds up the record player and we listen to his favorites, like "Rose-Marie I Love You" with Jeanette MacDonald and Nelson Eddy. Sometimes he chooses a record with Lotte Lehmann singing or a Puccini opera with Benjamino Gigli.

V

Mother's and Father's families don't visit us at the same time. When they visit, it is usually for a luncheon that lasts forever. We eat far too much. Afterward, we sit in the garden around a table under the big chestnut tree. Ilona brings the tray with coffee and lemonade. Odo and I listen to the conversation. Whether it is Mother's or Father's family, they only talk about politics. Except Uncle Carol, on whom I have a crush. Tall and thin, he is dashing and self-confident with his hat set at a rakish angle He smokes nonstop, is not married, but has a married woman for his mistress. When he visits us, I dress nicely and look very neat. Uncle Carol is a charmer with every female. He says I look pretty with the way I wear my hair. I blush and my heart beats faster.

My hair is long, thick, and parted in the middle. Mother says it makes my face look like the moon. I like the look of the moon. I can dream up all sorts of escapades. I wear my hair plaited in two pigtails, each fastened at the end with a brown ribbon that I tie behind the opposite ear, like a hammock. So my bun makes a small round cushion on my neck. I am supposed to brush and comb my hair every night before going to bed and every morning. I never do, I can't be bothered. I only plait my hair and tie a clean ribbon on each end. On Saturday I have my hair washed. It's a tragedy. My hair is full of knots, no comb goes through. It gets pulled. I am yelled at. I get slapped. It takes hours for Ilona and Mother to untie the mess. But I like to wear my hair this way. The pigtails look much thicker when they are not brushed and combed. I dream of hiding all sorts of things in my bun the day I run away to a place where the sea is blue and the beaches have no beginning and no end.

I am almost twelve when I go to school again. I am not sick anymore, and I play football with the boys. Odo says I am a great goalkeeper. I seldom let them score a goal. So each team wants me to defend the net. And two of the boys look at me with sweet eyes.

At school I don't have to study much. I pass exams with top grades. I have two good friends, Ada Goldberg and Elena Popescu.

Ada lives in the Jewish part of Bucharest. Their house is between the Synagogue and a kosher shop. Her father is a Rabbi. He always wears something on his head. Odo has a crush on Rachel, his younger daughter. Every time we show up, Ada's mother is in the kitchen preparing delicious meals, gefiltefish, matzoballs, cookies, and cakes. She feeds us as if we are starving. Besides the aroma of pastrami and cabbage and soup, there is much laughter and music. They never stop joking.

Elena lives next to the Greek Orthodox church. Her father is the Popa, the priest. The Popa is dressed in a long black robe and wears a tall black bonnet on his head. He is usually stroking his luxuriant beard and mustache. He sometimes plucks a hair out with two of his fingers and brings it to his nostrils. I watch, fascinated, wondering if he inhales his own odor or whether he enjoys tickling his nostrils with the hair from his beard.

At Easter he asks us to join in the ceremony. The church is warm with flowers, incense, candles, and singing. Afterward we go to the house where a table is set with arrangements of multicolored eggs—red, green, blue, yellow, and orange, with three tall sponge cakes, red wine, salami, and salt. It's all very festive. The best part is when we choose one egg, and with the pointed side we hit the other person's egg saying Christ is resurrected, while the person who holds the egg that's hit and cracked, answers, "It is true! Christ is resurrected!" Of course I cheat, even though it's Easter. With my finger, I cover the part of the egg that risks cracking.

When I meet with Ada and Elena, which is almost every day, we speak mostly about politics. The three of us are very interested in current affairs. We want to solve the world's problems.

In the morning, Father, on his way to the store, walks Odo and me to school. We drop Odo off and then we have our five-minute walk alone. We discuss the country's politics. Father is more worried every day. He says the Iron Guard with its anti-Semitic leader, Codreanu, is increasingly gaining the support of the Romanian people.

Then one day he explains that we are in great danger, that people don't realize what could happen. Too many of them think that Adolf Hitler is just a hoodlum whose influence will pass.

"It's foolish to believe that this is not taking on other proportions," Father insists. "It was an organized upheaval on the Kristallnacht, when the hatred for Jews erupted with such violence, destroying everything in its way. The night the Nazi youth broke windows and torched the shops owned by Jews. It wasn't just hooligans going wild." Father thinks the violence will spread, and it will be best for us to leave Europe for a place where the sun is always shining, where people sing and dance and run barefoot for miles on sandy beaches. And where they don't hate each other.

Mother comes to fetch us from school. First Odo, then me. I like to watch the two of them crossing the street toward me.

She looks so beautiful in her brown velvet suit and hat, her chestnut hair barely showing. It's lunch time and she is all made up. Her lips are crimson red as she smiles, walking in short strides and holding Odo by the hand. The three of us walk to Capsa, or to Dragomir, a fashionable meeting place, bar, restaurant, and delicatessen. We go straight to the counter. A second later, Mr. Vintila comes in. He wears a gray hat and holds a pair of gray leather gloves in his hand. He kisses Mother's hand, pats us on the head, asking how we did at school without expecting an answer, and orders the aperitif. Caviar on toast for the four of us, glasses of champagne for Mother and himself, and fruit juice for Odo and me. After that, we are left on our own while he laughs with mother. When we are finished, Mother orders a cheese, *telemea*, to be wrapped. I am entrusted with the package. After Father, Odo, Mother, and Aunt Josephine, I love cheese the most. Mr. Vintila sees us to his car, a wine-colored Buick with tan leather seats. The driver in dark gray uniform wears a cap and leather boots. He opens the door for us to jump in. Mother lingers another few minutes while Mr. Vintila says something which makes her smile. When the door of the car is closed on us, he tells his chauffeur to drive close to Romulus Street, where our house is, and to drop us at the corner. He never comes with us unless it is the last week of our summer holidays.

Every year, Father, Mother, Odo, and I stay at a hotel close to the beach so that I can have mud treatments to cure my rheumatism, which does not bother me anymore and is long gone. This way, everyone is happy having a vacation on the beach of the Black Sea, and for me, it's not a big deal to be packed daily from top to toe in mud.

After two weeks, Father has to go back home and return to the store. The next day Mr. Vintila arrives, and the only room available in the hotel is the room next to Mother's. There is a door between every room. Odo's room, my room, Mother's, and Mr. Vintila's. Odo and I have a conference, and we agree we must find out if Mother and Mr. Vintila, *hm hm hm*. But how, without raising any suspicion? I have a brilliant idea. After dinner when we bid Mother good night, she tells us she will take a walk to the casino and might be late going to bed. She asks us to close our door to her bedroom and tells us not to wake her up the next morning, she'll meet us later at the beach. Around lunch time.

As soon as she leaves, I pull out one of my long hairs. Odo holds one end and I tie it around and around the knob and the key of the communicating door between Mother's and Mr. Vintila's room. Next day we look for the hair. We don't find it.

VI

King Carol of Romania is with Hitler in Berchtesgaden when Codreanu, the leader of the fascist anti-Semitic Iron Guard Organization, stages a putsch in Bucharest.

He wants King Carol to abdicate and asks for the head of his Jewish mistress Magda Lupescu. Codreanu and other leaders of the green shirts are executed. Hitler is furious, and turns against King Carol. Rioting erupts in Bucharest, orchestrated by the Iron Guard. Mobs march on the Palace demanding the head of Carol and his Jewess. Carol abdicates in favor of his son Michael, and flees the country in the middle of the night on a special train.

1940. We have a cook and a maid. Ilona has left and has returned to her home village. Janos is now an engine driver on a train. On Saturdays he doesn't go to the pub anymore, and he doesn't beat Ilona either. He still visits us every other week. When he comes, he sits at the kitchen table with a bottle of wine, telling stories. He says he was *the one*, the engine driver on the special train ordered to stand ready for King Carol and his mistress, Magda Lupescu, to flee Bucharest at a moment's notice. I ask what happened. He sips more wine, scratches his messy black hair, and twists his unkempt black mustache.

"You should'a seen it," he says. "The train had a saloon car and eight other cars filled with hundreds of trunks."

"Trunks?"

"Them trunks were so full, some cracked open."

"Full?"

"Full of treasures like you never saw. Paintings, jewelry, gold, money all over the floor. Goddammit, there was so much of everything! All the country's money! And two automobiles in the coaches, ready to go." He swigs from the bottle.

"What happened next, Janos?"

"In the middle of the night I, Janos, was the one to drive the train out of Bucharest with King Carol and his mistress on board! Yah Rozalia!"

I clap my hands to encourage him to talk some more.

Then he waves his arms and tells how the Iron Guard found out about the escape and was waiting for them in Timisoara where the train had to stop to take on water for the engine. The train slowed down. Shots were fired. There was danger of Iron Guard men coming on board. Shots shattered the windows of the train and ripped into the woodwork. Magda Lupescu, for safety reasons, got into the bathtub in the royal suite of coaches. King Carol rushed into his mistress's bathroom and sheltered Lupescu's naked body with his own. He, Janos, the chief engine driver, kept his head and went full speed ahead through Timisoara station, risking running out of water. The train streaked passed the Guard. Taken by surprise, the Iron Guard could do nothing. Janos leans across the table and knocks over the empty wine bottle. I can't help asking how come he's here.

"Easy," he says. "When the train gets near the border, I tell Tudor, my friend who shovels coal, to take my place and slow down the train. Then I open the door and shout, you speed ahead full steam, and go, go!" His voice is getting louder. "Then I jump out. Get plenty wind on my face, roll over few times, and here I am." His eyes are unfocused. He shouts and sprays me with his spittle. He then closes his eyes and falls asleep.

Whether he is drunk or sober, his stories are full of adventure and excitement, and I don't mind his spittle.

Odo has his bar mitzvah. He is a young man now. At thirteen, a young man has to learn about sex. Father gives him money and an address. When Odo comes back, he tells me about the grim fifteen minutes' interlude with the prostitute.

I am Odo's best friend, and he confides in me. He says he has a crush on Ada Goldberg's sister Rachel, who is also thirteen. Her red blouse clings to her bosoms and drives him crazy. She is pretty and knows it. She is frequently grounded and has to stay home. Her father, the Rabbi, is old-fashioned and does not like his daughters to lead boys on. No good can come of it, he says.

January 1941. We are not allowed to go out of the house. It's quiet where we live. But the Légionaires, the Iron Guard, are on a three-day killing spree. A Pogrom is on in the Jewish quarter. They burn down Synagogues, rape, and torture women in front of their children and husbands. They go from house to house on the streets. One group of Jews is taken to the Baneasa forest north of Bucharest, and they are shot. Next morning gypsies come to extract the gold fillings from the victims' teeth. They find the bodies lying naked in the snow. News travels fast.

We now whisper when we talk and wonder what we'll do tomorrow. Mother and father are on the telephone in the other room. I hand Odo a bar of chocolate and watch him eating. He sets aside his comic strip book *The Adventures of Paturel*. He puts on his cap and snow boots.

I ask, "Where are you going?"

"To bring Rachel and Ada over to us."

I urge him to stay put, but he says he'll be back within an hour. I try to stop him. He pushes me aside and runs out through the back entrance, leaving the door slightly ajar. By the time I grab a coat and run after him, I've lost him. I am back home. I stand by the window waiting. I wait for an hour. Two hours go by. I go upstairs and tell Mother and Father that Odo has gone out to bring Rachel and Ada to us. Mother faints, and we look for the smelling salts. Father starts smoking one cigarette after another. We wait some more.

The doorbell rings five times. We freeze. Did Odo forget his keys? There are bangs at the door. The lynch mob is here! Father grabs a heavy cane and opens the small round window by the door. Cold air blows in, and he looks out. I can't wait, and I open the entrance door. A nun stands outside. She seems impatient and rushes in. It's Aunt Josephine, reincarnated as Sister Marie Josephe. She holds four crosses, each one dangling on a chain. Without a word, she puts one on Mother's neck, one on Father's neck, one on my neck. Father takes his off.

"Keep it for Odo," he says. "He'll need at least two of these."

"Where is Odo?" she asks.

We tell her what we know.

"God has abandoned us. Let's go, Rozalia! We'll have to find him quickly. I'm certain you know where he is."

She grabs me by my arm.

"Put your snow boots on," she commands. She throws a coat over my shoulders, a scarf on my head, and whisks me out. Father wants to come with us.

"You'll be in the way. Stay here, we are better off without you."

"I want to go with the two of you."

"Certainly not!" says Aunt Josephine.

"I'm coming with you," says Father, almost at the door.

At that very moment, Aunt Josephine, Sister Marie Josephe, bends her knee and gives Father an unsaintly kick right in his crotch. Then she pushes him away.

"You witch!" Father screams.

"A nun with a young girl, a goy," she laughs, "will survive. You stay here with Anca!"

While Father bends down in pain, she closes the door behind her.

"Hurry, Rozalia, we don't have a minute to lose."

Sister Marie Josephe holds my hand and strides along the snowy streets. Too fast for a nun, I tell her. From Strada Romulus, we take Bulevardul Mircea Voda toward the shores of the river Dambovita. We reach Strada Anton Pan with its small secondhand stores, and we see that all the windows are smashed. In the middle of the street, among the broken glass, are buttons, threads, needles, ribbons of every color. A carnival. On Mircea Voda, the same. We are in the Jewish Quarter. The Synagogue is still burning. No Ada, no Rachel, no Odo. Nothing, only desolation. In the Kosher Meat store, everything is upside down. A black dog sniffles at a sausage. Under a red checkered napkin, a hand is moving.

"It can't be true! This is a scene from the *Grand Guignol*, *Le Theatre de la Cruauté*," says Aunt Josephine.

It's getting dark. Between light and shadow. We cautiously approach the red checkered napkin. I lift the cloth. Aunt Josephine helps a young woman to her feet. Her dress is torn, one breast is showing. She raises her head with difficulty. Her face is bruised. Her hands hang helplessly at her side. Between her legs, a thin streak of blood. I take off my woolen scarf to cover her shoulders. She pushes me away and shouts.

"Go to the slaughter house to see what they have done! Savages! Fascists!" She spits into my face.

Then, I know that something terrible is about to happen. The heavy sky is filled with leaden clouds. We run on Calea Vacaresti toward Strada Abatorului. We arrive at the municipal slaughterhouse. Young men in green shirts are outside shouting, "Genuine Jewish Kosher Meat!" They have lit a fire. They are drinking and rejoicing. They won't let us pass. Aunt Josephine steps back and opens a side door. Belts and butcher hooks are hanging on nails. One axe is driven into a short tree stump. A push cart stands in a corner.

With the confusion going on outside, we manage to get through. We stop, horrified at the sight. Naked, mutilated bodies are hanging on butchers' hooks. Some have their bellies slashed, their intestines tied around their necks with the inscription of "kosher meat" on their bodies. Human beings who have gone through all the stages of animal slaughter on a conveyor belt. I close my eyes as tight as I can and hope that when I open them, the nightmare in front of me will have disappeared.

Outside, everything is in motion. Only the hanging bodies are still. I see Odo. I touch his body, cold and naked. I embrace that body. Helpless and desperate, I try to think what he felt before dying. Frozen and naked. Would he have wanted a less spectacular death, the likes of which could not even have happened in the Adventures of Paturel?

Aunt Josephine squeezes my hand. Tears roll down our cheeks. I want to take Odo down. There is a wooden box. I bring it close to where Odo is hanging. I try to reach the hook that holds him by his neck. I can only just touch his stiff, frozen body. I can't reach the hook. With all my might, I try to push Odo up. His body slides through my hands. I find another box to place on top of the first one. Aunt Josephine helps me climb up. Now I have Odo's head against my chest. With both my hands I push and twist him on one side. I am almost there. Then the box moves and I fall down amidst the newspapers and dried blood. When I raise my eyes toward Odo's neck, most of the lower part of the hook is showing. I want Odo down. I want Odo. I cry. I must have Odo's hook! Aunt Josephine steps on the wooden box, lowers Odo and, without a word, hands me the hook. I caress Odo's neck again and again and place the hook in the bun at the back of my neck. I'll keep it there with me, I'll never take it out. I am in terrible pain. A cold wind penetrates every part of me.

Tanks and regular army troops arrive. Arrests are being made. Soldiers take the bodies away. We are told to move on. I ask where they'll take Odo.

"All the bodies will be taken to the morgue," a soldier says. "Families can claim their loved ones there." The way they tell us this, it's as if they expect us to thank them.

VII

Ever since Odo died, Mother says she can't go on living, she can't cope with the loss. She asks me to dress in boys' clothes and wear a cap on my head when I go out. Tilted on one side, just like Odo. I'll do anything she wants so that I'll feel less guilty about her having lost Odo instead of me. We are desperately sad. As the days go by, Mother gets worse. She talks to herself and to Odo. She smells his socks and his shoes. She sits in the dark, her face turned to the wall. She has migraines and frequently throws up.

For hours I stay close to her, hoping she will put her arms around me. But she doesn't. When Father tells her, "Come to bed, Anca, it's late," she answers, "What can I do in bed? All I see is Odo's face, his blue eyes, his curly hair, his dimples." She keeps shaking her head.

A few days later she shouts and cries and tells us she wants to be with her sister Gisella in the country, close to Jassy, the town she came from. We don't know what to do anymore, so we end up doing whatever she wants. Father makes all the arrangements. He buys the ticket and makes sure Gisella will meet Mother at the station in Jassy. I pack her suitcase. The morning before she is to take the afternoon train, she cries and begs us to come with her at least for a few days. She says she can't bear to be without us on this trip. So the three of us board the train for Jassy. It is a nightmare. Mother has fits and keeps hitting her head against the window. We can't stop her. Father takes her in his arms to soothe her. After a few minutes, she starts to hit the door of the compartment with her fists.

Fortunately, there are no other passengers in the compartment. I don't dare to go to the toilet and leave Father alone. When the train stops in a station, Father pulls down the window to buy a few sandwiches and a couple of bottles of water. We feed Mother and hold her hand until we reach our destination.

Gisella, her husband Niculae, their four daughters—Irina, Ioana, Angela, Maria—(cousins I hardly know) are waiting for us at the station in Jassy. The girls are much older than I am and two of them are married, one to a doctor, the other to a landowner. No one recognizes me wearing boy's clothes and a cap on my head. We all embrace and go to their home, and there are tears before we sit down for dinner.

Uncle Niculae discusses with Father the Romanian version of Hitler's Nuremberg Racial Law Decree. It was King Carol's last decree before leaving the country. The decree was The Law Forbidding Marriages between Jews and Romanians of Blood.

Mother listens in silence. We all do. It is unanimously agreed that Mother should spend some time in the country with Gisella, Niculae, and their daughters, while Father would be better off returning to Bucharest where the unrest is less violent than in Jassy. The police and even the army in Jassy are competing with the Germans in their cruelty toward the Jews.

The next day, relieved that Mother will be well looked after, we are getting ready to leave for the station in Jassy, where we will board the train back to Bucharest. We go through the usual good-bye ritual. "Have a safe journey." "I hope to see you again soon." Much kissing. Many embraces. We then look for Mother. Where is she? We open the door of every room. Has anyone seen her going out this morning? No one has. We comb the house all the way to the top floor. We try the attic. She is there, hanging by her neck from a rope. Hanging just like Odo did. Family pictures are scattered on the floor. My heart hurts so much. Father covers my eyes with his hands, takes me in his arms, and cries with hiccups. He wails, "Anca, Anca!"

Uncle Niculae says we should hurry and leave.

"Leave right away! The authorities will have to be informed. I don't want them to find you here. Go now! I'll take care of everything and let you know what happens. Please hurry and leave!"

Father holds my hand as we run out in total despair. We flee on foot, not even knowing which way to go. We are bewildered, confused. Irina catches up with us in her car and offers to drive us to Jassy. She drives through the main street toward the station. There is unrest everywhere, especially in front of the police building. Irina lets us out at the corner of the station's main entrance. A two-minute walk.

We enter the first door we find open. On the rails in front of us there is a long trail of cattle wagons. The station master tells us we are on the wrong quay. To catch the train for Bucharest, we have to go out of the station and reenter through another door. We leave and follow his instructions. We are close to the door we entered, which is wide open. An avalanche of screaming people is being pushed onto us from behind. Jews. We can't get through. More Jews who have been rounded up are violently shoved with bayonets by policemen and soldiers. We are trying to swim against a wave of people. We are now sucked into the middle of this human sea. Father holds my hand and I hang on to him, afraid to be swept away. I hear desperate screams. Nothing coherent, as we all are jammed into padlocked cattle cars.

We roll around for hours. It is hot. There is no air, there are no windows. The doors are sealed shut. Most of the oxygen is sucked out. What's left is replaced by carbon dioxide vapors, perspiration, fumes of urine, vomit, and excrement. Everyone is shouting and screaming and pushing violently, gasping for air. It is pitch dark. Packed like sardines, after two days and one night without water or food in this torrid heat, many people have already lost their minds. Violence erupts in the far corner. I cling to father who is trying to protect me with his body.

I lean against the wall of the wagon and sit on the floor, in the midst of excrement. Someone vomits on my head. I try to remove the gunk from my hair and I feel the butcher's hook. Odo's hook is still in my bun. I push the vomit away with the sleeve of my shirt and untangle the hook. I hold it firmly in my right hand. With my left hand I try to feel where the wooden planks join on the floor. The train moves and I keep losing the crevasse of the planks. Finally, I can feel a bump between my fingers. With the hook I start hitting and pulling and hitting and pulling, not thinking that I could hit my other hand. Father clutches my wrist and takes the hook in his hand. He hits the plank and gives it a hard pull. A strip of wood starts to wobble. The noise of the wagons in motion and the screams cover the noise of the banging. I am soaked. With my fingers I feel a small hole. Father puts the hook in it and lifts the plank enough to make a crack. We can't talk or hear each other. The screaming is unbearable. He pushes my head against the cracked wood, and I take a deep breath. The air I inhale is disgusting but somehow I feel less faint. Father does the same. We take turns.

The train stops. I can't see anything. The roof opens. There are screams of "Water! Water! Water! Air! Air! Please!" We don't move. A soldier with a rifle on his shoulder and a torch in his hands counts the dead. He is slow closing the trap again until another man in a different uniform points a gun at him. Now, a young woman with a big belly is leaning on me. Her child could be born at any moment. There is a whistle and the train moves again, this time backward. I help the young woman to lean down toward the open crack. She tries but she can't, it's impossible to lean down with her big belly. There is no room to move her. Father slips his hand around her, puts her legs on his shoulder, and turns her on one side. He then pushes her head down toward the crack. With one nostril, she gets close enough to take a deep breath. Then another. Then more. Suddenly I feel there is hope. I feel that we'll make it. Two more minutes and she gives up. She shouts, "I can't anymore! To bring a child into this!" Her legs stiffen. The young woman's waters break and we are inundated. She stops breathing altogether. In his rage Father slams the hook against the floor. The crack is bigger now. I can put two fingers in it. We don't want anything to drip through and leave a trace between the rails, the guards will see it. On the other hand, at daybreak, if we survive, the light will come through the hole and will only create more panic and confusion for the victims. Father tears a piece of cloth from the dead woman's shirt and covers the hole. The train goes back and forth, the engine moving into reverse innumerable times between Jassy, Targu Frumos, and Podul Iloaei. There are short distances between each station.

I am dizzy. Father is shaking, and then he goes limp. I clutch his hand with both of mine and pull myself close to him. Every inch of me is glued to him as I tie my belt to his. Then I pass out.

My mind is blurry when the doors of the wagon open and bodies are thrown in a ditch. I cling to Father, afraid to lose him. I am too weak to move or to say anything. The bodies on top are crushing us. I am afraid to move, in case somebody sees us. What if they bury us alive? Horror-stricken at the thought, I push the corpse next to me with my feet, until I can see from the corner of my eye a piece of sky with a star, then two stars. I am about to sneeze when I hear a squealing noise, the sound of the creaky wheels of a wooden cart drawn by a horse. A voice says, "Hay! Hay! Hay!" Then everything stops. While the horse neighs, I stick my face in whatever I can and manage a noiseless sneeze. I hear footsteps, a man's footsteps. I can't see anything in the dark. The man talks to his horse. He uses swearwords I never heard before. Not only relating to a mother's genitals but many colorful ones extending to the entire family, the whole spectrum of humanity, the devil, and God Almighty. In between he exclaims, "Good God! How many shoes! We'd better hurry." He seems to be talking to his horse. "All those watches and rings and clothes we'll carry home! Let's start quickly before the Gypsies come to knock out the gold fillings. Old people have plenty of gold fillings in their teeth. Ha," he spits, "the bastards!" He starts swearing the whole gamut again.

A soldier passes and asks him, "What do you want with this rotten stink?"

"Come to see me in a little while. I'll let you know if I find anything."

"Good luck!"

"See if you can find me a blanket and a bucket of fresh water for my horse." He then laughs, "While I find a watch or two for you."

The soldier is back with the blanket and the water.

"Could you bring another bucket of water?" says the man to the soldier. "Here, keep this watch and take the ring for your woman."

The soldier leaves and I hear the man puff and swear as he removes shoes from the corpses. "Holy Mary!" He throws everything in the bucket.

My mouth is dry and my throat is burning. I am terribly thirsty. I wish I were a shoe. To be in that water for just a second!

"Motherfucker! So much vomit! So much shit!" The man pushes bodies aside. I can hear him throwing things either in the bucket or in the wooden cart. The soldier is back with more water. The man says, "Take that bracelet for your mother." The soldier utters some kind of blessing as he goes away. The man again pushes bodies to one side. He is getting closer. Suddenly he stops and leans down. I hold my breath. Father is on top of me.

"Master Dan! It can't be you!" The man tries to pull him out. But father is stuck to me by his belt. The man cuts the belt with his knife. "Jesus, you're heavy!" he says. "Are you dead? He lights a match and brings the flame close to father's nose. "Let go," he pats father's head, "Start breathing!" Father can't talk. He is limp. I can only see the man's back. He is taking an empty bottle from his cart. He fills it with water from the second bucket and holds it to Father's mouth. He has Father's head in his arms and makes him drink like a baby. The soldier comes back. This time there is someone else with him. The man covers Father with the blanket and puts him in the cart. The water bottle is left next to the horse, that kicks it. The bottle breaks.

The man is in the ditch again. He removes more shoes, then shouts to the two soldiers,

"What a mess! Not even the devil would want to be here!"

The soldiers laugh and leave.

The man lights a match. A few of the bodies that were already piled on one side slip down on me. The man lights another match. He interrupts his task. "What's this scarf doing here?" And, as he tries to untie the scarf Ilona gave me for my birthday, I open my eyes and whisper, "Janos." He holds his hand against my mouth.

"Shut up," he says. He lifts me up, lays me in the cart next to father, next to the shoes, next to the watches, the bracelets, the rings. He dips his dirty handkerchief in water, wipes my face with it, then makes me drink straight from the bucket. I am on all fours, like an animal, with my tongue out. I can drink and drink and drink. I hear soldiers approaching us. Janos covers me and father with the blanket and piles shoes and shirts on top of us. My head is swaying. Father is alive and so am I. The cart jerks over the ruts of an untraveled road. My ears are whistling. Then nothing.

VIII

I come to myself and open my eyes. All I can see is hay. Then a horse, then a goat, then three chickens. Then two eyes reflecting the daylight as if they were the beads of Aunt Josephine's rosary. A mouse.

Ilona appears with a cup of hot coffee and a slice of bread. She tells me to take two buckets of water from the well while she gets a brush and soap to scrub the filth off me. Father is already clean and in the house.

My whole body hurts. I have pains going in every direction, from my hands to my neck to my shoulders to my legs. I can hardly carry the water back from the well. After I scrub myself for a while, Ilona tries to untangle my hair with the dried shit and vomit in it. She keeps throwing water on my hair. She laughs.

"I've been wanting to do this for ages. Remember?" From the pocket of her apron, she takes out a huge pair of scissors and cuts. I look at my long plaits on the wet grass.

"We'll have to dig a hole and bury this in case somebody sees it and wonders where it comes from," she says.

I would like a bird's nest to be made out of my hair. A nest from which a bird could fly away. Fly toward beaches that have no end. But I say nothing, I only smile at Ilona who hands me a clean towel to dry myself. She helps me slip into a peasant skirt and one of her blouses and gives me a pair of wooden soles with large straps for my swollen feet. I can now go into the kitchen with her, she tells me.

Father is sitting on a bench by the table. He looks old and tired. His blond hair is almost gray. I sit next to him and caress his hand. Janos brings in a bottle of wine; and Ilona lays out white cheese, salami, and bread on the table. Father's eyes fill with tears. I try to comfort him, but he does not touch the food. Ilona puts cabbage, carrots, onions, potatoes, and a few bones to cook on the stove, saying that a warm soup will give him strength.

"A glass of wine or a shot of Tuica would be much better," Janos says.

I look out through the open door and see lines of string with clothes drying in the evening sun. So many pieces of clothing hanging, dancing in the wind. All sizes, all colors. Shoes and boots, last night's crop, are spread out on the grass, resting like tired birds. I fix my gaze on the few vine plants heavy with grapes, not yet ripe.

Evening is approaching. I help Ilona wash the dishes, sweep the floor, take the garbage out in the back. I have to go outside to the lavatory. By now it's dark. I light a candle to see where I am going. I open the door to the narrow wooden shack and spread my legs over the hole. With the candle still in my hand, I figure out what to do next without falling in. On my left, squares of newspaper are stuck on a nail. I wipe myself and start to cry.

Ilona insists that I sleep with her, but I'd much rather sleep alone on the straw in the stable. I don't mind the smell of manure. She has prepared hot milk with honey for me to drink before I slide between the sheets next to her. The bed is too warm. The heat reminds me of the train ride and I can't fall asleep. I can see Father, who is lying on a bench by the window. Janos covers him with a warm blanket and puts a pillow under his head. Then Janos locks the door, removes his boots, and throws himself on the bed, still fully clothed. A few minutes later, everyone else is asleep.

I curl up on the floor at the foot of Ilona's side of the bed.

The peasants say that when owls are singing at night in the trees, if you can hear one sing, it means that someone close to you will die. If this is true, a whole army of owls has been singing for me.

In the morning, Father has a distant look in his eyes. He stands in the kitchen by the stove while he drinks tea with lemon and listens to the radio. His face is anxious, his eyebrows drawn. Janos spreads butter on a slice of bread, cuts it in four pieces, and insists Father eat now, this very minute. I am moved by the way he treats Father. The rough Janos who used to beat Ilona when drunk, the Janos cursing and swearing in the ditch while removing valuables from the dead, this same Janos takes Father's hand in his and tells him not to worry. No one has to know we are here. He'll let no one in the house.

Months go by. Summer passes. I feed the chickens and learn how to milk the cow. I clean the barn where I sometimes like to sleep. I am not very good at chopping the wood. But I succeed in bringing laughter to my audience who watches me, axe in hand, missing the target most of the time. From chalk white, my cheeks take on a colored hue. I feel stronger. But Father is losing weight, his flesh and muscles are melting away. I sit as close to him as I can, hoping to inject him with some of my strength. He smiles and pats me softly on my head.

I help to dig a cellar under the barn. When it is finished, Janos covers the entrance with a wooden plank and spreads straw on it. Nobody can see it or will know where to find it. It's humid and cool, so Ilona can store strings of sausages, smoked ham, lumps of butter and cheese, and bottles of home-made

Tuica, a liquor made of plums. There is plenty of room on
the shelves for jars of preserves, which will be stored for the
winter. It makes me think of the big cauldrons simmering
with fruit and sugar which Ilona used to stir with a long
wooden spoon over an open fire until the mixture thickened.
There was that fruity aroma bursting from the bubbles. It was
childhood-autumn-garden-home. We were all there. Mother
and Odo . . . And now . . .

Now, we are surrounded by closed boxes, each containing
different items to be sold. Crates and boxes, separated by
contents. So many coffins . . . No identity. No names, just
signs. A circle for children, two half circles for women, and an
X for men. Boxes filled with skirts, trousers, tops, their linings
searched for valuables. Everything washed and disinfected,
then dried in the sun. Clothes of the unbaptized ones, the Jews.
Boxes and boxes of shoes and sandals with codes indicating
the size. Neat. Neatly packed.

Every week, Janos disappears with the horse and cart. He
goes to the markets in various towns as far as Vaslui where he
sells part of the crop removed from the ditch. Shoes, clothes,
jewels. Occasionally he also sells butter, cheese, eggs. The
crop from the land.

I hear Father and Janos talking about our returning to Bucharest.
They are worried about the peasants in the villages nearby who
welcome anti-Semitic actions and are helping round up Jews for
deportation. These peasants believe the Lord's punishment has
finally reached the Jews for crucifying Christ! Those Jews who,
for so long, have been killing Christian babies and drinking their
blood! The Germans are here to bring justice.

The future looks grim. We can't waste any time, the atrocities
are endless. The eighteen-year-old Michael, son of the toppled
King Carol, is only a figurehead king. The real power is in
the hands of the Nazi-backed military junta headed by the
red-haired cavalry officer, General Ion Antonescu, who suffers

from bouts of syphilitic fever. He appoints in his government several Légionaires, part of the Iron Guard of the assassinated Codreanu. The Légionaires are counted on to maintain order and to smoothly run the local economy, leaving the Germans to pump and transport the precious Romanian oil from Ploiesti. Meanwhile, the Romanian Fuhrer, Conducator Antonescu, is equally efficient in organizing the murder of a huge number of people under Hitler's program of genocide.

To the deeply religious and superstitious peasants, Codreanu is still present and alive in their world, though he was killed on the orders of King Carol. They believe he is the Archangel Michael's envoy on earth. They swear on their holy crosses that the tall, handsome Codreanu, dressed in white, rides a white horse through the Carpathian villages. They see him, their peasant god, everywhere. I am frightened by their fanatic religious ecstasy when it gets out of control. Codreanu's Iron Guard, the Légionaires, hung my brother Odo on the butcher's hook!

Father and I are lying on our backs, in the grass, looking at the clouds floating by. Our thoughts float with the clouds. We talk. Then we think and think. We decide. The time has come for us to flee. We have to return to Bucharest, so that we can prepare to leave Romania for safety. At present we have nothing. No money, no papers, no legal identity. It's dangerous.

"We have to get our papers and documents which are in the safe at home," Father says.

"How can we open the safe when we have no keys?" I ask. "Not even a key to open the front gate."

He pats my head to calm me down and tells me that there is a double of every key at the store on Strada Lipscani. That's where I'll have to go first. I'll find three keys hidden in a crevice under the second step leading to the entrance door. One key is to open the door to the store, another to enter the entrance gate at home, and the third to open the safe in the upstairs playroom. Once there, I'll have to remove a wooden trap behind Odo's old teddy bear, the one he slept with when he was little. Father squeezes my hand and we both hold back tears. With my other hand, I tear a small blade of grass and start chewing. My mind is on fire.

"Father, have some chlorophyll." I plant a kiss on his cheek and hand him some of the grass.

"You darling little rascal! What would I do without you?"

"And what will I do if you don't tell me the code to open the safe?"

"It's ODO. Put in the code, turn the key twice and the door will open. Everything is there. Money, papers, documents, passports, Mother's jewels, and a pouch to wear around your waist. Remove everything from the safe. The teddy bear has a hollow space inside it which can be reached from between its legs. Take it all, just get it out of the house. In the pouch, in the teddy bear, in a paper bag, whatever."

Father goes over everything again and again. Now, his voice is faint. He must be tired. He talks as if he isn't going to be with me for long. It's terrible! He worries about my being alone and penniless. Then he smiles and mumbles that Aunt Josephine will be there to look after me. And to cheer me up, he says we'll go away to a place where the sun shines on a luminous joyful town, where people laugh and dance to music on the streets. Where every day is lived as if it were a holiday. He wants to see me dance barefoot on the white sand of beaches that have no end.

IX

The horse and cart are ready to go. Janos has the reins in his hand. It's not light yet, and I feel darkness in my heart. We have to part. We embrace and kiss. Tears roll down our cheeks. All four of us. Ilona kisses Father's hand while he thanks her for all she has done for us. Her voice is humble and affectionate as she lowers her eyes, wipes her face with the sleeve of her blouse, and tells me that it was nothing. Nothing after all that Father did for her in the past.

It's my turn to embrace Ilona. I utter a torrent of unrelated words, anything to postpone the moment of letting her go. I talk and kiss her. I am in her arms, unwilling to tear myself away from the warmth of her body. In her simple way, she has protected me since childhood. Parting from her is parting with authentic, uncomplicated, simple life. I feel the loss already. It is forever.

Father and I are seated next to Janos in the wooden cart that rolls on the earth road toward the unknown. All the boxes and the dairy products are covered with a blanket. In about two hours we will reach Bacesti. Janos will set up his stand at the market where he can sell his goods. But he will take us to the station first. We will take the train to Bucharest. An eight-hour ride.

I watch Father from the corner of my eye. He looks good. Like a peasant should look with a *caciula,* a large cap that covers most of his head, and a sheepskin sleeveless jacket. I am quite proud of my own appearance. With the scarf tied under my chin and in Ilona's folkloric skirt, I look as if I have just finished plowing the fields. I want to remember everything. Every sound, every smell, everything I see. A hay wagon pulled by two cows. Birds in flight. They fly very fast and disappear. The smell of earth and moss. The squeaky sound of wheels in between the "Hai! Hai! Hai!" cries of Janos to his horse. A chicken strolling in the middle of the road. A rat crossing our path. A brook with clear water. A bloated dog floating on the river.

The sun is about to rise when we arrive at the station and I hear the train approaching. Janos has made arrangements with his friend Tudor, the stoker who drove the engine when Janos jumped off the train. The famous train that took King Carol and his mistress out of Romania. We are to travel next to the engine with Tudor. No tickets are necessary. No one will notice us. We look like all the other peasants. I carry a basket with hard-boiled eggs, tomatoes, a loaf of bread, a salami, *telemea* cheese, a small container with red wine, a pocket knife, and two bottles of Tuica, all covered with a flowered scarf. It's an early morning train that stops at every village. It's market day and the carriages are full. Baskets poke out through the open windows. People hang on the steps of the carriages. Nobody will notice us in this crowd. Janos helps Father climb into the locomotive. I am next. He says something to Tudor. His lips are tight when he looks at me. He attempts to wave, changes his mind, and leaves without turning his head. I am sad.

The locomotive starts puffing, and the engine catches speed. I feel the smell of coal, the sulfurous fumes. Something in me is burning. I can hear the wheels roaring. I reach out my hand to feel the air. I mustn't think.

Father's forehead is covered with sweat, and I wipe his face and make him sit on a box. He shivers. His head lolls slowly from side to side, his bluish lips grimace. The parted, bloodless lips make sounds, but the strained words cannot be heard over the noise of the engine.

A man with a red cap comes to talk to Tudor who points at us. He tells us to follow him into the adjacent wagon. My heart shrinks. In trouble again? I cross the adjoining platform, then hold out my hand to Father to help him cross. Can he do it? It shakes so much. He makes it. We are in the wagon for merchandise. No windows, it's dark. Father and I suddenly cling to each other. The thought of the cattle train . . . locked in for days, rolling back and forth. No air, no windows, doors sealed shut . . . How can we forget!

"You can sit wherever you like," the man with the red cap says. "Nobody will bother you. But before we arrive at any station and the doors open, you should return to the locomotive."

We go back and forth a few times. Finally, Tudor tells the man in the red cap that we are his relatives and we have to get to Bucharest. We have no tickets. Tudor winks his left eye. But we have a bottle of Tuica.

Until now I never knew of the persuasive power of plum juice. In no time we are shown into a first-class compartment with slightly shabby red velvet seats and a folding table. The shades to the corridor are instantly drawn and up goes an Occupied sign on the door. The man with the red cap says he will call us just before we arrive in Bucharest. Maybe we will have to return to the engine. But maybe not.

I put up the table and prepare our picnic. The menu is varied. Slices of salami, eggs, cheese, bread, a real feast. We drink the wine sBtraight from the container and pretend it's our Christmas dinner or rather Hanukah, to please Father. Our eyes are fixed on the window as we comment on the scenery that goes by. A peasant walks to the fields, a scythe on his shoulder. He waves, we wave back. Another stretches his arms lazily. Two women with sickles and hoes approach the train and spit at us. I pull down the shade as we enter the next station. But before the shade is completely down I see a girl my age kissing a young man good-bye. They kiss with eyes closed, mouth to mouth, body to body. It must be love, I muse. I hear the whistle of the train as it starts to move again. Father lies down, his head on the jacket, folded to make a pillow. Minutes later he is asleep. I stretch out on the other red velvet bench. Sheer luxury. Soon I am lulled into another world by the movement of the train and the monotonous noise of the wheels. A world full of love, no hatred.

There is a knock and the door opens. Just when I am riding a white horse, his wings spread, while multicolored rose petals rain on me. I open my eyes and see the red cap man saying that in another half an hour we will arrive in Bucharest. "You can clean yourselves in the toilet at the end of the corridor," he says. "There are no other passengers in this wagon, so you can go there anytime. Don't forget to tidy up the compartment before you leave."

"Thank you," I say. "What do we do when the train arrives in Bucharest?"

"Upon arrival, you can go straight out from your wagon on to the platform and meet Tudor in front of the locomotive. You'll have to wait for him there as long as it takes, as they are changing shifts." The red cap man salutes and wishes us luck before closing the door and removing the Occupied sign.

Soon we are at the station in Bucharest, and I help Father down the steps of the wagon. We are on the platform when I hear the announcement that a train for Jassy is about to leave. I remember that it was drizzling on the morning when we boarded the train with Mother, the three of us together. I recognize the graffiti on a corner of the bench, "Wishing you happy days." Father stares at me, his eyebrows raised.

"We'd better find Josephine first," he says, "She'll tell us what is going on, where everybody is." He takes a deep breath.

"And she can go with you to the store to fetch the keys. I think that's the best way."

His eyes seem to sink into his head, his arms fall helplessly at his sides. He is silent, tired, old. I make him sit down on the bench, and I tear myself away to wait for Tudor in front of the locomotive. It's early afternoon, bright and light outside. But inside, deep in me, darkness is deep-rooted.

Tudor appears. He looks different. He is wearing a clean blue overall. His face is shaved, his black hair is shiny, glued to his head with lotion. His moustache is turned up. He looks ready to conquer any woman's heart! Only the shadows under his fingernails reveal that he has been in touch with an engine. I can see the delight on his face when I tell him how smart he looks. He confides in me that he's going to meet his woman after he sees us off. He has promised Janos to see us out of here and to our destination; he knows we have no money for any transportation. He has to drive a truck with the merchandise that came with us and take it to the depot on the outskirts of the city. The boxes are already on a trolley. I help him push the trolley to where Father is seated. He lifts Father as if he is weightless and seats him in the middle of the boxes. I can't see Father anymore, but at every bump, I see the top of his *caciula*. We push the trolley through corridor after corridor. Doors open and close. People in uniform salute Tudor, and he has a word to say to everyone. Somehow, after numerous stops, we manage to reach the exit of the station. Outside, still pushing the trolley, we turn left, where a truck parks in front of us. The driver and Tudor exchange a few words and immediately begin loading the crates and boxes into the back of the truck. Father is hoisted on to the bench next to the driver's seat. The truck driver disappears into the station with the trolley. I hop in next to Father. Tudor, now at the wheel of the truck, asks where we want to go.

"Strada Remus. Do you know where it is?" I am uplifted at the thought of seeing Aunt Josephine again. In her apartment, surrounded with books, the samovar boiling with hot water for tea with lemon, served in tall glasses with silver handles. Sandwiches and cakes. To listen to her until I find a meaning to what's happening to us. She'll know what to do.

Tudor isn't familiar with all the street names, but he has no problem reaching the center of town, and Father says he'll guide him from there. The truck is sailing through Calea Victoriei across Bulevardul Regina Elisabeta into Lipscani. We pass Father's store. It's closed, shutters rolled down. Through the side mirrors, I watch the strollers and the passersby who cross the streets or step down from the sidewalks in front of the truck. There are many German officers in their shiny boots and Romanians in military uniforms. Most of the women, their faces with heavy white makeup and dark purple lips, smile while strolling along in high heels.

Now Father takes over. His voice is weak, and, with his hand, he points the way. When we reach Strada Romulus and pass our home, with locked gates and a soldier guarding the entrance, I feel my body being drained of its blood. I squeeze Father's hand. He shakes his head. A few minutes later we turn the corner into Strada Remus in front of the house where Aunt Josephine lives. We have arrived. The truck stops. The traffic behind the truck also stops. Tudor wants us to get out quickly, before a police patrol arrives. I take the last bottle of Tuica out of my basket and hand it to Tudor. I tell him it's all I have to thank him with and wish him *Sanatate* and *Noroc,* health and good luck. He helps Father out and drives away immediately, in a hurry.

We stand there for a minute. The evening is young. It's getting cool. I inhale the smell of cooking. *Sarmale,* cabbage leaves stuffed with hashed meat. Dinner is waiting for us! I feel intense hunger pangs, and my stomach makes lots of noise. I'd like to climb the steps three by three to arrive faster at Aunt Josephine's floor. But we have to go slowly, for Father is out of breath. He takes one step at a time. And we stop. He pauses. He coughs. On to another step. We are almost there . . . at my aunt's island of truth and peace. Away from the ocean of lies and horror which surround us. I am elated as I set my foot on the landing, and Father looks relieved. I ring the bell. I ring again. I knock. The door doesn't open. I wonder, should I go in? My hand reaches into the pot above the door, where Aunt Josephine always leaves the key for me.

"She must have gone out, and we'd better wait inside for her," I tell Father.

I have the key in my hand. There is something else. A thick envelope. I slip it into the pocket of my skirt to read later, once Father is comfortably seated on the blue sofa. I can't wait to enter. The key is in the latch. I turn it twice. I hear the familiar squeak when the door opens. It's dark, the curtains are drawn, and I switch on the light. I put my basket on the chair in the foyer. On the floor I see a notice in big letters that the electricity is about to be cut off. The same with the telephone. I look at the date. Three days from now. Strange. Aunt Josephine so precise, so organized, always on time.

Father starts to sway, his face is chalk white. I slip my arm under his, and we make it to the blue sofa against the wall. He flops down. I lift his legs, remove his *opinci,* peasants' shoes, slip a cushion under his head, and cover him with a wool coverlet, the one Aunt Josephine uses when she rests during the day.

I go into the kitchen to prepare a tray for the three of us. To surprise her when she comes home. But there isn't much of anything. A tin with tea leaves, another with biscuits, half a jar of *magiun,* plum jam, about ten lumps of sugar, *mamaliga,* Romanian polenta, noodles, four cans of sardines, oil, vinegar, salt, a box of matches, and two unopened bottles of wine, one white, one red. I decide to wait for Aunt Josephine to tell me where she is hiding the food.

I look around and feel a pinch of nostalgia. Books and more books. Shelves of books everywhere. I pick one out at random. *The Dictionary of Science*. It's dusty. Now I come to think of it, everything here is dusty. I'll have to help Aunt Josephine give the whole place a thorough cleaning.

I go back into the room to bring Father a glass of water. He is fast asleep, his mouth open. I decide to let him rest for a while. I reach for the envelope in my pocket and sit in the armchair by the light. I recognize Aunt Josephine's calligraphic handwriting. I read page after page, once, twice, three times until the news finally sinks in.

"Dear Child—I don't know if this will ever reach you. I heard from Aunt Gisella and Nicu about the horrors you have been submitted to. How your young life ended. Humanly, it's impossible to understand. All I hope for is that you did not have to suffer long.

I have prayed and hoped for a miracle. If you are here to read this, the miracle has happened. You and your father are alive. I wish I could be with you, to take you in my arms and make you feel protected and loved. There is nobody else in your family you can turn to. On your mother's side, they are all living in the dangerous parts of the country. Horrible atrocities are being practiced on Jews. So stay away.

On your father's side no one is left. Your grandfather Avram is dead. So is your uncle Carol. His sisters, Tony and Hanny, have left Romania with their families. I don't know to where.

Your father will probably attempt to leave for Palestine. However, my Rozalia, you will not be able to receive the entrance authorization for Palestine because your mother was not Jewish.

If you are ready to face the unknown, aim for America. I have been in touch with an American woman by the name of

Mary Jayne Gold. I have known her for a long time. She used to fly her single engine plane, a Vega Gull, all over Europe, having fun. In Palace Hotels in San Moritz, Biarritz, or the Italian lakes she led a carefree life, hopping from one party to another.

In the spring of 1940, after France was conquered by Germany, Mary Jayne joined the road of the Exodus. During this trip she met with the real world. She mixed with penniless refugees, desperate people threatened by death, misery, and internment camps. She couldn't stay indifferent to the cruelty of Nazism and joined Varian Fry, who had formed the Emergency Rescue Committee. They work out of Marseille. I have been in touch with her, and she knows about you. She promised she will do all she can to get you away from this continent which is on fire. To reach her, you must get to Marseille, the last of the large ports in the Vichy Free French zone. Mary Jayne Gold is an idealist. She has unlimited financial means which she is using to help a number of people leave Europe.

You will find it difficult to get out of Romania with the papers and documents you have. It will be hard to obtain officially an exit permit. If Leis Gunnard Iveson is still at the Swedish Legation, go to see him. He is a friend of a friend, and he will find a way for you to reach Mary Jayne.

I have joined a missionary group. I don't know where I will be sent.

Take anything you want from here. It's all yours.

Your Godmother, who hopes for a miracle."

With the letter, I find two copies of my christening certificate which I have never seen before. They are not the same. One states I have been baptized in the Greek Orthodox faith, the other confirms I am of the Roman Catholic religion. A note says, "From now on, always keep these on you." My Aunt Josephine certainly thinks of any eventuality!

X

There is pandemonium in my mind. Where do I start? Here I am, in the place where I have spent the happiest moments of my life; and all I feel is despair, confusion, and loneliness. I look at Father. His hair is thinning, he is growing bald. On his unshaven face, his cheeks are hollow. I can see that he is dying. He dies and dies a little every day. He mustn't know. I have to keep going and pretend I am fine.

From the linen cupboard, I take out the most beautiful pair of embroidered sheets. Probably they are part of Aunt Josephine's unused dowry. Pillows, pillow cases, eiderdown, woolen blanket. I make the bed. I put a couple of fluffy towels in the bathroom. There is a half-used cake of soap by the basin. I turn the tap. The water is icy. I throw the icy water on my face and throat. I'll have to heat the water to wash Father before he goes to bed. I find Aunt Josephine's pajamas and a warm robe. They'll fit him, he is so thin now.

I light a fire with the two logs lying by the fireplace. I manage not to fill the room with smoke. I watch the flames rising and listen to the crackling wood.

I set the table for two on a trolley. I cook the noodles and, with part of the leftovers from my basket, whip up a concoction worthy of a grand chef. I open the bottle of red wine. Tonight no *sarmale*, but after a couple of glasses of wine, my cooking will be tastier than *sarmale*.

I wash Father's hands and face with the heated water. He opens his eyes, surprised, drowsy like a baby woken from a deep sleep. Twinkling and moist, his eyes are as blue as the sofa. His face is flushed. He gets up, walks a few steps, and sits down by the trolley. We eat, looking into the fire as if nothing else matters.

After I have tucked Father into bed, I open Josephine's wardrobe and look for something to wear tomorrow. I try on a few of her dresses. I admire myself in the mirror and finally decide on a light gray woolen suit with a blue turtleneck sweater. The skirt is a bit long and loose, but I can hold it up with a belt. The brown flat heels are only half a size too big. Fortunately, it isn't the other way round and with an old piece of newspaper I can make them fit. On a top shelf, I find a large handbag the color of the shoes. I am all set. I look quite grown-up. Suddenly, I see a white sheet on a hanger. I lift the sheet and uncover Sister Marie Josephe's complete attire. The nun. Now I hesitate. But not for long. For the time being, I'll stick to my first choice.

I sleep like a log on the sofa. In the morning, after a cold shower, I feel clean and comfortable. I dress, then go into the kitchen. While the water boils, next to the radio, I notice an alarm clock which must have stopped ticking a long time ago. I wind up the clock and turn on the radio, hoping to hear the correct time on the news. On a tray I put a pot of freshly made tea, two cups, two lumps of sugar, and a plate with toasted bread, spread with *magiun* jam. The news is bad. With the war on, food is scarce and rationed. More decree-laws and government resolutions have been published in the *Monitorul Oficial,* the Official Gazette. Among other things, Jews will no longer have access to higher education, the right to hold public office or to practice legal or artistic professions, or to own radios. I can't hold back. I utter a series of blasphemous words, a vocabulary improved with the help of Janos. At the end of the news, I hear that the time is seven-thirty. I set the clock, switch off the radio and take the tray to Father. I enter the room smiling. "It's breakfast in bed, my darling." He sits up and leans against the pillows, his face illuminated by my presence. "You look so smart," he mumbles. "Plus I am spoiled with four-star service."

I set the tray on the bed. I put two lumps of sugar in Father's cup, and hand it to him. I kneel down by his side. I caress his emaciated thigh, his cheek, and kiss his forehead. He strokes my face. We sip our tea in silence. I wait for him to finish and take the tray away.

I am ready to go. Our hands clutch, unwilling to part. I am reluctant to leave.

"You know what to do and where to go?" Father whispers.

"Yes, don't worry."

"I wish you'd wait for Josephine to come home and go with her."

I tear myself away and close the door behind me.

XI

It's still early, very few people are on the streets. The town doesn't seem to be fully awake even though it's sunny. I don't have far to go. I want to avoid passing our house. I end up passing the church next to the house where Elena Popescu lives. I think about my best friends, Ada and Elena. We used to see each other every day. There is an odor of coffee as I stop in front of the door. For years, I could enter this house at any time. Elena, my school pal. All this is far away. A thousand years have passed.

I recognize two girls from my school who are waiting across the street, giggling. Each is wearing a black arm band with a swastika. I feel like vomiting. The door opens and Elena, with her satchel, comes out. She waves at the two girls and, with a straight face and an indifferent look, tells me to see the Popa in Church, he is about to finish the early service. She lowers her head, whispers without moving her lips, "Come back this afternoon. Let us know where we can reach you," and crosses the street to join her schoolmates.

I enter the church. The incense reminds me of Easter. The Popa sees me and makes a sign that I should follow him into the adjoining room. Before he says anything, he cuts a piece of *cozonac*, sponge cake, and hands it to me with a cup of warm milk. "Sit down, Rozalia. Eat first, then talk. You have lost a lot of weight." I do as he says. The warm milk flows down my throat, and the pandemonium in my mind starts clearing. I tell Popa Popescu what has happened, that Father is desperately ill, and that if something happens to him, I have no one to turn to, I don't know what to do. He plucks a hair out of his beard and rolls it between his fingers for a while. Then, the way he always did, he tickles his nostril with the hair. Even now, I think he looks impressive in his long black robe, his tall hat, and the big cross on his chest. I wait for him to say something after he stops the ritual with his nostrils. After a moment of silence, he takes my hand in his.

"You must get your ration card immediately. Meanwhile, come for dinner tonight. Enter the house through the back door behind the church. I'll go to see your father shortly after lunch with some warm food. Where is he?"

"In Aunt Josephine's flat. I'll be there to open the door."

I feel better now that I know the Popa will come to see Father. Also, the *cozonac* and the warm milk have given me the courage to carry out my mission. I walk with long strides and, in no time, I am in front of the store on Lipscani. The entrance to the offices is from the side, through a courtyard. A Romanian policeman comes along and asks what I am doing. "I have to go in," I say. "I need a length of material." "Out of the question," he replies. A young German soldier passes by. He salutes and smiles. I smile back. I speak to him in German. He grins. He tells me he is very lonely, and will I have a cup of coffee with him. "I can't go now because I have to get something out of the store," I say, "but the policeman won't let me in." My heart is beating very fast. The German tilts his head back, takes my arm, and marches me past the policeman to the steps which lead to the office door. The policeman shouts, "You little whore!" and spits. The soldier looks satisfied at having won his battle. He can go on to conquer other territories! He leaves, saying maybe some other time for the coffee. My heart is beating even faster.

I have to concentrate now, think of nothing else, remember every word Father told me. "You'll find three keys hidden in a crevice under the second step leading to the entrance door." I find them right away and wonder if I should go in. Maybe not. I'm in a hurry to get it all done and return to Father.

I put the keys in my pocket and walk away as fast as I can. Another ten minutes and I'll be in Romulus Street. Home.

When I reach the street, I find it difficult to advance. Traffic has been interrupted. There are a lot of police and army cars. I am told to walk on the other side of the street, to keep moving. However, a few people have gathered in front of our house. I join in and listen to what is being said. "Maria Antonescu, the wife of the Conducator Antonescu, is in that black limousine with small flags on the front fenders." I cross and get close to the gate without being stopped. In all the confusion, I want to try and open the small door next to the main gate without being seen. I am about to take the key out of my pocket when orders are shouted and room is made for the big gates to open. Guards on each side salute. The black limousine, followed by a truck, slows down as it drives past the gate. It stops at the main entrance door. On the steps stands a tall general. He must be at least a general, judging by all the medals on his chest and the many stripes on his intimidating uniform! Maria Antonescu climbs out of the limousine, and the general greets her with a friendly smile. He bows down to kiss her hand. She is rather short.

While all eyes are on the illustrious visitor, I take advantage of the commotion and sneak in. I walk straight on, make a right turn, and enter the house through the back door, only to find myself in the midst of six panic-stricken people. They rush back and forth, their arms full of clothes and kitchen tools. They shout at each other to hurry, to be careful. I recognize Ovid Macelaru, who used to be Chief of Police in Jassy and who was transferred to Bucharest with his family. I ask one of his daughters what's going on. From her half answers, I gather they have been given twenty-four hours to move out of the main house, and they are in the middle of moving to the servants' quarters. What were they doing here in the first place, I ask myself without finding an answer. Did they move in just like that? Convenient. It saves paying rent! My ignorance soon evaporates. The girls keep talking with excited voices. I hear about the CNR(National Commission of Romanianization) headed by Colonel Dobriceanu. Houses are confiscated from Jews and nationalized. I learn that now the colonel wants our house for himself. He'll even pay for it, a pittance of course, if he can't get it in any other way. "The valuables and the antique furniture will soon be confiscated," shouts one of the girls, dashing out with arms full of cargo.

I realize I am expected to feel sorry for Ovid Macelaru and his family who have to move out at such short notice. Imagine having to move out! Out of the house where I spent my whole childhood with my family! I swallow my anger and keep asking questions. Everything I hear is frightening, gloomy, hopeless. By now, my questions to Ivona, another of the three young daughters, are listened to with hostile politeness or are answered by a stony silence. I am eyed with suspicion. I feel like a trespasser and realize I had better move on. I hold back my tears as I walk through the corridor toward the staircase. I have to get to the playroom upstairs. Father told me, "With the key, open the safe behind the trap behind the teddy bear." But instead of climbing the stairs, I go on. I want to have a look at the dining room where we used to sit, the four of us, happy, laughing . . .

Exhausted, I slump on a chair against the wall behind the sideboard. I need a few minutes to get hold of myself. Through the glass door, opening on to the living room, I see Maria Antonescu pointing toward the two big Sevres vases, in opposite corners, each standing on a tall pedestal. They were

Mother's favorites, an extravaganza. Four men in blue overalls carry out the loot with care. The tall general with medals and stripes looks on, while he keeps talking to the wife of Marshal Antonescu, the Conducator. Sickening. I feel like screaming. I rush back toward the staircase.

I hold on to the banister as I tiptoe upstairs and see that the key to the playroom is on the hook where it always was. The door opens without the slightest noise. I lean against it for a few minutes. How quiet and peaceful! Through the big window, the sun is shining on the miniature doll's house, the stuffed animals, the electric train on the shelves. Reluctantly, I draw the curtain before I turn on the light. Two of the bulbs are burned out. Nothing else has changed. The spread on the sofa is not crumpled. Every toy is in its place. A room that has been spared. Even the faint odor of moth balls is the same, the way it was.

I wish I could linger for a while. Maybe someday I'll be back and then . . . I touch the keys in my pocket, ready to get going, when I hear footsteps approaching the door. I hold my breath. The door opens. The tall super-decorated general removes his cap.

"Rozalia, what's going on? What are you doing here?"

"I want to get some toys and photos," I stutter, my eyes glued to the floor.

"I saw you come in. I was afraid to say anything in case you panicked and were noticed. I didn't want to get you into trouble." He puts his arms around me. Some of his medals dangle in front of my eyes. "Silly girl, look at me!" I straighten myself up and my eyes meet his.

"Mister Vintila? General Vintila!"

"What a pretty young girl you've turned out to be. Like your beautiful mother. I do miss Anca," and he holds me even closer to the medals.

"You know about Odo and Mother?" I ask, afraid to move my head.

"Yes, I do. Anca wrote me a letter after Odo died. She did not want to see me anymore . . . She was in such despair."

"Yes. We all were desperate. Mother never recuperated from the pain."

"I know. I tried to reach her, but it was impossible. Finally, I telephoned her sister, Gisella, who told me what had happened. I still can't believe it."

I burst into tears. Not even a multimedaled general can watch a young girl cry. He makes me sit down in the armchair, gives me his handkerchief, and is ready to retreat, defeated.

"Take everything you want from here. Take your time. I'll send an orderly with a suitcase. In the room next to the laundry, the closets are full. It's getting cold. You'll need a coat and whatever. Have the orderly wait for you at the door. When you are ready, let him know. He'll help you carry everything down. I'll tell him to put the suitcase in the trunk of my car. Go with him and wait for me there. I'll join you as soon as I see you. We'll drive you out of here."

"Thank you." I dry my tears. "Can I pick some plums from the tree in front of my room?"

"I'll have someone fill a bag for you. I don't want to have you roaming through the garden. Here, have a candy." General Vintila puts a bar of chocolate on the side table. He produced it out of the pocket of his trousers, like magicians do. So generals with stripes and medals can do all sort of tricks!

"Thank you, General Vintila."

I see him close the door behind him. I wait until I can't hear his footsteps anymore, then I remove the teddy bear. I am nervous, tense. After trying two of the keys, the third one fits. The code is no problem. I don't even look at what is in the box when it snaps open. I put the pouch around my waist and start stuffing it with the cases holding Mother's jewels. But there is no room for the cases, so I take out the jewels, and wrap each piece in the newspaper I remove from my shoes, leaving the empty cases in the box. Money in different currencies, gold coins, papers, and documents are evenly distributed in the empty space between the legs of the teddy bear and in my handbag. I cuddle the toy, caress its brown fluffy coat, the pink face, and look into the glass eyes, the way Odo did when he was telling it his secrets before he fell asleep. I place the teddy sitting up, its arms and head between the handles of my bag.

There is a knock at the door. It's the orderly, saying he has put the empty suitcase in the next room. I have a last look around and see the family photo album on the shelf. I am not going to leave that behind, even if it doesn't fit into my bag. So with the album and the chocolate bar in my hand, my bag with the teddy over my shoulder, the pouch knotted around my waist, I walk out of the room dragging my feet. My shoes, without the newspaper, are now too large. My exit is far from elegant. The orderly doesn't seem to mind.

In the next room, I enjoy filling the suitcase. Every item is familiar. But I must hurry and not be nostalgic. I pack a suit for Father—shirts, ties, shoes. And of course, his gray hat. I'll wear it on my head so that it doesn't get squashed. I glance at myself in the mirror and see that it does look quite smart on me. I change into a pair of my own shoes which I find in the closet and throw an extra pair in the suitcase. Perfect. Ready.

Everything is in the trunk of the car. The same wine-colored Buick that drove us home after Mother and Odo and I had the aperitif with Mr. Vintila at Dragomir. The chauffeur nods as he recognizes me but keeps silent. I sit in the back of the car. The orderly opens the door for General Vintila who tells him something before he gets in. The orderly sits in front with the chauffeur.

"Put your head down, Rozalia." says General Vintila. I remove Father's gray hat and lean down as far as I can. He covers me with a cashmere blanket the color of the leather seats.

"Let's go," he orders.

We start moving. At the exit, the orderly rolls down his window and shouts to the guards to open the gate, the general is in a hurry. The magic works.

"Where to, Rozalia?"

"Left after the gate and then straight on until the next corner."

Three minutes later, the Buick turns the corner into Remus Street and stops in front of Aunt Josephine's building. General Vintila gives me a folded paper with his telephone number.

"Call me if you need any help or if you are in trouble." He slips something in the pocket of my jacket. It feels like money. More than I need to buy Father a newspaper. Lots more. I am ready to get out. But as the orderly opens the door of the car to let me out, I plant a kiss on the general's cheek. "Thank you," I say, embarrassed. He smiles at me, almost laughs.

I stand in front of Aunt Josephine's house in Father's gray hat, loaded like a mule with my suitcase, the brown paper bag with plums and the teddy bear in my handbag, and I watch the Buick vanish around the corner.

I can't wait to tell Father about my adventures. He'll be proud of my achievements. He'll laugh at the way I'm wearing his hat, with the rim down. He'll be glad I brought his razor so that he can shave and look smart when he dresses up in his elegant suit with the blue shirt and burgundy tie.

"I'm back! Mission accomplished!" I call, loud enough to be heard in the bedroom. No answer. I drop everything on the table by the blue sofa, and open the door. He is sleeping peacefully. I don't have the heart to wake him. I'll wait until the Popa comes with the food.

The doorbell rings, and it is the Popa, who asks to see Father. I tell him he is asleep. He removes a pot of warm food from the side of his robe and hands it to me. As I go into the kitchen to prepare the tray, Popa Popescu opens the door to the bedroom. When I return, all I can see from the door is the Popa's back in his long black robe and his tall black hat. He is standing by Father's bedside, praying. I set the tray on the night table and ask, "Is Father awake?" I look . . . I stare at the gray fleshless face. He is not breathing . . . He must have drifted off . . . He is dead. "Do you want to kiss him?" I hear. But that face and that body are no longer the face and the body of my Father. I cannot kiss. I cannot cry. Waves of inner tears inundate my heart. I remove Father's gray hat from my head and rest it at the foot of the bed, like a wreath.

The Popa calls the Rabbi who makes all the arrangements. There is no time to waste. The burial has to be within twenty-four hours.

The cemetery. The funeral. The prayers. I watch the coffin being lowered into the earth. After Odo's death, then Mother's and then the train-ride with so many corpses, I never thought I could feel a pain like this in my heart. There is a knife in my chest and only darkness in my head. Nothing matters anymore.

I stand there not knowing when God will show some mercy. Father does not even have his son there to read Kaddish, the prayer for the dead. A stranger with a hat on volunteers to read, moving back and forth during the prayer in Hebrew, which I don't understand. If Mother had been alive, she would have had every lamppost on every street leading to the cemetery covered in black. She would have wanted the world to know her pain.

The Rabbi sprinkles the coffin with dirt, and the gravediggers fill the grave. I think of Father's blue eyes, like Odo's. How cold and lonely he must be in his coffin. Moses, Christ, God, where are you? I hurt terribly inside. The ceremony is over, and I am told that, according to the ritual, I have to show my grief and tear off a piece of my blouse.

I run out of the cemetery never to return, never to pray again.

XII

Macabre humor. The irony of destiny. I pay Father's Jewish burial expenses with the money General Vintila gave me. It's only right that Mother's lover pay for her husband's burial. And without even knowing! With what is left over, I pay the electricity and telephone bills for Aunt Josephine's flat and buy a few logs. I have to stand in a queue for a long time to get a ration card.

Among the documents I brought from the safe, I find my birth certificate, my passport, and Father's life insurance. I obtain his death certificate and go to the offices of the insurance company. I present the paper which, in flowery print, states the huge sum Father insured himself for, on the day I came into this shitty world. "HA! HA!" is the answer, "you might as well use it as wallpaper!" I am learning something every day. I have entered the hall of mirrors.

Next I learn all about what can happen if one is half Jewish. The *gemishte*, the Germans term for unhealthy origin, mixed blood. Half and half. Mulatto Jews. Even baptized Jews are not clean, no matter how much detergent is used. They have to be exterminated. The ultimate solution.

I have to organize myself. I leave my ration card with the Popa's wife. Heavy and good tempered, she is a great cook, and I like to eat her food. I can pick up the pot with a warm meal anytime during the day on my way back to Aunt Josephine's flat. It's better for them if I don't eat with them every day. It's safer. I like it that way too. I can read while I eat. Sometimes I am asked to stay and share a meal, and Elena tells me what is going on at school. Sheer gossip. The gap between us grows wider each time I see her. We are worlds apart, another universe. How can I tell her anything, at this point?

Ten days have gone by and I am still sleeping on the sofa. Today I am sixteen years old, my birthday. Before putting out the light, I go into the bedroom. Father is omnipresent. I can see him lying there, his eyes closed, his cheeks hollow. My gaze goes from the crucifix above the bed to the crumpled white sheets I have been reluctant to change. The Jew on the cross and the crucified Jew on the crumpled white sheet.

In the morning, I decide not to indulge in emotion and self-pity. For two days now I have inquired in vain at the government office for passports, about how to get an exit visa. In the cramped rooms of a converted house, I have been sent from one counter to another. After I have stood for hours in a dimly lit corridor, one of the men behind a desk, with a big black mole on his nose, takes pity on me. He tells me not to waste his time and mine and to just go home. If I have nothing better to do, I can fill in these forms and wait for an answer. "How long," I ask. He answers by filling the air with ten minutes of bogus pontification and gibberish. Then he declares that it would be irresponsible to make any prediction. He winks, lights a cigarette with impatience, then shouts, "Next!"

I decide I had better go to see Mr. Leis Iveson at the Swedish Legation. I hope he is still there. I stroll around the streets for a while, trying to find my way without asking for directions. I follow the road traced in red on the map that fell out of the envelope of Aunt Josephine's letter.

At the end of an alley bordered by chestnut trees, I get to a small building with a garden. The shiny bronze plaque tells me I have reached my destination. I ring the bell, and the door opens immediately. I enter a room that is bright and clean looking. On the left, there are two rows of benches where about ten people are sitting, waiting. On the right, behind a desk, a blue-eyed blonde who looks to be in her thirties greets me. "What can I do for you?" she asks. The equivalent of the local bureaucratic language, "what the hell do you want?" "I have come to inquire about joining the Swedish Red Cross," I answer, careful not to reveal my real purpose which is to get out of Romania. She asks to see my birth certificate and any other identification, which I produce without hesitation from my carry-all bag. Then she starts to turn page after page in a thick book. Her finger goes from top to bottom, left then right. Meanwhile, I hardly dare to breathe. She stops. Her eyes betray her amusement. How many times a day does she hear the same story? "Is there anyone in particular you wish to see? What is the name of the person who recommended this meeting?" I tell her, and she writes everything down on a card in Swedish and hands it to me. I am about to go and sit on the bench and wait my turn. I see an open door where people are going in and out.

"No. Don't go there, go to the door that is closed, knock and go straight in. That's where you'll be interviewed." She smiles. "Good luck." Behind me, a family with a small child is waiting. I hear the blue-eyed blonde asking them, "And what can I do for you?"

I am seated at a desk opposite Mr. Leis Iveson, and I tell him my story. I feel my way around like a blind person tapping a cane, perceiving a step, a curb, or a puddle of water. I have no experience and have to make choices about a world I know nothing about. I haven't a clue what to answer when Mr. Iveson gives me a choice of various "legal" ways of leaving the country. I can marry a foreigner, I can bribe a highly placed official in the government, I can get a set of fake identity papers making me a national of one of a number of countries on this planet. As I am fluent in many languages, the last solution might be possible.

Maybe we will have to add a dash of corruption and bribery to this counterfeit cocktail. The bribes will have to be on various levels. To bypass the bureaucracy, to cut through red tape and get things moving. Anyway, because of my age, my papers have to be changed as I am too young to travel on my own.

Mr. Iveson looks so powerful; I can't possibly doubt anything he says. Especially when on the wall behind him a gallery of portraits vouch for him. Photographs of King Gustav V, Prime Minister Per-Albin Hansson, a young Raul Wallenberg, Folke Bernadotte, Gustav Forssius, Alfred Nobel, and many others. All of them have a compassionate expression in their eyes. The Powerful Viking behind the desk says that the Swedish authorities are doing everything they can to save the Jews. Large amounts of money from the private sector are being used in the name of justice and ideals. Being from a neutral country, they are negotiating and succeeding in saving lives. I don't know much about Wallenberg, Nobel, Bernadotte, and King Gustav V; but I'd like the whole world to be like them.

I am told to leave my papers, photographs, and a specimen of my handwriting in a few foreign languages with the blue-eye blonde and return the day after tomorrow. In the meantime, I should go and take some driving lessons in case I have to join the ambulance sector. It would also be useful for me to learn a few words of Swedish. He hands me a card with an address.

"I'd like to think about the problem of your being only sixteen and a girl," he says. "Are you any good at lying with a straight face?"

"No," I reply, "Never!"

He laughs. "Perfect," he says. "Most convincing, you are a champion." He adds that maybe I'll have to be a twenty-year-old man, he'll see what's available.

"Consulates and Legations in Washington, New York, London, Rio de Janeiro, and Marseille will be contacted. We'll have to wait and see." Yes, he understands that I want to reach

Marseille. He keeps writing. After a pause he tells me that I've been highly recommended, he does not say by whom. He opens a drawer by his desk and puts away the folder with his notes. He faces me, offers me a cigarette.

"No, thank you."

"Do you mind?"

"Of course not."

He lights his cigarette and takes a deep puff. My gaze follows the smoke for a second.

"You'll be alone most of the time," I hear him say in a low voice. He removes his glasses and looks me straight in the eye. "Do you have the perseverance, the courage, and the will to survive, no matter what?"

"Yes, Mr. Iveson."

"Whatever storms you'll have to brave, whatever waves will bar your way, until you swim ashore, you won't give up?"

"I won't give up, Mr. Iveson."

"Then, we'll have to get you out of here!"

I am about to say again, yes Mr. Iveson. But it isn't necessary. I am the living embodiment of the survivor. Puzzled by my own survival, I wonder if it hasn't just been a combination of sheer luck and the flexibility of a contortionist with an inordinate appetite for life.

My ears are buzzing. I can't hear anything else he says as I leave. I am walking on a cloud. After I exit the alley with the chestnut trees, I turn left on to the main boulevard. It's an autumn day, the sun is shining and angels are singing for me. I am not alone anymore.

Two tall SS officers in black uniform are walking in front of me. I don't want to pass them, so I slow my stride. Coming from the other direction, I see a very thin, elegant, not-too-young woman. She passes a church, makes the sign of the cross, kisses the medal of a saint hanging on her neck next to a cross, and, without any hesitation, walks on. As she approaches the officers, I can see there will not be room for the three of them on the pavement. To pass, she can step down into the road. But she doesn't. A collision will happen at any moment. Finally, the two SS have to step aside to let the stubborn-proud-toothpick-woman go by. She politely thanks them by saying. "I kiss your hand." And walks on.

I hear them laugh at the Romanian habit of saying thank you, hello, and good-bye all with the same *Sarut mana*. They stop and turn around to make some remarks in German. I can see the metallic look in their eyes, the hairless skin on their smooth faces, the blond hair under the peaked caps. The supermen in their striking uniforms, the death's-head and cross bones glittering on their caps. A black badge with the sign of a swastika on their sleeves. As the two SS are striding off, a flock of sparrows, not on their way to warmer shores, fly above us. Impressed by all this utterly superhuman power below, the birds show their appreciation and leave a good luck souvenir on one of the officer's caps. I'd like to ask, "How about the other one?" but they are gone.

The difficult part is being patient. The rest is easy. My driving is improving. So is my Swedish vocabulary. Every other day I report to the Legation. After a few weeks, I am ready to spend the rest of my life in this routine. An apartment to myself with books and more books. But also the fear of a knock at the door. My cell is comfortable, except that I am not free. At just sixteen, I am the inmate of a prison, waiting to escape. Time isn't on my side. So far, there is no solution in sight, it's impossible to leave. I am told that the Germans could occupy the free zone in France and if they do, getting out of Europe from Marseille will be out of the question.

On my next visit to the Legation, when I am already resigned to spending my life waiting, I am shown some counterfeit documents. Excellent samples. Stamps on the passport of a young man who looks just like me.

"The Swedish Consul in Italy, Mr. Westerberg, has been here for a visit and will be traveling by train to Milan with his secretary the day after tomorrow." Mr. Iveson tells me. Nothing else is said. However, I am attentive to every word, especially when it is casually spoken.

At first I have difficulty pronouncing my new name with a Swedish accent. But after a brief elocution lesson I make it. Then I have to practice my new signature over and over again. The Powerful Viking smiles, satisfied.

"Now, Johan, you will persevere, won't you?"

"Yes, I promise, Mr. Iveson."

"Come earlier on Thursday. We will have the right clothes for you."

"I have some, Mr. Iveson. My father's."

"If you use those, you'll have to remove the Romanian labels. Here, sew these on the inside of your garments. 'Made in Sweden.' I'll personally inspect you and your suitcase. We can't take the slightest risk."

"Thank you, Mr. Iveson. *Sarut mana*." I mean it.

"Your Romanian should have a foreign accent, Johan. Remember? One last thing, when you count, be careful not to count in Romanian. It's a method the Gestapo uses to know the real nationality of the person they are interrogating."

XIII

It feels like I am packing to go to boarding school, stitching labels everywhere. I hesitate between Odo's cap and father's hat. I wish I could keep both. It's so difficult to choose what to take and what to leave behind. Each discarded piece means parting from loved ones. It's agony when I get to the photo album. I can't take anything that indicates the places the photos were taken. Only portraits. The teddy bear, I'm definitely not leaving that behind. I check that there is nothing in the empty space between its legs, and I close the suitcase. I am learning how to become a spy. I don't like it. To be careful, to mistrust, to be afraid . . . I cut my hair but not too short.

We board the train in the evening. We are traveling in a first class sleeper. Mr. Westerberg has bushy eyebrows, countless wrinkles from smiling constantly and a space between his front teeth. He is alone in his compartment, and I am sharing mine with his secretary, Gustav, a good-looking young man in his twenties with a boyish face. He is very efficient and acts very much like a secretary should. I watch all his movements so that I too will learn to behave like an important person's secretary. At this stage, I'll be lucky to be taken for a second hand vice secretary. He handles the tickets with such assurance, sees that suitcases are in the right cabin, tips porters, and the man with the red cap carries the diplomatic pouch and keeps a worried eye on me.

After Mr. Westerberg and Gustav have finished using the bathroom between our compartments, it's my turn to get ready for bed. I remove all my clothes and slip on Father's big blue sweater. My legs are showing. I haven't a smart blue pajama like Gustav who is sitting on the bed below, waiting for me to open the door.

"Would you prefer to sleep in the upper berth or the lower one?"

"I don't care." I reply.

"Unless you would like to sleep with me in the lower one, it is preferable for you to climb up. If there is a control during the night, I can deal with it without your having to appear." I prepare myself to climb the ladder to my berth. "Just a moment, Johan, I'd like to kiss you good night." And he takes my head between his hands and kisses me on my mouth. He draws his whole body toward me. I close my eyes. My first kiss. I see in my mind the boy and the girl kissing on the platform when I was with Father in the train to Bucharest. They kissed eyes closed, mouth to mouth, body to body. Just like now. I hear the whistle of the train. In spite of all the excitement, we each sleep in our own berths.

Next morning we laughingly decide to be very careful. The Nazis do not tolerate homosexuality among the clean Aryan race. "Don't you forget it, Gustav!" "Don't you forget it, Johan!" When the train stops in Milano, I notice through the window the handsome Carabinieris with big black feathers on their hats. Everything is behind me, I think.

We leave our train. The station is crowded with packs of soldiers in helmets and guns on their shoulders. There is gunfire in the distance. Luftwaffe airplanes drone in the sky. A woman with a child in her arms runs to catch a train. Two black shirts grab her, hit her. She hands the child to a passerby and screams insults at the young bastards who drag her by her hair and slap her. The child cries "Maminha!" with its arms extended. I can't think straight. I put my suitcase on a bench, open it, and take out Odo's teddy bear. I hand it to the child who stops crying and hugs the toy close to his breast.

Mr. Westerberg is already on the train leaving for Rome. Gustav is furious, ready to kill me. His eyes are full of thunder as he hands me two tickets to Monaco and the rest of my papers.

"What a way to act, for someone who has to pass unnoticed! Hurry, Johan, to quay five! Be sure to catch the train without any other heroic gestures." He runs to join Mr. Westerberg in his compartment.

I notice an elderly man walking toward me with a silver tipped cane. When he is near me, he leans on my shoulder and says, "I am Clas Haglund. Let's go. You'll help me walk and care for me. Do you have my train ticket?"

Clas Haglund? Train ticket? By now I am a veteran in dealing with unexpected events. But I am still shaken by emotions. It all goes so fast. I try to understand and concentrate. Of course, the ticket is in my hand, I see his name on a note clipped to one of the two tickets.

"Yes, I do, Mr. Haglund." I pick up my bag and his briefcase and we are off to quay five. Once there, I act like Gustav did. We board the train for Monaco. I have no change, but fortunately there is no one to tip.

We are in a first-class compartment. We don't talk to each other as we are not alone, and we pretend to read books in Swedish. Sitting across from us, an Italian officer is smoking next to a woman in a low cut décolleté. Her cleavage is most promising. At every movement of the train her breasts inflate, blow up, burst out. It's hide-and-seek. I wish I had boobies like hers! After a quick look at her almond green eyes and her shoulder-length curly dark hair, my bewitched eyes are back staring at the balloons. The officer's face is swelling with pride as he takes her hand into his, to show us that she belongs to him. The luscious woman smiles, satisfied, and winks at me. I am ready to smile back and wink when I remember I am a young man who will certainly get into trouble with a jealous Italian lover. And an officer on top of it. But I must have a guardian angel. At the next stop, they leave the compartment with a short good-bye, and get off. I still wish I had boobies like hers!

Mr. Clas Haglund asks me to lower the window and buy sandwiches and beer from the vendor outside the train with the liras he gives me. "Stay close to me, and wear your cap." The ticket inspector opens the door. I hand him the tickets, which he punches. My heart is beating in my throat. The train moves again, and I doze off, exhausted, partly from the beer and partly from fear. I hear a powerful noise like an explosion. I wake up with a start. Panicked, I peer out of the window. The door opens. Customs. Italian, French, German uniforms. I have to open my suitcase. A nasty smile every time they get to the women's clothes. They say in every language, "Transvestite of course."

A few minutes later we have arrived in Monaco. I am almost disappointed. The trip is over. Mr. Haglung and I leave the train and go to the Hotel Terminus which is across the station. I check in and leave my suitcase there. Mr. Haglund pays for two nights. "Come with me," he tells me. "You will have to find your way around here. A-l-o-n-e." He gives me a map of Monaco. "As long as you stay within the border line, you are safe. Be careful not to step even with one foot on to the soil of Beausoleil, or Cap d'Ail, which is France. People have been arrested and deported for being absentminded and making this mistake." Though his voice is harsh, I am not afraid. I'll emerge from this chaos somehow!

We walk toward the port. On the right, he points toward the palace, high on a rock. The houses on the road to the fortress are strung together in a multicolored necklace. There are boats in the harbor. The turquoise water is clear, and the light air has a faint odor of iodine. I feel an overpowering desire to giggle and to shout my relief. But I only smile politely.

It's cocktail time. We are sitting at a small table in the hall of the Hotel de Paris.

Mr. Haglund has come down from his room. "We can't talk upstairs because everything is bugged, listened to, and reported," he tells me. "There is a file on everyone."

By the second glass of wine, after a look at the ornate ceiling and the marble columns, I am entertained by the merry-go-round. Talk of ballet, opera, candle-lit dinners, with violins playing, it's unreal. I don't give a hoot anymore about German, French, Italian, or any Eskimo officers.

The bar starts to empty. Elegantly dressed bejeweled women escorted by equally elegant looking men, some in uniform, head toward the exit. They laugh and, on their way out, stop by the revolving door to rub the balls and lifted knee of the bronze equestrian statue of Louis XIV. Mr. Haglund responds to my raised eyebrows and inquisitive look by telling me about the superstition of gamblers who rub the horse's parts to bring them luck, before they head for the Casino. I excuse myself and go toward the revolving door, intending to touch the ping-and-pong without being seen. I am ashamed even to believe in this. But it can't harm me. I need all the luck I can get.

At the revolving door, I stand undecided. At the bottom of the steps, I see a car stop in front of the hotel. A young German officer with pale-gray eyes steps out of the Opel, removes his cap and his coat, and leaves them in the car. The doorman at the entrance opens the other door. Out steps Miss Gorgeous Blonde, in a long, tight, white satin dress, her pale skin showing abundantly. She trails behind her a long white fox stole, like a dog on a leash. She has the strangest walk. Her body moves sideways, then in circles, as she approaches the revolving door. She is now next to the horse. The Pale-Gray-Eyed-Aryan-God says something to Miss Gorgeous-Blonde-Mae-West who curves her body, tilts her head backward, and breaks into guttural, contagious laughter. He puts his arm around her waist. They enter the elevator. The door closes. My mouth is wide open.

The doorman who sees my disarray, fills me in with the gossip. "They usually have their dinner in her apartment," he tells me. "Sometimes, after midnight, they come down and cross the Place to the Casino. They only return to the hotel in the early hours and are not seen again until late lunch time." He thinks that the pale-gray-eyed officer must be an important representative of the Wehrmacht. "On special occasions, he arrives with a black Mercedes-Berlin. He always parks his car at the same place, in case he has to leave urgently. There, right in front, ready to go. He only has to turn the key. The damn arrogant SOB."

How can I resist the temptation? I think a lot about the Opel during dinner with Mr. Haglund. We are seated in a crowded and noisy little restaurant where the odor of food predominates. I fill myself with *tagliatelli* to start with, before I attack an *osso buco* and find enough room for a *tiramesu*. Thinking about the Opel hasn't made me lose my appetite. Mr. Haglund looks on amused. His only comment is, "Fill up, it might be your last decent meal for a while."

We walk down by the water. It's late, the streets are half empty. A car slows down, then moves on. I start to talk. I say what's on my mind. I could drive to Marseille and hope to be there in four or five hours, not going too fast. Mr. Haglund asks if I know which way to go, which roads to take, and which to avoid. We sit on a bench under a lamppost. From a briefcase I have not seen before, he brings out a folded map of the south of France, showing the way to drive to Marseille. He gives me the briefcase. "You should have it handy," he tells me. "It will make you look important." He's also put in a tightly rolled duffle bag in case I have to get rid of my suitcase.

Then he faces me. "Do you know how to drive an Opel? You did say an Opel, didn't you? Do you know where the lights are, where to switch on the motor? The clutch, the accelerator, the brake? How to open the trunk, the glove compartment? You can't afford to hesitate in case you are stopped and asked to open or start anything." I feel I am drowning. I have never even seen an Opel before. My expectation of the great adventure, my getaway, fades. Pity the exhilaration can't last. There is more. "You must be sure you have enough petrol. It'll be difficult to stop and fill up on the way. Ask the man at your hotel, the one with the beard, to buy two additional cans of petrol." He hands me a note written in a language no living person could understand. "Here, show him this, he'll know what to do."

How will I ever know which is which among all the learned words I am being bombarded with? I have to know each one of them in case I am asked to open the trunk or show my documents. So we walk around until we find another Opel, parked close to the port. There I have my lesson. Another avalanche of words. It isn't easy to concentrate after dinner. I feel sleepy. I am overwhelmed and devastated by what I have to face. I am unwilling to return to reality and long to escape into the paradise of the leisured, the fairy land I have been in for the last few hours. I am only sixteen!

XIV

Now, at the Hotel Terminus, the man with the beard and I exchange knowing glances when I pass him. Since I handed him the note in Esperanto, we have our secret.

I sleep late, rest, eat in my room, revise every detail, imagine all sorts of circumstances. I even see myself being caught, tortured, soaked in blood, my head under the guillotine. Serves me right. "Thou shalt not steal." Not even from the men who enjoy a feeling of complete power over their victims?

Dogs can smell when you are afraid. I shall not be scared. It is one o'clock in the morning. My suitcase and the cans of petrol are downstairs behind the desk. I walk in haste toward the Hotel de Paris. The Opel is there. A few joyous guests enter the revolving door and joke with the doorman. I am next to the car. I open the door. I throw my briefcase on the seat. I put on the officer's cap and coat and slide in. I am in front of the wheel but I am too far away. My legs aren't long enough. I wiggle to get closer. Never mind . . . later. I turn the key. Stabbing my forefinger on the button to the point of dislocation, I start the motor. I remember to let the handbrake off. The car jerks only once before I drive it smoothly around the Place. The clock over the entrance to the Casino says one-thirty. I almost forget to switch on the lights. I think of the Pale-Gray-Eyed-God coming down the steps, purple with rage, looking for his car. I feel an indescribable satisfaction. Besides

being a thief, I have also become mean. Very mean. I wonder if
my pleasure comes not only from the knowledge of the power
I have over an enemy but also from the accomplishment of
an impossible mission.

At the Terminus, I put on the brakes. The bearded man is
there. He shows me how to open the trunk as he loads the
two cans and my suitcase. Then he adjusts my seat, opens the
glove compartment, and takes out the papers for the car. He
whistles with admiration at the impressive document, stamped
and delivered by the German military authorities in Paris. The
"Ausweiss" is signed by General von Briesen. "Show this at
the barrage." He winks as he closes the door.

Driving on a road I don't know, in a car that is not mine,
that I have no right to even be in, is ridiculous. It's crazy! I
don't even have a driving license!

Cold sweat runs down my spine when I am stopped at the
first barrage. But all I have to do is show the "Ausweiss." My
officer's cap, coat, and my gloved hands provoke the click
of heels, as I salute. My foot is on the accelerator. I am off
to Marseille, a town known to me only for its soap and the
famous French anthem. Nothing makes any sense, not even
the Marseillaise makes any sense. Incredible that a song of the
Army of the Rhine, composed by a young officer in Strasbourg,
should become "La Marseillaise"!

Coincidence, unreasonable coincidence of circumstances
made the volunteers from Marseilles on their way to Paris
sing it at every place they stopped. By the time they marched
through the streets of Paris they electrified the crowds with the
patriotic words and their warm southern voices. The song from
Strasbourg was given the name "La Marseillaise," instead of "La
Strasbourgeoise." Senseless. Just as bizarre as being saved by
the American Mary Jayne Gold, someone who has never even
seen me before. Why? Why wasn't I left to die slowly with the
rest of them suffocating, killed for no reason on the train?

For weeks I have been on a swing, pushed back and forth, reaching higher and higher, until nothing matters anymore and fear has disappeared. I have joined the Evil Ones. I am dressed for the part. I feel strong and confident and have to avoid self-pity and self-justification, to forget all sensations and emotions. I'll have to start with the death of feelings and the death of thoughts. Will the death of men be next?

The headlights of the Opel are painted blue, leaving only a thin crack through which the light beams through. I have to drive very slowly on the tortuous road which runs along the coast. Again I am stopped at a barrage and show the papers. I am in the so-called Free Zone of France, highly controlled by the Germans. The Vichy Government is no more than a puppet state.

I have to build up my hatred and keep my eyes on the road. After Nice, I stay away from the coast and drive over back roads. I follow the directions on the map. I pause and check. If I lose my way, I won't have enough petrol to even reach Toulon. I pass through little villages with squares shaded by plane trees. I would like to bring these moments to a standstill. Mingle with the locals, listen to carefree talk. Learn to play the game of *boules, les pétanques,* among the short-sleeved players, the way they do in the novels I read. But cafés are empty at this time of the night, and there is no one around. I have to hurry, pass Fréjus, and cut in through the hills of the Massif des Maures.

Daylight is timidly teasing the sky when I stop outside Toulon. I take off my cap. With care, I put the gloves in the pocket of the coat and leave everything on the back seat, the way I found it. I hope pale-eyed-Siegfried will appreciate this. The car's tank is practically empty. I remember my good manners and empty the last can of petrol into the tank. Had I been part of the underground, the Resistance, the Combat, the Franc-Tireur, the libération-Sud or one of the other groups, I would pour the petrol all over the Opel and strike a match. The trouble is, I have no match and I am hungry. So I walk down to the main road, sit on the edge with my suitcase and briefcase, and devour the sandwiches the man with the beard prepared for me. What a let-down from being, for a while, a Wermacht officer with pale-gray-eyes!

The mistral is blowing. It sweeps the sky of its clouds into clean-clear blue. An infinite mirror of blue. I am on my back, my head leaning on the suitcase. I have no idea how far I am from Marseille, but guess I am somewhere close to Evenos. I feel lazy. I hope for a miracle.

Beginner's luck! A delivery truck slows down, then stops.

"Salut! Bonjour! What's a young lad like you doing on this road at this unearthly hour of the day?" The truck driver is animated and grins with a mocking smile. "Going to your office Sire? Joining the Navy in Toulon?"

I give him a tall story, sparing no details, about the accident I have had. How I abandoned the car, which was on fire in the bushes, after being chased by hoodlums who were after my briefcase.

"The briefcase is nice, but why the hell would anyone want the damn thing?"

"Because inside is a rolled-up map which shows how to reach a certain place in Marseille . . . A treasure is waiting there for me."

I watch the man attentively, his big hands on the wheel, and shoulders wide as a wardrobe. I'd hate to have him squeeze my neck.

"Jump in," he says, "if this isn't too low class for you! I have some deliveries to make on my way to Marseille." He is evidently impressed by the French Francs I hand him. It's the first time I have used the foreign currency I removed from Father's safe.

Sitting in front with my briefcase and suitcase under my feet, I listen to the exuberant driver. He talks and talks, telling me an even taller story than mine in his soft drawl. It's difficult not to listen to such a colorful storyteller. With dancing eyes, a trim dark moustache, he is at the same time bleak and funny, florid and fierce. Obviously, neither of us believes the other, but we both enjoy the exercise of fibbing.

His name is Marius. Marseille is overcrowded. Rooms are difficult to find. When found, they can only be rented for two days, with prices increasing as fast as the demand.

We stop. Typical-Perfect-Marius gets out. He says that if I pull each bag to the edge and put it on his shoulders, it will save him climbing up and down on to the truck. Besides wanting help, I suspect Marius is having a private joke, given my thin frame. But I'll show him! I drag a bag to the edge without lifting it and, with a push, make it land on the big shoulders. The trouble is, there are a lot of heavy bags to drag to the edge and push on to his shoulders. As if to spite me, he carries them like feathers to a back door where someone pays him. All I can see is a hand. It's cash and carry.

What a relief to sit down again in an empty truck with my eyes fixed on the road! Marius says that we now deserve a Pastis.

At the entrance to Marseille, he parks in front of a bar. I am carrying my suitcase and briefcase with me as we enter. A young man with an apron is drying glasses behind the counter. Colorfully labeled bottles in all shapes and a large percolator are on the shelf under the picture of a jovial-looking woman. On the opposite wall is a moleskin banquette next to a beaded curtain that hides a door. Marble rectangular tables with chairs are arranged indoors and outdoors on the pavement. On the awning it says "Chez Fanny."

We sit at a table which is neither in nor out. "This way I can see what's going on," says Marius. I ask him if he knows how I can get to the American Consulate. He laughs, pouring down his Pastis mixed with water.

"If you are trying to get a visa for America, you are here for a while! Thousands of people are waiting. There is plenty of time for another aperitif."

I hear the whistle of boats in the distance. Men in overalls come in from the street. Some stand by the counter, others sit at tables. They all seem to know each other, and they all speak at the same time. I am the only one who is listening. I learn about the locals. Instructive gossip. After a short time the bar empties.

Marius gets up.

"Are you leaving?" I ask.

"No, young man, wait for me here."

He walks toward the back of the bar, pulls the curtain, and disappears behind a door. After a few minutes, I see him in front of me. Then again he disappears behind the curtain and reappears by the truck. I rub my eyes, convinced I am plastered. Drunk from all that Pastis! How otherwise can the truck be full when I left it empty?

Everything is confused. It's yes and no. Empty and full. Truth and lies. Illusions and reality. I'll go behind the curtain and see for myself what's going on. I have had enough of this double identity. I'll find out where I can wash up and change into my own clothes again. Back to Rozalia. Good-bye Johan.

A gendarme walks in. He knows everyone. Except the funny-looking thing sitting alone with four empty glasses. He stands next to me, frowns, and asks for my papers. I produce the documents which he examines by turning all the empty pages. There is silence, then a short *hm hm* as he hands them back. Under the circumstances, I'd better stick to being Johan for a while longer.

Soon the French policeman finishes his drink at the counter and leaves. I drag the suitcase and briefcase with me toward the back of the room and open the door behind the curtain. I stare at the big space filled with closed bags and cases, each with a number. With her hands on her hips, the woman in the picture above the counter bosses everyone around in a loud voice. Marius and another man are hoisting bags and cases as they vanish through a back door.

The woman sees me. She comes close to me.

"Hey, handsome, where do you think you're going?"

"I'd like to clean up and use your, whatever . . ."

"That's all?"

"Yes, Madame."

"Not Madame! I am Fanny. And you?"

"Johan."

"Kraut?"

"Not Kraut."

"Then what the hell are you waiting for? Do you need a hand, or what?"

The men are back, they start laughing.

"No thank you, Fanny." I am nervous and baffled.

"Move on. It's there in the back. Afterward, you can wash up at the sink in the kitchen."

"Thanks, Fanny." I head toward "The Whatever."

"Leave your junk at the door. There isn't room for all of you inside!"

As soon as I see the door, I foresee a terrible problem. I face the door like a man faces the enemy. With suspicion. It's a half door, one that swings open. Once inside, you can see what goes on outside. But, the glitch is that your head and legs can be seen by any passerby.

I have to concentrate. Use trigonometry. My nationality is already at stake but now my sex is at stake too. My dilemma is how to lower my pants without drawing suspicion. Even Hamlet wasn't in such a mess! How will I manage? Acrobatics? Here I am, like the captain going down with his ship, staring at the white enameled deck on which I stand, my legs apart. If I remove just one leg of the trousers, it'll certainly be a mess.

Removing both legs is safer. How will I ever walk out of here with my head up? I didn't count on this. I envisaged everything, even the guillotine, but I was not prepared for this. What's the use of being a learned egghead and not being able to cope with Fanny's loo?

After some acrobatics, with the suitcase standing guard smack in front, I take a chance. No one pays any attention to my turmoil.

I can't wait to be Rozalia again in a world where things will be simpler!

XV

It all happens so fast. Once more I am seated next to Marius. This time he doesn't talk. He seems to be deep in his thoughts. It could also be that, after the reasonably good lunch we had with Fanny, he is sleepy. When he finished loading, all he said was, "Let's go." He knows where I want to go, so I assume he is driving me to the American Consulate. I'll finally be able to inquire how to reach Mary Jayne. We drive for a while. It seems we are going back toward Toulon. Close to a railway, a sign says LA POMME. He turns left and drives through a big gate to the Villa Air-Bel. We are in a gigantic park with cedar trees, greenhouses, a fountain in the middle of a water basin. A few people sit around a table, laughing. After we pass them, Marius shouts greetings to no one I can see, "Salut, Max. Salut, Andre . . ."

He suddenly puts on the brakes. "See those trees? Max hung his paintings on its branches. It was a very successful exhibition! You should have seen the auction!"

"What auction?"

"An auction to sell paintings."

"Who's Max?"

"He left with Peggy, before the others."

"Who's Peggy? What others?

"They called themselves Surrealists. A lot of fun!"

I think he is either drunk or seeing ghosts.

"I can't see anyone. Who are you greeting?"

"It's habit. It brings me luck."

"For what?"

"To get paid when I deliver."

"What do you deliver?"

"Don't ask questions." He removes the cover from the loaded truck. "Come on, give me a hand." He jumps down, expecting me to do my job. Push and kick the bags one by one so they land on his shoulders. "Watch out for the numbers. Stop at ten."

When he returns for the next lot, I ask if he has been paid. "Not yet," he says. "I liked it better when Janette was there. She used to pay immediately, even before I finished unloading. Janette was so pretty and soft-spoken, like nobody I have ever known . . . an angel, an American angel."

"You sound as if you have a sweet spot for her. Is she your girl?"

"I never had the slightest chance with her. She was in love with Robert."

"Robert?" he does inundate my brain with a lot of names! "Who's Robert?"

"A minor gangster, like all of us. Before joining the local underworld, he deserted the Foreign Legion and fought with the Liberation army." Marius draws a last puff on the cigarette hanging from the corner of his mouth. Between his thumb and forefinger he stubs it out with a twist and aims it from a distance into the vase standing by the door. I imagine what he could do with a rifle.

"What happened to Janette?"

"During Maréchal Petain's visit to Marseille, Andre, Varian, Daniel, and Janette were arrested and held incommunicado on the ship Sinaia."

"But I thought Janette was an American?"

"Even Varian was American."

"It doesn't make any sense. America is not at war."

"The Marseille police didn't want any trouble with the Vichy Government so they wanted them out of the way during Petain's visit here. They would have liked to get rid of them forever. We finally managed to let the American Consul know where they were. He got them out. He rescued them."

"Well, what happened next?"

"Varian and Janette were escorted to the Spanish border and sent home to America. They were forced to leave Marseille for good."

I have no idea what he is talking about. He keeps throwing information and names at me as if to test me. Or is it to test my patience or to confuse me? Does he think I know who these people are and that I am involved with them? Unless Marius has something up his sleeve. But what if all he wants is to show off and drum up publicity for himself? I'll soon find out.

I tell Marius how important I feel knowing him. He, who knows all these people. This is history. It would make a good movie. But at this point, all I want is to get to the American Consul who will reach Mary Jayne who, I am sure, will solve my problem.

"Marius, when we are finished here, can you tell me where I can find a place to stay tonight? Also how to get to the American Consulate?"

"Don't waste your time. Fanny can put you up for a few days if you help us. You can pay when you get to your treasure."

"What treasure?"

"The one that's on the rolled-up map in your briefcase."

And we both burst out laughing, and we laugh and laugh until Marius says we need an aperitif to rest from all the laughing.

We drive into Marseille and leave the truck in the Vieux Port. Again I drag my suitcase and briefcase to a cafe. At the corner of Baili-de Suffren, we sit outdoors at "Au Brûleur de Loups," I drink a lemonade while Marius has "his usual." What concoction is his usual? A mystery, like everything else. At his insistence, I take a sip of "his usual." My tonsils roast in my throat. I extinguish the blaze with the lemonade.

It doesn't take long for me to realize that I am right in the middle of the melting pot of intellectuals and refugees fleeing Europe. Besides an entrance visa to North or South America, refugees need an exit visa from France, and a transit visa for Spain and Portugal, both neutral countries. The other escape route is by sea from Marseille to North Africa and from there to another intermediate destination like Martinique. But one has to be careful, as the Germans are patrolling the Mediterranean Sea and there is no network to help the refugees in any of the ports upon arrival.

A lot can be bought on the flourishing Marseille black market, and here I am, sipping a lemonade with one of the men from the shady underworld. Not only does he seem to know his way around, but he has innumerable ways to get there. He admits it's a question of how much. With my looks, the elegant briefcase, and my well-cut suit, I should be able to work my way out, he tells me. In short, he thinks I am loaded.

While Marius is gulping down his third dynamite, he manages to talk to everybody who passes us. They stop, say something, he says fine. Makes a note on the palm of his hand with a pen.

When the palm of his left hand is full of notes, he takes mine. I ask why he doesn't use paper. He says, "You'll find out. Start learning a few of the rules. Never list names or addresses on paper. Certain subjects can only be discussed in a bathroom with the water running. If you have to leave a written message, a good place is in a tube of toothpaste."

I feel like a dog watching with concentration the bone to be thrown. Waiting, waiting, my entire being vibrating with excitement. People walk by, and I hear orders for unrelated objects. Passports, visas, bread, sugar, butter, meat, coffee, oil, milk, chocolate, cheese, coal, wood. "Croquefruit" is a favorite after passports, visas, and tickets.

I like the name Croquefruit. I wonder what it is, maybe it's a secret code. I ask. To my great disappointment, I hear Croquefruit is a piece of date paste coated with ground almonds. While making notes on my palms, Marius explains how this business started. The goal of its founders was to provide work for leftist militants, artists, exiles, and Jews who were put out of work by the racist decrees of the Vichy regime. A very resourceful man, the intellectual running the enterprise, changed raw material into a tasty temptation, the Croquefruit. Given the restrictions, food was in great demand. In the long run, it turned into a gold mine. Marketed throughout the region at two francs apiece, they were at times five million morsels behind in orders.

"Do you want to meet some of the artists and make some money while waiting for your passage? I can arrange for you to work with them." He looks me in the eye, scratches his ear, deep in his thoughts. "Or maybe you could help me in other ways. Let me think. Ah oui!"

I find it best to keep quiet while my head goes from side to side like a crazed windshield wiper following the comings and goings.

Days go by. I am now a fully fledged black market wheeler dealer, living in a world where men and women risk their careers and their lives. Cutting deals, falsifying papers. My new life is bursting with events. I also find out that Marius was not on that road accidentally when he picked me up; he had received orders to look for me. From his double-talk, I understand the bearded man at the Hotel Terminus had a finger in it. It's useless to ask Marius to answer anything directly.

However, it is through him that I hear about Varian Fry, the young American who volunteered to come to France as the

representative of an American relief organization. His mission
was to help rescue a number of intellectuals who were on
the Gestapo's blacklist and in great danger of being deported.
They were known critics of Hitler, and there was nowhere in
France they could hide and avoid capture.

Fry needed all the help he could get. He enrolled in his
team, among others, Mary-Jayne Gold who, instead of returning
to New York, stayed in Marseille to work with Fry. She called on
Daniel Bénédite, a French friend, to help with the organization.
She used her unlimited finances to fund the rescue committee
and actively took part in dealings to save people from being
deported to concentration camps. The Germans complained to
the Vichy Government who, in turn, annoyed by the success
of Fry's organization, complained to Washington.

Meanwhile, the State Department in Washington instructed
its Consulate in France to reduce the quotas for issuing visas.
But . . . but . . . in spite of all these instructions, Marius tells
me not to worry. The vice consul in charge of visas at the
United States Embassy in Marseille, Hiram Bingham, is openly
defying the orders of the State Department. Instead of turning
refugees away, he is issuing visas to Jews so that they escape
the internment camps. Harry, as Marius calls him, works closely
with Fry.

When I go to see him to ask for a visa, Harry Bingham
advises me not to wait around in Marseille for long. Shy and
modest, he apologizes for not being able to stamp my passport.
"To enter the USA, you'll have to tell the truth and use your
Romanian nationality. Your request for a visa will have to be
on the quota reserved for Romanians. You could go to a South
American country and wait there for the American Visa as it
might take a while."

"The Swedish Legation in Bucharest has already advised
its Legation in Rio de Janeiro of my possible arrival there," I
tell him.

"The Brazilian Consul is a friend of mine," he tells me, and he calls the Brazilian Consul. "Please . . . immediately . . . it's urgent . . . Romanian . . . a relation of someone very remarkable." I can only hear words here and there. I can't thank him enough. I could go down on my knees. It warms my heart to meet someone like Harry. He says, "I just find it painful to watch the long line of individuals around the blocks outside the embassy being treated like cattle. Bullies should be stopped."

It's strange the way my daily life is evolving. Whatever I want to know I "just ask Marius." I call him the concierge of the port of Marseille. He is a walking encyclopedia, specializing in past and present local eclectic activities. He takes me along on his deliveries and involves me in his wheeling and dealing. I am part of this world where wrong is right. Delivering to the hospital medication and food obtained on the black-market might be wrong, but when I think of the lives it saves and the money made, I have to admit, it makes me happy. Especially when it is used to buy someone's escape from a camp.

Today the truck parks at the Paradis clinic. I am going to help Marius unload but not the way we usually do. He doesn't want to be stopped at the entrance or be seen by any of the nurses. They could give us away and inform the police.

I jump down and open a door behind the cedar tree. I stand for a few minutes on the threshold of the clinic basement, peering into the dark until my eyes can see. Now I help Marius unload. When all the packages are neatly stacked against the wall next to buckets filled with medical equipment, I step inside. It smells of ether, chloroform, disinfectants. I have to wait there for Marius to enter the clinic through the main entrance and reach the floor upstairs.

After a while, I hear a grating noise. I see a platform being lowered on a heavy metal cord secured at the second floor. I hope it's well secured. I put the buckets on the platform and whistle for Marius to pull the cable. Up and down goes the platform with its cargo, until all the packages and buckets are upstairs. After the platform and the cord have disappeared, I close the door behind me. Exhausted, I lean against the truck and wait.

An hour goes by. No Marius. Odd. I go to the reception desk where I am told that the man I describe, the one with the thin moustache, is visiting the patient Victor Brauner. "Visiting hours should be over in ten minutes. You'd better remain downstairs so as not to miss him."

Marius resurfaces. He wipes his forehead with the sleeve of his shirt and tells me he stopped to visit Victor, who is very ill. He thought it would cheer him up.

"The receptionist mentioned you were with Victor Brauner," I tell him. "Is he the surrealist painter?"

"Yes. Victor used to visit the villa on Sundays when the Surrealists met to play games."

I am bubbling with excitement. I want to know more. I torture Marius with a hundred questions until I can piece together how Victor Brauner with Andre Breton, Oscar Domingues, Wilfredo Lam, Jaqueline Lamba, Max Ernst, Jaques Harold, and Andre Masson decided to produce drawings for a new pack of cards, filled with symbols and colors, which they called 'Le Jeu de Marseille.'

"Are they still here?"

"They left one by one as soon as they received their visas. Victor failed to get a visa on the Romanian quota."

"Are there any other Romanians around?"

"Tristan Tzara."

"Tzara, the founder of the DADA movement! How thrilling! Any chance of meeting either of them?"

This time Perfect Marius, in a dictatorial tone says, "You are a Swede, Johan! Don't you forget it! The French police work with the Nazis. So stay away from meeting anyone from this group!"

As events unravel, I find out that the Villa Air-Bel, named by Victor Serge "Château Espère-Visa," was the gathering place of Surrealists who had fled the occupied zone. Everyone was waiting for visas. Writers, poets, painters, all waiting to leave. I am not the only one in the queue.

I begin to understand what Marius told me when we drove through the gates of the Villa Air-Bel for the first time. What had sounded like gossip then is now clear. That Max is Ernst, Peggy is Guggenheim, Andre is Breton, Janette is Mary Jayne Gold, and Varian is Fry and I should not bother to try finding any of them because they have left. Everything sounds definitive. Like an amputation. The more I hear about them, the more I am overwhelmed by their courage. How Fry succeeded in staying a year when his permit to remain in France was only valid for three months. Even though the French authorities kept a close watch on him and his activities, he infringed every law there was, to do what he believed in. He arranged escapes from French internment camps, forged papers and passports, orchestrated illegal border crossings, and his faith in humanity made him stand up to his peers. He succeeded with his team in saving thousands before being expelled from France as an "undesirable foreigner." When finally forced to leave, Fry said he not only remembered the faces of thousands of refugees he had helped out of France, but he thought of the faces of thousands more he had to leave behind. I feel like crying. I understand there isn't only hatred in this world. I will have to persevere and survive. The problem is how.

Without Mary Jayne Gold and Varian Fry, I find myself in a windowless corridor. It's dark. Every time I think I have found an escape, the door is bolted.

I apply for the Brazilian visa. I have to show I have the means to buy a passage to get there and produce an affidavit stating that, once there, I will be able to work and will not have to beg. I must wait for an answer. Meanwhile, I can't book a passage on a ship leaving Marseille. For that I need a French exit permit and, besides the Brazilian entrance visa, I need a transit visa of the country I'd cross to get to my destination. Once I have all the documents together, I can buy my passage on a ship. But ships are so few, they are fully booked. By the time I'll get to book my passage, at least one of the visas will have expired and then, once again, I will have to wait in line while my money is running low.

Police raids are more and more frequent. I am confused. I don't know which passport to show. I decide to use the Swedish for the French, the Romanian for the Brazilians and, when in doubt, neither.

While I wait, I ponder the route I will have to take. I try to be in the port whenever there is a departure of refugees. I watch them board an old cargo ship after standing in long lines surrounded by policemen. They have to pass brutal inspectors and listen to racist insults. I am not very encouraged.

These are terrifying moments for so many of the refugees, waiting to hear if they have obtained a permit to leave, or are being sent to a concentration camp. Waiting to hear whether America will declare war on the Axis and if the Allied liberators will arrive in time.

Worst of all for me is not to have anyone to complain to and grumble with. Though by now I should be an expert in preparing adventurous escapes, I wish I had someone close to share my inner turmoil with. To tell me to make up my own mind or spend the rest of my life hiding in Fanny's attic.

XVI

I pay the rent regularly to Fanny. First for days, then for weeks. It's over a month now that I have had this room in the attic. I can come and go as I please through a trap on the floor under the table. A ladder leans against the wall in the courtyard next to the lavatory and the shower. An old, slightly rusty bicycle stands ready for a getaway or for urgent deliveries. No one besides Fanny and Marius knows I am here. Now I need enough money to pay the boat fare and to buy the many cartons of Camel cigarettes to bribe officials at the customs. I have been consulting Harry Bingham and Daniel Bénédite who has been in charge of the "Centre Américain de Secours" since Fry was expelled. Both favor the Spanish rather than the Marseille route and encourage any means to get out, provided I stay away from the impossible, legal red tape. I should leave as soon as my Brazilian visa arrives.

The time has come to untie the pouch around my waist and take out Mother's jewels. I remove the wrappings one by one and arrange each piece on the table. It's hard to decide which one to sell. Every piece has a life of its own, a meaning. Maybe I should sell the diamond brooch, which takes up the most space and which I never saw her wear. Father gave her the brooch shortly before Odo was gone. That's when we were still all together, in front of the fireplace, listening to the gramophone playing.

Marius says he can help. He takes me to a back street store behind the Canebière. There a man is seated in the dark. He wears a pince-nez which he removes. With a magnifying glass, he examines the brooch. It's an autopsy. During the dissection, he counts each stone and measures the large ones. He says the color is blue-white and speaks of numbers and of carats. I am learning a new language, but when he says that it's worth very little because the Marseille market is flooded with people selling their family jewels, my interest fades and so does my hope. Marius says, "Forget it! This is a unique jewel because it can be taken apart and worn in two pieces. I know just the person who will go wild when she sees it!"

The man with the pince-nez says he wants to think it over as I, the young man, am so nice. Perhaps he could pay just a little more. Marius mutters that he can't stand the SOB's who take advantage of the misery of people in need. I watch with admiration, tongue in cheek, this outburst of Marius's uprightness. Do what I preach, not what I do! He grabs my arm and we leave, with the brooch of course.

Marius wants to show the brooch to Lily, also known as Marie-Louise Countess Pastre. While he drives, I wonder about what kind of dump Marius is going to take me to this time. At Cap-Rouge we enter Montredon, a huge estate surrounded by high walls.

We pass several houses before we reach the main part of the castle. Men and women stop their activities to wave at us. They all seem busy with a multitude of occupations such as croquet, playing chess, singing. Three violinists are tuning the cords of their instruments next to a table where tea is being served in a samovar. Nobody pays any attention to us. Marius parks the truck at the side of the building. Then he takes my hand and, with a self-assured stride, walks me up the steps to the main entrance. At the door, Elie the butler greets us and tells us that the Countess is in the little salon listening to music.

I hear a desperate "Mario! Mario!" Someone is in danger! Numerous poodles surround us. I am ready to rescue the woman who is crying out for help before it dawns on me that I am listening to Puccini's Tosca. I am being swept into an unreal world of mystery and poetry, then swirled up on to a glistening stage.

We are led into a formal room with a grand piano covered with a shawl and silver framed photographs of the Countess in the company of important and famous people I should recognize but don't. With a finger to her lips, she tells us to keep quiet. With another sign, she indicates where we should sit and wait. We wait. Seconds after the last note is played, Countess Lily stands up, tells us that music is her life, it must be her Russian blood, and if I am a musician, I can stay as her guest for as long as I'd like.

She goes on to say that she is planning a special festivity in a wooded vale in the park. A musical event under the direction of Manuel Rosenthal with an orchestra made up exclusively of Jewish musicians who are not able to work due to the Vichy laws. She pays large fees to the artists and, if I am any good, I can start right away, and become one of her permanent house guests. Her enthusiasm is boundless. Marius tries to interrupt. She says she will not accept a refusal. All I can foresee is another failure to find the money for my departure. It's my last chance. I bravely take the brooch out of my pocket and lay it on the small table covered in red velvet. The last rays of the sun shine on it. The stones sparkle like fireworks, taking on a life of their own. A miracle. Lily stops talking. Stares for a minute. Says she must have this marvel now, for tonight. "How much?" "That's all?" "Your mother's?" She rings the bell. Where is the handbag? Oh! The naughty poodle is sleeping on it.

Never in my life will I forget the black crocodile handbag. It opens like the huge mouth of a crocodile from which appears a bunch of rolled notes, held together with an elastic band. She hands it to me. Then she hesitates. I hold my breath as she plays with the brooch, taking it apart and putting it together again. She pins it between her voluminous breasts, then admires herself in the mirror next to the windows which open on to the terrace. From the mouth of the crocodile, she removes another bunch of notes and slips it into my other hand. Then she turns to Marius. "Please ask Elie what else is urgently needed for tomorrow besides the cases and cases of champagne." She is bubbling with joy as she goes out through the French doors leading into the park. She joins her guests. Marius pats me on the shoulder to bring me back into this world. He tells me that Lily's revenue from the aperitif Noilly-Prat is being put to good use!

The super-generosity of the Countess is not enough to remove my fears. I clutch the two packs of rolled bills. I have no idea how much money it represents. But I don't know what else I'll need, what my future expenditures will be.

I am still in shock about my good luck when I climb into the truck next to Marius and watch him write notes on his palm after speaking to Elie. I show Marius the bunch of bills. "Before anything else, I want you to take whatever you want. It's your finder's fee."

He takes one bill.

"That's all?"

"Yes, that's all for now. But when you leave, I'd like you to give me your briefcase."

I stare in disbelief. "Of course, Marius! What a strange request!"

"Someday the war will be over. That's when I'll be elected Mayor of Marseille. I'll even have a football team of my own. I'll need to look very important, so I'll carry your briefcase!"

He lights a cigarette and is silent until he parks the truck in front of Chez Fanny.

"Do you need a hand with the loading?" I ask.

"Not now. Go back to your room and start studying the map showing the roads that cross over to Spain. The 'goats and smugglers' trails through the Pyrenees. When the time comes for you to go, you should be ready to leave right away."

"So you won't have to wait very long for my briefcase!"

And he laughs. So I laugh as well while I climb up the ladder to my room in the attic.

For some unknown reason I have a hunch that I should get ready, but for what exactly, I still have to find out. I take out the map and the duffle bag from the briefcase. It will be easier to carry the bag than the suitcase. I transfer everything into the duffle bag which has two handles and a gadget which means I can wear it on my back like a rucksack.

With a certain amount of nostalgia, I slip the suitcase under the bed. Father's suitcase. I'll have to leave it behind. I unfold the map on the table and study attentively the route I'll be taking. When it gets as far as Perpignan, I notice a piece of the map is missing. I turn the briefcase upside down and shake it. Out falls a black cardboard lining and the rest of the missing map of Spain and Portugal. I shake some more. A thin paper, folded to the size of a stamp, lands on the floor. Intrigued, I unfold the delicate paper with great care. I read the recipe. It's a formula in algebraic symbols about how to cook special dishes. The ingredients to be used are enumerated. I am flabbergasted. I suspect this must be the reason Marius wanted my briefcase with the double lining. A perfect hiding place. However, the formula on the folded paper must have a meaning other than how to prepare a Mediterranean ratatouille! So my meeting with Marius was not accidental. I was the carrier of documents. He knew all along everything about me, Rozalia.

It is a brief visit on the day when I stand in the office of the Brazilian Consul, Carlos Alfredo Bernardes. Through almost the entire ceremony of his handing me the passport with the Brazilian immigration visa, I stop breathing. For a moment I think I'll never breathe again. He tells me that arrangements have been made for me to leave from Porto, on the coast of Portugal, and upon my arrival in Rio de Janeiro, I'll be taken care of.

I shake hands with him. I have a peculiar feeling that makes it impossible for me to talk. He also says nothing further. At times like this, words have no meaning. I only say, "Thank you." He says, "Good luck. Take good care not to miss the boat."

I see Marius right away. He gives me a pair of sturdy walking shoes, fills my pockets and bag with packs of Camel cigarettes, and asks me to give him in a hurry another trinket or two to sell. This time it's mother's earrings and a bracelet. The next day he arrives with the money. He takes part of it to pay for the cigarettes. The rest he hands me in different envelopes. He has changed some of the money into the foreign currencies I'll be needing on my way to Porto. "I'll drive you as far as I can and leave you at the place from which you'll have to walk. No paths. You'll have to climb over the mountain. Are you afraid?"

"Of course not . . ."

"Well then, why the hell are you sitting here looking white like a virgin's bridal gown?" he wants to know.

My stomach rises in my throat and I am sick with fear. There is no use arguing with Marius. As promised, I quietly hand him the briefcase. Then the folded paper and my suitcase. While I put on the walking shoes, he unfolds the paper, reads it, ponders for a while, then tears it into little bits, puts them in the plate that is lying on the floor, lights a match, and watches it all disappear.

Parting, always parting, always in transit. No suitcase, no person can accompany me on the unknown route. Again I shake hands. Again I say nothing. Again I feel words have no meaning. Again I stand alone watching the truck disappear with Marius.

I start climbing. No path is in sight. I have memorized the route and hope I don't make any mistakes. I go through vineyards. I climb once more. There are only rocks. Stones roll down while I continue walking, hoping to get to Spain before dark. Hiram Bingham and Daniel Bénédite both rehearsed with me the road I am taking. They stressed the importance of finding the Customs right away, to avoid being shot at as a smuggler. I keep climbing, when finally I hear voices. It's almost dark. I venture into the Customs house and make my grand entrance. In perfect Spanish, I say, "I have found out that there is high duty to pay on cigarettes and have decided not to take them with me. I'd like to leave them here." I throw the whole bunch of packs on the table. Packs come out of every pocket of my duffel bag. The men don't hesitate to grab the cigarettes, while one of them stamps my Romanian passport. While I am at it, I'll have the Swedish one stamped as well. No problem. No one even looks at my name or at me. Though my legs are shaking, I leave as fast as I can without running. I am down the mountain in no time. I am in Spain!

In spite of my interest in the arts and especially in paintings I decide not to stop in Madrid to visit the Prado Museum. Without wasting any time, two days later I arrive by train at Porto de Leixoes, in Portugal. My fear is dissipating. I am leaving Johan behind. I watch his Swedish passport float on the water for a few seconds before sinking into the Atlantic Ocean forever. I am free to be Rozalia again.

BOOK II

Looking For Josephine

XVII

It is early evening when the Bahia sails from Porto de Leixoes. The lights twinkle as I look behind. It's foolish, I think, to look behind. I am standing on the lower deck with many other men and women. We each hold on to our small bags. There are fewer passengers on the upper deck where the price of the cabins is more expensive. We go down to the galley where we are handed a cheese sandwich and a banana on a small tray. I sit on my bag, afraid to lose the few belongings I have left. My papers, photographs of Mother, Father, Odo, Aunt Josephine, a few others, sandals, some toiletries, and summer clothes for when we land. My passport, the name and address of the Swedish Ambassador, seventy-three dollars, two gold Napoleons, and a diamond ring are sewn into the pouch attached to my waist under my blouse.

The officer in charge shows us to our cabins next to the boiler room, below the kitchen. Each cabin has twelve bunks. There are four cabins. Two for the men and two for the women. Even the married couples are separated.

"I don't want any problems on my ship," the captain says. "I want you to understand from the beginning that I will use any means I have to, for you to follow my orders. Unfortunately, some of you will have to sleep two or even three in one bunk because the ship is overloaded. Showers are available once a week."

During the first two days, we all try to get along with each other. It becomes increasingly difficult when the temperature soars to over one hundred degrees and we are sleeping three in one bunk. Keeping order provides the greatest challenge. At night, we stuff our clothes in the cracks of the hull to keep the rats out. The mattresses are full of lice. Food and water are scarce, and it is impossible to have more than a weekly shower. There is no medical attention for us passengers. We use a rusty bucket for our necessities, after which, through a porthole, we lower the bucket on a rope. We have to be precise in our calculation, not to lower it too far and lose the bucket, or have the wind and the waves splash the contents back on us. Each time I feel I am on a trapeze, concentrating before making the salto mortale. Twice a day we are invited on to the lower deck to walk for half an hour. We are asked not to mix with the passengers who sit on deck chairs in the sun. With the gorgeous sea around me, I try to imagine Rio with its beaches and what it will be like to be there.

For almost thirty days we, the human cargo, are jammed against each other on this floating nightmare. I lie awake at night, wondering how much longer the journey will last. When we sailed from Porto, we expected to be in Rio after two weeks. When asked about a date of arrival, the officer on board tells us that freighters are capricious. "One never knows for sure, but we will land soon."

Finally on a Monday morning, our boat stops outside Rio's harbor. A loudspeaker tells us to be ready for the ferry, and that we are being separated into three groups. First are the ones who have a visitor's visa, then the ones like me who will enter on an immigration visa sponsored by a Brazilian or a resident of Brazil, and then the ones who are already Brazilian citizens. My group is the first to board the ferry, which takes us to Ilha do Governador.

I can think of nothing as I inhale this moment which I have been dreaming about for so long. I walk down the gangplank. I am on land and it's sunny. There is a breeze coming from the sea. There are trees and flowers and birds and butterflies.

The Immigration Service consists of two tables in the shade of a big tree. I line up at the first table. The man who sits behind it is a mulatto. I hand him my papers. He looks me in the eye, smiles, and asks if I had a good trip. Then he stamps my passport, hands me a leaflet and a paper the size of a postcard. In a book he writes my name, age, the color of my eyes, and so on. I move to the next table. The man behind it stamps the card with the leaflet and says, "*Felicidades*, Dona Rozalia." I answer with the few words I know in Portuguese, among which is thank you. He smiles. I guess it must be my accent.

I follow the arrow which leads to a barrack with showers. A fat woman in a white uniform hands me a small piece of soap and a towel. The soap smells of disinfectant. I understand from her gestures that I should also wash my hair with it. "Leave your papers with me, on the table. First you have to be disinfected and deloused." She points to a basket where I can throw out my dress. I do as I am told. But before entering the shower booth, I roll into my towel the seventy-three dollars, the two gold pieces, and the ring.

After the shower, I hand in my towel and recover the papers and my carry-all bag. A woman medic examines me, gives me all sorts of shots, writes something on a yellow paper, and says, "Dona Rozalia, you'll be OK." Everyone here calls me by my first name, and nobody seems to bother about the family name. It sounds friendly. I like it. I have passed my entrance exam. I take a clean pair of panties and a dress out of my bag. The rags I was wearing are already in an incinerator. I emerge feeling cool and dressed to face the new world.

I join the rest of our group. We are invited to help ourselves to food laid out on a long table in the shade of two

orange-colored umbrellas. Rice, black beans, farofa, carne
secca, fried bananas, oranges, and mamao. We can eat as much
as we want. We are given paper cups from which we drink
first water, then coffee, with plenty of sugar.

It's heaven to sit on the bench under the coconut tree and
look at the sea while I wait for my sponsor to arrive with the
authorization to enter Rio. I would like to share my feelings
with someone. I think of Father with whom I dreamt about
all of this. And Mother. And Odo. And Aunt Josephine, whom
I hope to find someday, alive.

XVIII

Germans occupied the free zone of France on November 12, 1942. The people of Marseille were taken by surprise. The Germans arrived noiselessly at night while the mistral was blowing, covering the sounds. The armored cars, the tanks, the side cars, the machine guns quietly crushed any resistance. I made it out just in time.

Barbu Catargi, Romanian attaché at the Swedish Legation, and his Swedish counterpart, Niels Larson, arrive on a motorboat. They are both good-looking. Catargi with dark hair, brown eyes, soft traits. Larson is blond with blue eyes, strong features but not quite a Viking. They walk straight to the authorities. All the necessary papers are ready. They are shown to where I am seated, waiting for them. There is a polite exchange of greetings. They help me on to the motorboat that starts up immediately. I am arriving in Rio with two handsome young men without military uniforms. A good omen. When the boat is tied up at the pier, and we climb out, Barbu Catargi says he hopes I'll be happy with the arrangements which have been made for me. He hands me a folder as he leaves. I am beginning a new life.

The car drives Mr. Larson and me toward Copacabana where I will be staying. On the way, Mr. Larson points out the tourist attractions. In the two years he has spent in Rio, he tells me,

besides the warm climate and the beauty of nature he admits
to his fascination with the Brazilian humor. The people's joy of
living, their day-to-day happiness. "Smiles and music are part
of their lives. They have an unbelievable indifference to their
own poverty," he adds. "And great ingenuity to get around
any law. A disdain for set rules. There is always a way, just as
with the Italians, *aranjarse.*" He tells the story of a Brazilian
who applied for a license to import eight hundred pairs of
shoes from the States. He couldn't obtain the necessary import
license or the hard currency for it. So he shipped to Brazil eight
hundred shoes of all sizes and colors for the left foot only.
Upon arrival, the merchandise was held up and confiscated by
the customs according to the existing law. After one month,
the confiscated shoes were put up for auction. Needless to
say, nobody bid for the shoes except the sender. The sender's
bid was ridiculously low and successful. The rest goes as
expected. The next shipment of shoes, for the right foot, arrived
shortly afterward. The same operation was repeated. "There
is a different code of ethics in Brazil," says Mr. Larson. "It is
fun and greatly admired to fool people here, especially if it is
the customs!" The car stops on Avenida Copacabana in front
of a small two-story chalet surrounded by modern apartment
buildings.

Dona Ruth meets us. She is a small woman, very tanned,
with a languorous voice that emits many loving nouns and
adjectives. *Meu bem, meu anjo, meu amor* (my treasure, my
angel, my love). At the end of every sentence she says, *Si Deus
quiser* (with the help of God).

The place is called a Pensione, but it is not a real boarding
house. It's on two floors. Only the rooms on the second floor
are for rent. It's more like a big apartment. There are five
lodgers. I will have my own bathroom attached to my room.
But two of the lodgers have to share their shower room. Rent
is due each week. Breakfast is served downstairs, next to the

kitchen. At night, we are allowed to snack on the cheese, goiabada, and bananas of many different qualities—*oro, prata, agua.* Oranges are cut so that the only way you can hold them is by the bottom peel, while you suck out the juice and throw away the pulp. You make orange juice in your mouth with your teeth. Occasionally, there is another kind of orange called *lima,* with a sweeter taste. Next to the biscuits there is a box like a piggy bank where we are supposed to leave a few cruzeiros after we have helped ourselves to food. If anyone cheats and doesn't leave the money in the box after cutting a slice of cheese with *goiabada,* there won't be anything to nibble on when this is finished.

Dona Ruth assures me that I will not meet the other lodgers, as they all have different schedules. She runs the Pensione with one maid. "It brings me a nice income," she tells me, "but I am very choosy with my lodgers. It's important to keep the respectability of the Pensione intact. Before I accept a new boarder, I check on his or her references. If anyone misbehaves, they are given twenty-four hours to clear out."

I have no references, and my first month's rent has been paid in advance by the Swedish Legation. It will be deducted from the salary I will earn by doing translations and giving lessons to Ambassador and Madame Hesselvicks' two young sons.

Mr. Larson leaves me in my room, explaining that he will come back tomorrow morning, after eleven, to drive me to work. "You'll get acquainted with your duties and meet the people you'll be working with. Meanwhile, you can either rest or go out for a walk. Turn left, then left again, go through a square—the Lido—straight toward the Avenida Atlantica which runs for six miles along the sandy beach." He gives me one hundred cruzeiros for which I sign a receipt, in case I want to buy something from the vendors on the beach: sliced pineapple, coconut milk, and, most importantly, a straw hat. His last piece of advice before leaving me is, "Be careful in the sun. It's very strong. Better wear a hat and cover your arms and shoulders."

I remember that during the holidays, when we were at the beach, we rubbed suntan oil on our bodies. So on my way out, I stop in the kitchen and spread cooking oil abundantly on the parts that will be exposed to the sun—legs, arms, and nose. I realize I don't smell very nice. Actually, I stink. But once out on the street, I don't care. I get the cold shoulder from a passerby, and a dog barks at me in an unfriendly way. I buy my straw hat and walk, almost run, on the wavy mosaic of the Avenida Atlantica. I see all those bodies on the beach. The colored umbrellas. Some people play volleyball on the sand, others play *futebol*, soccer. Acrobatics. Bodies, bare feet, friendly laughter. I am in heaven.

The first thing to do in heaven is to take off my sandals and lift up my skirt before wetting my feet in the Atlantic Ocean. I feel like Neptune—so powerful—when, suddenly, a tall wave knocks me and my inflated ego down. There goes my straw hat. Now I feel more like a wet duck, but at least I don't stink anymore. I dry myself in the sun.

When I return to the Pensione, the humidity is thick, and I feel the stinging of sunburn. Dona Ruth is in her room with the door open. She smokes a corn pipe and asks me to come in. On a dresser are small statues of the Virgin, Saint Sebastian, and a crucifix. Blessed saints on postcards lean against the wall, and a candle burns on a plate. She smiles. "You look very burned, but don't worry." She hands me a white paste to put on my nose and all over the parts that sting. "Drink a lot of liquid, Dona Rozalia. Be careful not to dirty the furniture with the white paste when you get to your room." I already envisage sleeping standing up tonight so that I don't get the ointment all over the sheets, or I could sleep on the floor so that I don't upset Dona Ruth on my first night in her Pensione. "Drink a lot of water," she insists, and she follows me into the kitchen.

I take a cup from the shelf and pour some tap water. She stops me. "No! Not this water! Don't drink this!" Perplexed, I look at Dona Ruth who points toward a stone filter. "You must only drink water from the filter." She explains at length the mortal threat of tap water. The sewage system. The heavy rains. The putrefaction. In fifteen minutes she has transformed a Paradise on Earth, into Paradise Lost. I manage to abstain from laughing aloud while I think how Dona Ruth would have fared on a one day cruise on the Bahia.

I go to my room with bottles of filtered water and oranges. It's pleasant. The furniture is simple, functional, shiny, and brown, upholstered with a nondescriptive print in a smudged, practical, nondescriptive color. The two big windows are on opposite sides of the room. One looks out on the Avenida Copacabana, the other onto a small court surrounded by the back part of apartment buildings with balconies on each floor. The balconies are open enclosures with laundry hanging out to dry. I can see the laundresses scrubbing sheets against the inclined stone part of the large basin, the *tanke*. There is one faucet of cold water for each *tanke* and each balcony has two *tanke*. One to scrub in, and the other to leave the laundry to soak overnight. There are small piles of laundry soaking in the sun all along the edge of the balconies. After rinsing, the sheets are raised on a string to the ceiling to dry.

I watch this procedure while I drink the filtered water and eat oranges. I spend a sleepless night, trying to figure out how to look my best when I meet my new employers. From all the oranges I sucked during the night I now have the runs. I'm not religious, but at this point, I am convinced that only God can help me.

God helps me. My interview is not a disaster. My schedule at the office is explained to me. I meet Madame Birgitta

Hesselvick, a Scandinavian beauty, who is the wife of the Swedish Ambassador. She is kind and discusses literature with me. She says she is impressed by my references and hopes that I will enjoy my work. She would like her sons to have an eclectic education which, it appears, I possess.

XIX

Teresopolis is a resort less than two hours by car from Rio and much cooler during the summer heat. Most of the city's well-to-do have their country homes there. At weekends, there are parties, luncheons, and dinners around swimming pools. On Sundays, most invitations are for a late lunch of a *feijoada* which consists of black beans with all sorts of smoked meats and sausages, rice, *farofa* and many other dishes. Drinks are for the most part *cachaça* and beer.

I am at the swimming pool with the two Hasselvick boys, Lars, eleven years old, and Bertil, ten. We are showing off, doing acrobatics on the trampoline. Then we dive and chase each other under water. When I am on firm ground again, my eyes red from the chlorine in the water, I remove my swimming cap, and in my black one-piece bathing-suit, I jump up and down on one foot to get the water out of my ear. In front of me stands a man with a glass of beer in one hand and a cigar in the other. He looks like an El Greco portrait. Elongated, with dark penetrating eyes, dark hair, a straight nose with big nostrils, and a sensuous full lower lip. He is not only good-looking, but he has an air of whimsical elegance in his blue shirt and slacks.

"Would you like a towel?"

"No, thank you, I will dry in the sun before Lars pushes me into the water again."

My nose is running. He puts his cigar in his mouth, hands me his handkerchief, and says I can keep it. I blow my nose and put the handkerchief under the swimming cap on the deck chair. I notice his watch, a reversible Le Cultre like Father's watch. It's four o'clock.

"How old are you?" he asks.

"Seventeen," I snap, "and you?"

"Thirty-eight." With a condescending voice he adds, "Too bad you are only seventeen!"

"Why?"

"Because I can't marry you until you are eighteen without your parents' consent."

"Too bad, I don't have any parents to tell me that you have very naughty eyes."

I think, "the cheek this man has!" and I jump into the pool. When I emerge he's gone and I'm glad.

The butler brings cake and lemonade and says that the guests have left. But we linger on, and I tell the boys about the adventures of Odysseus, the way Aunt Josephine used to tell me.

On Monday morning we drive back to Rio. The ambassador asks me if, after next weekend, I could stay on for about ten days in Teresopolis to do some important work translating for him. French into English. His secretary will drive up from Rio every other day to work with me for a few hours. It would be of great help to him, and he hopes that I will not feel too lonely. Fernando and Esther, the keepers at the *sitio*, will take care of all the household duties. I am thrilled to be on my own. I am eager to plunge into research in books and dictionaries. I feel I've hit the jackpot. But I have to wait another week.

For two days now, I am alone at the *sitio* in Teresopolis. The house is spacious. The furniture is modern and comfortable.

The only time I leave my desk in the library is when Esther brings in a tray and insists I eat while everything is still warm. She puts the tray on the round table by the window. She won't leave the room until I sit down and try her food. She grumbles that I am too thin and spend too much time with books. When she comes back to clear away the tray, she checks that there is nothing left on the plate. Then, she asks if I need anything, and I don't see her again until dinner at seven, when the same ceremony is repeated. By eight, she draws the curtains and closes the shutters, and I can work in peace until late into the night.

At nine, I open the glass door and the shutters. Through the wire netting that keeps the insects out, the room is filled with an unfamiliar scent. For another hour, I am buried in my papers. Then I hear a voice say, "This is a kidnapping. If you don't shout, nothing bad will happen to you." I immediately hide the papers I am working on under the blotter and look up. A masked man is pointing a gun at me. He is wearing a black hat and a cape.

"Zorro?" I say. I know I should be frightened but I am curious. What a story to tell the boys!

He does not answer. Then, with the gun pointing at me he says, "Now, walk quietly in front of me, or I'll tie you up and carry you out."

I walk ahead of him on damp grass. We take a short cut to the entrance gate. He opens the iron gate, pushes me out, and closes it carefully. In the lamplight I am surprised to see a thoroughbred horse with an elegant saddle. The man unties the horse. Without any warning, he covers my head with his cape. Before I know it, he is in the saddle with me in front of him, galloping away.

After a while, I ask, "What is it you want with me?"

"I don't like to ride alone, I thought you'd like to join me."

He stops at the entrance of a greenhouse, opens the door, and tells me to sit on a bench. He sits next to me, lights a cigarette. And then I see it. The Le Cultre watch.

"Will you hand me your gun before it melts?" I burst into laughter and tear off his mask.

"May I introduce myself, Henrique Moreira Cardoso." He turns on the light. We are surrounded by orchids. An infinite variety of orchids.

XX

Henrique Moreira Cardoso teaches me how to ride bareback. "The best time is at night," he tells me, "when the heat is down and palm trees move their branches against a spray of shooting stars. When the moon is big and red. When mosquitoes buzz and mixed odors fill the air." For a week, I ride for hours every night. I can now hop on to the horse without the slightest effort.

"Now, there's only one way for you to completely relate to the horse," he says.

"And what way is that?" I look at him, surprised.

"Ride naked."

"What, naked?"

"Yes, besides your boots. You have to keep them on because, in some places, there are ticks in the grass and there's also a worm which, if it enters the skin, can only be removed by freezing."

I take off my clothes. Henrique hardly looks at me. He rides by my side. For another three hours, I ride, rubbing against the horse's spine. The rough trot slaps me in the crotch and bounces me from side to side. My back is straight, my knees press the horse's sides. I am sore. I wish I had a pillow or a towel between my legs. I want to give up. The horse's spine hurts.

"It hurts too much. I can't do this any more," I yell.

"You can't stop now," he laughs. "Go on, arch your back more!" and he whips my horse to make it go faster. The sky breaks lose with torrential rains. Thunder. The horse gets excited.

"Wiggle your lower part, your *bunda*!" Henrique shouts. "Samba to the tune of the wind! Can you feel the rain glide on your body?"

It pours. A vale of water is coming down. I see Henrique dancing his horse around mine. He grabs me by my waist and sits me on his horse, astride in front of him. I am facing him. My back is against the horse's mane. The horse breaks into a faster trot. Henrique penetrates me. Again and again and again. The horse trots on. I can only hear whispers, mutterings and moans.

I am finally alone. I stand naked in the bathroom in front of a long mirror, and I examine my body with great curiosity. What has changed? It hurts me to pee, and I ache in a place inside me, a place I never felt before. I smile ironically and see a wicked look in my eyes. I shrug my shoulders. Big deal! Now that I have done this as well, what's next? I can't help but think. If only he knew. No matter what I do or let him do to me, I can't erase from my mind the slaughterhouse, the train ride, Mother hanging from that cord, and Father's soulful-looking eyes when he left for good.

Yet Henrique brings me an intoxication I find hard to master. There are moments with him when I feel that nothing else matters. That I am beyond mourning—beyond tragedy. I am tempted to yield to those moments of relief from myself when I can transcend my pain and start healing. As if by magic, he has the power to make me overcome the agony of my loss. We know nothing important about each other. However, he did tell me that he is not simple, that he is a hunter who knows how to domesticate the most ferocious jaguar. He can make it enter willingly into a cage that only he knows how and when to open.

He calls me Oncinha, baby jaguar. The metaphor is enough for me. I know before I experience it that he'll try by every means to trap and cage me into his phantasmagoric world.

I must not see him again. I must go on with my life and determine the course I want to take. I have to master my own destiny, to know what to do and what to aim for. I won't let myself take refuge in some empire of the senses. I must stop seeing him. I must not see him again.

And I see him a week later. I don't tell him he is the first man I have made love with. I don't tell him I love him which I don't know if I do. He doesn't tell me he loves me either. He says it would please him no end if I would not wear my panties when I meet him. I say it is too hot anyway and it suits me fine. He says it's important to feel the urge of our bodies, to let our senses talk for us. We don't talk much otherwise. There is no time. Words seem useless. A look, rain, thunder, a parrot swinging on a branch. Almost anything stirs up the lust that draws us together. Words only start to flow once we are riveted to each other. We then confide aloud the absurdities of our imaginations which are without limits.

I ride side-saddle for our meeting today. Henrique wanted us to be dressed all in white, for the purity of our inner thoughts, he said, and smiled. I wear a long loose white skirt with my blouse, tied in a knot at my waist. He wears his white shirt unbuttoned, with white jodhpurs and his black boots. We wear identical straw hats. We ignore each other. I steal a look at him. He looks terrific. At times he opens a passage through the woods to let me pass. Occasionally he lets the branch of a tree run up and down my back, to remind me he is still there.

We arrive at our usual meeting place, the first *botequin* where the path ends. The owner greets us from behind the counter. We tie our horses to the pole next to a low wooden hedge and we go straight to the table in the shade. The owner brings us two *cafezinhos* and two *cachaças*. He pulls the key to the back room out of the pocket of his shorts and places it by the sugar bowl.

"*Ate ja.*" He takes off his flip-flops to crush a fly against the door as he disappears. It is very hot, siesta time. Not even the dog is outside. We remove our hats and sip the *cafezinho*, drink the *cachaça*. We watch the sky through the leaves and the flowers of the flamboyant tree without touching each other. Perversely, we let our desire grow into exasperation. The perspiration is running down his chest. My hair is moist. He surveys me sharply and does not take his eyes off me. I get fidgety. He hands me another *cafezinho* which the man has brought us. He takes the spoon, dips it in the sugar at the bottom of my cup and puts it in his mouth. He slowly licks the sugar off the spoon, his eyes fixed on me. Each of his movements seems to be coming from some internal force. He does not budge. I want to leave. I get up, turn my back on him, and take a step in the direction of my horse.

"So long," I say casually. I hear the noise of his zipper. He pulls me back, folds me over the table, lifts my skirt, and with one hand turns my head to the side. With his other hand he parts my buttocks, a ripe apricot, and penetrates me from the back.

"So you were going to leave! Right? You wanted to ride away! Didn't you? Here, take it!" He clings with both hands to my breasts while he humps me from behind like a dog.

A few minutes later, he pulls my skirt down, lifts me up in his arms, takes the key next to the sugar bowl and carries me indoors.

"My trophy," he says, as we pass the sleepy man at the counter. In front of the room he turns the knob and opens the door. He gently puts me down on the bed and starts undressing me. The door is wide open.

"Don't you mind if someone sees me like this?"

"Let them watch and applaud. What we have together is a masterpiece." He laughs. "I'll be back in a second." He leaves the room and opens the door even wider. He comes back with a plateful of jars containing vinegar, oil, salt, and pepper. He says he is ready for a salad, and he locks the door from the inside.

His clothes and boots are on the floor. He is kneeling next to me. He holds the jar high up and tilts it in such a way that the oil splashes between my breasts. He then slides his hands on my body from top to toe. When he is finished oiling every part of me, he rubs his body against mine until we are both slippery, rolling over each other like two eels.

He is gentle and tender as he gives me my shower, washes me, rinses me, dresses me, and puts on my makeup. He asks me to sit on a chair by the open window while he puts on his clothes. With his arm on my shoulder, we walk out and pass the counter. He leaves the key with a note on the plate. The man says, "*Muito obrigado, Doutor Henrique.*"

In Rio, a few days later, I meet him downstairs at the entrance of the Pensione. I am all dressed up. He opens the door of the Mercury Convertible, and I slide in next to him. I give him a peck on the cheek, and he pinches my *bunda*. I would like to go to a nightclub and see something of Rio's nightlife. He puts the top down and says that I am too young to go to a nightclub. But maybe some other time, when we are bored with each other.

Meanwhile, he suggests, we *will* have dinner at a place by the sea. We drive on the avenue along the beaches and take the road up after Joa toward Barra da Tijuca. He parks the car at the door of the restaurant. We walk on wooden planks to our table, close to the sea. We hear the roar of waves crashing on the sand. We peel the large broiled shrimps and eat with our fingers, then rinse them in a bowl with slices of lemon.

We take off our shoes to walk on the wet sand. Waves break at our feet, abandoning seaweed with its strong odor. Henrique picks up a bunch of fresh slippery seaweed in his hand and rubs it on my thigh.

I let him palpate me internally and externally and discover with amazement the delights of his touch. The light of the moon picks out the gleam in his eyes and his teeth as he thrusts his head backward. He stops at nothing. He holds my head with both hands. He sinks deep inside me. Back and forth until I almost choke. Grains of sand are also in my mouth. We roll to the music of the sea foam mixed with the foam of our excitement. Between water and shore, the sea washes our foam away. The lights of Rio are glittering along the coast.

XXI

Three months now. I call Henrique "Amante," Lover. He has rented a studio in Copacabana next to my Pensione so that we can meet anytime during the day and occasionally spend the night together, when parting seems impossible. I have to be early at work, and at the rate we are going, I'm not getting any sleep. Every day he grows more intense. Henrique now wants to know where I am and with whom, whenever I am not with him. He says he has to be able to find me at any time. It's not Romeo and Juliet. It's more like hell, infernal and sublime. At times it's poetry. Like Baudelaire's "Les Fleurs du Mal." There is no end to his fantasies and now even mine. I am hardly ever at the Pensione. Only to shower and change my clothes.

"I'm tired," I say. "We can't go on like this."

"We have to masturbate before we meet. That's all."

There are evenings when we can only see each other at midnight, after his dinners and unavoidable social obligations. Then he's in a bad mood, especially if I arrive after him. He says that the next time, if I am even one minute late he'll strangle me. Or maybe just punish me in such a way that I'll never be able to leave his sight. When he is in this state of mind, he keeps speaking without waiting to hear an answer. He unbuckles his belt and cracks it on the table.

"You are nothing but a little girl, you little animal! You are not even domesticated! I want a real woman! You aren't yet ready for all I want to do with you. You are too young for me!" His eyes glitter, the corner of his mouth is turned down. He talks on and on.

I get close to him, put my arms around his neck, rub myself against his body, and whisper in his ear, "Will you teach me how to became a woman? How to be ashamed of nothing? How to want more and more without any boundaries?"

As I talk, I can feel him grow. He then relieves his anxiety on my dress.

"No boundaries?" he asks and puts the palm of my hand against his mouth.

"No boundaries."

"None?"

"None."

"Then come with me, I'll show you a part of Rio you have not seen."

"I want to change my dress."

"No, you must keep it on like this."

He changes into casual clothes. He takes a few bills out of his wallet and puts the money in the pocket of his trousers. He slides his hand under my arm and leads me to a taxi parked around the corner. "Lapa," he tells the driver. It's two in the morning.

We are walking in the red light district. The lowest there is.

A street prostitute comes up to me. She's big and black. She sticks out her tongue and wets her lips, then does all sort of contortions with her tongue.

"Anything a man can do I can do to you," she says and urinates, standing on the curb of the street.

I hear a raucous voice coming from one of the cubicles.

"Are you new here? Taking our business away, hey?"

In the row of cages, one next to another, some of the bamboo blinds are down. Leaning at their windows, each prostitute shows what she can do. Her specialty. A mulatto with bleached hair nods with an inviting smile. A fat white woman with permed red hair leans forward, her breasts in a demi-bra appear ready to fall out. A blue-eyed doll, thin and wrinkled, flat as a board, with a red bow tie round her neck and a short red apron tied to her waist, throws her head backward while, with her hand, she touches herself under her apron . . .

"Anything you want I can give you," says one with black-laced boots. Her laddered black stockings are held up by a worn garter-belt. She holds a whip in one hand and a chain in the other. She wears a military cap and cracks the whip against her boots.

"Interested?" asks Henrique.

"No thanks."

"Do you want to come inside and watch?" says the mulatto with bleached hair. "Which one of you is going to watch?"

"No, no."

"What, no watching, no doing?" She removes her bra. "It's late. Come on. Half price for you with your daughter."

A drunken young sailor approaches the big, fat prostitute. He says he can give her twenty cruzeiros. That's all he has left. It's closing time, he argues.

"For twenty cruzeiros what do you think you'll get? Crabs, that's about all you can get for twenty cruzeiros!"

"What? Crabs?" The young sailor looks surprised.

"You don't expect silk worms for twenty cruzeiros, do you!" she laughs.

Henrique goes toward her and hands her a bill of a hundred. Leaning on the windowsill, she opens the door without leaving her stool. She lowers the bamboo curtain. "Come," she tells Henrique. "Bring the girl in as well." Henrique grabs me by the hand as I try to draw back.

"So you wanted to see it all!" he says to me. I try to pull away; he won't let my hand go. With his other hand he grabs the young sailor by the neck the way one holds a puppy and pushes him through the opened door. "Cheers," he says. He chuckles while he lets me walk away.

The prostitute watches us with bored contempt. He follows me but keeps a distance, pretending we are not together.

We meet at the pharmacy, the medical center at the corner. The prostitutes each have a card, a license. They regularly have to undergo medical examinations for venereal diseases.

"Do you have enough for now? Do you want more?"

My curiosity grows like a soufflé with every word he utters. He takes me around to ill-famed places and explains in detail what they do there. When my eyelids flutter, he says, "Shall I go on?"

I learn much about life with Henrique, a life in which the frenzy of lovemaking becomes a primary occupation. Every evening he has something new in store for me. We look at pornographic pictures and drawings. He tells me the ones he likes and wants to know the ones which arouse me most. When I don't entirely dare to show my excitement and resist him by saying that I can't just be a slave to sex, he slides his hand on my fur and, with his fingers in me, checks my reactions.

"Liar, you little hypocrite. Look me in the eye." He takes me in his arms and whispers, "I want to love you like no one ever has or ever will. I'll love you in such ways to make the whores in Lapa blush. With me, you'll forget the world."

It all sounds like a song. I think he is insane. I feel too weak to stop and too weak to go any further. But I can't back out. I'll do whatever he wants. Whatever his eyes tell me to do.

He has bought me two dresses. A white one and a black one. The dresses are tight and cling to my body. I need him to zip me up. He also chooses my shoes. I now wear very high heels. I have trouble walking without looking where I am going. He wants me to comb my black hair straight and flat against my head. He puts on my makeup. A deep red lipstick on my mouth and black mascara on my eyelashes. He is right. I look stunning like this and, of course, older. He wants me to drive everyone crazy when he takes me out or to a party. He now takes me to his parties. And as soon as men gather around me and I enjoy myself, we leave.

When we meet, I have no idea what to expect. Anything can happen.

Tonight, after dinner at the Bec Fin, we drive up to the Corcovado. At the foot of the Statue of Christ, he kneels down. He stretches his arms the same way as the Statue of Christ does, looks up to the sky, and tells me how I'll soon enjoy and love everything he is dreaming up for me. He tells me that I'll be free from the chains of my past the day I have no other thoughts besides yearning to be with him.

"You will then be close to insanity," he says.

"Aren't we already there?"

"No." He shakes his head. "We haven't even started."

The way he talks, I think he's ready for his next move. I can hear the flutter of wings, going to and fro between expectation and fear.

In silence for a few minutes, we look at the view of Rio at our feet.

"A nightcap?" His voice is cynical as we are driving back to Rio. His eyes glitter maliciously. He turns the car off the road and puts the brakes on. "I will drag you on your high heels into the forest and use every part of you for hours while you scream helplessly," he says. "I'll let you scream until you have no other thoughts besides yearning to be with me."

"No way," I laugh. "No way!" I scream. We hug.

XXII

Now he has a new one! He doesn't telephone me twice a day anymore. He is frequently late. Friday he doesn't show up. I wait half an hour and then leave.

Three days later he phones and apologizes, telling me how busy he was at the office. How terribly sorry he is to have neglected me.

"I hadn't noticed," I tell him. "I didn't think we had a date. Didn't you say you'd be away for a few days?" I keep my voice charming and gay. "Is everything all right at the *fazenda*?"

"What? Is that all you have to say? Don't you care? Haven't you even noticed my absence? Weren't you worried?"

"Why should I have been worried?"

"Did I hurt you?"

"Of course not," I laugh. I am immune. I think to myself, how can he hurt me when no one can ever hurt me?

"I'm coming over. Be downstairs. I am taking you away with me." His voice sounds short, sharp, and final.

"Sorry, Amante, I can't make it. I have a lesson."

"When do you finish?"

"Not before seven."

"It's two o' clock now. What kind of a lesson is that?"

"Psychology and manners, Lover."

At seven he storms into my room at the Pensione. Takes me in his arms, slides one hand down my dress. I melt.

"Your lips aren't even parted, your legs aren't even spread apart! You are wearing panties! Haw dare you!" He pushes me away, turns on his heel, and goes toward the door. "I'm off to the *fazenda*. By tomorrow, if you can stop your nonsense, Cosme will fly you over. Be ready by eleven." The door closes behind him.

I hate myself for letting him treat me like a yo-yo, back and forth, up and down. I forget about dinner and try to read. I can't. I think of Henrique and wonder why he has to torment himself and me all the time. I think of the gray years of my adolescence, back there in Romania, when events were so violent. Why must he, for no reason whatsoever, create additional torment to endure?

It's Saturday morning when I hop into the two-seater Beechcraft Plane next to Cosme, the pilot. He straps me into my safety belt and pulls the throttle. The engine roars. We fly low enough over the *favelas* (shanty towns) to see the houses made of mud and straw. Multicolored clothes are drying in the sun. Children stop playing to wave at us. A young boy beats a drum made out of an empty container. Two girls dance. An elderly man sits in the shade smoking a corn pipe. The plane climbs up as we leave the shores of Rio behind. For almost an hour we fly over large areas of fields, some planted with corn, others with mandioca. Miles of coffee shrubs. White cows graze in a pasture and drink by the river. The plane passes through a cloud, the cows disappear. Now we fly over a forest, then an alley of houses. Then we fly over an enclosure for horses. Another enclosure where pigs are bred. Cosme tells me that Senhor Henrique owns all this land. He points out the houses of the farmers who work there. "About five hundred people," he says. "Senhor Henrique built the church, the school and the hospital for them, even a store."

We are landing on the fairway. Henrique is there waiting. He smiles. He holds a branch of wild white orchids, the color of his open shirt. I think flowers are so unlike him. As I jump out of the plane, he throws the orchids at my feet. I am in his arms.

"Oncinha," he says, "Will I need a cactus for today?" We laugh and hug. He murmurs in my ear, "No panties?"

"No panties, Amante!"

Maria, the maid, comes running over to us with the message from Consuelo the cook that lunch will be ready in an hour.

Henrique hands her my carry-all bag.

"Maria, show the Senhora to the blue guest room."

We watch each other for a moment. He squeezes my hand with unusual warmth.

"I'll meet you at the house for lunch," he says. "I have prepared a dish you've never had before, especially for you. *Cozido*, a Brazilian stew, you know." He laughs. "You'll see, you'll like it."

I follow Maria along the stone path, lined with banana trees. We reach the house. In front of the entrance are two colossal trees with vanilla vines and strings of orchids hanging from their branches. The windows of every room open onto the verandah that runs along the U-shaped house. Maria opens the door for me, and I enter a large hall. The furniture is dark and heavy looking, made of jacaranda wood. I walk across the room behind Maria. I can hear my steps on the stone slabs as she opens the latticed door for me, through which one can see and not be seen. On my right, the door to the blue guest room is wide open. Every piece of furniture is carved in dark jacaranda. A cedar treasure chest is at the foot of a large four poster bed. Under the mosquito net, I can see the fine embroidered linen sheets. An antique pew sits in a vaulted niche. A white nightgown with many rows of white lace and a pair of high heeled white slippers has been laid out. Two tall silver candlesticks stand against a wall, framing a painting of Salome dancing. Maria sets my bag on a chair, shows me the door to the bathroom, explains how I can get to the outside dining area where Senhor Henrique will be having lunch. She asks if there is anything I need, and leaves.

I take a quick shower, brush my hair close to my head, and put on a touch of lipstick before I slip into a sleeveless cotton dress.

A few minutes later I enter the outdoor dining niche. Trails of flowers climb the walls. Henrique sits in a wicker rocking chair by the hammock which is hung between two wooden beams. The shade feels cool. A green field lies at our feet, stretching as far as the eye can see.

He stands up, pulls out my chair, and smiles.

"Fold up the back of your dress so as not to crumple it, and sit down, Oncinha. We have *Cozido* today, remember?"

I fold up the dress and he pushes the chair under me. I'm ready to sit down.

"Ai! Oh!" I jump up.

He pushes me down on the hot pad on the chair. The boiling hot pad on the chair.

Maria comes in and leaves the food on the table. Henrique tells her to go away.

He puts a piece of meat and a *chouchou* on my plate.

"Eat. Sit still and eat. I'll have you boiling hot when . . ." he fills his own plate, looking me in the eyes. He then smiles, full of mischief. "Are you drooling? Will you now remember to be boiling hot, your lips apart, no panties ever again? You will remember, won't you?"

With both hands he lifts me and sits me on his lap with my legs spread out. He nibbles at my neck and murmurs, "Arch your back and move while you are boiling hot. Just the right temperature," as he turns me around. He is rocking his chair back and forth with himself in me. "Keep moving, he says, move faster. Don't stop." Then, with his napkin, he wipes off the traces of the *Cozido* and lies me on the hammock.

"I'll be back. Wait for me here."

An hour later he is back at the wheel of his jeep.

"Are you all right?"

I nod yes.

"Jump in. Come closer. Hold on to me. It's going to be a shaky ride." He presses his foot on the accelerator. The jeep jolts along. He drives for miles, making occasional stops to check on the various generators. He explains that the *fazenda* has its own electricity and water from its three wells. Whenever we pass a group of peasants, they remove their hats. He stops to talk to one and the other. He has a notebook in his hand and keeps making notes. At every stop we make, he is handed sheets with numbers, which he examines thoroughly in seconds. I watch this man whom I have not met before. Sure of himself. Conscious of the way he looks. Master of all those people.

The jeep jerks along the road for another fifteen miles before it stops at the entrance of the stables. Henrique also breeds racing horses. In front of a big round building where horses mate, the groom is at the door. He says we should not go in now, especially not the Senhora. The stallion is about to mount the mare.

Henrique asks me if I want to watch. Without waiting for an answer, he pushes me in through a side door. He lowers his voice and murmurs obscenities in my ear while the stallion performs. Then he turns his back on me and speaks to the veterinarian for a few moments. After which he takes my hand and hurries me toward the jeep. He seems upset. I ask him why.

"Your nipples are showing through your dress. It's time for you to wear a bra."

"You, the exhibitionist? Amante, you must be joking!"

"No, I am not."

"Jealous?" I ask.

He puts his right hand on his heart.

"It hurts," he says. "You don't know how much it hurts. It never hurt like that before."

"Am I the one to hurt you?"

"You hurt me every time I see you and every time I don't. My mind is ablaze with the thought of you. My body is in pain when I am not in you."

"Amante, it doesn't have to be like this. Why do you continuously have to alternate between cruelty and gentleness, between euphoria and gloom?" I caress his hair then his bushy eyebrows. "Could we simply just be happy and laugh?"

"Impossible as long as you refuse to do what I ask."

"But I always do whatever you want me to do."

"No. You don't."

"What else do you want?"

"Come to live with me. You are my woman, my wife, and only death can part us."

"Please, Henrique, give me some more time. I am not ready yet. I still have a few things to work out."

"Now, Oncinha, now!" and he steps on the accelerator. The jeep moves on.

At dinner he is quiet. There are clouds on his forehead. Between spoonfuls of coconut ice cream he says, "A few days ago, I obtained a divorce in Uruguay from my wife, Carla. We have been *desquitado* for over two years." He explains that in Brazil, a Catholic country, there is no divorce but a legal separation called *desquite*. Most Brazilians who want to remarry divorce in Uruguay after obtaining their legal separation in Brazil. "The second marriage is illegal in Brazil but valid in any other non-Catholic country. Someday the law will have to change. So many Brazilians just go ahead and remarry many times. A good lawyer does what is necessary to protect the second family. The only legal heirs are the children of the first family."

"Tell me about your children," I say.

"Carla," he replies, "has two boys, Geraldo and Conrado, and a girl, Ariana, from her previous marriage. In the future, I might myself bring up a boy, the way we do in Brazil. The procedure is called *de criacao*. He is treated the same way one's own child would be."

"Are these children *de criacao* ever legally adopted?"

"Some are."

"When do you see Carla's children?"

"I'll have all three children stay with me over Christmas. I don't want to separate them from each other or from me. They are too young."

I don't ask if Carla will be there as well. All I want to know is that Henrique will not interfere with my plans for Christmas. I have accepted the invitation from the ambassador and Madame Hesselvick to go to the *sitio* in Teresopolis. They have asked me to stay with them during the children's summer vacation and until after Carnival, during the months of January and February. I am welcome to stay with them all the time, but if I can't, two days a week will do. When Mademoiselle has her days off.

I tell Henrique about the plan.

"I am pleased to know that you won't be working every day from Christmas to the end of the Carnival," he replies. "We'll spend New Year's Eve together, and you'll see all the *macumbas*, black magic, on the beach. We'll dance during Carnival until our feet drop off." He stares at me, his voice intense. "By then you'll be eighteen, old enough to realize your life is with me."

The dark clouds on his forehead have disappeared. Henrique sees me to the door of my room.

"Wear the white nightgown laid out on the pew. For the servants, you know. I'll see you in a little while, Oncinha."

He leaves. I wait for him all night in the white nightgown.

Next morning is Sunday. Maria brings me a breakfast tray, with two coffee cups and two glasses of orange juice. A white orchid on my plate. There is a knock at the door. I am surprised by his courtesy. He respects my privacy, I say to myself. When the door opens, Henrique is all smiles. He is wearing a purple robe over white pajama trousers. A white scarf is tied around his neck.

He is freshly shaven. I can smell his Kneeze lotion as he sits on my bed, drinks the orange juice, and waits for me to do the same.

"Did you sleep well, Oncinha?"

"Yes, wonderfully well, thank you. Your orchid is beautiful. Thank you, Amante. How did you sleep?"

"Fine. Put the orchid in your hair behind your ear and get ready for church."

"Church?"

"Yes, church. It's Sunday."

"I don't want to go."

"We'll see."

He removes the tray from the bed and puts it on the table by the window. He pulls out a long white scarf from the pocket of his robe.

"Now put your hands together and pray. Pray that I don't strangle you today."

"All right, I pray that you don't suffer too much if you don't strangle me today." I burst out laughing while he ties my hands together with the scarf.

He turns the radio on, and to the beat of the music, he dances with me toward the antique pew in the corner of the room.

"Now kneel on the red velvet," he says, removing his scarf. I am on my knees and he binds my eyes with the scarf. I see nothing. I am not laughing anymore.

"Now pray," I hear his threatening voice. "Pray to me. Your only God. You must be blind to all but me. Do you understand? Your faith in me must be blind like all faith is. Tell me you'll do what I ask you to do." He does not expect an answer as he obsessively goes on. "You are not going back to Rio tonight. You are staying here. You'll live with me all the time."

"I have to be at work early tomorrow morning." I attempt to free myself.

"You'll have no other work from now on."

"No, I can't. Not yet."

"Yes, you can."

"Please, Amante, let me go! I need a day life as well."

"Stubborn! Someday you'll come to your senses. I'll kill you if you don't!" He pulls my nightgown over my head, spreads my legs. With both hands he holds my hips. "Now arch your back, tremble with rage all you want. You will not free yourself of me. Do you understand?"

I end up understanding.

He is furious and will not remove the scarves binding my hands and my eyes. "You deserve to be in the basement where the slaves used to be chained. What would you have done then?"

"Just what we are doing anyway," I answer.

With the belt of his robe he ties my hands to the pew. He picks up the receiver of the internal phone by my bed and tells Cosme to be ready by four to fly me back to Rio. "That's what you want, Oncinha, don't you?" Next he calls Maria and asks her to put a tray with fruit, cheese, *goiabada*, and a bottle of red wine on the table outside the bedroom door. No one is to disturb him until he rings. I hear him bolt the door. Draw the curtains.

"Now it's only you and me. I'll see to it that when you leave you'll be crawling on your knees." He removes the bandage from my eyes and lights the candles in the silver candlesticks. "So you can see better," he murmurs, clenching his teeth. He does not stop. I can't even catch my breath. I am on a marathon. He opens a drawer, takes out a corked bottle, and uses the bottle to move in me. I finally collapse. He unbolts the door and brings in the tray which Maria has left at the door, then bolts the door again. He removes one of the lit candles from the silver candlestick and slides it in me. He leaves the candle in me. The hot wax drips on my legs. He pours the wine into a glass. He drinks from the bottle while he holds the glass of wine to my lips. I sip the wine. He says, "Hurry." He sets the glass and the bottle aside and moves the candle in me to the rhythm of a samba playing on the radio. "I'll move the candle inside you until you make me stand up again," he says.

"Please, Henrique, stop."

"No way. Unless you stay. I'll keep at it until the last minute when the plane will fly you back to Rio."

"Please, I . . . ," and he shuts me up sticking a slice of *goiabada* in my mouth, mixed with his desire which is hardening and growing back.

At three-thirty he unties me and carries me into the shower. The water feels good and soothing. He holds me up against him and says maybe, before I leave, I should have another dose, some more of what we already had or something I have not had before. The beast, I think, is capable of doing anything to get his way. But I can still turn on the cold water to cool him down. And I do. I can't stand up. Henrique carries me to bed and calls Maria who brings him a pair of slacks and a clean shirt. He slips a dress on me, brushes my hair, then tells Maria to open the doors while he carries me in his arms to the plane.

"Until tomorrow night."

"Tomorrow night?"

"Tomorrow night at eight, be ready."

The Beechcraft takes off. Henrique waves the white scarf. Then, with a smile, he brings it to his eyes, pretending to wipe away his tears. He has such a satisfied look on his face. The beast. The clown. He has had his weekend of fun. I can't even move. Why is he like this with me? I think—if I can think at all—is this his idea of a wedding? The white gown, the white orchid in my hair. A rehearsal. Or is this a warning? The setup for a rape and another one of his fantasies? I want to forget my past nightmares and not be reminded of them. I look out as we fly over land and water. I fall asleep.

Cosme leaves me at the door of the Pensione. I manage to enter my room on my own. I throw myself on the bed and do not move until next morning. I am late for work. My knees shake all day long. At five I am back on my bed enjoying my solitude. I sleep soundly until I hear the siren of an ambulance that stops in front of the Pensione. I feel so much better. I look out from the window on the Avenida Copacabana. Parked in the middle of the street is an ambulance. A doctor in a white coat, a stethoscope hanging from his neck, says something to another man in white. From the back of the ambulance they take out a stretcher. People are gathering to see what's going on. Traffic has come to a stop. The crowd grows in size. I go downstairs. It's eight o'clock. Henrique should be here any minute now. The door opens, and Doctor Henrique and his ward, Cosme, put down the stretcher in the hall. Before I can even open my mouth, Henrique lifts me up and lays me on the stretcher. Cosme and Henrique carry the stretcher out.

"It's the height of rush hour," Henrique mumbles. "The traffic couldn't be worse. Cars are only crawling along. It's the only way to be on time." He covers me up to my eyes with a white sheet. "I made a reservation in a *churrascaria* in Leblon. I am hungry. Aren't you? I'll just make sure that you are hungry too. First, I'll examine you." The stretcher goes straight into the ambulance with Doctor Henrique by my side. He draws the curtains, opens a bottle of champagne. We laugh and he hugs me and, with the second drink, examines me thoroughly. He keeps examining me so thoroughly that the ambulance shakes. We hear the people who have gathered around us. They say it must be serious, the accident was terrible. Different stories are being told. One person saw the knife that went through the chest. Another heard the bullet that went through the head. Fortunately, none saw the doctor examining the victim. A deep, thorough examination.

When the ambulance stops shaking, the doctor smears some of my lipstick on his hands and opens the doors. With a large piece of gauze he wipes off the lipstick from his hands, shakes his head, and pushes the crowd aside. "Make room and let the car pass. It's urgent," he says. "Let's go."

Since the arrival of the ambulance, the traffic has stopped altogether. The streets ahead toward Leblon are empty. He drives very fast and I am carsick, lying on the ambulance bed. At one point he stops to let Cosme out.

When we arrive at the *churrascaria*, he removes his doctor's coat and stethoscope. We sit outdoors at the table. We don't wait for the food. Henrique has placed his order in advance to be ready at eight-forty-five sharp. All kinds of grilled meat, sausages, fish. A gargantuan meal from the outdoor grill. Our appetites are astoundingly good and our mood has improved.

The moon has many phases. Simultaneously it can shine and be dark.

XXIII

My avidity for wanting to see and know too much has given me dark circles under my eyes. Henrique says that it's about time I had a real honeymoon. A few days on our own. We are to go to Paqueta, an island where no cars are allowed, only bicycles and carriages, drawn by horses. We are not taking his boat which is moored at the Yacht Club. There will be no sailors around. He'll show me real life. In peace.

We take the ferry at Praca Maua. It is crowded. Before the sun reaches its high point, we go up on the deck where they serve *cafezinhos*. A soft breeze blows from the sea. In the distance I can see the Sugar Loaf, the beaches and the mountains we have left behind, and my heart grows agitated.

"Oncinha, look. Look that way," Henrique says and takes my hand in his.

Next to a basket, full of green salad, a man sits on the floor. He could be a fisherman under his strawhat and with his trousers rolled up to his knees. Impassive, he puffs smoke out of his mouth. No cigarette is visible. He turns his head in my direction. Instead of his nose and his mouth, I see a big hole. Leprosy. Half of his face is mutilated. The man digs his hand in the cavity where his mouth must once have been and takes out a cigarette. He makes a loud noise with his throat and projects a ball of spit that lands close to my feet.

I am shipwrecked. Henrique squeezes my hand and whispers in my ear that, from now on, nothing else besides the two of us has any meaning.

We step down from the ferry into a horse-drawn carriage. The man says he will take us to the hotel which is only minutes away. He takes the longest route to reach our destination. We don't mind. We are drunk with joy, sun, and peace. We see the brightly colored small wooden boats in red, yellow, pink, and aqua lying on the sand, oars next to them. A barefoot fisherman with a strawhat sits on a wooden box mending a net.

We check into a small hotel under ridiculous fake names. James and Joyce Shakespeare. We sit on the veranda at a table with a paper table cloth. The owner brings different plates of food which he sets in front of us. Sweet potatoes, rice, black beans with *carne seca*, *farofa*, finely chopped green salad, shrimps, fish. We drink beer. Then he brings us Minas cheese with *goiabada* and *marmelada* and cream of avocado with a taste of vanilla. Henrique holds my hand and feeds me with his spoon. Each time he puts food in my mouth, he kisses me and says it tastes better this way. We laugh and joke. And for the first time, we talk quietly about ourselves.

He has his arm around my waist as we go to our room. Nothing fancy. Bed, two chairs, table, and behind a yellow curtain, a pole with four hangers and a shelf. The walls are white, and the tiled floor has a yellow mat on each side of the bed. Henrique closes the shutters and switches on the electric fan on the ceiling. He helps me take off my dress. We shower and then slip under the cool white sheets. He stretches out his arm. I put my head on his shoulder. He pulls me closer to him, and with his hand on my breast and mine on his chest, we fall asleep. When I open my eyes, I hear a church-bell ring four o'clock. He does not open his eyes when he looks for me under the sheet. He gently strokes me until I cling to him. We make love to the tempo of a slow fox trot, as in a dream. Never before has he been like this with me. He kisses my neck and my mouth with care, as if afraid to hurt me. Our movements are slow, and we are quiet. Languorously quiet. Not a word. It is peaceful, and I love him.

When Henrique opens the shutters it is evening, but it is still light outside. He puts his small suitcase on the table and takes out two pairs of blue shorts with matching shirts and a pair of flat-heeled sandals. He sets the smaller-sized shorts and the sandals on the chair beside my bed.

"It's for you, my love. Your honeymoon trousseau."

"What, shorts? You don't mind if I wear them?"

"Only while we are here. Two days OK?" he laughs.

We leave our room and rent bicycles.

We hold hands while we cycle around the Island dressed like twins in our blue shorts and shirts. The thrill of discovery prevails. Finches and giant tortoises hundreds of years old. Parrots, yellow butterflies, orange butterflies with black spots, white butterflies with blue stripes. Flowering bushes. Bougainvillea in different shades from pink to purple covering verandahs and houses. Flamboyant trees with orange colored flowers and coconut trees are everywhere along the road. The fauna and the flora seem astonishingly indifferent to our presence. The red sun sets on the horizon. Henrique finds a large shell on the sand and brings it close to my ear. I listen to the music. It sings.

Strange how happiness, like anger, comes on all of a sudden.

We have dinner by candlelight under a palm tree. He runs his fingers through my hair and utters sweet nothings. Between each course we kiss as if we have just met. We cycle back to the hotel. It's early when we go to bed. His deep kisses run like water down my throat. We make lavish plans, warm promises, we talk late into the night. Finally, we love each other to sleep.

XXIV

Ambassador Gustav Hesselvick and Madame Birgitta Hesselvick have already left for their *sitio* in Teresopolis. The chauffeur, Waldir, is to drive me with their two sons, Lars and Bertil, and their numerous suitcases, packed for a two months' stay in the mountains.

I am glad to return to reality. To lead a normal family life. There is much love flowing from parents to children and from children to parents. The children are well behaved. They sit up straight, go to bed early, and are kind to the servants. Between balls, parties and official dinners, Madame Birgitta Hesselvick devotes much of her time to her children. She follows their studies. She has discussed with me their curriculum which she wants to be in French and English. Their Swedish studies can be followed by correspondence which arrives and leaves regularly by the diplomatic pouch.

We arrive at the *sitio*. The maids and the valet unload the car. The ambassador and Madame show us the house. Christmas decorations are in every room, on every table and on every door. It is very festive. Even the fireplace, which is only lit in August, is filled with the Crèche and all the little animals. Red stockings stuffed with gifts hang on the fireplace. A pine tree, as high as the ceiling, is covered with silver and gold tinsel which glitters in the last rays of the afternoon sun. We are looking at the colored balls, the angels, the stars, the cookies, trumpets, ribbons, and all the unopened parcels under the tree. The children are enchanted, and suddenly, I feel the warmth and enchantment of a home. Another two days and it's Christmas Eve.

During the day, I take the boys to the swimming pool or we go riding in the woods nearby. On alternate days we speak French and English. While we are having fun, I try to slip in something instructive. I tell them the story of the Count of Monte-Cristo. I encourage them to ask all sorts of questions while we fly a red kite high in the sky. When we come back to the house for meals, Monica, the maid says my *noivo*, fiancé, phoned. Henrique can't always reach me by phone because the lines are bad and I am out most of the time. I have asked him please not to phone. I have promised I'll call him. I don't want to interrupt this wonderful feeling of unperturbed joy. This family is so civilized and so full of warmth.

After dinner, evenings are spent in the study. As the butler serves us coffee, there is soft background music. It reminds me of the evenings in my childhood, when all four of us were together. When Father was winding up the gramophone to play "Rose-Marie I Love You."

Madame and the Ambassador are very tactful. They never question me about Romania. They tell stories about the various countries in which they have lived. They possess the art of conversation—to talk about a subject and not about oneself. But this evening, the ambassador asks me, "Is there anyone in your family you'd like to see? Anyone you miss?"

I think of Aunt Josephine. How I need her. She is the one person who could sort out the cobwebs in my brain and tell me what to do when I am sinking into Henrique's paranoia. She could explain so much to me. I tell them about Aunt Josephine.

The ambassador rings the butler and asks him to bring a pen and a pad. He takes notes. Name, age, where she was last seen. More and more details. He removes his glasses and says, "We'll find her."

I can't believe it. I have tears in my eyes. I try not to cry when I thank him. It feels so good to be talking like this, to be human again. To have kindness surrounding me—without the violence.

Two days before New Year's Eve, Waldir drives me back to Rio. I have spent eight days in a haven of joy and peace. Until March, I will be going up to Teresopolis two days a week to teach the boys French literature while Mademoiselle has her days off. I have been asked to translate some papers into English and French. Nothing much. By now I am fluent in Portuguese, which was easy for me to learn because of my Italian, French and Latin. So now I can also translate from Portuguese.

Back at the Pensione, Henrique is waiting for me at the entrance. I would have liked to have an interval before readjusting to him. A pause before entering his universe again.

XXV

There is darkness in Henrique's eyes when we enter our studio in Copacabana.

"It was too long to be without you."

"Amante, we have two months ahead of us to spend all the time we can together."

"Besides the two days a week when you are in Teresopolis." His face tightens." I can't even go up there, now that I've left the *sitio* to Carla and her children." He lights the candles spread at the edge of the rectangular table. "Lucky you. No way I can check up on you. Who knows what you do up there?"

At one end of the table there are no candles, only two small silver trays. One holds a pot of honey and the other is covered with a red napkin. He unzips my dress and lets it fall to the floor. He takes off his shirt, holds me tightly against him, kisses my eyelids, and then sits me on the table between the two silver trays.

"Lift the red napkin."

Under the napkin is a thick gold chain. He puts it round my neck. It's heavy.

"It's beautiful. It's too much. Thank you, Amante! I love it!"

He looks at me and smiles. "Oncinha, I told you so."

"What do you mean?"

He kisses my mouth and opens his arms. "Come, enter your cage, Oncinha!" He strokes me behind my ears. I purr like a contented kitten. "Happy?" he asks. I nod.

He fills two glasses with whisky. I don't want any whisky, so he drinks both. Then he says, "Look for me, Oncinha, undress me!"

I put my hand on him. Nothing. Then I open his belt and unbutton his trousers. He is not there.

"You can do better than that, Oncinha! Come on! Make it come alive!" He puts the honey on his organ, grabs the chain and pushes my head down. "Lick it off, Oncinha! Love it! Love it! Nothing is immoral if it helps to perpetuate love."

He puts the honey on my body and plays with me for a while. Then he says he is tired. We take a shower. He presses me close to him, holding the necklace. We go to bed, and I see he takes a pill. He wants to sleep. But he doesn't let me go, he clings to me. I wait until he falls asleep. I think it is just as well to have an early night because tomorrow is New Years' Eve.

Next day, I leave Henrique at the studio in the dark. He says he wants to rest, that he will fetch me this evening. We'll see *macumbas* and the ceremony for the goddess of the sea. I should dress in white and think of three wishes. He will bring the candles and buy the necessary white roses. I am full of excitement looking forward to tonight. I enter my room at the Pensione. On the floor is a letter. It has a childish handwriting, as if it has been written with the left hand. It is a poison pen letter. Whoever has written it is convinced that I have bewitched Henrique with my love potions. It ends with threats. If I do not renounce Henrique, the most desirable man in this city, I will be harmed in many ways. There are big interests at stake and I am advised not to interfere. I am disturbed by this anonymous letter and wonder who the author could be.

To wipe away these thoughts, I take particular care when I put on my makeup and try a new hairdo which shows off my necklace. I am dressed in the long white gown when I hear the doorbell. I go downstairs thinking that Henrique has arrived earlier than agreed. I answer the door. There stands a clean-looking tall red-headed young man with a pinkish face and deep-set piercing green eyes.

"Do you speak English?" His voice is hesitant and shy.

"Yes, I do."

He points at the newspaper in his hand. He looks me straight in the eye and says, "I'll take it."

"Take what?"

He does not take his eyes off my mouth.

"The room. It's in the ad."

"Oh! I'll call the manager." I am about to burst out laughing.

"Do you live here?"

"Yes."

"Never mind the manager. It suits me fine. Just what I'm looking for," says Tom Huntington in one breath.

That same evening Tom moves into the Pensione.

Henrique is late arriving. He looks so good in his white clothes. He is wearing a sweetly mischievous smile. I decide to say nothing about the letter or about his being late.

He gives me white roses and takes my arm. We walk along the beach. Flickering candles in small paper boats are everywhere on the sand. Among beds of white roses floating on the sea are more candles in paper boats. Henrique says I should make my three wishes now, light three candles, and throw three white roses into the sea. My gift to the Queen of the sea, Imanja. I am not supposed to tell anyone my wishes, it's bad luck. I make two wishes that are good. To find Aunt Josephine. That the war will soon be over. And one wish that is bad. That Hitler should disintegrate, drop dead. Henrique throws the rest of the flowers into the sea one by one. They join the floating white blanket, lullabied by the ripple of the water. I wonder if he has made a wish.

We are surrounded by music. Islands of people dressed in white. We are drawn toward a gathering where some of the women are wearing white turbans. Drums are beating, a high priest called the *Pai dos Santos*, and a fat *Mae dos Santos* are marching and dancing in a circle. The beats are loud, the dance and the shouts intense. The dancers move every part of their bodies. Beautiful expressions of pleasure and ecstasy are on their faces. Henrique says that later they will drink the blood of a sacrificed cock. It's black magic. I feel the beat of drums in my whole being. Henrique ties a handkerchief on my wrist and sprays on some perfume. He asks me if I like the odor. I have no idea if I like it or not, but I know I feel elated while I smell it. I want to dance, I am not tired, and I enter the circle. Henrique pulls me out, sprays more perfume on the handkerchief, and to the drum beats, plays me with his hands as he would play an instrument. His eyes play, his body plays. We are glued to each other. In a frenzy.

My two days a week in Teresopolis upset Henrique. He says when I am not with him he is overcome by a feeling of anxiety. He doesn't mind if I am in another room, but he needs to know that I am there. We spend most of our time at the *fazenda*, mostly in his rooms. When he is busy I read in a hammock outside the window where he can see me. If he has to go out he asks me to come with him. The night before I leave for Teresopolis he tells Maria to prepare the blue room for us. I know what to expect. But he is not as angry as he was the first time. And I see there are tears in his eyes when Cosme flies me back to Rio.

When I return from Teresopolis he is waiting for me at the Pensione. So are the weekly poison letters under the door.

Today I see two burning candles at the main entrance, next to a doll with pins sticking in it. The maid at the Pensione tells me to be careful, that this is very dangerous. The doll looks like me. Bad things can happen. I must have a serious enemy.

A week before Carnival we are staying in Rio. We go to see the Samba schools, *Escolas do Samba*, where people of the same neighborhood, usually a working-class community, gather on a regular base for rehearsals and samba nights. At Carnival the people come down from the *favelas* in their costly, colorful costumes. The chariots each have a different theme. All year round the participants have been preparing and have spent all their savings on three days and four nights of joy, fantasy, music, dance and extravaganza. Henrique takes me to every ball. It's one night at the Gloria, another at the Copacabana Palace, the Municipal opera house, the Yacht Club, and, in between, some popular ones where nobody knows him. He keeps spraying my handkerchief with the *lança perfume* for me to smell. We enter the sea of people marching, dancing, and singing to the rhythm of the drum beat. I keep dancing, unaware of time or place. I am not hot, though my dress is wet with perspiration. I don't feel my feet. I am floating. Henrique sprays my legs and my back. It keeps me cool. I am in the midst of a wave of people intoxicated by the nonstop music. I march into this collective intoxication of crowded bodies, raised hands. Nothing else matters. I have lost Henrique. Three mulattos are dancing around me. One of them, his limbs and body twisting as if he were made of rubber, is dancing in front of me. Another is shaking his hips in an almost seated position. The third one holds me by my waist. We dance as if we are in a trance. It's almost morning. The music has not stopped. A young man with dark hair, in a red shirt open on his hairy chest, has replaced the one who was holding me by the waist. He is very close to me when he sings *o que e que a Bahiana tem*. Henrique finds me. I can't stop moving to the music. It's as if I'm drunk. My hips move on their own, and I shake my shoulders like the natives. Henrique tries to take me by my waist. But I move and shake in circles. He sprays *lança perfume* on me and tells me to calm down. The more he sprays me, the stronger I feel the drums in my stomach, the more energy I have. Impossible to stop.

The sun is rising when we return to the studio. I am still singing and moving, so Henrique turns on the radio. He half fills a glass with whisky and drinks it slowly while he removes his clothes. Then he lights a cigarette. After a few puffs, he turns the radio up to maximum. I am wild with desire. I can only see his body, and I am naked against him, shaking. "Here, Amante, take as much as you want! I'll show you!" I can't stop. I'm not tired, even twenty-four hours later. But he is. I wake him up again and again. Then I ask.

"What is in this spray?"

"Ether mixed with cheap perfume," he laughs. "If you go on for another few days you'll like it so much, you'll miss it when you can't have it."

"Where do you keep it?"

He points to a big unopened box. I open the box, and one by one, I throw the metal sprays out of the window. I don't care where they land. Anyway, it's a Brazilian habit to throw things out of the window! Even burning cigarette stubs that land on a brand new convertible.

"Here's to your *Imanja*, here's to your *pai dos santos*, here's to your *mae dos santos*, to your *macumbas*, the poison letters."

When I am finished, I know I'll miss this state of euphoria, where everything seems possible. Where nothing can frighten me. Where I am not alone in this world. But I must face reality.

I have no parents. If I want to survive, I have to be my own parent and put an end to self-indulgence and, consequently, to self-destruction.

Henrique, in a lotus position, puffs on a cigarette and chuckles, "Am I next, Oncinha?"

XXVI

A week after Carnival, Ambassador Hesselvick calls me to his office and hands me a three-page letter.

"I think we've traced your Aunt Josephine," he says triumphantly. "She was last seen in Recife, where she was running a nursing school next to the *Igrejinha das Fronteiras* (the tiny Frontier Church).

I can't believe it. I thank and thank him over and over again, but I think it is not enough. I wish I could give Ambassador Hesselvick the Sugar Loaf, the whole mountain, to show my gratitude, instead of the box of chocolates I plan to send.

Inevitably, I keep asking questions. The ambassador calls in Mr. Larson from the Swedish Legation and asks him to spend all the time it takes with me to explain how to get to Recife to pursue the search for Aunt Josephine.

"First, you have to see Dom Helder Camera."

"Dom Helder Camera? Who is he? Where can I find him?"

Mr. Larson sits me down and describes Dom Helder as a courageous priest who is part of the group of Latin American clerics who call themselves Liberation Theologists. He has been accused of being a subversive agitator, a misguided dupe in the hands of the communists, the priest steering his parish to rebellion.

I can't wait to tell Henrique the news. When I do, he asks "What are you going to do about it?"

"I would like to go and see Dom Helder who, I am told, can direct me to where Aunt Josephine might be," I tell him.

Henrique says he first wants me to meet his mother, Dona Edithe, and his sister, Dona Silvia, whom he adores. They will arrive in Rio from New York within the next ten days. He also wants to move into the new house he has bought in Leblon. The restoration is complete. "I'd like to show you how your rooms have been decorated. Bedroom, dressing room, study, and your own bathroom. Of course, you will only occupy these rooms when I am old and tired, or when one of us is playing hard to get." Meanwhile, he expects the usual treatment, which means "stay close to me and don't leave my sight."

"Are you putting me on a leash?"

"I am." With one hand, he pulls me by my necklace and draws me to him, then kisses my mouth for a long time.

A few days later, I speak once again to Henrique about Aunt Josephine and how much it means to me to find her. He pats my head the way one does with a domesticated animal and says, "It can wait." By now, I am nervous and tense and am starting to have health problems. I don't know who I can ask to recommend a doctor. I think it might be a gynecologist I need to see.

Henrique and I have dinner. I feel sick. Reluctantly, he drives me back to the Pensione. After he kisses me good night at the door, I ask him if he can give me the address of a doctor.

"Why?" he immediately asks.

"I want to know the reason for my discomfort."

"When I want a child from a woman I take her to a desert island to make sure the child is mine." He grabs my arm very harshly. "With your experience! I was informed about the men you saw in Teresopolis!"

"Stop it, Henrique! I'm not asking you for a diagnosis. All I'm asking for is the address of a good doctor. Are you saying that I'm pregnant? I have no idea what the problem is. You have no right to talk to me like that." I tear myself away from him. "Are you going to give me the address? What are you trying to say? That if I am pregnant, the child wouldn't be yours? I'll tell you what, if I am pregnant, I will name the BASTARD after you!"

He raises his bushy black eyebrows in surprise. He slaps me across the face. He jumps in his car and drives away. Dazed, I stand alone. At my feet, next to a burning candle, lies a doll punctured with pins.

I am on my bed, undecided what to do next. Cry, continue to be furious with Henrique, or both. I feel sorry for myself. I am glad there is no one here to see how I feel. There is a knock on my door. It's Tom Huntington, my neighbor.

"I heard you come in, and I thought you might like this." On a tray he carries a bottle of scotch, soda, two glasses, and nuts. "May I sit down?"

I nod. I have tears in my eyes. My cheeks are burning. Tom places the tray on the low coffee table by the window and sits in the armchair next to it. He pours the scotch in the two glasses, adds the soda, and brings one glass over to me.

"Here, drink this, you look as if you need it."

"Thank you, Tom." I get up from the bed and sit on a chair in front of the dressing table. I can't help but see in the mirror how I look, like a cocker spaniel that has been in the rain. My eye makeup and lipstick are smudged. One side of my face is red and swollen.

Tom keeps talking about his trip. He has just returned from the Amazon River. Before that he was in Minas Gerais. He is a mining engineer. His work, for a well-known American multinational the name of which I don't catch, takes him all over the interior of Brazil in search of minerals. He has a sense of humor, and when I tell him some of my theories on life, he takes out a piece of paper and a pencil and pretends to take notes, while he blushes. He is young. Probably only twenty-five.

The scotch is working on me. I feel much braver. I don't feel shy. I tell him I believe in premarital relations. His face gets terribly red. I give him a whimsical look, lower my voice, and chant.

"Would you buy a car without trying it out beforehand? Wouldn't you run it at least a couple of times around the block?"

"I must make a note of that one!" he laughs.

We both end up laughing a lot. It's almost eleven when he leaves the room.

"I'll be in the Parana region for about five days," he says. "Can I take you out for dinner when I return?"

"Yes, I'd like that."

XXVII

I am in the shower when Dona Ruth sticks her head in to tell me I've received a basket of yellow roses. There is an envelope with it. I quickly dry myself and go to read the note. Henrique writes that he has made an appointment for me to see Doctor Jose Campos, and I should phone the doctor to confirm the time and date. I read on, hoping he'll apologize. He doesn't. I give the yellow roses to Dona Ruth who showers me with an avalanche of endearing words. Then, I call about the appointment. A nurse answers the phone. She knows the doctor is expecting to see me. Could I stop by anytime today to give her a sample of my urine and blood? The appointment with the doctor is the day after tomorrow, if it's all right for me to wait that long. It is all right. After a good night's sleep, I feel my misery is fading.

On Wednesday morning, the doctor asks me first to sit down and tell him what's the matter with me. I answer all his questions, then he says I should take off my clothes and put on a white gown. I sit on the examination table. He pokes my knees, and one by one they jump. He asks if I hear voices. I say, "No, do you, Doctor?" He looks at my eyes with a flash light, then it's my nose, my ears, a wooden stick on my tongue. "Say ah! Say thirty-three." He listens to my chest. "Stop breathing, cough." He has his ear against my back. Then he pokes and knocks some more. I forget what we are doing, and I ask,

"Who is it?" His hands are poking me under my ribs, before he attacks my belly. Then, he says, "I must examine you internally so please, spread your legs, Dona Rozalia." He puts jelly on rubber gloves and goes for my plumbing. It isn't quite what I'm used to. He's finished and says I can dress.

He is at his desk writing out a prescription. I sit opposite him, waiting for the verdict. He hands me the results of the blood and urine tests. I have an infection, he tells me, and my plumbing is inflamed. I am anemic and stressed out. "If you follow the prescribed treatment you should feel better in about ten days." He pauses. "Do you know the precautions a woman has to take?" I admit I have no idea. He says, "As long as you have relations only with Henrique, you don't have to worry about getting pregnant. Henrique is sterile. As an adult he had mumps with complications." I am speechless. So why did he make that awful scene? Why did he have to humiliate me? He knew that I could not be pregnant by him. Did he really think I was fooling around?

Doctor Jose Campos asks if I have told Henrique that he was the first man to have known me intimately. I answer, "He never asked, I didn't think it was important for him." Doctor Jose Campos shakes his head. "Here is your prescription. Take it easy for a while. Also, please give this prescription to Henrique. He should take two pills twice a day. While he's taking them he can't drink alcohol, of course. You can take the same but only half a pill once a day when you feel blue. See my nurse on your way out and have her explain what a woman should and should not do." He gives me an *abraço*, a hug.

"I have a daughter your age," he adds.

After a session with the nurse on the subject of intimate hygiene and its derivatives, I ask her to mail the prescription to Henrique. At this point, I don't ever want to see him again.

My rage has simmered. My health improves. Another two weeks and I will be able to go to Recife to see Dom Helder and find out more about Aunt Josephine. Tom Huntington says he has to go to Bahia anyway. He can take "a long cut" and go further north to Recife with me. It would be fun not to be alone on this mission. I have been given three weeks off from work.

I still think of Henrique. The more I try to understand, the deeper are the contradictions. I go out with other people, but I talk about life the way Henrique would have talked. I have not known a man before him. So I have never questioned his behavior, his continuous sexual urge. I have surrendered unconditionally to him. What has happened?

A whole month and I haven't seen him or heard from him. He hasn't been seen anywhere. The studio where we used to meet is empty. The *sitio* in Teresopolis is occupied by Carla and the children. Cosme tells me he hasn't seen Henrique at the *fazenda* for a month. His secretary, Maria Rita, reluctantly tells me he's traveling abroad and will not be back for another month or so.

I miss him. I walk the streets where I think he might be. Maybe I'll run into him casually, I think. It's late, almost eleven. I am at the corner of Rua Duvivier on my way to the Pensione. A man is behind me. My heart beats fast. Finally. It's him. I turn my head. A voice says, "This is a holdup," and the masked man points a gun at me. I smile. I say to myself, "He is back to his nonsense again."

"Backward, against the wall!" he says, sticking the gun into my ribs.

I realize it's not Henrique. He is shorter. I obey his command. I am confused and frightened. This is all I need!

"Say something!"

"What? Anything?"

"Talk to me. Tell me who you are."

"What do you want?" By now I am terrified. I have to be careful what I say.

"Just keep talking."

"Talking? About what?"

"Tell me things. Tell me what you did today. Then it'll be my turn."

I think fast. His turn? To do what? To rape me or shoot me? I have a little money on me. I hand it to him. He pushes my hand away. Maybe it isn't enough. He lowers his head and now the gun is against my cheek.

"I'm not joking!" his voice is impatient. He coughs. He lowers the gun for a second to spit. He takes a handkerchief out of his pocket to wipe his face. "Come on, walk. Move to your left. Over there."

I back up a few steps and we start to walk. When we get close to a lamppost, I can see him. An old man, a mulatto with white hair. He doesn't look poor, he is neatly dressed.

"I don't understand. What do you want from me?"

"I want to talk."

"Is that all?"

"Yes. Just that. Talk. At my age, no one wants to talk with me anymore."

I am stupefied. It seems to be the only motive to his crime. A man has to use a gun to rob someone's time, to steal a few seconds of their attention. He explains that, if nobody has the courtesy to willingly give him even a moment of their time, he has to obtain it at gunpoint. He can't spend the last days of his life without meeting others, eye to eye, to reveal his inner thoughts.

We find a bench on Avenida Atlantica. We sit down. I talk, telling him an imaginary life, full of lies. When I see that he is sleepy, I take my leave. He squeezes my hand and says he hopes to meet me again. I answer that it would be nice when we next meet, to sit and talk somewhere pleasant and forget about the gun and the holdup.

"Not like that, Senhora," he says with a happy smile. "Please, let me threaten you with a gun. It's so much more fun! I enjoy it a lot more this way!"

I meet him again. This time without fear.

I wonder if in crime and in love, there is a moment when one's fears are left behind.

I think about Henrique. Could it be that his mad passion endangered the stability of his mind? How unbearably lonely he must have been, craving a relationship in which one meets the other without fear.

Yes, fear. My fear of loving. My fear of losing. His fear of loneliness. His fear of happiness which he systematically destroyed. Always testing. Never trusting. Capable of plucking out the feathers of a phoenix rising from the ashes.

I am overcome by anxiety. I'm not going to wait for Tom's return. I need someone on whose apron or lap I can cry, but I can't go around with a gun like my new holdup friend. I've waited long enough, every minute seems like ages. I must move and find her. Aunt Josephine is alive. Soon, I'll see her. There is nothing that I want more.

I have to work out the practicalities for this trip. How to get there? Plane or bus? Money? By bus it's cheaper but the trip could take two days, perhaps more. I will also need money for food. Up till now, between the Pensione and my work, I have not spent anything on food. I'll just eat bananas. I ask Mr. Larson at the Swedish Legation to help me find a place to stay when I arrive in Recife. Maybe with the nuns. I doubt the stay will be for long. The moment I find Josephine I'll be staying with her anyway. She will know what to do, she always knows. I have three weeks off. Excitement flows over me. Mr. Larson is a dear. He solves every problem. He gets a cheap ticket by plane through the Legation, gives me an advance on my wages, and tells me not to worry if I can't be back in three weeks. But not to stay away more than four. He will write the necessary explanations to the ambassador. "Your plane is leaving tomorrow for Recife. Go home and pack." I take my leave with mountains of thanks. I say good-bye with tons of affection and gratitude to the ambassador and his family and all the Swedes in the world!

At the Pensione, I ask Dona Ruth to rent out my room while I am away so that I don't have to pay in my absence. Then I start packing a small duffle bag for my adventure and a big box of my belongings to leave with Dona Ruth for when I return. I slip a note under the door of Tom Huntington's room. If he still wishes to take the long way and meet me in Recife, my address will be with the nuns at the convent next to the dispensary. I'll be there by Thursday, twelve days from now and will wait for him for three days. If he can't make it, I'll see him in Rio when I get back.

XXVIII

Recife. I have bubbles in my stomach. My fear is great; it's beyond my understanding, beyond my strength. Something important is about to happen. I enter the small convent. I am expected, Mr. Larson has seen to it. A young nun shows me the cell I am to occupy and all the facilities. Food is across the road. Doors close at eight in the evening. I'm given a schedule for prayers I don't have to attend. I can instead roll bandages and do other similar tasks. Wake-up call is four-thirty. Mass at the Igrejinha at six.

I lie naked on the narrow bed close to the floor. A wooden cot with a thin mattress. No sheets. No pillow. I cover the mattress with my large white towel. It's hot and I can't fall asleep.

At five o'clock the next morning, dressed in a khaki skirt, a tee-shirt, and sandals, I watch the sun rise from the sea. Under a palm tree, a man is selling green coconuts. He is chopping holes in the coconuts to get at the sweet, clear milk. Another vendor is pushing a cart with oranges and corn cakes.

By six o'clock I enter a wooden Catholic church near the sewage canal. A small old man is coughing as he prepares to say Mass. He is Dom Helder.

"Em nome do Pai, do Filhio e do Espirito Santo." His voice is soft and slow, his hand rises gently, into making the sign of

the cross. A small ringless hand, the same milky coffee color as his cassock. His only adornments are a wooden cross and a tiny white dove he wears pinned to his robes. His face is wrinkled. His ears stick out. The fragile-looking man begins his day in front of the unpainted wooden altar. Radiance floods his face, and he smiles when he gives Communion. He holds the silver bowl of wafers. His fingers hover over the bowl before he selects each wafer, as if he is searching for a particularly fine one. He lays the wafers into the open mouths, gazing gently into each face.

I wait my turn. I am the last in line. "May I see you alone, Father?"

"Wait for me next door, my child," he replies.

I go there after the service. It is his home, a house of three small rooms. A nun is there preparing his frugal meal. I ask if I can help. She gives me a knife and some potatoes to peel. I ask many questions. The only answer I get is that Dom Helder wakes up once at two o'clock in the morning and, for a while, writes poetry and letters on the table in the other room. Then he goes back to sleep and wakes again at five-thirty, to the first singing of the nuns. He sleeps in a cell-like room, the size of a large cupboard which has room only for a narrow bed.

I am peeling the last of the six potatoes when Dom Helder walks in. I get up. I am intimidated. I wipe my hands on the towel by the sink.

"What is it, my child?" he takes my hand, "Come with me, where we can talk."

I follow him into a bare-looking room. Through the open window the sun is shining on the wooden crucifix, a lonely ornament on the white walls. A wire with a single bulb hangs low from the ceiling next to sticky paper dotted with a few dead flies and mosquitoes. With his small brown hand he points at one of the wood and straw chairs, indicating where I should sit. He sits opposite me. Between us is a wooden table with stacks of papers, an alarm clock, two glasses and a bottle of water. He gently pushes everything aside and takes both my hands into his. His eyes look into my eyes.

"What shall I call you, my child?"

"Rozalia." I manage to smile.

"Now tell me, Rozalia, what has brought you here?"

"I am looking for my Aunt Josephine. She used to be a nun. She was called Sister Marie Josephe, and she is also my godmother. I have no other living close family besides her. I'll do anything to find her . . . more than anything else in the world I want to find her. Ambassador Hesselvick told me she was alive and that you could help me . . ." I ramble away without stopping to breathe. I am terrified of his answer.

"You look pale, Rozalia, have some water." He lets both my hands go, pours water into the two glasses, hands me one, and sips his water slowly, shaking his head.

"Dom Helder, what is it? Is she alive?"

He leans forward and says softly, "I haven't seen her for over three months. But that's not unusual for Doctor Maria. She frequently travels from one place to another."

"Where does she usually go?"

"Wherever she is needed. She has opened dispensaries in many villages."

"And how does she move from one place to another?"

"Sometimes by bus, other times by boat, mostly on foot. Even by helicopter."

"By helicopter?"

"Jovelino, the *fazendeiro* from Amazonia, sends her his helicopter whenever there is an emergency at the *fazenda*."

I feel as if my head is under water. Can I emerge? I'll have to learn about her life here. I have to be patient. Soon, I'll hold her in my arms.

"Where do you think I can find her now?" I ask.

"It isn't easy to find her. She moves around a lot. She is afraid of nothing. She is very special. The Indians trust her. The Jangadeiros love and respect her. When she was in Ceara, I was told, she wanted to go with the fishermen on their Jangada, from sunrise to sundown. She wanted to find a way to help this black population of fishermen. So brave. They wouldn't have her at first. No woman has ever been on a Jangada." He drinks more water and wipes his mouth and the moisture on his forehead with a handkerchief he takes from the pocket of his robe. "Can you imagine what it's like to be in the sun all day, not knowing if the catch will be enough to feed you? From sunrise to sunset with no shade, on a raft made of six logs connected with wooden pegs. Hardly room enough for three people. A raft with a small cotton sail on its short mast, a wooden rudder, a barrel of water, and a rock as an anchor?" His voice sounds tiny and buried, and with his fingers, he touches my hand.

"Did she finally convince the *Jangadeiros*?"

"Of course. She has a way with people!"

"Have you seen her since she came back from Ceara?"

"I am not sure where she was coming from when I last saw her. At times she visits between two stops. She updates me on her work. It's a lesson in courage and perseverance. She keeps organizing dispensaries for the poor, then trains a local person in the basics of first aid and nursing. She does the rounds herself for a while, before she's off to the next place."

"What shall I do? Where do I start?" My heart is sinking. I feel numb. Hope is vanishing.

"From the dispensary here you can get a list of each village she has been to. Plan to go to each one. Upon arrival, contact the mayor or his assistant on my behalf and ask for any information they can give you. Somehow, someone will lead you to her. If everything else fails, you can go to an Indian settlement not far from the Amazon River. You'll have to look it up on a map. A few hundred Indians live there in a dense jungle forest. Doctor

Maria goes there now and then. Jovelino the *fazendeiro* sends her his helicopter whenever she asks. You might have to do the same. It's impossible to reach the place otherwise. Don't go there alone. Leave it to the end, as a last resort."

Dom Helder stands up. It's time for me to go. He cups his hand on my forehead, mumbles a short prayer, gives me his blessing. I am not sure what to do. Maybe I should kiss his hand. But I don't feel like it. He must have felt my confusion. He takes me in his arms. Gives me an *abraço*.

"Thank you for your help," I tell him.

"If there is anything else you want to know, you can reach me every morning at the same time at the same place."

I leave. I am outdoors. I can feel the tropical humid heat. My mind shoots in seventeen parallel directions at once. I am hungry, which is confirmed by my rumbling stomach. I buy a bunch of banana *d'oro* from a vendor on the street outside the church. I keep eating one after another while I am wondering what to do next. But first I have to find a place to throw the six banana skins. I look for the vendor, thinking it would be a good idea to ask him to dispose of them. There should be an after sales service! But the vendor is gone. Our ideas seem to differ. So I am most uncivilized and throw them in the sewage by the Igrejinha.

I turn right, cross a small road. There are colored shacks made of wood or earth, and on each side, cloths are extended on a cord. A dog sleeps in the shade of a broken three-legged table. Under two palm trees, children play football. There are blacks, mulattos, Indians, and whites. All are barefoot, running after the ball. The ball comes my way. I can't resist and I shoot it straight between the palm trees. I used to play football with Odo and his chums. Then I was the *porteiro*. I don't realize what I am doing until I hear, "Goal!"

Now the children are pulling me by my skirt to join them. They all talk at the same time. Their enthusiasm doesn't cool off, they won't let go. I tell them, "I have things to do but some other time perhaps."

"No way. It's important. We are preparing for a match against another neighborhood. If you join, you can be our center right and we are sure to win. What could be more urgent?"

"I am looking for a Doctor Maria and I have very little time," I explain. "I have to go to many places where she usually goes if I want to find her."

The shouts stop. Silence. One of them comes forward. "I am Joazinho." He rolls his big black eyes at me and says, "After the match, we will all help you to find her." I can see myself going through the North of Brazil like the Pied Piper with the youngsters behind me. One village after another, then through the jungle. Throwing one child after another to the crocodiles until they let go of my skirt. They are still clinging to me when Joazinho tells me about the last time he saw her. "It was a while ago. She came to disinfect and bandage the leg of my father who had fallen off a scaffold. Doctor Maria was very tanned, telling stories about her trip to Fortaleza."

"Do you think, Joazinho, that Doctor Maria went back to Ceara?"

"No, she said she was heading in the other direction."

"Have you seen her again?"

"No, we haven't seen her since."

At least I can now eliminate the search in a certain area, if I am to trust Joazinho. I manage to free my skirt without the help of crocodiles. And careful not to be drawn into a new adventure, I find my way to the dispensary.

The door is open and so is the window. I'm hazy from the heat as I walk in. I can hear the muted sounds of the street. Alzira, a short woman on the plumpish side, with dark brown skin, greets me with a large smile. She appears to be in her thirties, looks happy, wears a white skirt and a white tee-shirt. Her flip-flops squeak on the worn wooden floor. She brings me a *cafezinho*. I feel alert again after I gulp down the strong sugary black coffee. A young black man, Waldemar, in white shorts and tee-shirt, busies himself with a package from which he takes out medications to put on shelves. He marks each item in a book on the white table.

I tell my story which they listen to with great interest. When I finish, I am handed a list of every place where Doctor Maria has opened dispensaries. Waldemar produces and unfolds a large map of the region, showing the states of Ceara, Para, Maranhao, Pernambuco and Bahia. And another map, of part of the Amazon River between Manaus and Ilha de Marajo by the Atlantic Ocean. The Indian settlement Josephine goes to is toward Altamira and the Xingu River. At this point, I am a geography wizard. So many places, so many possibilities. I rub my head, hoping to dissipate the labyrinth in my mind.

After the third *cafezinho*, Alzira lights a cigarette as she refolds the map of the state of Bahia and Ceara. "Doctor Maria would definitely not be there now. We would have heard from her." I stare at the remaining maps and think of Josephine in the midst of those innumerous streams and rivers, spreading like nerves through miles of swamp.

"No highway. In certain parts there is just an earth road. It's argil, the color of burnt orange," I am told by Waldemar. "You can take the maps with you."

A woman walks in with her son. Alzira changes his bandage and gives the mother a pill. Waldemar writes everything in a book O JORNAL. Other people come through the open door. I depart, thanking Alzira and Waldemar for their help.

The heat is stifling. I drag myself back to my cell in the convent. I intend to leave the maps and papers there before roaming around Recife. I want to think and imagine what Josephine's life is like in these surroundings, so unlike her. No books. But bandages, smells of disinfectant, perspiration. Flies, mosquitoes, cockroaches. Perhaps even snakes. Once I am in my cell, I can't resist the temptation of a cold shower which is at the end of the corridor. There I scrub myself and wash my hair with the big chunk of soap that will have to last for the duration of my trip. I dry by using the draft from the open door so that the towel won't be wet when I lie on it. Of course I risk someone seeing me. But I have to make a choice.

It feels sheer luxury to lie on the dry towel extended on my cot. Before I know it, I fall asleep and dream of visiting Recife looking for Josephine. And just when I am about to find her, I wake up to the sound of singing nuns.

I dress in the same clothes I wore all day. Not crisp and clean. I'll do my washing before going to sleep. For now, I have to hurry across the road if I want to have something to eat before the place closes. Once there, I take my time and talk to the man behind the counter while I eat rice and beans. Without any warning, it starts to rain.

"I'd better go. It's closing time anyway. How much?"

"Whatever you wish." I leave some change. "With the help of God I'll see you tomorrow," are the man's last words as he locks the door behind me.

I don't have far to go. The rain comes down in buckets, panels of rain so thick it looks like fog. It washes away everything. Only a few seconds and I am already walking across a stream littered with leaves, empty bottles, oranges, and . . . my banana peels.

Extra washed and rinsed in biological rainwater, my wearing apparel dries on two hooks I discover behind the door. With this distracting view before me, I drift into oblivion until the morning.

XXIX

In khaki slacks with a long-sleeved shirt and a man's strawhat, I am ready to face hours in the sun, if necessary. The duffel bag is neatly packed with plenty of mosquito repellent, a flashlight with an extra battery, my towel, soap, comb, toothbrush, toothpaste and my "entire" wardrobe. The maps, the list of dispensaries and a small jar of aspirin and one of quinine are in the side pocket. I close the door behind me. With my lightweight bag, I go toward the chapel. I wait for the nuns to finish their morning prayers and singing. As they come out, the Mother Superior sees me. I can hear her asking the young nun what this boy is doing here. I am happy I can fool a mother superior. I remember when *my* mother wanted me to dress like Odo. Now, passing for a boy will make it easier for me to comb this vast area in search of Josephine. It's safer for a boy to go from one distant village to another.

It's five in the morning as I take my leave from the nuns, thanking them for their hospitality. Whatever change I have, I drop in the tin box by the gate. After a few wrong turns, I find the Estacao Rodoviaria where I catch the next bus which leaves on time at six. I pay the driver who hands me my ticket. The nail on his little finger is over an inch long. Only on the one finger. I wonder what he uses it for. To clean his teeth? To scratch his ear? To blind an enemy in a fight? Preoccupied with my queries, without having the guts to ask, I quietly go and sit in the back of the bus. I take the maps and the list of dispensaries from my bag before I slide it under the seat. I unfold a map on my knees. With a pen, I circle each location on the map from the list. I plan to go from one place to another for the next eight days. If I'm lucky enough to find Josephine right away, I can return to Recife with her and await Tom's arrival.

The engine is loud. I can't doze off. I look out of the window. I can only see orange-red dust. The long-nailed driver makes an abrupt turn to the right. Now we are moving on a very bumpy trail between rows of banana trees. We pass a stream. A man in a ragged straw hat which hides his face is fishing without a rod. The line is wrapped around his hand. Another hour goes by and we pass a few shacks. In front of the last one, I see a scruffy-looking man sweeping piles of dead cockroaches two inches long into a heap. I close my eyes. I don't want to see anything more until we arrive in Bezerros, my first stop.

At Bezerros, I get off the bus with my duffle bag. I ask for directions to the dispensary and follow every instruction I gather from anybody in sight. By some miracle, I reach my destination. I hope to leave my bag there and use their facilities. A note on the door says I'll have to wait, whoever it is has left for a short while. But I can't wait, I'll burst. I look around. No one in sight. I go behind the dispensary. There is a yard with a small arena. Feathers and blood. On one side two cages, each with a cock. I turn my back to the cages and let my slacks fall down. I cookoorigoo. The cocks cookoorigoo back. A trio. Tonight, they'll fight to the kill. I feel utterly alive again. I go back to the dispensary. Now I don't mind waiting.

After a good half hour, a copy of Alzira arrives to open the door with apologies. The dispensary is smaller than the one in Recife. Alzira 2, ready to give her life for me, can't help with my search. "I suggest you see the mayor or his assistant in case they have any news. You can leave your bag behind the curtain and sleep here tonight in a hammock. If there is an emergency, you can call me at the house," she points to her house across the street. Then she gives me the key to the dispensary. "Throw the key under the door in case you leave before I arrive tomorrow." She coaches me on how to get around. "If your trip to the mayor is not successful, go to the church and pray. Next door to the church you can profit from the magic of the Candomblé ceremony which will be held tonight. Most of the faithful ones attend both Candomblé and Catholic Mass."

To impress Alzira 2, I tell her, "The drumming and the chanting carry me into a trance, where I am taken over by the spirit of an *orixa*." I can see she is impressed. I am given an extra piece of bread with the *café com leite* and an orange.

When I get to the mayor's office, I have to wait for the assistant, who's supposed to be there later. The day is spent going from one place to another, from one person to another then back again. Ping-ponging. Each time I am offered a *cafezinho*. I even share a meal of rice and beans. Everyone knows Josephine but no one knows where to find her. I finally make arrangements, with the mayor's assistant, to leave the next day for the second destination.

It's almost evening. I can see the light falling from the sky in waterfalls of transparent blue. Sitting on a bench, in front of an open door, a man works with a knife on a chunk of wood. I stop, curious to see what he is doing. I ask. He sets aside his knife, lights a cigarette and explains he is carving narrative messages on blocks of wood. Would I drink a *caipirinha* while he tells me more? Yes I would like to. He talks about the origins of the *literatura de cordel,* when traveling folk poets recited verses about real and imaginary characters. Now these poems are carved on blocks of wood with bold and naive prints. He is working on one he names "The Woman Who Put the Devil in a Bottle."

I am on my second *caipirinha* when I hear the rest of his story. It's about a woman who does so much for the poor and the sick. She fights evil. She bottles the devil. And she is real. I ask for her name. He says that I couldn't have heard of her. Yes? He tells a long story about saved lives. About her incredible courage. I just have to listen and wait for the end. The languid pace of his voice reaches new heights when he finishes by saying, "It's Doctor Maria." He makes my day. But he does not know where to find her. The same answer. The same words. Still it feels soothing when, back at the dispensary, I am lulled to sleep in my hammock thinking of the woman who bottled the devil.

My Pilgrimage continues. By bus, by horse, by mule. It's the same at every stop. Alzira 3, Alzira 4, Alzira 5 . . . A crucifix. Always identical answers. But I have an idea. I'll make my own version of the woman who bottled the devil. At each stop, I find paper and pencil. I start to draw, illustrations of what I want to say. I leave a WANTED poster at each dispensary. If anyone sees or hears about where to find Josephine, they should let the mayor know. As I continue, the pictures become better and more moving. I am starting to like them myself; I discover a pleasure in drawing. Next to the visual message, I add decorative details—flowers, fruit, animals, doodles. Anything that attracts attention. It's easier for the ones who don't know how to read.

It's the last stop before returning to Recife. I have accomplished nothing. I am no closer to finding Josephine than I was ten days ago. Ten days of yearning and missed connections. An exercise in waiting, hoping, and disappointment. All I have achieved so far is to know more about her. But it is not enough. I am not her biographer. I have just one urge, to have her arms around me . . . To sit on her lap. Is it the warmth of a human body I'm missing, now that Henrique is gone? Do I miss him?

I do. My forehead is hotter than a frying pan. My knees feel weak. I must be hallucinating.

The bus stops in a small village. I have been two days without a shower. I check my bag into a public bathroom, undress, and stand in the shower for at least fifteen minutes. A place a dog wouldn't even pee in. Leaving the shower, I feel dirtier than when I went in.

Before returning to the convent in Recife, I have to see one more mayor's assistant—a man I hadn't even heard of until yesterday. He is my only remaining hope to find Josephine in these parts. Another wait. Another *cafezinho*. Another avalanche of empty words full of love. Repeatedly I am told, "Why be in a hurry to reach a goal and finish anything? In time, life will finish it for you in any case. Time? What is time? Time is only time. Nothing is urgent."

I'm so tired. I can't think straight. I am trembling and perspiring like a horse after a race. I can't hold down any food. I need to lie down. My brain is boiling. My muscles are yelling with pain. But I have to wait and wait. The room is an oven. The heavy, sticky heat wades in through the open windows. And somewhere in this immense country, with its jungle, its swamps, its rivers, its little villages, somewhere is Josephine. If I find her, how will she react? For the first time it occurs to me that the answer could make me feel even more rotten than I am feeling now.

The last thing I remember is reaching for the aspirin in the pocket of my duffel bag while a man hands me a glass of water. He is reciting stories about Doctor Maria I have heard before, only adding a few new endearing words.

When I open my eyes it's the next morning. A big black cleaning woman tells me I have been sleeping on the sofa in the mayor's office. She is the one who will take me to the bus leaving for Recife. "So you better hurry. Would you like some coffee before you go?"

"I can't gulp down anything, but a visit to your facilities would be helpful." She takes my arm and practically carries me to the small clean bathroom. She shows me which chain to pull for the head shower and which is the one to flush the toilet.

"On second thought," she says, "there is no time for you to shower." She points at cut newspaper pieces hanging on a hook next to the window. "I'll stay behind the door while you get ready. You are too weak to be alone." She's right.

My newly found black-fairy-godmother carries my duffle bag. She instructs me to lean on her with all my weight and walk slowly. Somehow we make it to the bus. She hands me a bottle of water for the trip and gives me an *abraço,* saying *vai com Deus.* At this point I'll go anywhere with anyone. I hand the money for my ticket to another pinky-long-nailed bus driver. It must be part of their uniform or the sign of some secret cult. But I feel too weak and miserable to care. I drink all the water from the bottle and swallow an aspirin. The constant vibration throughout the trip makes me lapse into a half sleep. I awake when the one long-nailed driver calls out "Recife." It's hours and hours later. The nausea is gone.

The driver helps me off the bus with my duffle bag.

By some miracle, two nuns are walking by. I follow. I can't walk as fast as they do. I finally ask for the help of every saint I've ever heard of. The saints and the nuns hear me and come to my rescue. Half crawling, I make it to the convent.

Once there, formalities are simple. Mother Superior takes a look at me and doesn't seem to like what she sees. My appearance is such that in no time I am carried into a cool cell and a wet terry cloth towel is placed on my burning forehead. I have to swallow a kind of chicken broth from a freshly cooked *canja.* It's nice. It feels good to have something warm inside me. I hear that I don't have malaria, but am dehydrated and am suffering from an undefined illness. I am left alone to rest.

A large jar with water is put next to me with the instruction to drink it all. I am not to leave the cell. At the bottom of the cot is a pot so that I don't have to recycle the water. How thoughtful!

Next day. Is it next day? I am not certain which day it is. Overcome with anguish and humiliation, I bite my lip to avoid crying in front of Mother Superior. She is standing by the door in front of me. There are two men behind her. I hope they aren't taking me to hospital. She tells me my fever has receded. She pats my arm. It's over. I can go.

One of the men comes forward, leans down, and attaches my sandals to my feet. He dresses me in no time, as if he has done this forever. I am too weak to even open my eyes. I feel terribly lazy, limp, and lost. And the cell is so dark.

"Honey, where's the rest of you?" he throws me over one shoulder like a parcel and walks toward Mother Superior. "I am Tom Huntington. I'd like you to meet Peter Conrad, a geologist who works with me at the Compania Mineradora e Hidroelectrica." He hands her a folded paper. "For the next week, the three of us can be reached at the Pousada do Bom Fin by the sea. It's all written down. I expect our patient to recuperate her strength by then. I hope you don't mind my taking her away."

Mother Superior agrees with everything he says, probably pleased to get rid of me, a girl who has not attended Mass even once. Peter Conrad is carrying my duffle bag, and Tom Huntington is carrying me. I am swept away. I can't get my thoughts in any order. I lean on his pectoral muscles which are testing the strength of his shirt buttons. The mining engineer in shining armor saving me from a life in darkness with nuns. No dragon in his way. He'll have to make do with what there is. And there is plenty.

"Honey, don't worry. From now on we'll take care of everything. Just concentrate on getting well."

He places me like a china doll between the two of them on the front seat of a truck. Peter is at the wheel, and Tom has his left arm around my shoulders so that he can hold me. The truck, a Ford, is jungle-ready with its large tires, shields of wire mesh over the headlights, and a noisy engine. Peter drives the Brazilian way. Imaginative. Improvising. No rules. Ignoring all lights and signs. Like everyone else. I have one hand clenched to the window frame, the other holding on to Tom. My heart stops at every intersection.

The race comes to an end at a *botequin,* close to our destination. Now the three of us are sitting at a table in the shade.

"What will you have, honey?"

"Anything, as long as it's not a *cafezinho*!"

"How about some shrimps?" asks Peter, and I nod. Peter is a wiry short man with curly brown hair. American, he is fluent in Portuguese and stingy with words in any language he chooses to speak. I learn that he has been almost everywhere in Brazil, having worked for the *Compania* for the last ten years. Tom says I can talk freely in front of him, that Peter knows why I'm here.

Tom brings my duffle bag and puts it under the table. He takes my hand into his and tells me that he and Peter are ready to hear all about my adventures. The owner of the *botequin* serves us three Brahma *chope* beers with our *camaraos,* shrimps, and *palmito,* palm tree hearts. In his old gym shorts, old tee-shirt, and cheap rubber sandals to protect the soles of scarred and hardened feet, he gives us a wall to wall smile.

I talk and talk, sparing no details of my misfortunes. They listen, order another round of beers, and ask to see the maps. My Odyssey becomes more and more muddled. I notice they shake their heads and talk to each other very briefly. As a result, I am hardly consulted. I am told.

I am to stay at the Pousada by the beach for a whole week. Eat, sleep. I will spend my days drawing as many posters as I can in between dips in the sea. I'll be provided with all the materials I need: paper, colored pencils, whatever, available from the office of the Compania in Recife. Peter and Tom will have to leave an hour before dawn each morning. They have to fly by helicopter as low as they possibly can, before humidity sets in and visibility becomes nil. Under trees and vegetation in various locations, tons of minerals, gold, copper, manganese, and nickel are there to be located. Each of their findings will then be indicated on their map and evaluated.

In the evening, after a stop at their office, they will drive through Recife with my daily posters. The plan is to leave a poster at every *botequin,* dispensary, and food store they know. Someone, they say, will guide us to Josephine and contact the Compania.

The way they talk, it sounds like an election campaign. They are so organized. They plan to visit and leave the posters at the various orange groves and sugar and tobacco plantations owned by the *latifundario*, the landowners who usually live far away, giving their orders from Recife or even from Rio de Janeiro. Peter knows of a village, Piloezinhos, in Paraiba, where there is a nun, Sister Valeria. She is part of a group within the Catholic Church which favors overthrowing or at least undermining the present government. Peter wants to hang some posters in the village square, where the donkeys are loaded. "The richer peasants live there in blue or yellow houses with roofs made of red clay tiles," he says. "Behind the coconut and banana groves, on the hill, are the stick-and-clay houses with no doors, no windows, earth floors, and roofs made of banana or palm leaves. These are the landless. The chances are that, at some point, Josephine would have been involved with them."

I'm not in the mood to talk. I just let things happen, and everything seems to go according to plan. At the Pousada facing the sea, two rooms are waiting for us. Each one has two single beds with mosquito nets. One bathroom for us to share. Everything looks clean. It feels cozy and secure. I spend my days in the shade drawing furiously most of the time. In the evening, Tom and Peter go for a swim before dinner. I join them when I feel strong enough. We have our meals outdoors in our bathing suits. There are two other guests. The owner does the cooking, mostly sea food and rice. I help to clear our table. Before going to their room, Tom and Peter take my drawings, give me a peck on my forehead, and evaluate my physical progress. According to their latest bulletin, I look so much better every day.

At times during the night, when I open my eyes, I see Tom in the dark. The moon is shining through the open window. He touches my forehead lightly with his hand, pulls up the sheet to cover my shoulders, and adjusts the mosquito net. Then he sits on the other bed for a while before he tiptoes back to his room. Occasionally, he lies down and falls asleep but is gone by the time I wake up in the morning. Neither of us mentions anything.

By the end of the first week I hear that the Compania is inundated with orders for additional posters. Peter and Tom have a ball. I don't understand, why are they laughing and joking? What's happened? I learn that the posters are selling fast. Before returning home, tourists and Garimpeiros are buying them as souvenirs to bring back to their loved ones. The *Compania* will have to branch out into this new activity. I am disheartened at first, then I join in the laughter. We each have a *cachaça* to celebrate this nonsense.

On the radio a new samba is playing. The words in English are something like "We're all looking for the Compania of our dearly loved Doctor Maria." And we drink one more *cachaça.* The three of us end up dancing to this new hit. If only Josephine could hear it and show up! Peter has enough of our nonsense and retires. Tom asks if I would enjoy a midnight swim while the moon is big and red. For luck, he says. He will come to wake me.

After the *cachaça* and the dancing and the laughter, I hardly have the energy to remove my damp bathing suit before I fall into bed. I pull the sheet over my head and fall into a deep slumber. I am still half asleep when Tom wraps the sheet around me and carries me toward the water. He lays me down on the sand. He takes my hand. "Whenever you are ready, darling." He is wearing his bathing trunks. His body is even whiter in the moonlight, and his hair is even redder than the moon and he smiles. He helps me to my feet. The sheet falls. Strange how it doesn't bother me. It was Henrique, he instilled in me not to be ashamed of my nakedness.

Tom says he must be dreaming as we walk hand in hand into the sea. The water is now up to my waist. I can still feel the sand under my feet. Then a current, an empty hole. Nothing. I am floating on my back. I see his eyes, his mouth. The light dims, at first only slightly, as he holds my head with both hands. His face is close to mine, and he kisses and kisses my face gently. My eyelids first. When his lips touch mine, I am in his arms, holding on to him. A white wave washes us ashore. I would like to stay here, lying on the wet sand, listening to Tom saying in his soft voice that he loves me madly. But he goes to pick up the sheet we left on the beach. He helps me up and ties the sheet around me like a white sarong.

Now he slowly draws me toward him. He kisses my mouth. His kisses flow down my throat. And I kiss him back without even thinking why I do. I lean on his shoulder when we walk back to the Pousada.

"I love you. I really do." His hands hold my waist as he plants a kiss on my forehead. "I can't wait until I see you again, my darling." Then he closes the door behind him as he goes back to his room.

"Damn the gentleman in you!" I think to myself. "The Anglo-Saxon-Puritan!" But somehow I feel quite well and healthy again. I sleep until very late the next morning.

In the evening, I am glad to see Tom. But he looks as if he hasn't slept. I feel sorry for him. We glance at each other like conspirators. When Peter is around, we act as if we hardly know each other. As soon as he turns his back, we steal a kiss here and there, a caress, or a wink. At last Peter says, "I don't mind if Tom sits you on his knees as long as you both stop pretending. There is nothing to be ashamed of. It's about time. Tom has been talking about you, Rozalia, for ages, since he first met you. What's the big secret?" He laughs. "I've had enough of our Puppy Romance." I get an elegant kiss on the hand from Peter who has our next move all planned out. He'll fly with us into the jungle and leave us at a spot he knows by the Amazon River. He will continue with the pilot to the Hidroelectrica which the Compania is building in the neighborhood of Altamira. He will wait for us there.

Tom and I will have to travel briefly by canoe on the Amazon River, the shortest way to reach the place where Josephine is most likely to be. Peter has already made arrangements with one of the few Indians who speaks Portuguese. "The Indian will take you in his canoe, then guide you to the tribe in the vicinity of the Xingu River. You'll have to take presents for the tribe, plenty of mosquito repellent for you, and a few tins of food and water in case you have any unforeseen problems. Rozalia, have you been vaccinated for yellow fever and malaria?"

"Yellow fever yes, malaria no. But I have been taking quinine pills and carry them with me."

Peter doesn't want to hear about my pills. Vaccination is a must. So be it.

XXX

A week later we take off. After over three hours in the air, the pilot announces that we should get ready to jump out fast. We approach a clearing at the foot of a hill. He doesn't want to touch down and risk getting stuck in an area that might have been flooded after the rain, he tells us. Soon, we circle over a gap in the trees and see an Indian waving a grass flag.

Tom opens the door and jumps to the ground. It's my turn. It isn't very high, but the air displaced by the helicopter ruins my landing. There goes my performance on the circus trapeze! I end up in Tom's arms. He's holding me close to him so that I won't be blown away. Peter throws out the packages and bags, and the chopper leaves. Now we are alone with the Indian who doesn't wear a straw skirt or have red stripes on his forehead. He is bare-chested and wears green shorts. His black hair is long. We examine each other for a brief moment. Then he smiles. "Follow me," he says. I am relieved that he does speak Portuguese, it would be hopeless otherwise. He offers us a big leaf which contains something to eat with our fingers. It's white and delicious. We never find out what it is. It's getting dark. Before the mosquitoes start their dance, we spray ourselves with the repellent.

Tom and the Indian carry everything except for my duffle bag which I am clutching with both hands to my chest. I won't let anyone touch it, I feel as if my life depends on it. By the time we reach the Amazon River, it's night. Our Indian pulls the canoe out from the bushes. He checks that no anaconda, boa constrictor, or any other reptile, including a crocodile, is taking a nap in or around it. Then he arranges the parcels so that there is enough room for us all. I am included with the parcels because he asks me to sit at one end without moving. Tom jumps in as soon as the tip of the canoe reaches the water. The Indian gives it a last push and takes his place at the opposite end from me. He starts to paddle, one left, one right.

We are already in the middle of this wide river. I can't believe I am not imagining it all. Here I am, gliding on the dark water, down the Amazon in a canoe made out of a narrow tree trunk, paddled by Our-Indian. I am inhaling every moment with all my senses. I look, I hear, I smell. I am overpowered by the silence. There is nothing besides the clip-clap of the paddle and a huge red tropical full moon. We are not to move or put our hands in the water, which is infested by piranhas. Suddenly, I hear a terrible, desperate scream. Drifting toward us, on a Victoria Regia, the giant white water lily, sits a baby *onça,* the Brazilian jaguar, king of the jungle . . . helpless. The roots of the flower must have loosened when, at night, the baby *onça* came to drink. There is nothing anyone can do. No one. Nothing. Only watch. I think of Henrique who called me Oncinha. I feel I myself am drifting toward the unknown.

Hours later Our-Indian says *agora,* meaning "now." We are nearing the edge of the river, and we seem to be closer to the forest. He jumps out and pulls the canoe over the wet earth. Tom follows, ready to help. I am next, then the packages. From behind the bushes, two Indians appear. They have red stripes on their faces and straw skirts hang from their waists. Our-Indian talks to them. A young woman appears from behind a tree and looks at me with interest. She is bare-chested. After a long deliberation, Our-Indian tells us to wait. The woman disappears into the woods. We hand the two tribesmen the presents we brought for their chief. Tom is holding my hand. Maybe he understands my fear. We look at each other. There is nothing to say. I know we are being watched.

More Indians appear. Then more. They are curious. Our-Indian is constantly talking with the one who is obviously their chief, and their discussion takes a long time. I can hear their voices and see their faces. They stand in front of an oval ring of huts, each hut covered with neat rows of straw reaching almost to the ground. Our presents are at the feet of the chief who seems to be listening to Our-Indian. Finally, Our-Indian comes back to us. In Portuguese he tells us that we are allowed to spend the night there. But we are not to come near the tribe or touch any of them, as white men only bring diseases and death. And Tom looks extra white. The only white person the chief trusts and admires is Josephine. Occasionally, Our-Indian reports, the chief even asks for her advice. We will be allowed to leave in the early morning when we will be guided by two Indians with painted faces to the place where Josephine is to be found. From there, Our-Indian will walk with us to the Xingu River where we'll wait to board a boat which will take us close to Altamira. He will come with us as far as the river. It is impossible to find our way alone.

In a few minutes, Tom and Our-Indian unroll one of the small packages we brought with us. They fit the poles together and erect a miniature tent for one-and-a-half people, which is our situation. One blanket, a mosquito net, bottled water, and canned marmalade. We enter the tent. I cuddle into Tom's arms and wait for the sun to rise.

It's before dawn, kind of light dark, before the sun rises. I unzip the mosquito net and wriggle out of the tent. I stretch my legs and my back. I ache all over. I am reassured that my body is still whole; I have not yet been chopped up. I walk toward the river where, the night before, I saw the Indians bathe. I remove my boots and everything else and imagine I am soaking in a luxurious bubble bath. The power of imagination is working, and I end up feeling refreshed. Through the bushes, I see many black eyes watching. But I am far too thin to be tasty enough for anyone's meal. Unruffled, I put on my clothes and return to the tent to find a loaf of manioc and fruit on a large leaf next to Tom. He smiles and looks comfortable, waiting to share our breakfast together. All this is nothing to him. So I pretend it's natural for me too.

We are ready to leave. Our tent is folded. We spray ourselves with repellent. Tom offers to carry my duffel bag, but I refuse.

"Why are the Indians barefoot while we are wearing boots to avoid the snakes?" I ask.

"Indians see everything. They can see even a very small snake," says Tom.

We start to walk in a line the way Indians do. The trail is narrow. One Indian with a painted face walks at a certain distance ahead of us. Again we are warned not to get near any of them. The spirits will blame us, the white man who took their land away, for any accident. Or disease. Or death. Our-Indian is different. He walks in front of me and Tom behind me. The other painted Indian follows Tom. At a distance, of course. The painted ones occasionally make bizarre sounds to each other. At times Our-Indian translates their meaning into Portuguese. Other times he doesn't. We stop. More sounds. Our-Indian doesn't bother to translate or tell us anything. With machetes, the painted Indians cut left and right through bushes, making room for us to pass. Tom and I are silent. As we walk I hear sounds I have never heard before coming from the forest. My thoughts are taken up by the immediate dangers. Jumping over a branch or a root, avoiding slipping on a rock or something unexpected falling from the trees.

After over an hour's walk, we reach a stream snaking through the rocks. Then we pass through an opening into a small field. The Indian in front of us puts up his hand. We stop. He points at the rusted propellers and at the bones next to them. "Josephine," he says. I stare.

A pile of bones. Two skulls peeping through the grass, and a third on a branch swaying rhythmically like a puppet. I am ready to faint. I want to yell. Instead I stumble. I want to cry out, instead I nearly knock over Our-Indian.

The air is suddenly cold. The last time I saw Josephine, she was in Bucharest, surrounded by her books! Now all I can see is bones, scattered in a jungle in Brazil. Tom tries to take me in his arms and mumbles something in my ear. I push him away. I kneel down by the stream and splash my face with water. Reality hits me. I wish I could scream like the baby *onca*. I can't. The *oncinha* is floating. There is nothing one can do but watch.

I have already lost Josephine once. Losing her again is different, it feels definitive. I am frozen, isolated. This is terrifyingly real. It dwarfs everything else.

The rust on the propellers tells me that the chopper must have been there three months or more. That's when Josephine was last seen.

"Does anyone know when the chopper crashed?" I ask. "How did it happen?" I get nowhere.

"The spirits must have decided this." I am told. "They have their reasons."

Why are there only skeletons, I wonder? Why no clothes? Was the flesh eaten or has it decomposed in the heat? All sorts of scenarios are inventing themselves in my mind so that I can surmount the deep cuts I feel in my heart. Anything to postpone facing what I am seeing. Could it be that the chief didn't want Josephine to leave? Or that he wants to keep us, the white enemy, away from her? Am I being heartless not to embrace the bones? Which ones are hers?

"We can't stay very long," says Our-Indian. "We must reach the Xingu River before sunset. The boat will be there waiting. I'll leave you as soon as you are aboard. Do not go anywhere without the captain's guidance. It's dangerous. You could lose yourselves. There are many rivers that run into each other."

Again I look at the bones while I listen to Our-Indian. There are too many bones for the three skulls. When I turn around, the other two Indians have vanished. Tom is holding my hand.

"*Vamos*," announces Our-Indian.

We start our march toward the river, and I tag along like a zombie. I walk through the dense foliage and keep plowing ahead, not knowing where I am going but knowing I have to keep walking until I do know. I decide that I will return to Rio as soon as possible. I am far away in my thoughts when Our-Indian cuts our way into a clearing by the river. We have reached our destination.

Now we have to wait for the boat, a *chalana*, to arrive. I sit on my duffle bag while Tom argues with Our-Indian who wants to leave us to fetch his canoe. I am not in the mood to talk, but, at this point I say half a dozen swearwords in Romanian, the kind to beat a sailor's vernacular. Our-Indian smiles and shakes his head. I must be polite and smile back. Tom asks what I said to make Our-Indian stay and look so happy.

"It's a secret. A magic word. Trust me."

He trusts me. But the Spirits of the Witch Doctor don't. Suddenly, we are hit by torrents of rain, and darkness blinds me. I can't even see Tom who is standing right next to me. The violent storm doesn't last, it's over, and the afternoon sun returns.

The river is littered with leaves, branches, and debris. Down the bend, I spot a floating box about three meters wide by ten meters long. It's our boat. It is flat-bottomed so it can transport cargo and take knocks from debris. It even has an engine. I can hear it.

The *chalana* pulls up to where we are standing. Tom talks to the captain. He gives him our bags, helps me aboard, and jumps into the floating-box. I repeat the Romanian swearwords to Our-Indian. Again he smiles, before disappearing into the jungle.

I shake hands with the captain. His uniform consists of shorts, tee-shirt, flip flops, and two missing teeth. Under a real captain's cap, his long messy oily hair shouts for a shampoo and unforgiving scissors. He is very much the master of the boat.

"My instructions are clear," he says. "Besides bananas and the two of you, I am to take no other cargo. So there is plenty of room. You better sit on the wooden benches and enjoy the scenery."

We sit like guests at a tea party and fall into the seductive slow rhythm of the forest that glides past us as we wend our way upstream. Two more hours and it will be dark. At the end of this nerve-racking, frenetic day, the only thing we can do is to watch the travelogue in front of us. Cobalt-winged parrots cluster on the branches of trees. Birds rise in the air and then descend in a wave of turquoise, red, yellow, orange, and green. Two white throated toucans ignore the monkeys jumping from one branch to another. Butterflies, in numerous colors, with black polka dots, flutter above a huge turtle resting on a log. Alligators thrash through the shallow water. An anaconda watches us with disdain.

The sky and the water are clear as the *chalana* turns left into a narrower branch of the river. We are motionless. I can't say anything to Tom. He doesn't say anything either. Words are useless. He pats my shoulder. I am glad he is here with me. I'll always remember him being here with me.

Surprise, surprise. All goes according to plan. Peter and Tom are the greatest organizers. Next morning, we are in the helicopter going back to Recife. My head is cluttered with images of my jungle adventure. All I want now is peace and ease, no complications. I wish I had a family, but I don't. There is no use crying about it.

Another three days and I will have been away from Rio and work for four weeks.

"Tom, I will have to return to work." I am shouting to make myself heard over the noise of the chopper.

"Everything has already been arranged," Peter casually shouts back. "You have a reservation on a flight from Recife to Rio at four o'clock this afternoon. A room at the *Pensione* will be ready for you upon your arrival, confirmed by Dona Ruth over the telephone."

"Thank you, Peter, I am grateful to have all these arrangements made for me. I am so tired."

We land at Recife airport and we all get out. Tom and I will lunch at the airport restaurant before I board my flight to Rio. Peter hugs me and says "Good luck. I know I'll see you again soon." He tells Tom he'll be back after four with the car to drive him to the *compania*. Then Peter climbs into the helicopter and takes off. I have tears in my eyes. Grateful tears.

I wash and refresh myself in the airport washroom before I enter the restaurant. Tom has done the same but is already seated at a table by the window when I emerge.

I sit across from him. He holds my hand.

"I'll miss you, my darling."

"I don't know what to say . . . I don't know what I would have done if you hadn't been there with me." I am touched by Tom's devotion. His trying to console me for the loss of Josephine, the last link to my family. It was only yesterday when I finally found out. It feels as though he has been by my side for ages.

"I wanted to be with you. It was important to me as well. I wanted you to know you were not alone. That you could rely on me."

"I find it difficult to understand why you are doing all this for me."

"I can explain. It's easy. But I wish we could be in a different setting. Somewhere with candlelight flicking around us. I would order a bottle of the finest champagne and the most exotic food flown in from all over the world."

I look at Tom in disbelief. Everything he is saying is so unlike him or what I know of him, up to now. He stands, takes my hand, and makes me stand too.

"I love you more than life." He kneels down, looks with intensity into my eyes. He kisses my hand. I caress his cheek with my other hand.

"Will you share my toothpaste with me for the rest of my days?" he asks.

"What toothpaste do you use?"

"Preferably yours."

"If that's how it's going to be, I'd better say yes. Anyway, it's the best offer I've had in weeks."

"I'm so lucky, my darling!"

"Would you like to get up from kneeling now and let me kiss you?"

We fall into each others arms. It is a Hollywood kiss, the longest one on or off screen. Eyes closed, bells ringing in my ears . . . and clapping. Nonstop clapping. Bravo! Bravo! *Felicidade!* The other clients in the restaurant won't stop applauding. So we bow to the audience and sit down at our table, next to each other. We seem to be glued together, in spite of the heat.

The waiter takes our order. Sandwiches and beer. We laugh.

XXXI

1946. In Romania, the Conducator, Antonescu, whose troops carried out the mass killing of Romanian Jews, is executed after being convicted as a war criminal by the Communists who deposed him. I can just see him standing erect between my mother's two large Sevres vases which his wife had, five years earlier, removed from our home.

Dona Ruth is at the entrance of the Pensione when I arrive, smoking her corn pipe. The way she goes on about how she missed me, I am surprised she has survived my absence. "I have put you into another room that is slightly larger and slightly more expensive," she tells me. "It is next to Senhor Tom's room. And the bathroom has a window. The cardboard box with the belongings you left behind is already upstairs. If you need any help, I am here for you. But to start with, you look much thinner than when you left, and before anything else, you have to eat." We go to the kitchen. The table is set. "You have to share a meal with me," she says.

It isn't a meal, it's a feast. Meat, vegetables, rice, salad, and dessert. And Guarana to drink—as much as I want. "Thank you, Dona Ruth."

When it is over, she won't let me help her with the dishes. She takes me by the arm and leads me upstairs to my room.

She even helps to carry my duffle bag. She opens the door and gives me the key. I see, on the little table by the window, six white roses. The note says, 'With you for ever, from the Compania.'

So Dona Ruth has been warned by My Knight in Shining Armor to take care of me. What else does she know? What has been said over the telephone? I'd better not ask.

After an *abraço,* the door closes. I open the cardboard box and hang up my clothes for tomorrow. The unpacking does not take long. I find my chunk of soap and spend the next twenty minutes under a hot shower. Scrubbing and scrubbing. Shampooing. When I am finished, I dry myself with the big fluffy towel. Then, before wrapping it around me, I look at myself in the bathroom mirror. I have not changed much since I left. Only the things around me have changed. Lately, I have lived in a present that didn't seem to have a future. From now on it will be different. I am too sleepy to think straight or to prolong the pleasure of being back here. I am numb. I fall into bed without drawing the curtains, without thinking. I've got a long day tomorrow.

In the morning I take particular care in dressing and looking as civilized as possible before I meet Mr. Larson at the Legation. Though I am among the first to arrive, I sense a certain agitation at the office. The phone doesn't stop ringing. Everyone is in a hurry. Mr. Larson greets me and politely inquires about the outcome of my trip. I inform him of the result as briefly as I can.

"I am sorry to hear about this," he tells me. He pauses. "The ambassador and his family have been recalled home. They will be leaving in about three weeks. There will be a good-bye party a few days before their departure. You will have to help wherever you are needed."

I start rushing, helping with the packing, with last-minute translations. With the children's homework. On the days that follow I am the first to arrive in the morning and the last to leave at night. The departure of Ambassador Hesselvick and his family is the closing of a chapter in my life. They represented an island of peace, serenity, sanity, and normality. For almost two years they have provided me with a refuge of stability while I shared Henrique's unstable Universe. I am very sorry to see them leave. I'll miss them—the boys, Mrs. Hesselvick, the ambassador. I would have liked to tell them about Tom, to ask for their advice. Now that I am alone, away from Tom, I am not sure I want to marry him. We haven't even been intimate. I really believe we should try it out first. We are both so young. I'll be seeing him in another ten days, and I'll tell him then.

On the day of the good-bye party, I am wearing an elegant dark blue silk cocktail dress, one of the last presents I received from Henrique. I have been asked to stay within reach of the ambassador and Mrs. Hesselvick and to keep an eye on the boys. It is most important that nothing should go wrong. I immediately start bargaining with the boys. We are to avoid a last-minute diplomatic incident. I force them to wear ties. In exchange, they can watch an American Western tomorrow evening, with all the trimmings—popcorn and plenty of ice cream.

After I have achieved a happy ending in my negotiations with Lars and Bertil, their beautiful mother is relaxed and smiling. In a lavender gauze dress, she stands next to her husband to greet the guests as they arrive. Soon the crowd of friends spreads through the double doors of the reception room on to the terrace where tall palm plants have been placed for the occasion. Waiters navigate among us with trays of hot canapés and glasses of champagne. As the evening goes on, everyone seems to be having a good time. They all enjoy themselves more and more. Nobody cries in spite of the fact that unanimously it is said, "How sad, how terribly sad it is to part."

At one point, Mr. Larson joins me. He is with a happy-looking man with heavy-rimmed glasses, a good humored teddy bear, not dressed for the occasion. During the introductions, Mr. Hatvani, who has just arrived from Paris and doesn't speak a word of Portuguese, asks me to call him Lazlo. I start speaking English then move into French, inquiring about his preference. Soon I find out that he has a staccato way of talking, with a heavy Hungarian accent in whatever language he speaks. His sentences are colorful, and he doesn't always bother about the use of verbs. So I go for the few Hungarian sentences I learned from Ilona and Janos back in Romania. Lazlo's round face lights up as soon as I show off with my restricted knowledge of his mother tongue. Between drinks and canapés, I learn that he is an artist who has been teaching art at the University in Budapest. World events have driven him to Paris where he has opened a studio of textile designs. He began by selling his designs to the French industry, then expanded into the British and Italian markets.

Mr. Larson, who had left us to mingle with other guests, is back with us.

"Lazlo is one of the most successful creators in the textile design industry and has been highly praised in a letter of recommendation from the Swedish consul in Paris," Mr. Larson tells me with his usual straightforwardness. "Lazlo would like to cover the South American market and is in need of an assistant. Imperative requirements are languages galore and a knowledge of art and literature. He wants to avoid people without imagination. An impediment to his creativity." Then Mr. Larson casually adds, "I think you two will hit it off."

After a few skoals he leaves us standing there, looking at each other in amazement until we both burst out laughing. How undiplomatic, I think. Mr. Larson will never make it to be an ambassador. But, in the meantime, I am so grateful to have the prospect of another job ahead of me.

"When shall we meet?" asks Lazlo.

"Thursday, anytime after the departure of the ambassador and his family."

"Five *heures* at *le* Gloria Hotel. *Zimmer* 345. *Igen?*"

"*Da. Da,*" I say to the poly-linguist teddy bear. "Skoal."

On Thursday, in room 345 of the Gloria Hotel, I look with delight at the designs Lazlo removes one by one from a big green folder before laying them on the table. Each sheet represents a different colored design. When he speaks of "color combinations" and "repeat," I don't know what he means. I don't want to interrupt and ask and show my ignorance. So I keep nodding my head. And Lazlo keeps talking in his inimitable way. I am not Professor Higgins in Pygmalion; I don't need to correct his speech. Somehow, I manage to understand him, especially when it comes to "You know sort of Gustav Klimt. Or pre-Columbian. Or Victorian influence. Or Renaissance." A waterfall of words that instantly have a meaning for me. "Loose Romantic-Geometry-Futurism." As he talks, I see images in my mind. Without a word, he hands me a pad and a pencil. I start to sketch ideas that come to me while he shows his designs. He then explains how each color is printed on a different screen. How a drawing, when repeated and connected, becomes an overall pattern.

Two hours later we sip our *mate* tea. Lazlo asks, in a goulash of languages, if I can come in the morning to help him. "I have two appointments with owners of large printing mills close to Sao Paulo. You will get a better idea of how clients act. What they want. They will each be accompanied by their respective stylists. They will first look at everything before choosing the designs they wish to buy."

Of course I'll be there tomorrow for this new adventure in an unfamiliar world. Fashion? I can't make head or tail of what it's about. Lazlo, confident in my capacities, tells me not to worry. If I like working in this field, he is ready to discuss financial arrangements.

I step out of the Gloria Hotel. I am on a cloud. I catch a bus that stops on the Avenida Copacabana in front of the *Pensione*. I get off, thinking about the whirlwind of colors and ideas I have been immersed in. Squeaking brakes and a variety of swearwords remind me I have to look left and right when I cross the road.

I parachute myself back to earth and enter the Pensione. Dona Ruth hands me the phone as I walk in. It's Tom.

"I was worried, my darling, that you had already forgotten me."

"Who is it?" I pretend I am out of breath.

"Tom. Remember me? The one whose honorable proposal you have accepted."

"I don't know anyone by the name of Tom. You must have the wrong number."

"I doubt it. You are the right number for me, the only number. And the best number there is!"

"And how would you know?"

"I've been reading books."

"Speaking of books, I've been thinking about it."

"What has the wise darling been thinking about?"

"That you totally ignored my principles."

"Which ones? I've been filing all of them with much care in my filing cabinet."

"Remember? You don't purchase a car without trying it out first?"

"If that's your desire, I am willing to oblige. And by the same token I promise not to mention the word 'marriage,' a word that does not seem to be in your vocabulary, until after the mayor has delivered the piece of paper with the legalized proof."

"Where and when do we run the car around the block?"

"You cold unromantic woman! While I yearn to have you close to me and . . ."

"Don't say it."

"Will a weekend in Aguas Lindas do?"

"It'll do."

"I can't wait to have you in my arms. Hm! I'll say no more!"

"You are a darling!"

Many endearing words go back and forth. When we finally hang up, I realize I didn't tell Tom about the possibility of my new job or my doubts about marrying him.

These must have slipped my mind as soon as I heard his voice. If that's what he does to me, maybe I care for him more than I think. He is so stable, reliable, uncomplicated, and fun. I wonder how I'll feel after our weekend together.

There are stars and a full moon, and I am not sleepy. I walk to Avenida Atlantica and sit on a bench. I watch the waves breaking on the sand. I wish I could share my expectations with somebody. Someone with whom I am not emotionally involved and afterward would never see again. The way one confides in a stranger on a train, when all becomes clear and simple. But there is no train, no stranger and nothing is simple and clear. Instead, I buy myself an ice cream Chica-Bon.

Every morning I arrive early at the Gloria Hotel. I am eager to learn all I can from Lazlo. I am an ignoramus in this jungle of fashion. I am present at every meeting, fascinated by this new experience. Lazlo gives me a list of people to call. I arrange all his appointments. Everyone is interested to see the new collection freshly arrived from Paris. When clients show up, Lazlo is calm and smiling. I watch all his movements. At times he sits quiet as a Budha and utters just one word here and there, while he shows them the variety of patterns. At other times, he jokes with the stylist or with the big boss. I translate everything he says, not being able to judge what is pertinent and what is not.

By the end of the week, most of the collection is sold and he has more orders to be sent from Paris at a later date.

"Lazlo, may I suggest that, instead of sending anything from Paris we sit down and paint a few of the patterns already ordered, right here and now. If you can explain and demonstrate how it's done, I'll help."

"I am surprised that you choose to work late into the evening rather than to go out for a pleasant meal and show me the lights of Rio. But I am impressed that you don't take your assignment lightly," says Lazlo in a comprehensible English.

After two sessions, the prognosis is that I am rapidly becoming a textile designer. Lazlo is so pleased by my progress he lets me finish whatever he has initiated. By the time he is due to return home, he instructs me on how to deal with his clients.

I am hired. The financial arrangements are excellent. A salary and a commission on sales plus all expenses paid. We are to start next month when his new collection will be shipped from Paris. If all goes well, I can eventually organize an office here or in Sao Paulo. We'll see. For the time being, I'll tell no one about my plans. No one.

XXXII

It's a perfect day on the afternoon when I sit in a jeep next to Tom, ready for our "honeymoon weekend." Dona Ruth has packed a small basket of food I am forced to take with me. She insists that I am starting to look more like a boy with breasts, than a woman. So terribly thin, she mumbles. I am finally convinced she'd hate Modigliani and adore Rubens. Whenever she catches me, I have to chew on something.

I wave her a special good-bye. Tom draws me closer to him. "It's only the beginning," he says. "The rehearsal for the honeymoon!"

Strange, I don't feel the seriousness of the step I am about to take. I just think that, having been deprived of any fun in my adolescence, I am now entitled to make up for it and have loads of fun. I am looking forward to these few days, whatever the outcome. It's wonderful not to have to think. To let light, happy moods roam.

According to instructions received from Tom I carry nothing with me besides my large handbag in which I have tucked an extra bathing suit, a comb, a toothbrush, a soap, and a towel. A blue sarong tied over my blue bathing suit, flip-flops, and a man's strawhat complete my wardrobe. Tom's is as spare as mine. No excess baggage. I can't remember ever having experienced such freedom.

After an hour's drive, we stop at the end of a road. There is sand and a wooden plank. A dingy with an outboard motor is tied to it. A fisherman sits on a bench next to a big turtle at least a meter wide. I get out of the jeep, and Tom parks in the shade of the tree next to the *botequin*. He talks to the fisherman and hands him an envelope.

Against the sun, I see Tom coming toward me. He is all smiles, tall and quite good to look at. We walk toward the plank. He helps me step into the dingy and immediately starts the outboard. The fisherman unties the cord and throws it to us. Tom holds me by my waist, close to him. With his other hand he is steering. The dingy catches speed, and the water splashes us. I sense that something different from what I have known before is about to happen.

We are approaching an island. The turquoise-blue water is so clear that I can see the bottom of the sea, where a variety of different colored fish swim among the weeds. Leaning down as if to greet us, branches, heavy with flowers in yellow-orange and cyclamen hues, pierce the luscious green vegetation, and with their shade protect us from the sun. At the end of a short dock stands a blue cabana surrounded by a veranda. Nothing else. Tom attaches the cord of the dinghy to a tree. He says, "Woman, stay with me." With two fingers he unties my sarong. "Man is crazy about you." We both laugh and kiss and laugh. Whatever we were wearing falls on the floor of the dinghy.

Thereafter, I always claimed that Tom laughed me into bed. Only it wasn't in bed. But in clear translucent turquoise water with yellow and blue fish swimming around us.

Bubbles on small waves caress our limbs. And we chase each other to the bottom. Then up again. For hours. Close-gasping-interlaced, then slipping away, then back. Until exhausted, we stumble into the cabana and, on the straw mat, love each other to sleep.

Twice a day, an invisible hand provides a tray with fruit—*mamao*, avocado, pineapple, bananas, cheese, yellow or white, dry biscuits, and bottles of mineral water. And we, drunk with the joy of discovery, taste each other continuously. Each time feels different, though always seasoned with sea salt. Tom says he wants to love every inch of me. I feel I am on a survival trip, and our bodies have a life of their own. Impossible to part. Sometimes his caresses feel like wings, or unexpectedly, I sense an octopus all over me when he crushes me with his weight.

When are we ever going to stop? Not even while swimming in the cold water at night. Not even when wearing those masks and palms we found on a shelf in the cabana. It's Adam and Eve with palms swimming straight into lust again. Ridiculous!

During the whole weekend we are stingy with words. Mostly it's "Woman, bring it over here" and "Man, oh, man! Take it."

When it's time to leave, we finally retrieve our clothes left behind in the dinghy.

"I didn't quite bargain for such an overdose," I say, planting a kiss on his chest. That's as high as I can get standing on my toes.

"I guess it's too late to apologize. But, darling, it's our honeymoon after all. Fifty years from now you'll be sorry you grumbled and suggested rationing my impulses."

"I have to admit you are quite wonderful!"

I have just realized that, for the duration of this weekend, Tom has not driven the car around the block as agreed. Instead, he raced at Monza—way ahead of any expectation. Everything was perfect. He made all the arrangements; he took care of every detail. There has been nothing for me to do but enjoy every moment.

It's after midnight when we tiptoe back into our rooms at the Pensione. Tom says, "You can choose my room or yours to sleep in. But it is out of the question to part now." He takes me by my waist, smiles down at me, and asks, "Do you consider me satisfactory?" I nod. "So will you make an honorable man out of me and give me your passport, birth certificate, and whatever papers you have so that I can take care of it first thing in the morning?"

I hand him what he is asking for.

He says, "Is that all?"

"You can have more and more of me if you ask. But in my room please."

He asks. Before I can say yes, we are under the shower. And as soon as we slip under the clean sheets into the bed, it's yes, yes, again and again.

Through the *compania* Tom makes the necessary arrangements for the mayor to marry us within eight days. I am a bit frightened at the speed at which events are developing. But Tom reassures me, "I am not the kind to hesitate when I set my mind on something. Nothing will slow me down now. Too late."

We keep both rooms until the wedding—for appearance's sake. I ask Dona Ruth to be my witness and Peter is Tom's best man. I wear a red printed silk suit the day of the wedding, and Tom looks terribly smart in a beige suit with a blue shirt and a wine-colored tie I chose for him. We even have rings, inscribed as they should be. Tom thinks of everything. After we have tied the knot, it's time to have an elegant meal at the Bife d'Oro with our two witnesses. Champagne and all.

We now have to discuss the prose of daily living. Where shall we live? It's not a problem, it's quite simple. We don't want to stay away from each other. Tom says he can take care of me with the salary he makes, especially as I am not extravagant.

"Rubbish," I say, "I am extravagant! What if I want one of those straw skirts of the painted Indians? Will you buy one for me?"

"Later, much later, only if you wear it to dance the Hula Hula at our golden wedding celebration!"

For now, everything is fine with me. I have time, I am happy, Tom is fun, and life with him is continuous laughter. I am on vacation. A vacation from responsibilities. Anyway, I have to wait for the new collection Lazlo will send from Paris. It won't arrive in Rio for at least another month. I decide to follow my own impulse and join my new husband in his nomadic life. From motel to motel.

So far this life suits us. Even Peter has fun whenever he joins us for dinner. After we finish eating, I attempt to have a fifteen-minute civilized conversation with Peter. No way. Tom takes me in his arms and says, "Good night, Peter, see you tomorrow."

I can hear Peter laugh as my impatient young husband puts me to bed. Lights are frequently out at nine. There are times when, during the night, the light is switched on again, after I hear "I love you more and more, woman."

Of course Tom leaves at four in the morning. But he is back in the evening as eager to love me as on the first day. There is permanence, security, routine in our way of life even though we are permanently on the move. But his love is there. I love his love. Enduring-steady—serene.

During Tom's absence I fill my days. First sleeping late, that takes care of at least four hours. Then the rest of the time I play house. I busy myself with the laundry and invent all sorts of meals. Like the Garbage Omelet I make with all the leftovers. My specialty. I am delighted with the praise and encouragement I receive. At dinner, I set the table with a flower and a description of the menu on a piece of paper I tear out of Tom's notepad. Illustrations are frequently ungastronomic but mostly related to our life together. It's laughter-love-bed. The other occupation I am particularly interested in is Tom's socks. Washing socks. I wait until there are enough of them.

The best part is how to hang socks. It's an art to know how to dry socks in a motel room. I am an expert at solving the puzzle. To Tom's delight, when he opens the door after a day's work, he has to fight the battle of socks before he can reach me. There are many variations. Around the lamp to the window to the door on a string. Or from the door to the ceiling to the bed to the bathroom. Depending on my inspiration, there is always a message. And only Tom knows how to interpret it. He appreciates my housewifely qualities. He wants to name me Woman of the Year. I know that no one in the world would agree with him. But he must have his reasons.

After three weeks of playing wife, I feel I am on a treadmill. A lot of mileage going—going nowhere. Monotonous. I'd like something to change before life gets boring. Laughter, joy at lovemaking isn't enough. But Tom doesn't see it my way. "We are together, isn't that enough?"

"No, it isn't. Not for me anyhow." I want to return to Rio and start organizing the textile design project. The new collection will be arriving any day. I want to see what I can do with it. How can I explain all this to Tom?

Today the wind is blowing more than usual, whistling against the loose shutters. I am irritated and nervous from lack of sleep and too much noise. Tom has been in the bathroom for ages. He is particularly lively this morning at four, ready to board the helicopter.

My body is aching all over. My eyes, half closed, are roaming around the plain motel room. The strapless brown sandals are on the dull linoleum floor. On a chair is my duffle bag. The going-away bag, packed with the essentials. Ready.

Suddenly, I have only one wish. To get out of here as soon as possible. What am I doing with this well-balanced, clean-cut boy, the opposite of everything I have ever known? Lately, I submit to his caresses with the tolerant patience of the pet that has never been quite domesticated. Yes, I still love the look in his green eyes moist with desire, but I must get away from this or choke. I turn my face into the dank sour-smelling pillow. I pretend to be asleep and wait for Tom to leave. After a kiss on my neck, I hear his footsteps reaching the door. I feel a twist in my heart. I want to run to him and kiss him good-bye. As on every other morning. Instead, I sink my face even deeper into the pillow as he closes the door behind him with care. Careful not to wake me.

I throw a wrap around my sunburned shoulders. I look for the schedule of flights leaving for Rio which Tom keeps next to his note pad. There is a direct flight at nine, this morning. If only I can make it! Across the road from the motel, a bus is leaving for the airport in forty minutes. I dress in a hurry. I am out of breath, running for the Olympics. Quickly, the pad and the pen. In a frenzy, I write. No time for illustrations.

"Dearest darling, I just can't take it. It has nothing to do with you. I am not leaving you, my darling. But I can't stay buried in a ditch. I have to get out or choke. I am leaving for Rio. I didn't have the courage to tell you this in person. I was afraid of changing my mind once your arms were around me. By staying, we will in time suffocate each other. For our love to last, there must be another way where we can grow independently and still be together. There must be a solution. Think about it. I can be reached anytime at the Pensione. Please understand!

Woman"

And Tom does understand. He is on the telephone that evening, talking as if nothing has happened. He asks if I had a pleasant trip and suggests we meet next weekend. He'll know in a few days where.

I can't believe my luck. In contrast to Henrique, Tom lets the light shine in on me. I can bloom to the utmost if I so desire.

He doesn't want to be an impediment. He says he feels for me that rare kind of love in which one loves the other more than oneself. His happiness depends on my being happy, wherever that happens to be. I am euphoric. I am given the opportunity to wallow in a relationship without hurt or thorns.

Every morning, there is a letter from Tom. And every evening, minutes before nine, he rings to wish me good night. Sometimes he chats for a while, completing an episode from his letter. Details he omitted. As time goes on, we start sharing our fears and our joys.

I am so used to this schedule that when I have no mail in the morning, I miss it.

I don't complain. I answer some of his daily notes. Almost all of them. When we meet, there are no dark clouds to be chased away or problems to be solved. No arguments. Time is short. We want to make the most of it. Plenty of laughter and love!

Not even Dona Ruth is a problem. She is happy when she sees us. How romantic, she giggles, puffing on her corn pipe. And Peter says he wouldn't hesitate to tie the knot with his eternal fiancée, whom none of us has met or seen, if he could have our kind of arrangement.

XXXIII

I rent one room with a telephone from a lawyer whose secretary I share. It's a light and airy space. The desk and chairs are included in the rent. I buy on credit the bar stools and the large unpainted wooden table, high enough to show the designs. The sign outside the door says RB. Pronounced Arbee or Erebe.

With my initials on the office door and on the letters I sign, all indications are that the office is run by a man. A woman? Impossible. No two-legged female in Brazil works independently at anything important! I won't be taken seriously if it's known that I am a woman. A girl is even worse. Later maybe. Much later. All meetings end the same way. "Why does a good-looking girl like you spend her time cooped up in an office, when you and I could go out for dinner and have fun?" I am ready to scream. I can see Tom laughing, "Good try, but now back to reality." I won't accept that kind of reality. I am determined to find a solution. If I managed to get out alive from that ditch after the train ride from Jassy, this isn't an insurmountable problem. While I ponder on this predicament, ideas inundate my mind. Finally, I decide to make the rounds of the art school at Rio's University. I initiate my first market research—searching for the ugliest boy or girl I can find. I ask to visit all of the classes. After a thorough investigation, I hesitate between two candidates. They are both ugly enough to cause retina damage. Neither of them could be anyone's plat du jour (dish).

For peanuts, I hire the boy who can also draw. I will pay Luiz Carlos da Rocha his monthly wages out of my own salary. I am pleased with myself. I have surmounted the main hurdle. Now to the next hurdle. This afternoon, at the customs, I have to clear the package of designs which has just arrived from Paris.

I take a bus that goes all the way downtown after the Praca Maua and stops in front of the customs. I enter the offices and inquire from a man in blue overalls what I have to do to receive my package. He hands me a bunch of papers and smiles. Flabbergasted, overwhelmed by the many forms to fill in, I stare at him, then frown in desperation. Formalities are so complicated! It will take ages. I can't be bothered. I leave, saying I want to think about it.

I hail a taxi to the Pensione. When we arrive, I ask the driver to wait for me. He trusts me and waits. I run to my room and change into a white suit that clings to my body. Barefoot, without stockings on my suntanned legs, I dash back downstairs. I carry in my hand a pair of white shoes with very high heels. A small handbag, with two decks of cards and most of the partly pledged remainder of my first month's salary, is firmly clutched under my arm. The car takes off. I put on my lipstick, then my shoes. The taxi driver says I look beautiful. A booster in times of need. He sails through the streets as if in a gymkhana, ignoring all red lights. With a jerk on the brakes, he stops at the entrance of the customs and charges me for one way only. A good omen. I am ready. I am impatient to prove my expertise.

An hour later, I am playing a lively game of poker with the men. I am careful not to win, no matter what hand I have. I manage to lose a big chunk of what is left of my salary. But I pat myself on the shoulder as I leave the premises with the package of Lazlo's designs. The nice customs officer who pocketed my money calls one of their trucks and helps to load the heavy box. I promise to be back. "No forms to fill in," are my last words to my poker partners, who laugh. I sit in front with the driver. High heels and all. Quite a sight. I wish Tom could see me. I hope nobody else does.

I have been writing letters to every client on Lazlo's list, announcing the arrival of the new collection of designs from Paris. I let Luiz make the appointments. I feel so grand as clients arrive from Sao Paulo, not knowing who the boss is. Am I the one to work for Luiz or vice versa?

In the meantime, I notice with great interest which designs the clients pause to admire before they set aside the ones they wish to buy. I write their comments in a notebook. Each day I learn new words in the complicated terminology: Jacquards—Wovens—Warp—Chenille-Ottoman-Surah-Link-Weft. I look them up. Many of these words are not to be found in a civilized dictionary. I end up by understanding. Support=ground=material.

Up to now, I had no idea what kind of material anything I wore was made of. And when I hear it's 45 percent one thing and 55 the other, I feel humiliated. I am nothing but an amateur! I am surrounded by people who know so much about things I don't know! I'm good at languages, but this is a tough field to understand. What saves me from giving up and running away is my ignorance. It's the total ignorance of an amateur that gives me the courage to go on.

I keep repeating my findings to Laszlo over the phone, which designs sell best with the Brazilians and the Argentineans. I am learning about the needs of the market from the comments made by clients. There is room for a less sophisticated line of designs. Small and simple, with as few colors as possible. Inexpensive. Maybe for furniture and bed linen. Quantities, I keep hearing. I tell Lazlo about my discoveries again and again. He thinks I am doing very well with what we have. But he doesn't mind if I try something on my own. Why not?

By now I have received my second month's salary. I am intoxicated with the success of Lazlo's designs. Tom, in whom I now confide, is supportive and doesn't ask more than I tell him. With Luiz helping with clients and keeping the books, I'll find the time to branch out. It's the right moment. If I fail, I don't have far to fall.

Ready to face my eventual failure, I buy a large drawing pad, tempera colors, brushes. The containers for mixing colors and washing brushes are provided by Dona Ruth. The discarded marmalade jars are her contribution to my new enterprise.

Strange is that feeling when, after all the preparation, I am faced with nothing but a white page—ready to be brought to life. Shy, uncertain of attempting that first stroke, I am terrified of ruining the clean white space. I close my eyes. Think of Yeats who succeeded in automatic writing, I tell myself. And off I go. I dip the brush in any color, then smack it on the paper. Stroke after stroke. My hand moves, then halts. I open my eyes. It won't do. It's not even good enough to line a garbage can. I'd better forget about automatic painting and leave that to the great modern artists. I mustn't be discouraged and give up so soon. I'll have to find something else. But what?

Maybe the motifs I used for Josephine's posters. People liked them, they bought them. I had illustrated the posters with flowers, leaves, doodles. A simple and direct approach. I take a smaller pad, less intimidating. I draw a few of the motifs and carbon copy them many times. I cut them out one by one and make an arrangement with the pieces. I then glue the result to another small sheet which, again, I carbon copy a few times. Now I have quite a few bouquets to cut out.

On the ex-white intimidating sheet of the large pad, I have brushed one color top to bottom. By now it's dry. I am ready for my first masterpiece. On the colored background, I paste the cut-out bouquets falling over each other. I like what I see. It looks all right so far. But I have a problem. How to color the white cut-outs? I have heard often enough that less color is better for quantities. Cheaper to print. I've heard stylists speak of color combination. What shall I combine with what? I am not going to take a chance and ruin it all by combining colors that scream for help. So I play it safe. I take one color and mix it once with white. I fill in a space, then add more white to make it paler. Then I add a dash of red and continue to fill each space. And so on. From lavender, to turquoise, to light blue. On a soft blue background, it's a happening in the same tonality.

The first stylist who sees it claps her hands. "This is the next new trend!"

I nod.

"*Camaieux*," she says.

I nod.

"Of course it's *camaieux* for the next season. You can't hide anything from me, Arbee!" Her long earrings shake.

Again I nod. "Right you are. There is nothing anyone can hide from you." But I'll have to look up what all of this means.

I phone Lazlo in Paris and tell him about next year's fashion trend, according to the enthusiastic stylist. He roars with laughter. I am ready to be fired. Instead, his hearty and ironic laugh becomes a deep bark of pleasure. Reassured, I join his booming laugh.

Next day the boss of the stylist for whom I am an open book arrives from Sao Paulo to see me. It's urgent, he tells me, he is in a hurry. I open the folder with the designs, ready to show him the entire collection. He says not to bother. "I only want to see the one in *Camaieux*." I lay the page on the table, fearful of his reaction. He looks at it intensely. I am fastening my seat belt, ready for the verdict. He doesn't say anything for the longest minute before signing an order for five more designs of the same family. Different colors and various other motifs in this style, he insists, leaving it all entirely up to me. Included in this unexpected knockout package deal is an invitation to the mill in Sao Paulo. "You'll have to be the one to make the presentation to our American client. It could very well develop into a huge order. Miles and miles of printed cotton for the furniture market. Would you be interested in royalties?"

What does one do when one doesn't have a clue about what to do? Answer, think. Keep thinking until you know. So with a wall-to-wall smile, I say, "I'll think about it." And the more I think about it, the more the Sao Paulo wizards get keener for me. And the keener they are, the more I think. Day by day, propositions and conditions are becoming more interesting. In the meantime, with the help of Luiz, whom from ugly duckling I promote to my carbon-copier-in-chief, the extra five designs are ready. I shiver with anguish as the date of delivery approaches.

I call Lazlo. "Help! What shall I do?"

"Don't panic. Use some learned language to outdo the technical jargon. People in this trade love new words. The more incomprehensible the better." I translate Lazlo's Goulash of words.

"Even academic words?" I ask.

"*Igen*. Academic *mots* is *perfectione*."

"Something like postmodernism, or mannerism?"

"*Perfectione*."

"No other 'ism,' I guess. Such as communism, fascism, rheumatism?"

"Better *nem*."

As if one problem isn't enough, Tom phones. He has been promoted. The *compania* wants him to supervise their interests in the Middle East and in Asia. A position of great responsibility.

As an incentive, his wife is allowed to join him at any time on his trips, all expenses paid. What do I think and how do I feel about this? My reaction is immediate.

"Congratulations, darling! I am so proud of you! Of course you must accept. Will you join me whenever you can?"

"This we'll have to work out later. We'll see." And we decide to meet in Sao Paulo after I have faced the Almighty at the mill.

The day of reckoning arrives. I courageously step into the limousine which is waiting for me at the airport in Sao Paulo to drive me to the Martinezzo Factory. I am wearing my white suit, so as not to clash with any print or color I'll show. Clever, I think, but I dress in white more out of superstition, remembering the result of the poker game. I carry the tube with the six designs in *camaieux*, a word I have now learned how to pronounce with the greatest of ease. And an elegant attaché case, black, trimmed with tan leather. A leftover from Madame Hesselwick, before the family left to return to Sweden.

At the entrance, I am met by the Know-It-All-Stylist who relieves me of the long tube. After an affectionate greeting, she escorts me through a number of "short cuts" straight into the lion's den, the conference room.

In a sumptuously decorated area, with wood-paneled walls and thick beige carpet, I am introduced to a dozen people. They are firmly anchored on tan leather armchairs around a long *Jacaranda* table. Besides the psychic Stylist and her Almighty boss, I don't know a soul, and I find it impossible to retain any of the names I hear. The faces are blurred, as if I've put a veil over everyone. Cigarette smoke fills the hazy space.

I set my attaché case on the table, where a card with the initials RB indicates my place. I mustn't be nervous, I must appear calm and collected. How terribly difficult when I am so frightened! I meet Almighty 2, the Important American Client and his vice president. I am seated next to Almighty 1, who sits next to *him*, the client.

Everyone grows silent. All eyes are on me. I have to say something. How shall I start? I size up Almighty 2 who looks to be in his early fifties and has the frame of a healthy football player with a crew cut dark hair, a turned-up nose, and a lot of perfect white teeth he doesn't hide. On his wrist is a watch that indicates the time in every part of the world, the day, the month, the year, and many other useful bits of information in case one has a sudden attack of amnesia.

I have to be impressive in my opening line! But my tongue is stuck, my mouth is dry. I mustn't panic. I twist my toes in despair. I am intimidated, but the toe twisting does it. I remember a saying that every human being has the same unavoidable necessities. And I see in my mind the image of Almighty 2 sitting on the john. Like everyone else . . . it helps. He is human after all. Now I am finding it easy to talk to him. A flow of words. He seems pleased with what I say and that I speak English fluently. Will I do my presentation in English? he asks. I have no idea what a presentation is. Not even in Romanian. While I am getting ready to use my "isms" as advised by Lazlo, the stylist, her long earrings still dangling, is speaking about the novelty in these original *camaieux* designs. She is the one to have inspired this new style. No one can stop her. She finds names for anything she sees while explaining the importance of this new trend. Even I end up convinced that the designs she is showing are great. And the ground, meaning the fabric or material used, will definitely make the designs a smashing success. End of story.

Two waiters, each with a tray of *cafezinhos*, make the rounds, as Almighty 1 says a few unforgettable words.

"Today's success in business is almost impossible without collaboration. You have to work with someone who listens to what you really need and who, together with you, defines realistic objectives. Someone committed to helping you achieve faster, better, and more sustainable results." Everyone in the room claps their hands in approval.

Almighty 2 is convinced. While orders are being discussed, he demands that the "someone" should be RB, the young designer. He wants her in charge of supervising production and delivery. RB will be the one in contact with the Americans. Almighty 2 will deal only with her. A person whose English is fluent, so that misunderstandings will not be possible. My eyes are ready to pop out when I sign the agreement. My collaboration in exchange for royalties on each meter sold.

XXXIV

Nothing can match the ardor I feel. With my feet firmly planted in mid-air, from now on I feel that anything can happen. I spend two days a week at the mill in Sao Paulo and report to Almighty 2 on the progress of his order. I also see other clients to show Lazlo's designs. My relationship with Tom is solid, and it's fine with me. I can make my decisions rapidly, without asking for his approval or his opinion on anything. He has the same advantage. We can both progress without feeling guilty or abandoned. There was a moment of uneasiness after I explained why I couldn't accompany him on his Middle Eastern and Asian tour. But that dissipated at the end of the weekend we spent in bed . . . talking it out. As a result, we decide to get a place we'll name home. We'll meet there at every opportunity we have. When? Soon.

Almost a year passes. I spend more and more time at the mill in Sao Paulo. Now it's three days a week, sometimes even four. The reason is that Almighty 1 died in a car accident. His son, Baby-Almighty, has taken over the running of the family business. The family's origin being Italian, the young man has many links in Rome. Whether he's chasing actresses from Cinecittà or simply enjoying himself, he is determined to spend as little time as possible in Sao Paulo.

At first, I am asked to look at the foreign correspondence and answer letters once in a while. Then, one day, Baby-Almighty, with a huge smile, his eyes fixed to the floor and clinking the change in his trouser pocket, asks me to supervise all the correspondence. For that, I'll be very well remunerated, of course. Consequently I am getting acquainted with every department, including bookkeeping. My personal financial situation is flourishing day by day. There are royalties on the designs sold to Almighty 2. There is salary and commission from Lazlo's textile designs. Luiz is now in charge of the Rio office while I am away. He refers question to me, after which I refer them to Lazlo in Paris, who Goulashes his answers back before I give Luiz instructions. Life is great. Tom and I can start looking for a home. I feel the world is mine.

And that's usually when the bad witches are marching in. And marching in they do! Without any warning.

I am at the mill drinking my third *cafezinho* of the day, while dictating the correspondence to Mirella, the secretary. Without knocking, the young man from the accounting department rushes in. He is agitated, his face is on fire.

"We have to get hold of the boss quickly. It's urgent!" He tells me.

"I haven't a clue where he is. Why?" How would I know where to find Baby-Almighty?

"The bank is stopping all further financing. There is a huge overdraft. They say not a penny more! Don't you know where to find him? We must find him!"

I have no notion of what he is talking about.

"Can you tell me more? Calm down and explain yourself."

"The bank's delegate is saying they can't trust the playboy anymore. The faucet is closed. Someone has to talk with the banker!"

"How about one of the directors?"

"They have all left for the weekend."

"On Thursday?"

The accountant then explains that without the bank's financing, even my project with the Americans will stop. Most of the drafts, the contract, and the letters of credit have been used as collateral. Up to this moment, the only figures I have followed are the ones regarding my royalties. I can't understand how it is possible that, with the turnover of the mill and the money I have been earning, my dreams can vanish so suddenly.

It is impossible to reach Baby-Almighty. I try to ring him. Again I try. Then I even try his playmates, mentioned in the scandal newspapers. After giving it some thought, I wonder if Baby-Almighty could do anything anyway under these circumstances—buried as he is among feathers in the Opium Den (he was the one to inspire Fellini's *La Dolce Vita*, years later.)

All other attempts failing, I contact Peter at the *compania* in the Bel Horizonte office. The telephone line is bad and my explanations even worse. The only thing I understand is "get the accountant to give you all the figures for the last three months. Ask for justification for each item."

"But, Peter, I haven't a clue about bookkeeping."

"All you need to know is that there are two columns. In one money is paid in, in the other money is paid out."

"Got it so far."

"At the end, when you add up each column separately, the results have to be the same. If not, you are in trouble."

"I'm not so sure I understand that part. But it's a start."

"By the way, which bank is it?"

"Zezinho, what's the name of the bank?" I ask the young nerve-racked accountant.

"Banco Universal, Dona RB."

Peter is duly informed and says he'll see if he can find out more from the bank. He knows one of the directors.

Zezinho, Mirella, and I spend the next three days, which include the weekend, in one room at the mill. We take turns going around the corner to bring back sandwiches and Guaranas from the *botequin*, as we can't afford to interrupt our research. Fortunately, I have with me my elegant briefcase which nobody has ever seen me open. In it are two pair of panties, two tee-shirts, and toiletries. I am all set. Tom has been warned by Peter about where to find me, which he does daily, renewing his offer to make out of me a kept woman.

In a frenzy, we go through the accounts, flipping page after page, pointing at figures for which we can't find any justifying paper. There are incomprehensible invoices to clients which have been paid but not registered. Invoices registered but unpaid. Invoices unregistered and unpaid. Even Zezinho, who is the smallest fish in the accounting department, is stunned. The accountant-in-chief is away. For any further explanation, we have to use our own judgment. "Definitely there is something rotten in Sao Paulo!"

On Monday morning, Peter phones. I summarize my findings and he does the same. His contact at the bank has told him, off the record, that with the present setup at the mill, they are stopping all financing. They won't even talk anymore with the present owner, the sole shareholder. However, should any of the younger employees come forward with a rescue plan, Banco Universal is willing to listen. It has to be a new team willing to work and take risks. New blood. New organization. According to Peter, my name is on the favored list.

"Why not give it a shot?" he says, "Prepare yourself first. Go to every department. Comb the enterprise from top to bottom. Then arrange a meeting with the banker."

Is Peter crazy? He must know something he hasn't told me. Would he, who is so organized, send me on a wild-goose chase?

Ten days later, we finally get hold of Baby-Almighty on the phone, and he is informed of the latest developments. His answer is, "Do what you can." He doesn't seem the least bit concerned, the Gerente-Director tells us.

I am trembling with fear about what lies ahead. I have an appointment with the banker at eleven-thirty today. I must discuss a loan. How will I ever be able to impress him with my kindergarten knowledge of finances?

With the help of Mirella and Zezinho, I have prepared an impressive, bulky file. In it, I argue that by reorganizing the commercial setup, the mill could be self-financed and very secure within four to five years.

I arrive at the meeting ahead of time so that I can rehearse my opening line without being overwhelmed by the surroundings. I am shown into the impressive office by the secretary. She immediately brings a *cafezinho* and chats with me while the telephone rings nonstop—unanswered. Minutes later, the Diretore makes his fussy entrance, apologizing for being so busy while he hands a bunch of papers to the secretary, who disappears.

"So you're the highly recommended RB," he says, thrusting forth both his hands.

"I have heard so much about you too, Senhor Flavio. I am delighted to meet you."

"Please sit down." I move toward his desk, but he points toward the settee and two armchairs round a coffee table covered with magazines on economy and finance. I sit down. He buzzes. A waiter comes in with sandwiches and beer. We talk. He speaks of politics, literature, philosophy. A lively conversation follows. I forget what I have come for. Ideas go back and forth while we munch on our food. After one hour, I point to my bulky file.

"Would you like to look at my findings? There are a few suggestions on the changes that I think should be made to reduce costs and increase productivity. Basically, there is a lot of sloppiness, especially in the commercial department. It's such an easy target for unscrupulous employees. There is no one to supervise the catch-all-you can that goes on."

"Interesting." He looks at his agenda. "Would next Monday be all right with you, Dona RB, for an emergency board meeting at the mill?"

"Anything you say is fine with me."

"Then ten-thirty, Monday, the thirteenth." He calls his secretary and instructs her to make the necessary arrangements for the board meeting at the Martinezzo Factory. Then he turns to me and asks if, by Monday, I can make a report of my findings. Not more than six pages, including the conclusion and remedies. And produce ten copies.

"Carbon copies are my specialty," I say. We both roar with laughter. I am the only one to know why.

The board assembles in the same conference room that, a year ago, I had entered on tiptoe. I sit next to the banker who chats pleasantly while the others take their seats. Two lawyers are also present. One for the bank, one for the mill. Even Baby-Almighty is there. Until the last minute, nobody knew for certain whether he'd show up at all. I wish his father, Almighty 1, had given me a green light to sack him with all the others. But Senhor Flavio has provided me with lesson one. First, plan to seize the majority. Second, clean up the house. Then make some real profits.

So I shut up. But I wonder at the way everyone around this table looks and acts alike. Everybody has a healthy tan and wears a tie and a dark suit. They shuffle papers, pretending everything is just fine. Remarkable. They must have been carbon copied as well!

The meeting starts on a friendly note. Balance sheets. Performance. Predictions. The banker exchanges notes with me after each speech. They mostly end with "wait and see."

Baby-Almighty looks happy, so do his directors. If the banker can be convinced to continue financing the mill, everything is possible. One director even argues in favor of an additional investment for a new department. He turns to me to support his opinion. "Will you please describe the enormous potential in the American market?" I can't suppress a smile. Senhor Flavio gives me a nudge with his elbow and says "Now." I open my briefcase, remove the ten copies of my report, painfully prepared with Mirella and Zezinho. I am careful to close my briefcase quickly, given its usual emergency contents, before I hand the copies around. Nobody even glances at my report as it's folded and set aside. All that work for nothing! I am hurt. My masterpiece seems to be a flop in presentation and in substance.

I stand up, take Senhor Flavio's copy, flip three pages, point at paragraph 2, and set it open in front of him. Next I take a deep breath and say, "In my opinion there is no need for any financing which is not covered by a draft, a letter of credit, an invoice, or other collateral, as explained on page 4 paragraph 2." My report is suddenly being unfolded. All heads around the table are inclined over it. Everything is quiet except my heart which is pounding like crazy. I reach for the jug of water to fill the glass in front of me. My hand is shaking. The banker takes the jug from me and, while he fills my glass, looks at me, and says in a whisper that everyone can hear. "*Formidavel.* Don't be afraid. Go ahead." Then the Gerente-Director stands up. With an ironic grin, shared by a few in his audience, he stares at me. "My dear, since you seem to have the answers to all our problems, why don't you just take everything over and work it out yourself?" My heart sinks, missing a beat. But only for an instant. I have no idea how to proceed. I have been put against the wall. Senhor Flavio comes to my rescue. "Now RB, leave it to the lawyers and myself." My back straightens. The game has caught up with me.

The board meeting is adjourned until four. Meanwhile, the two lawyers and Senhor Flavio meet with Baby-Almighty in his private office. I am told to wait in a small adjoining room until they call me. What is going on, I wonder. Every now and then, Senhor Flavio or his lawyer rush out and mumble something in my direction, pretending they need my consent. They draw a few puffs on their cigarettes before they hurry back into the mysterious room, closing the door. Back and forth they go. As a fairly good poker player, I guess they must be bluffing until some deal is struck. Lawyers always dream of a quick settlement instead of a nagging litigation.

Then within seconds I am called in. It all goes so fast. I am hardly seated when I am asked to read carefully the conditions in the initial agreement before I sign. They have a lot of territory to cover yet. This is only the first step.

Conclusion, Baby-Almighty is left with 20 percent of the shares. The bank another 20 percent. I have 60 percent of the shares in my name, with broad discretionary powers. But until I can turn the whole organization around, my shares stay in the custody of the bank. For this I am given four years, at which time I'll be able to negotiate the purchase of the remaining shares from Baby-Almighty and the Banco Universal.

At four o'clock, while the announcement is made, I am already thinking about reducing costs. I'll have the accounting department closed, keeping only Zezinho. Let the bank do the work of the two columns. All this goes on in my mind while I watch a wasp on the bald skull of the Gerente-Director. I do hope he won't be stung before I fire him with all the others.

BOOK III

Anaconda

XXXV

Rio de Janeiro, July 28, 1967. Thousands of government workers were given the day off for the funeral, but they preferred to flock to the beaches. The solemn salute of gunfire every ten minutes went largely unnoticed. Thus, followed to the very end by the unpopularity that had been his lot in three years as an honest but uncharismatic President of Brazil, Humberto Castello Branco last week went to his grave at the age of sixty-six, victim of a plane crash in the fifth month of his retirement.

Wrapped in a white cotton bathrobe on that bright Friday morning, I recline on the turquoise chaise-long, my breakfast tray on my lap. I am not going to the office and I am not attending the funeral either. Deep in thought, I look out of the window, hoping to see sailboats leaving the yacht club for the open sea. Nothing moves. Not a mast against the perfectly blue sky. No waves. I sip my orange juice, swallow a multivitamin, listen to the news, then gaze into the mirror at myself. Rozalia, Johan, Oncinha, RB, I have acted so many different roles. Simultaneously, I have changed roles and costumes. From Hamlet I leapt into Rigoletto, from Eastern European refugee I jumped to multinational textile magnate, from Henrique's passion and instability, I landed in the stability of a secure marriage with Tom.

In any role I have played, I have always stayed alert and present, ready to learn—whether the learning was cerebral or erotic, obscure or direct. But what I see now reflected in the mirror is a middle-aged, young-looking old woman. In my late thirties, I am not as skinny and flat-chested as I used to be. I have fewer angles and more curves, even on my cheeks. I still wear the same short black hair, flattened to my face. My eyebrows are slightly raised over my brown eyes as if I'm questioning my life. I've been thinking about Tom.

How, in spite of being away from each other most of the time, after twenty years of marriage we are still a unit. How we manage to have independent activities, and when we meet, not to talk about our businesses, or the color of the carpet in the living room. Why are we faithful to each other? Why don't we fight? For all the wrong reasons, I tell myself. We have no time to waste when we are together. We have overcome the daily incomprehension most couples experience. We know each other so well we can anticipate what the other will say.

However, I have kept silent about the story of my childhood. I am part of the school of silence. Silence on events Tom hasn't witnessed or experienced. I am from another planet. I can't expect someone who has not lived my kind of life to understand the tortuous, deep-rooted pain I still carry within me.

The phone rings. No doubt it's Tom, calling to say he's coming home tonight.

"Hello, my ever absent husband! I was just thinking of you."

I hear a low sad laugh. It isn't Tom, yet it is a laugh I know. I feel a bolt of energy, but I can't place the laugh.

"How are you, Oncinha?"

His voice is the same. Time has not changed the timbre or pitch or the current of amusement swirling under his words.

I have not heard from Henrique since that day two decades ago when he left me alone just as suddenly and completely as he had once filled my life. In spite of the relief I felt being free from his intense possessiveness and the wild excitement, I have often wondered why he disappeared without a trace.

As time went by I was busy in my new life, building my business empire and having a serene and fun marriage with reliable-steady-secure Tom. I hardly ever thought about Henrique. But when the thought of Henrique had been completely erased from my memory, he suddenly reappeared when I least expected him. His name was in the news daily, as his activities as a benefactor of society were reported. He now played such a large a role in the public imagination that even Dom Helder Camera was quoted as saying at a Sunday Mass, "If Brazil had five people like Henrique, poverty and misery would be eradicated."

Luckily, the newspapers didn't know that the middle-aged head of the chain of textile mills had, as a young girl, been romantically involved with the most generous and powerful man in the country!

"Oncinha? Are you still there?"

"Henrique. What a surprise! It can't be you!"

"Who else? I was thinking of you and decided I must see you right away. It's urgent."

"Urgent?" I laugh. "After all this time?"

"Very urgent! Please RB tycoon, have lunch with me!"

"But, Henrique . . ."

"Today, Oncinha. It can't wait. I'll send my car to pick you up at one o'clock."

"Wait . . . wait a moment, Henrique." I put the breakfast tray on the side table and fiddle with the belt of my robe. "How do you know I am not expecting someone? How do you know if I'm free for lunch? You don't even know where I live!"

"Oncinha," he says quietly, "I have known where you have been every moment of every one of these years."

He hangs up.

We are seated on a big terrace overlooking the sea. In silence, we just sit and look at each other. After all these years, he seems even more attractive. His gray hair, his tanned face, the intense gaze in his eyes. He is tall and slim in his white suit. I am also dressed in white, a habit from when I used to meet him. I'm wearing the heavy golden chain he put around my neck that day, in one of his unexpected ceremonies. For years I didn't take it off. It was a symbol which was meant to unite us. Now I am wearing it on my left wrist, twisted three times next to my watch, in the latest fashion.

I feel as if I have been in a doctor's waiting room for a long time. When the door opens to let me in, I can't remember what I'm here for, what I want to know and what I want to say. I am embarrassed and I can't help it. But I'd like to find out what has happened during all this time and who he has become.

His fingers touch my hand.

"Are you happy, Oncinha?"

"Very happy to see you, Henrique. You look terrific. Even better than years ago."

"No, that's not what I mean." His eyes don't leave mine. "I'm asking if you have found happiness."

I know he is really asking if my life has been a happy one, if my choices have been good ones, if fate has not been too unkind to me.

"Happiness? Is happiness possible? Are *you* happy?"

"I feel glimpses of happiness—when passion, madness, and love are strong and new!" He looks away and shudders. "The way I felt with you . . . when I thought it was impossible to give you up." His face quivers, and he closes his eyes. "I don't know of any other kind of happiness."

"But, Henrique, doesn't your work bring you any exhilaration?"

"No. Not for long." His voice is low.

His answer throws me off guard. Not just that Henrique is unhappy, but that he is willing to admit it. I put my hand over his. He smiles for a moment, staring at the chain on my wrist.

"I am not sure happiness is possible," he murmurs. "Or perhaps, maybe it just isn't possible for me."

I pull my hand away. I don't know what to say. I have never seen him this way before. My mind scrambles to find a way to change the subject, to cheer him up.

"Henrique," I say avoiding looking him in the eye, "you have the reputation of being a genius. You are admired and loved by a whole population. You create so many things! I've read about the hospital you've built, the schools for children, the homes for the elderly." I feel an urge to stroke his face to reassure him. But I don't. "Isn't that enough?"

"Not for me."

"Why, Henrique? Why? What's happened?"

"When you walked through the door of the Pensione, I felt such a terrible pain . . . The pain was unrelenting." He lights a cigarette and stares at the smoke for a while. "I was down. I felt dead, I was not in charge of myself anymore. I just let things happen.

Then I had a long period of self-pity. I came out of it by gradually reinventing myself and my life. I threw myself into work to fill the emptiness and loneliness. Like an alcoholic. I didn't stop. I worked with passion, longing for satisfaction. And my anguish eventually eased. I was safe again. But I missed the state of intoxication I felt with you."

I have to think fast of something to say. Anything to avoid entering Henrique's Universe.

"There are rumors that you'll be nominated for the Nobel prize. The man who has everything and still wants more." I smile and he smiles. We are safe again. Away from pain and recriminations.

I can feel a breeze caressing my bare arms. The sky is purple now. The waiter does not dare to come near us. He knows he'll be handsomely tipped for leaving us alone.

Henrique keeps talking. I continue to be silent and look at him. He talks, describes, confesses. I listen and watch the movie he wants me to see. He talks in the present, as if I've been with him all this time. He fills the gap of the missing years.

The political changes brought the military to power. The junta rapidly issued decrees suspending the political rights of suspected subversives. Thousands were arrested. Democracy was on the shelf. Henrique was suspected. He became agitated, stressed. Meanwhile, his ex, Carla, reappeared in his life. She was so understanding, sending him little notes on a daily basis. An avalanche of love and devotion. She takes care of everything around him. She was full of concern and attention as she ironed out his daily life. All he had to do was sign the checks. She came to the office at lunch time every day with a delicious meal, accompanied by an excellent wine. This gourmet "still life" was served on a big silver tray with a white linen mat and napkin, embroidered with his initials. Quite a change from the sandwiches he used to grab between meetings. And there she was, sitting on his desk, legs crossed, with such a naughty look in her eyes and tons of devoted love. He found it difficult to resist all the attention. He wanted to discuss this with his sister Silvia. There was nothing he couldn't discuss with Silvia. Since their childhood, she had always been the one he could laugh with. She was his closest friend. For his birthday, he took a trip be with Silvia and her husband Armand, at their property in the South of France. Claudia, their daughter he adores, was also there. This, for him, was a Jacuzzi of rejuvenation.

"After a visit with my sister, I'm ready to face King Kong with my bare hands." He gets into a boxing position and laughs. "She is such a stimulating person and yet she is soothing and understanding." He sits up straight in his chair and lifts his chin.

His mouth takes the shape of an ironic downward smile. "On the morning of my birthday I receive a theatrical cable from Carla. It's filled with "Thank you for existing" and other statements of that magnitude. I show it to Silvia. My dear sister bursts into laughter. In the end, I had one of the most enjoyable birthdays ever."

While he is speaking, I want more than once to intercede. To coordinate his stories. He has told me too much for someone who has just reappeared. Why is he telling me all of this? I know from the newspapers that he remarried Carla. What is he getting at?

"Does Silvia ever come to Rio?" I ask.

"She's here now. She always wanted to meet you. Come for dinner with your husband, the day after tomorrow. Eight o'clock at the house in Leblon. We are having a few friends you'll enjoy meeting. A couple from Switzerland."

"I'll find out if Tom can make it and let you know. He'll be back tonight."

"No excuses. You'd better both be there. It's an ultimatum, Oncinha!"

"Then we'll have to come! I'll tell Tom he has to visit your famous house which is so lavishly described in every decorator's magazine! I'm convinced he'll be impressed and report at eight."

After lunch, in the late afternoon, I stop at the office. I pen in my diary, Sunday, thirtieth, at 8:00 p.m.—Dinner Leblon—with an interrogation mark. I suspect Henrique wants something in addition to inviting us for dinner. Something urgent. But what?

It's almost eleven o clock. Tom will soon be home. I am in bed, in my flimsy nightgown, reading *Risk and Opportunities* by Thomas Huntington. I had no idea my husband had written a book! How does he know all these things? With all the degrees he holds, no wonder he has all the answers. But I have difficulty following the author in his statistical studies. However, I enjoy reading the chapter on "The Good News and the Bad News."

When Tom comes home after an inspection trip in the field, he usually heads straight into the shower in his bathroom. By the time he comes out, it's too late for dinner, so I have Fatima prepare a trolley with the kind of food we can nibble at. This is our routine. At times, I am asleep when he opens the door without a sound and tiptoes into the bedroom. Tonight, he pokes his head in first and asks, "Are you asleep?" I slide his book into the drawer next to the bed and say, "Come in, my man!"

It still makes him smile when I call him "my man."

"Sorry, my darling, to be so late."

He is bare-chested with a towel wrapped around his waist. He runs his fingers through his thick red hair. I notice he has grown a thin moustache since I last saw him ten days ago. It makes him look older and more assertive. If he had any white hair it wouldn't show on his white skin.

When Tom is in the field, he wears a polo shirt over his jeans. So from the elbows down, his arms have a darker hue where the sleeves end. He says it isn't the sun but all those tattoos done by the Indians. "Remember?" he'll ask me. "On the Paranà River, on the border of Bolivia!" He stretches his arms now as he stops by the glass doors that open on to the balcony. For a few minutes he lets the night breeze caress him. He turns to look at the sky, and I see the back of his head tilted upward. He fills the window frame with his wide shoulders. He is tall and his legs are firmly planted on the floor. Solid like a mountain, I think. No wind can make him sway.

Now he comes toward the bed. His side of the bed. He lets the towel drop and slides under the sheets. He opens his arms and I move right in, my head on his shoulder.

"And what did my tycoon wife do today to make her look so lovely?" He strokes my hair.

"I didn't go to the office. I had a luncheon date."

"A luncheon date? Business?"

"No. With Henrique. He called me out of the blue."

A shadow passes over his face. "What did he want?"

"He invited me to lunch, to invite us both to dinner on Sunday."

"Do you want to go, Rozalia?"

"Only if it amuses you, darling."

"Why not?" he sits up. "Who else will be there?"

"His sister with her husband from France and another couple from Switzerland. And of course Carla, his wife."

"I think we'd like to meet the Rascal's wife, wouldn't we? I've heard she's quite something!"

I pretend not to notice his remark and look into his eyes without blinking.

Tom smiles a smile that has no lips. "Did the professional home wrecker try to convince you that your marriage is dull? That life with him would have been more exciting?"

I laugh a little, wondering if he is worried or upset.

"Does it bother you, darling?"

"Should it?" He raises one eyebrow in a familiar gesture. "How does a husband know what a wife is doing with her days when she is not at the office?"

"And how does a wife know what her husband is doing when they are apart? In the compartment of a train, between the wings of a plane, in a cocktail lounge between a martini and a Cuba-libre?"

"Trust, Rozalia darling, trust."

"Trust? You can only trust a husband when he is in his coffin, at least fifty feet underground!"

Later that night, under the sheets, Tom's fingers lightly touch my breast. When I turn toward him, he gives me a good night peck on my cheek and puts the lights out. What? That's all? After ten days away?

XXXVI

Tom drives the Mercedes to the door where a valet takes it to the parking area. We walk up a few steps and the door opens. Carla is there to greet us warmly. She is a pretty, charming, smiling woman, an inch or two shorter than myself. A small white organdy apron is tied around her hourglass figure, her hands are up as if she is drying her nails. No introductions are necessary. She knows all about us. She greets us with an *abraço* that couldn't be more affectionate. "I am so glad you could make it. Come in. I just finished in the kitchen." She is heavily perfumed, manicured, and her hair is impeccably groomed, nothing out of place. The makeup man must have just left.

Henrique smiles ironically when he greets us and murmurs, "With seven servants and a chef, Carla cooks for us. Caviar and toast."

"Pucci, I do it all for you," she says this with a note of coqueterie in her glance and in her voice.

Pucci laughs and greets Tom with an *abraço* as if he has known him forever. No doubt he wants to impress on Carla that it is Tom who is the invited guest, who happens to bring along his wife, RB.

I can't help a wall-to-wall smile, when Henrique follows with Tom as Carla shows the way. She walks with sinuous grace, like a panther, as she removes her little apron and hands it to the maid. We enter the mahogany-paneled library, adorned with books, all bound and classified. In a white jacket, the butler is waiting with a tray of canapes.

When Silvia walks in, we all turn toward her. She is sunshine. At the slightest provocation, her smile becomes laughter, a noiseless laugh as her head tilts slightly backward. She hugs Carla and says something to Henrique who starts to laugh. Armand, her French husband, does his hand kissing before joining his wife, now standing next to me. Silvia does not say the usual "I've heard so much about you," probably to avoid upsetting Carla who evidently does not connect me with the Eastern European girl Henrique once knew. When Carla introduces the Baron and Baroness Armand de la Tour du Roque, the baroness says, "De la Tour du Roc and Roll—please!". They do not take themselves seriously.

For an aristocrat, Armand de la Tour du Roque looks far too healthy. Nothing decadent about him, unlike most of the others in the Gotha—the who's who of the aristocracy. Besides hunting, shooting, and fishing, he is normal. A short moustache, sandy hair, slightly tanned skin, tall. He is not thin. Food, as for every Frenchman, is one of his joys—and it shows. However, he isn't fat, and he seems to be attentive to his figure. Impeccably mannered, never ostentatious, he shows great interest in the people he talks to. It doesn't take long before he and Tom are deep in animated discussion. Armand is going to Patagonia for the first time, and Tom, who had been on an exploration mission there, is telling him all about it.

Everybody is standing, talking, waiting for the guests of honor from Switzerland to arrive, when four young people walk in. The two young men and the girl are Carla's children, and the ten-year-old boy, Antonio, is Henrique's child *de criacao*. They are well behaved and greet us politely, then each goes off in a different direction. Antonio embraces and clings to Silvia as if he is searching for refuge. Geraldo, dark haired, Italian looking, goes straight to Henrique. Conrado and Ariana, who both resemble their mother, surround her. Carla cannot take her eyes off Conrado, clearly her favorite. Now we, the grown-ups, have to be polite as well. We comment on the youngsters' nice manners. There is a satisfied look on Carla's face. Everything is perfect. It isn't easy to resist her charming ways, her cooing, her thoughtful and affectionate gestures. How attentive she is to what each of us is doing. She even notices the kind of canapes we choose. She tells the butler which ones to pass round again and to whom. She graciously moves among us, without neglecting her children, in this image of perfect hostess, mother and wife.

It all fits so well with the setting. A spectacular large window, taking up the whole wall behind the desk, frames a very manicured, multicolored tropical jungle from which a range of lights bursts into the room. A Chesterfield leather sofa and four inviting armchairs surround a coffee table on whose center stands a tall flower arrangement. I learn from Carla, who seems eager to seduce Henrique's friends and family, that this is Henrique's inner emporium. Nobody can come in unless invited, and the children have to wash their hands before they enter, in case they touch one of the numbered editions.

The butler announces, "Professor Alter and Doctor Gastel have phoned to say they are on their way. Their plane from Zurich arrived late. They will be at the house shortly."

"Professor Alter is the famous psychiatrist from Zurich and a fierce opponent of Freud," explains Henrique. "Doctor Gastel, his wife, had helped build and run our hospitals and research centers. She is in charge of the neurological department."

I stand close to the ladder, leaning against the library shelves, so that I can read the titles of the books. The majority are on philosophy, physics, psychology, and psychiatry. I am amazed. I never suspected this side of Henrique, but with him, one never knows. Surprises are his motto.

From the corner of his eye, Henrique scrutinizes my reactions. The same old Henrique!

Without a word, he hands me a first edition of James Joyce's *Ulysses*, saying, "Have a look at this. It's in remarkable condition." I take the book over to the window where the light is streaming in. I am enthralled. It must be five minutes before I turn around and peer into the dimly lit room. I see the two guests of honor who have just arrived, greeting their hosts. Henrique takes me by the arm, "Come and meet Doctor Gastel and Professor Alter." I look in that direction. They are both of about the same height and on the thin side. Professor Alter has white longish receding hair, a small beard, and penetrating blue eyes. As my eyes adjust to the change in light, I drop the book on the table, astounded. Henrique is up to his tricks again! The elegant white-haired woman, tall enough not to have to wear high-heeled shoes, in a wine-colored dress and a string of pearls, is the spitting image of Aunt Josephine with pale pink lipstick and glasses.

I must have had too much to drink! The butler has been following me with cold champagne to wash down the caviar served by the maid. I must be drunk! With all the excitement, I had better hang on to Tom, I know I can count on him. But I can't see Tom. My eyes are blurred by a veil of water. I'm trying to stifle my emotions. Seeing Henrique's books must have reminded me of my childhood. I don't know what to say. I'd be a fool to tell Doctor Gastel, "You look just like my Aunt Josephine" or "May I hug you—I've been longing for this moment." How stupid, Aunt Josephine would never forgive me. After all she taught me, how could I act like an idiot when I have the opportunity to be with two of the great minds of our times?

Henrique introduces me as "Mrs. Huntington, alias the mysterious RB who is the brain behind the string of textile mills, while her husband busies himself building electrical dams around the world, to be able to support his wife!"

Fortunately, dinner is announced. One by one the four young people quietly disappear. We enter a formal dining room and pass a Chippendale table which could seat twenty-four. The walls are adorned with a trompe l'oeil view of Rio bay. At the far end of this room is a cozy dining area like a gazebo. A small crystal chandelier, with a dim light, hangs over a round table set for eight. Silvia, who has placed us, sits between the professor and Tom. Carla is between the Professor and Armand. I am between Armand and Henrique. Doctor Gastel is between Henrique and Tom.

Four silver candlesticks surround a centerpiece of yellow roses. The four Baccarat glasses before each guest sparkle in the candlelight. Limoges plates are placed on embroidered cream mats. The number of knives and forks on the sides of each plate suggests that many courses will be served. In spite of the opulence, there is an intimate, informal breeze in the room. I can see that the professor and the doctor have been here before. Silvia announces, "Armand is an expert on wine tasting. But tonight, nobody is to act as all wine snobs do and pass useful information on the fruit in the wine or the taste of the oak barrel!" Then she turns to the professor and asks, "How can you distinguish between real and fake, between truth and deceit, between lies and imagination?" The answer comes like a shot.

"There is no difference," says the professor, "Reality without fake does not exist, nor fake without reality." He turns to Doctor Gastel, "Why don't you explain your theory about imagination?"

"The person who imagines is not necessarily a liar," she explains. "Take a writer who constructs the world he creates. The props are necessary to decorate the scenery described. In reality, the situation does not exist, is nowhere to be found, but by looking for it, a writer enters into the world he has created. The props he includes are for his own amusement."

Intimidated but fascinated, I take a sip from one of the glasses in front of me and venture, "I suppose this would also apply to an actor who, before a performance, is invaded by anxiety and insecurity, but as soon as he is onstage, he relaxes. With his imagination, he enters into the role he is interpreting and it becomes his truth."

"Yes. It's the power of one's imagination. It's like Utopia."

The professor stops eating. "We are frequently on a small island of truth in an ocean of errors and lies." He gazes at each of us intensely with his blue eyes that seem to look through us like x-rays and adds, with a smile, "If you can understand everything I say, it means that I have not explained myself properly."

I hear laughter and then my mind wanders. To another universe. Another life—a past full of horrors and atrocities. Odo. Mother. Father. Josephine. I can't take my eyes off Doctor Gastel.

As the evening goes on, no one pays much attention to the exquisite food and vintage wines.

Coffee is served in the big drawing room. Silvia comes near me and asks, "Any chance of seeing you alone?"

I'm surprised. "Whenever you like."

"Tomorrow? Where?"

"Come to my apartment on Rua Ruy Barboso at one o'clock, for lunch," I tell her. "I have to catch a plane for Sao Paulo at four. Is that all right with you?"

"Fine. Not a word to anyone. All right?" Silvia smiles and walks away as if her feet hardly touch the floor.

I'm startled. What is this all about? What else can I expect tonight? I feel I'm on a roller-coaster. Strong emotions have been surging through me, one after another. By now I have a splitting headache.

Tom, to please Carla, asks to see the rest of the house. Carla takes Doctor Gastel by the arm, saying, "You haven't seen what I've done to our bedroom." Tom whispers in my ear, "You look pale. Any problem?"

"No, it's nothing," I whisper, as we go up the stairs. We enter the bedroom. The large bed faces a window looking out over the garden to the sea. There is a short passage to a little sitting room. It is easy to see who sleeps on which side of the bed. The door to the right opens to a boudoir dressing room and a pink marble bathroom for her and, to the left, a dressing room and a wood-paneled bathroom for him.

"You've done a terrific job, Carla," says Doctor Gastel. "Your decorating skills are remarkable."

Doctor Gastel looks at me and, out of the blue, takes my pulse. She says to Carla, "This young lady's pulse is beating very fast." I admit to them that I have a headache.

"Do you have something we can give her, Carla?"

"Look in the medicine chest." Carla points toward her bathroom door. "Take RB in there and see if you can revive her—meanwhile I'll show Tom around the rest of the house."

I'm impressed at how neat everything is. Embroidered towels, all initialed. On the shelves under the mirror is a variety of large perfume bottles, bath-salts, dried flowers in a silver container. A little silver tray, two glasses, and a thermos jug with iced water sit on a small table by the door. Doctor Gastel pours the water in a glass, opens the medicine chest, finds the aspirin, takes out two, and as she is handing them to me, she stops. She reopens the medicine chest. I can see what she's looking at. A complete A to Z set of antidepressant and hypnotic medication. On the top shelf, separate from the other medicines, are three tall glass bottles labeled "Benzadorepin. JHB. For Henrique." I look at Doctor Gastel with inquisitive eyes. She looks back at me and says, "Benzadorepin plus alcohol is very dangerous."

XXXVII

It's early morning when we leave our Leblon Hosts (as we unanimously decide to name Henrique and Carla). I still feel shaky and disturbed when I enter the Mercedes and sit next to Tom. He drives with one hand stroking my knee as if to comfort me. On the Avenida Atlantica on our way home, he says, "The sea is also agitated. But even high waves break on the sand . . . I understand."

"You don't understand!"

"I do." But in fact I don't think he does. Nor do I. He is silent for a moment and I can hear the regular sh of the waves. "You can love more than one person in your life, Rozalia." he says.

"I know."

"But in marriage love is different. Time doesn't count. Years go by and one still sees the person with the same eyes as when one first met."

"Like the day you walked into the Pension*e*?"

"To me you'll never look older than the young girl I first saw when she opened the door . . . in a white dress, a golden chain on her neck."

We reach Avenida Ruy Barboso, and he drives straight into our garage. The back elevator takes us directly to the apartment. There are three latches on the entrance door. Tom, very expertly, knows which one to use first. He is an engineer, after all. The door is hardly closed when he takes me in his arms, kisses my neck. "Honey, my darling, finally home!"

"Quite an evening, I'm not myself yet." I smile and cuddle up in his arms.

Usually, as soon as we are alone after being out with friends, we have our laughs and make our zany comments. But this time there are no laughs, no comments. There is much to assimilate. A seesaw of unusual events is going through my mind. Henrique's family, Henrique's books, Silvia wanting to see me alone, the medicine chest filled with psychotic drugs, Doctor Gastel. I can't stop thinking about that resemblance to Aunt Josephine. So much is stirring up my past, memories I have tried to forget.

"How is your headache, my love?" Tom asks.

"It's still there."

He picks me up in his strong arms and takes me into the bedroom, lays me on the bed, and takes off my shoes.

"Is your headache real or does it mean 'no duty dance'?"

"I'm just tired, darling. I have a headache, maybe a Henrique-headache."

He does not answer and just keeps looking at me. I see his eyes moist with desire, or is it doubt? I'm thinking, headache or no headache, tired or not tired, this evening or not this evening, Tom is leaving early in the morning for Canada. He will be away for eight days.

"To hell with my headache," I say and unzip my dress.

Tom doesn't wait. He lifts my skirt and is already in me. We are on a journey of discovery. No time for words of endearment. No talking. Only our bodies are talking. In a frenzy of passion we are all over each other before we reach a climax.

Like an open faucet we want more and more. Again and again. My headache is gone but not that feeling of almost desperate desire. Is it because we did not talk, we did not laugh, we only felt? Has Henrique possessed us? When dawn breaks, our bodies are entangled, and we are still wearing our evening clothes.

The sun is rising from the sea.

We shower. Tom dresses, I wrap myself in a robe, and we have breakfast on the balcony. Fatima brings in a tray with hot coffee, *mamao*, cheese, marmalade, and toast. Without uttering a word she disappears after discreetly nodding her head.

"Amante," I say, touching his ruffled hair. Suddenly I stop. I realize that I used to call Henrique by that endearment.

Tom kisses my hand "You are incredible. I still can't get enough of you after all the years."

The telephone rings, announcing that the car is downstairs.

"Gosh, it's already seven! Quickly," he says, "I'd better leave before your husband comes home from his binge with the boys!"

And we are back to our old selves.

I go to the door with him, and we part with a chaste good-bye kiss. He slips his hand under my robe, plucks a pubic hair, puts it in his wallet, "For luck!" he says. And we laugh as we always have done.

"If that's what an evening with Henrique and Carla does to you, we should see them more often."

"Or maybe less," as he plants a kiss on my neck and leaves.

I'd like to go back to our room and prolong the fulfillment I feel. But I have no time to linger in bed, to enjoy the taste of our night. At times, I wish I could put up a sign in my life saying, "Please do not disturb under any circumstances." Also, I'd like to disconnect from the evening in Leblon. But I must be ready for Silvia when she arrives. I call Maria, our cook, and give her the menu for lunch. Then I say instead, "Do whatever you want but make it as short a lunch as possible. Remember I have a plane to catch."

There isn't much else to prepare. The household is run efficiently by Fatima, with clear instructions about guests who might arrive unexpectedly. A spare room with its bathroom is always ready to be occupied.

Tom and I are extremely careful to keep our privacy intact.

We each have our own dressing room and bathroom which makes us rather civilized. It's our private domain. It's taboo. No one enters these sacred rooms unless invited. My dressing room has a desk. We never use the dressing room to sleep in, though there is a sofa bed in case one of us has a cold or is sick. For the last twenty years, we have only dared to be sick when we are away from each other. We don't fight or sulk at night or whatever couples do when they take a pillow, bang their bedroom door, and go to sleep in another room. We decide to have the conjugal tantrums in the intervals when we are apart. After so many years, it seems to work.

At times, Tom telephones on the hotline from his room to mine to ask, "Goddamit, where are my damn socks?" So that I come over. Other times I call and ask, "Have you called me about your damn socks?" Of course, the socks are not the sole purpose of our meeting. On those memorable occasions, the sofa bed is used.

Fatima comes in with a vase filled with yellow roses. She hands me the card that has arrived with it. I read, 'Looking forward to see you. Silvia'

"Where would you like me to put these, Dona Rozalia?"

"Try to find a place in the living room, Fatima. I'm just finishing looking through some papers for my trip. I'll be with you shortly."

I'm ready for my usual inspection tour before my guest arrives. Flowers are everywhere, and room has to be made for Silvia's bouquet.

"Fatima, try over there, at the other end of the living room. There, by Senhor Tom's music room."

Tom's music room is the library. He listens for hours to his records there, mostly classical.

The *porteiro* announces on the house phone that our visitor is on her way up. The bell rings impatiently twice before Fatima can open the wrought iron door.

Silvia walks in like a sunny bubble. That huge smile on her face makes it impossible not to like her. She has a light that glows from within. A curl of her blond hair covers the corner of one of her dancing green eyes. Her elongated body, in a blue silk blouse over impeccably cut linen slacks of the same color, moves in long strides, hardly touching the ground. Peeking through her sandals, the red nail polish on her toes matches perfectly the color of her lipstick and her fingernails.

She stops long enough to give me an *abraço*, the equivalent of a warm hug, and shoots on toward the large bay windows overlooking Urca and the Sugar Loaf.

"What a view! Look, a boat is leaving the yacht club."

Suddenly, she turns and sees the photo on the table next to the yellow sofa. Tom and I are standing with the Jivaro Indians. She laughs, and her burst of laughter sounds like a bird song.

"Drink?" I ask.

"Yes, please. A Guarana will be fine."

After last night I am tired and have little patience for chitchat. I am eager to know the reason for Silvia's anxiety, or her wanting to see me. What does she want to share with me? We don't have much time.

"Forgive me for being abrupt, Silvia, but please tell me what is it you wanted to see me about?"

She gulps down her Guarana. "It's about Henrique."

"Yes?"

"You are the only person besides me that he trusts."

"I didn't know that."

"For years, Henrique has from time to time had bouts of depression. Between his ups and downs, he has long periods in which he is happy and well. Now his doctors say that if he suffers another depression, they would like to try a few sessions of electro shock treatment."

"I'm so sorry for him, Silvia. What does Henrique think about this?"

"He says he will give it a try if he can have it done in your home."

"Why? That doesn't make any sense."

I am stunned. I have often wondered about Henrique's irrational behavior, the intensity with which he lives, like a forest being gradually consumed by an inextinguishable fire. The blaze is far too strong. It's safe to watch from a distance but not to get too close. Impossible not to be burnt.

Silvia puts an arm around my shoulder. The silk of her blouse, with its faint smell of lavender, feels smooth against my neck.

"Rozalia . . . What is troubling you?"

"I don't understand any of this, Silvia. Why doesn't he have the treatment in a clinic?"

"Because it would immediately be known all over town."

"But how does Carla feel about him having treatment in my home? She's so devoted to him."

"You don't understand. Carla shouldn't know about it."

"Why not? Don't you like her?"

"It's not that! I just react to her like to a scratchy woolen sweater." She smiles, looks me straight in the eye, and murmurs, "He wants no one besides you. He insists he can't trust anyone else."

I think about Tom. How can I keep this from him? It wouldn't be fair. Yet it would also be unfair to tell him something so confidential about Henrique. I have to give Silvia some kind of an answer. It's difficult to get involved, and difficult not to get involved.

I take her by the arm as we go into the dining room. "I will have to think about this."

We sit down. Oblivious of the view, oblivious of the efforts Fatima has made to set the table with the colorful plates matching the flowers in the center of the table. In silence, we pick at the shrimps with avocado. After that, I can only hear the clatter of plates being changed. I have no idea what we are eating. Deep in my thoughts, I don't even know how we came to sit on the veranda of the living room to drink our *cafezinho.*

"Strange how memory behaves," I finally say. "We hide things from ourselves, we suffer both from remembering and forgetting the past." I am caught in that painful contradiction where I have had to remember and have had to forget. "I had to put things away where I couldn't find them or I couldn't have survived."

"Yes, I know from Henrique how your relationship was full of fears and joys."

But I am not only thinking about Henrique, I am thinking of the fight within myself. To be able to forget. To be able to survive the past.

"Did my brother tell you anything about Carla?" asks Silvia.

"Yes. Mostly about the reason they resumed their life together. Yesterday evening they seemed to be in a bliss of contented happiness."

"To the spectator, maybe. *Querida* Rozalia, there is a lot I'd like to talk to you about." She has an imploring look in her eyes.

I check my watch and see that I hardly have any time left to get ready. The car is downstairs waiting. Zair takes my briefcase and the files I'll be reading on the plane, when Silvia asks, "May I use your phone?"

"Of course, there by the door."

She dials a number while she adjusts a lock of hair. "Hello, my love." The receiver is on her shoulder next to her face. "I'll be late for dinner." Her voice is low and sweet. "Don't wait for me if you have something better to do." After a pause, "But don't elope with anyone, because I'm coming back." She laughs and hangs up.

I ring the bell for Fatima, who comes to open the door for us.

"I'll be back tomorrow evening, in case Senhor Tom telephones," I tell her.

I am ready to say good-bye to Silvia. "Can I drop you off somewhere on my way to the airport?"

"Thank you, I'd love that. Can I tell you where I'm going once we are in the car?"

"Mysterious, aren't you? Or is it mischief?"

"We'll see." She lifts her arched eyebrows.

The front elevator takes us down to the main lobby. Zair sees us and opens the door of the Mercedes. We are about to enter the car as he reports, "Traffic was terrible this morning when I drove Senhor Tom to the International airport. We almost didn't make it."

"Zair, we are going to the National airport this time, and we'll drop off Dona Silvia on the way."

"Well, Silvia, where shall it be?"

"I'm coming with you," she says, giving me her huge smile.

"What? All the way to Sao Paulo?"

"Yes, *querida*, all the way to Sao Paulo, unless the plane makes a stop elsewhere."

I am entertained by her extraordinary spontaneity. Just like Henrique, unpredictable. Could it be that there is a lot more she wants to talk about? I am not sure I want to hear it all. And then, I won't be able to read my files during this forty-minute trip . . . But I don't think I have a choice.

We arrive at the entrance of the airport where we have our own parking place. I give Zair my ticket with instructions to purchase one for Dona Silvia. But by some unexpected miracle, Silvia has a spare ticket to Sao Paulo in her pocket! She triumphantly hands it to Zair.

Her seeming disarray isn't very credible. A good pretence, a great performance! She evidently came prepared for this "spontaneous" decision. I suspect it is important and am impressed by her courage and ingenuity.

By the time we board the plane we act like old friends, enchanted with each other's company. We fasten our seatbelts. Silvia's anxiety is obvious. She talks too fast in a high-pitched voice. I take her hand and pat it gently. "What is it? Tell me."

"It's about Carla."

"What about Carla? I know very little about her. I remember she had an Argentinean first husband with whom she had three children. Is she having any problems with him?"

"Not that I know of. Well, not now."

"What do you mean?"

"According to Carla, her first husband forgot to tell her before they married that he was an occasional homosexual. On top of which, whenever he was in his heterosexual moods, he was frequently unfaithful to her. So a few years and three children later, Carla looked around for a better *sistemazione*."

"A new *sistemazione,* a new arrangement?"

"Yes. Preferably a bachelor who was very rich, very intelligent, and very much in love with her, even if she had to stand on her head to get him. She had a try with Edgar Abboudi, the banker, who was ready for a fling but not for the real thing. Then she was introduced to Henrique. A week later, she moved in with her three children . . . it worked for a while. A family with lots of children was a novelty for Henrique who could not have any himself. Then they separated. Then Henrique met you and divorced Carla, leaving her very well provided for. When the two of you split up, he went through a very agitated period. He overworked, started numerous big projects, and he must have told you how eventually he remarried Carla in one of those dubious Brazilian arrangements. Now, after all these years, I strongly suspect that Carla has taken up with Abboudi again."

"What do you think she's up to?"

"In my scenario, Abboudi would like not only to screw Henrique's wife but, with her help, screw Henrique out of his fortune. Or maybe it's the other way round. It could also be that Carla, with Abboudi's help, will take Henrique to the cleaners."

"Well, well, that's quite a scenario! Either way it sounds terrible!"

"It is! Especially since my mother, Dona Edithe, and I have most of our assets tied up as partners in one of Henrique's successful enterprises. We trust him implicitly and have never bothered to check on what we receive on a regular basis."

I listen intently to Silvia and try to paste together last night's events, at the dinner in Leblon. All the pills in the medicine chest in the bathroom. The psychiatrist Professor Alter, the neurologist Doctor Gastel. The books on psychiatry, psychology, and philosophy that were in Henrique's library. His interest in building those neurological hospitals.

"Are you insinuating that, due to Henrique's psychic instability, people around him are trying to create a web of circumstances which would eventually justify their actions?"

"Yes. He's already reacting in a way which shows that he's doing what he's told to do. The next day he doesn't remember anything. He's taking pills day and night. He's afraid of his own moods. He's afraid that when he is euphoric, he might do something to harm his family and his empire. That's what the people who surround him keep telling him. And more and more medication is at his disposal."

"But, Silvia, everything you are telling me is frightening. I didn't realize what was going on. Do you have to deal with this alone?"

"Yes, Rozalia, I can't discuss it with Armand. He wouldn't understand. In his world one just doesn't do certain things."

"Have you tried to speak to Henrique?"

"Impossible. When I'm around, Carla doesn't even go to the bathroom, so as not to leave him alone with me. No chance of seeing him without her being there. Once, at a party, he managed to tell me that he was worried about a new will he had made in which Carla and Antonio, his son, were his only heirs. He was not sure he had done the right thing. He also began telling me that he had a touch of diabetes. Before I could say anything, Carla was there. With a smile, she asked where should we dine that night."

"How frustrating!"

"Yes, Rozalia, I am desperate. Henrique's resistance to a strong-willed influence is decreasing. It is easy for anybody to influence him, even in a negative way. He could be induced to make plans or take actions which are against his will."

"At this stage, do you think his condition is likely to deteriorate?" Without waiting for an answer, I bombard Silvia with more questions, "Is there any chance for him to get away from it all and improve? Is this why you wanted him to have his treatment away from Carla?"

"Yes, it's his only chance."

XXXVIII

The plane is landing. For a moment, I feel guilty leaving Silvia who, with a brave smile, is heading toward the next plane back to Rio.

I have to return to the arid reality of every day. Away from Hitchcock's plots. I can't let myself go. Should I do that, it could change the destiny of the thousands of people who work in the various enterprises I have created.

To this day, after so many years, I still can't explain the story of my success. The events were mostly a series of accidents and chance encounters. I improvised as I went along. I worked with enthusiasm and just went ahead. I ignored my inner struggle between what had been and what could have been. And I kept going forward.

Now, with a determined step, I hurry to meet my assistant, Senhor Luiz Carlos da Rocha, who has arrived in a company car, a Brazilian-made Ford. He's come a long way since the days when I selected him from the art school as the ugliest boy I could find! He relieves me of the briefcase and the file I am carrying. On the way, as we drive through the outskirts of Sao Paulo, we discuss the evening's schedule. "After the meeting in the boardroom, we'll have to take the eight foreign visitors out for dinner," he informs me.

"Have they already seen the mill and studied our organization, Senhor Luiz?"

"Yes, they have, Dona RB. They seem very interested and keen to invest in the company."

"We'll see."

It's already five o'clock when I walk through the offices, greeting everybody by name. I make it a point to remember everyone's name when I ask how they are. I even listen to their answers.

I stop at the little bathroom next to my office to comb my hair and powder my nose. I already feel better. Invigorated, I enter the boardroom. Everyone stands up to greet me. I am being congratulated on the results of the recent developments of the company. Praising the dynamics of my achievement, they say their research reveals that this is the most exiting and potentially rewarding investment in the coming decade. I'm flattered, mildly so, as I gather that they have something important in mind. Whatever it is, apparently they want it very badly. In the last year and especially now, with all the improvements, the business is attracting a lot of interest from prospective foreign partners. Recently, a number of delegations from Germany, France, Spain, Holland, and Japan have visited us. Projects are being discussed with companies of these countries.

Anyway, this meeting is not final. Between translations, I have no idea what to do. So I nod every time they say something and look at me. I am expected to know everything. I keep my poker face and wait to hear what they have in mind. When they get to the core of what they are ready to offer, I'll talk. Meanwhile we exchange smiles, nods, glasses of mineral water, *cafezinho* with a lot of sugar. They know about the markets and the growth of our national sales. They also know about the framework and why I decided to radically restructure the sales system. I have created a network to control and monitor the whole chain from production to retail sale and distribution. So far, I think I have achieved my objective. And everyone in the room knows it. We adjourn. I stand up. The meeting is over.

Senhor Luiz has arranged transportation for our guests in two cars. We are having our dinner at the *Churrascaria*. He has placed the order in advance to be ready for eight o'clock, so that we don't have to wait. We sit outdoors. The table is loaded with all kinds of grilled meats, sausages and fish cooked on the outdoor grill. Local music adds to the evening's program. Senhor Luiz, with his cheerful bonhomie, makes sure that our guests feel in the heart of typical, colorful Brazil. He clearly loves to be surrounded by people and orchestrate the entertaining. I am delighted that I don't have to talk too much, as I can hardly keep my eyes open. Fortunately, besides the *cachaça* in the *caipirinha*, there is enough liquor to open a tavern. The evening is a success. The Japanese guest Mr. Yamamoto, the German Herr Danziger, the French Monsieur Duvernois remove their jackets, loosen their ties, and dance on their own to the rhythm of a Samba. The *caipirinha* has had its effect. Fortunately, I don't have to see them the next morning with their hangovers.

When I am finally alone in my hotel room, Tom telephones to give me the usual boost before I put the lights out.

Next morning, at seven, before going to my office, I stop by the mill. I can hear the hum of the plant. The machines and the long printing tables are already in motion. There is a whirl of activity. Workers stand at the end of each table. Smocked technicians leaning over pitchers of dyes, carefully calibrated, are experimenting. Long broad sheets move along conveyor belts which stop regularly so that layer after layer of pattern can be pressed into what will soon become the finished product. I am pleased that the expertise and reputation of the enterprise are well developed.

I am ready to see the new samples in the styling department, and there I listen attentively to what each of the employees has to say. The stylists, the sales persons, the head of production. Then, after a little hesitation, I point to what I believe will be the market's demand. I am often blunt, quick to reach an assessment. I have some opposition from Paolo, one of the stylists, who is having one of his artistic tantrums. I'm trying to calm him down, but he persists. So metaphorically, I have to throw some iced water on his head. Then I say, "Enough, Paolo. You can't win." I go on for a while. The head of the sales department doesn't agree with the head of the production department who, in turn, doesn't agree with the stylists. My role tends to be that of diplomat. I keep everybody away from each other's throats. By now I feel I need a rest, maybe in an asylum.

At nine o'clock I'm in my office, which is elegantly decorated. I can't remember which one of the stylists decided that I was entitled to have the kind of office that fits my status. Both the floor and the ceiling, sheathed in smooth steel, polished to a mirror finish, create a dazzling effect. The reflective surfaces overhead and under foot make the space look large and intimidating. As I come to think of it, physically I don't fit in this room at all, I'm far too thin. A stout figure with a prominent belly would give more weight to my position and to the sign on the door which says President.

I lunch with the director and Zezinho, the accountant, and listen to their complaints.

I like our little dining room at the office where simple healthy meals are served which don't make me feel sleepy afterward. And I don't have to rush through traffic to be back at my desk where Mirella, my secretary, is waiting. She is perfect for me. She doesn't talk unless talked to. She is always ready to take dictation and prepared to relay my instructions to each department.

She asks what to do about the thirty-five-page business letter from Japan.

"Let me read it."

Mirella hands it to me. I turn page after page. The text, in English, is close to a kind of poetry. It talks about how another year has passed and the snow on Mount Fuji has melted and cherry blossoms are blooming, and after thirty-five pages of description, it ends regretting that we could not do any business deals together.

"Ready, Mirella? Here is my answer." I dictate. "Dear Sirs, Thank you for your letter. We wish to inform you that the motto of our enterprise is YOU PAY, WE SHIP. YOU NOT PAY, WE NOT SHIP. Very truly yours."

Mirella, usually impassive and used to my outbursts, withholds her laughter but can't resist a faint smile. On my way out I tell her not to worry. "You'll see, by return mail they will open a letter of credit for the full amount we have asked." I remember when Aunt Josephine taught me philosophy and psychology. Now, when I have to deal with unusual circumstances, those lessons are quite useful.

Senhor Luiz knocks at my door to say that, if I wish, he will gladly drive me to the airport. It is his polite way of saying that if I want to catch the seven o'clock plane back to Rio, I had better leave right away.

I'm ready. The car drives straight up to the plane, a courtesy arranged by Senhor Luiz's connections at the airport. I climb into the plane and doze off during the trip. Zair meets me in Rio to drive me home. As soon as I enter the apartment, the phone rings. It's Tom. My rock, secure enough to be married to a successful woman. There is no competition. We are somehow partners in all we do together. Then the phone rings again. It's Silvia. Then I disconnect the phone. I take a long bubble bath and have a light supper in bed.

I am glad to be alone in our big bed, stretching out as much as I can in the cool crisp white linen sheets. Above the white upholstered headboard, hangs one of my drawings. A nude woman with long hair. Only one breast is showing. Repeated in a mirrored gallery, it looks like a tapestry of breasts and Tom loves it.

On the opposite wall hangs a Man Ray print that I love. The red Lips dominate the whole room. A drawing in pen of three women bathing on a beach, by Dorival Caymmi, the Brazilian composer, hangs between the glass doors that open onto our breakfast balcony. For a double room the furniture is spare. There is a Louis XVI commode with silver framed photographs of Odo, Father, Mother, Aunt Josephine, and Tom's parents who also passed away before we married. A chaise-long covered in aqua reps and two white upholstered chairs stand next to a round table fitted with a white skirt to the floor. Simply framed drawings by Diego Rivera and Di Cavalcanti's portrait of his wife who looks like Greer Garson in Mrs. Miniver's Rose, hang above a small Louis XVI table where we leave each other notes of approval or disapproval.

When I'm alone, the curtains are never drawn so that I can see the sunrise and the sunset from my bed. I never tire of looking at that big orange ball of fire in movement entering into the sea. And when the sky becomes a potpourri of numerous shades, I feel an astounding inner peace.

XXXIX

We frequently see the Leblon Hosts while Silvia and Armand are in Rio. We even have them for dinner at our home. At first I wasn't too keen to give in to Henrique's curiosity to invade our territory. But Tom, so secure, gets a laugh out of my reluctance and finds ways to embarrass me into agreeing to see them. He claims that when Henrique is around, I make myself look more beautiful and that my voice becomes terribly sexy. I call Tom a middle-aged pervert who has obviously fallen for Carla. The irresistible Carla, who has seduced him with her cooking. So after some more teasing, I give in and we spend more and more time with them.

Tom and Armand enjoy each other's company and always seem to have a lot to talk about. On the other hand, Tom and Henrique have a different relationship. When together, they laugh at each other. Henrique teases Tom whenever he can. He seems to enjoy exasperating my husband. When Henrique asks Tom what we would like for Christmas, his answer is, "Definitely your head on a silver platter."

A few days later, Henrique sends Tom a large package. When he opens it, there is a small package in it with a note, "Please forward this little token to RB. I have decided to keep my head for another week. Hope the enclosed will do as a substitute." Tom hands me the little package and waits for me to open it. Stupefied, I find a pair of diamond earrings mounted in gold. The card says "Happy Anniversary, Oncinha, remember?"

He's done it again. Tom reads the card and, as expected, asks what the anniversary means. Frankly I have no idea. But if I tell the truth, it could create some doubt in Tom's mind. I'd better tell a tall story.

"Oh! I remember now, how in the middle of the Amazon forest I found a tribe of Head Hunters. I managed to keep my head. And by making some extraordinary signs, I showed them a method that could be used to shrink heads twice as fast. They liked me and adopted me. So when the tourist season started, they put me in charge of the sales department. It wasn't an easy job. I was made to understand that tourists would buy the shrunken heads in all sizes as souvenirs. I am about to make my first sale when I hear a voice saying. 'I'd like them gift wrapped.' And who do you think was the buyer? Henrique, of course. Now at least you know how we met."

"I do understand," says Tom taking me in his arms. "It's definitely a day to remember!"

We both try on the earrings. I think they look better on me, but Tom doesn't agree, and he says that I should eventually return the gift. I'll be damned if I will. I know only too well that Henrique did this to create some spice in his life and, if possible, some trouble in ours.

Next time when we see the Leblon Hosts, Tom wears one earring, and I the other.

"What a pair those two are! They share everything! Aren't they adorable!" comments Carla, who isn't part of the game.

Henrique and Tom, both amused, keep a straight face. None of this matters anyway. They are ever so polite to each other. Carla tells me she has no idea what is going on. She busies herself with the guests from Sao Paolo who are to be wed shortly, while we, involved in having our own fun, pay little attention to what goes on. Before we know it we have the honor of being invited to the wedding of the year by Esther and Jonathan, the future bride and groom.

It all happens so fast. There must be some kind of mistake. But it's too late to refuse after accepting the gold rimmed, printed invitation with our names on it.

I wear a light lilac dress and a cloche hat for Esther and Jonathan Abboudi's wedding in Sao Paulo. Tom is also jazzed up for this big social event. After today, Edgar Abboudi will be the only available male bachelor left in the wealthy banking family. Another brother, Max, is already settled, and Isaac, the eldest, stays in Switzerland. The four Abboudi brothers and their four sisters, of Lebanese origin, are Brazilian citizens and have a few other passports and nationalities at their disposal. Sephardic Jews, they are devout people, whose father and grandfather made their fortunes financing the camel caravans. Tom and I have never been to a Jewish religious wedding, let alone such a grand one. When we married, it was a civil wedding with no fuss and we went to Aguas Lindas for a week. No trousseau. No luggage.

This one is a Hollywood production. The black air-conditioned limousines carry the crème de la crème of friends and enemies who have traveled from Rio, Brasilia, Buenos Aires, Montevideo, New York, Geneva, Israel and quite a few Middle Eastern places.

I see Henrique at the far end of the ballroom next to Jonathan, the groom. English-educated, Jonathan runs the family's banking operation in Brazil. The intensity with which he and Henrique talk makes me understand that Henrique is on their future client list. With a lingering smile, her eyes half closed, Carla is talking to Edgar Abboudi who has the reputation of having a brilliant mind. His small frame is topped by a large bald head, his eyes placid and heavy lidded. His movements are slow. Everyone knows that the great love in his life is an Italian Countess. But on and off, as I learned from Silvia, he has been having a sporadic affair with Carla. She has been chasing him for years, during and between marriages.

The large family which the bride and groom have gathered together is full of affection, family ties, and closeness. I recognize the value of a culture based on happiness. The band is playing. Tom is by my side, squeezing my hand. We each understand how the other's mind works. We laugh and enjoy all the nonsense around us, without having to explain or say much. He is always my best audience. It is impossible to be bored when we are together.

In her elegant Paris couture gown, Carla sees us, waves, and comes our way. Edgar Abboudi gazes down the hall as she walks away. We are amused when in her usual melodramatic way, she tells Tom how wonderful she thinks he is. All this because he once showed his surprise at the absence of any decent paintings in her house. "This place, so filled with all the fineries money can buy!" he had said. It didn't take long. When we were next having dinner in the Leblon House, we were shown the new acquisitions, bought at a London auction. We were even shown the catalogue of the sale, with the prices of acquisition:

> Leger "Le Clown" at. L 12 500—Klee "Helldunkel Stude" at. L 3 500—Klee "Cotes de Provence" at. L 9 500—Bonnard "La Promenade des Jeunes Ecolières" at. L19 000—
> Braque " Papier Collé" at. L 17 000—Picasso " Le Peintre au Travail" at. L 13 000—
> Van Gogh "Après L'Orage" at L19 000.

Tom had laughed and patted her on the shoulder, "Carla, it's not that you weren't complete before, but now you're the greatest. What a buyer! You'll never be out of a job. Did you

get the loot wholesale?" She had been pleased, and had planted
a kiss on his cheek. "Thanks for the idea."

"Don't forget the insurance."

"Done."

Before the evening had ended, Henrique asked Tom if he
had any other great ideas. Then he had taken him aside to
talk about a project.

That same evening, Carla had taken me by the arm to show
me the garden she'd just had designed by Burle Marxs, the
famous landscape architect. We stopped by the rocks. The
water was running in a tortuous way between stones. Patches
of green and flames of orange, red, and yellow erupted from
the tropical plants. Hidden lights gave the scenery a beauty
that left me speechless. I listened to the water hitting the rocks.
In a passionate voice, followed by soft innuendos, I heard, "I
love Henrique so, so much that I don't know if I could live
another day if something happened to him."

"What are you worried about?"

"I don't know. I just couldn't live without him. If something
happened to him I'd kill myself." She touched her forehead as
if to prove her despair. She ran her fingers through her hair
and pulled at a mesh of her fringe which fell back as soon as
it was removed. The new twenty-four carat diamond ring from
Boucheron caught in her fringe. I helped her untangle it.

She sounded so sincere, I wondered if she believed what
she was saying. So melodramatic, in contrast to my life with
Tom. Of course we'd miss each other if death parted us.
But we would not kill ourselves. We have laughed so much
together. We could reminisce about all the laughter we shared
for a long time. We recognize the futility of most things and
navigate through daily tasks with humor.

I believe that we have the best marriage in the world. We
spend about six months a year together, the rest of the time
Tom is on a plane. We manage, however, to speak on the

phone on a daily basis. Sometimes more than once. With the change of time in some parts of the world, it isn't always easy. Children? Oh. Yes. We have put them off for next year. And that has been going on for the twenty years of our marriage. We will soon have to do something about it. But we have so much fun when we are together. And even when we are apart, our lives are full. We don't miss the diapers yet.

XL

After Silvia's stories about Henrique, I decide to lunch with him whenever he calls. It's usually a last-minute arrangement. My office is on Avenida Almirante Barroso. One of his offices is on Avenida Franklin Roosevelt, so we are within walking distance. We meet for lunch at the Jockey Club on Avenida Rio Branco, also just around the corner, and we talk mostly of our work or we discuss politics and keep the conversation very unromantic and businesslike. I wait for him to confirm what Silvia had told me, but so far nothing. I can only detect a certain anxiety each time before he swallows a pill. Occasionally, I notice a blank look in his eyes. He seems to perk up toward the end of the meal when he repeatedly thanks me for accepting his invitation. Surprised at his humility, I wonder what happened to the arrogant Henrique. At times, he even tells me that I clear his mind and arouse in him the desire to live life's promises. I don't think I fully understand the nature of his anguish. I want him to talk and open up to me, but the Jockey Club is hardly the place. I tell him, that if he'd like to, next time we have lunch together, he should fetch me at home. We could go to some outdoor restaurant. He likes the idea. We decide for Tuesday next week at twelve-thirty, unless we hear from each other to the contrary.

Tuesday, twelve-thirty. I wait for Henrique. He is late. Very late. Cascades of water are pouring from the sky. It's a never-ending waterfall. The radio announces that the *favela do Bonfin* is slowly disappearing under mud and water. The soil is sliding away from its hill. There is nothing to hold the *barracas,* made of mud with straw or wood, from sliding away. The earth is washing away everything, and people with it.

I worry about Henrique, about his perennial flirtation with death. I call Cosme, his assistant, who tells me that of course Henrique is there at the *favela do Bonfim* with his trucks and all the help he can gather. Ambulances, warm food. I don't think twice. I jump into my car and drive toward the *favela.* The impulse is stronger than reason. Who should be saved first? Henrique, Henrique. I leave the car at the corner. I have to walk. I see him right away. There he is with his sleeves rolled up giving orders, pulling out malnourished children from the waste the rains wash down. He covers them with blankets, comforts them, then carries them himself toward a truck that goes off to come back for a new load.

Formidable, this man, so different from the Henrique apparently incapacitated by recurring depression. He orders me to bring him more blankets from the truck. To lift a branch to make room for the stretcher to pass. He is totally in charge, even after the police and the army arrive. I do what he tells me. We are all drenched, and the rain doesn't stop. They count the dead and the wounded. Hours go by, and the last truck leaves. It's dark. Henrique looks tired but says he feels fulfilled. He walks me to my car, holding my arm so that I don't trip on all the obstacles on the ground. Broken chairs, tables, something that might have been a bed, pots, and pieces of a puzzle that, put together, could have been part of a home.

We reach my Mercedes. He opens the door for me, then closes it before I have time to enter. He takes me in his arms. Our wet clothes touch. He presses me against him. It feels familiar. "Thank you, Oncinha, for being here today. It was important that you were with me on this occasion." On his face I can see he still has his dimple, but now it competes with his baggy eyes. I pull myself close to him. I can smell the earth and the rain and the mud on our drenched clothes. Every inch of me is glued to him. I cling to Henrique as if I am afraid to lose him. We are both too tired to say anything. We cry, tears mixed with rain, water mixed with each other's tears. I say finally, "Father." Horror-stricken, I am afraid to move in case I lose him. My mind is on that train and on that ditch Father and I were thrown into before Janos found us. I thought I could erase that nightmare and forget. Impossible with today's catastrophe, the mud, the fear of Henrique dying. I can still feel the pain and see the image of Odo hanging on that hook. The hook I put in my bun. That hook I used to open the board in the train so that we could breathe.

"If only I could do something to help you breathe."

"Just be there, Oncinha. Why be scared?" Henrique asks. "You can only die once."

Oh please, whoever you are, don't let Henrique leave as well. It has taken me years to lay brick on brick until I could build a tall tower, a tower which reached the peak of the mountain. So tall that I could see life from above, could evaluate most relationships and be immune to new pain. If Henrique dies, another part of my life dies. The bricks will fall to mix with earth and mud until the tower crumbles. Nothing will be left, only bricks and mud. No trace of the tower. I am dizzy. In my mind the image fades.

"Henrique, please let me help you, if I can. I don't think you ever knew how important you were to me. Aunt Josephine opened many doors in my mind, but it was *you* who carried me over the threshold."

"How I loved you! That mixture of enchantment, excitement, and exasperation."

"Henrique, don't."

"Did you think that I could just walk away, take a shower, and wash it all off ? Yes, I was far too complicated. You were far too young. You wanted to find your way. And then it was Aunt Josephine you had to find. I felt betrayed. I couldn't bear the thought of your wanting to find her. At all cost, even if you had to leave me. I felt threatened."

I am shaking. My clenched teeth make a peculiar noise.

"I wanted you to take me to Dom Helder Camera in Recife," I utter. "I wanted to be with you when I hoped to find her."

"Instead you went with Tom."

"Yes. And she was gone. We followed every trace we could think of. We left messages everywhere. After three weeks of combing Recife we went into the jungle by the Amazon. We reached a tribe who showed us the remains of a helicopter, with bones and skulls. We finally gave up."

"Oncinha, in the safe in my office there is a letter for you which I wrote years ago. At the time I thought it should reach you only after my death. I'd like to give it to you soon. Maybe when I next see you?" He takes my hand gently and says, "Now I'll drive you home. I'll have Cosme pick up your car. You'll have it by eight tomorrow morning washed and sterilized. No trace of our meeting today."

He's right. I am exhausted. I sit next to him in his jeep. There are no doors. He holds me with one hand so that I don't fall out at the curbs. He stops and lets me out at the building next to where we live. Strange, this sudden change. What do we have to hide?

Next morning, I read the newspapers. "O Globo" is full of the *favela* catastrophe, with pictures of Carla, perfectly groomed, bringing Henrique hot coffee at the scene of the disastrous earth-slide. How dramatic.

Vadim, Carla's entertaining and talkative masseur, has a crush on Fatima, our maid. Occasionally, he comes by on his

way to work, has a copious breakfast in the kitchen before
six-thirty, and tells the staff all the gossip. He always asks if
Tom or I would like a rubdown. It's usually, "No thanks." But
today is the day. My body aches. Come in.

He sees the newspaper with the photograph of Carla on
the floor. And off he goes. He excitedly explains how, if it
hadn't been for him, this would never have reached the "O
Globo" on time. "How come?" I ask. He explains that it is
he, Vadim, while giving Dona Carla her daily massage, who
updates her about the terrible disaster. By then it is too late
for her to join Henrique, who is already home. Besides, she
has no idea where the *favela* is. He tells me how, as soon
as he finishes massaging her, Dona Carla wraps herself in a
big fluffy towel and goes to a chest of drawers. Out comes a
photograph. She smiles and shows Vadim an old picture of her,
handing Henrique a cup of coffee. Would Vadim, on his way
home, drop off the envelope at the "O Globo" for the social
columnist? Besides the photograph, there is a note asking the
columnist to pass the story on. I listen and do not utter a word.
Once Vadim has gone, my body doesn't ache any more and
I laugh and laugh.

I mustn't forget to tell Tom all of this.

XLI

The newspapers speak daily of Henrique. He is a genius. He doesn't even need to rehearse his speeches. He has mastered the craft of holding an audience enraptured when he talks. People gather around him and listen to what he says. He asks them to go to his hospitals to get free treatment, and they go. He decides to build new homes for those who have lost theirs. He imports any available fabricated houses he can find. He is immersed in a tornado of achievements. He hardly sleeps. He controls other people's reality without realizing he is the one who is controlled.

Carla calls me at the office. She says, "I have a hard time taking Henrique the way he goes on. I am leaving for New York." I know from Tom that Abboudi is there. "I'll be back in a fortnight. Would you and Tom look after Henrique, while I am away? It's important!"

"Why?" I ask. "What's happened? Wouldn't it be better if you stayed?"

"Not after what he told me last night."

"What?"

"He wants to leave me."

"Out of the blue? So sudden? Did he give any reason?"

"He'll never leave me alive, do you hear me? Tell him that. I'll never let him go." Carla's usual soft voice takes a turn. It's like thunder.

"You sound like an anaconda."

"What's an anaconda?"

"A reptile that wraps itself around its prey and crushes it."

"That's right. I'll never let him go alive."

"Perhaps, Carla, you should stay and be there for him. It could be a phase that will pass."

"If only I could find out who it is this time!"

"What do you mean?"

"It's simple. Years ago, when he went nuts for a young girl, I did all sorts of things."

"Things? What things?"

"You won't believe me. It works. Dolls with pins. Poison letters . . . black magic."

"Come on, Carla, if anything did it, it was your charm." I say this with my sweetest voice. The bitch. So it was she who had been trying to frighten me, back at the Pensione!

"Do you really think it was my charm?" I can picture her wiggling, flattered by her favorite subject.

"Yes. I am convinced. Anyway, let me know what you decide. I have to leave you now. There's a call waiting on the other line. It could be Tom." I hang up before I tell her, "You are the kind of person capable of killing your parents, then asking the judge for clemency on the grounds that you are an orphan."

It wasn't Tom on the other line. It was Henrique from around the corner.

"Oncinha, any chance of having lunch today?"

"If it's early and short I'd love to. I have to be in Sao Paulo before three."

"Are you staying there overnight?"

"I don't know yet. Anyway, I have to be back in Rio tomorrow by one."

"I propose to the busy RB the following: lunch in one hour at the Casa dos Pescadores, the restaurant next to the airport, and a leisurely dinner tomorrow evening, preferably without Tom."

"Henrique, evenings are not advisable. I don't think Carla would like it."

"Carla is leaving tonight for New York."

"I know. She told me."

"When?"

"Just before you called. She was not in the best of moods."

"I don't understand what else she wants from me. I have done everything to protect her financially. Nothing seems to be enough. I was convinced by her advisers that I must take precautions not to act foolishly when I'm euphoric."

"Shall we talk about it when I see you? You are doing so many wonderful constructive things. Even if you do a few foolish ones, does it matter?"

"It seems to matter. I am told how dangerous it could be. What if I purchase a new factory, another money shredder . . . which I might regret? I can't trust anyone, not even myself. Especially myself, I am told."

"You sound upset."

"I am. I have transferred my shares in Mondial, the holding corporation, to Stelhio, my director, to make sure that the whole setup is safe."

"Safe from *you,* the founder, the one who built it all?"

"Yes, safe from me in my periods of euphoria."

"Haven't you done enough?"

"It doesn't seem like it. Now Carla also wants my shares in Banco Universal!"

Banco Universal . . . ?

"Henrique, I think I'll return to Rio tonight. Even if it's late. I'll cancel tomorrow's appointments and see you anytime for as long as you like. But for now, let's relax over lunch. I'll see you shortly."

I'd like to have someone throw buckets of cold water over me. I find it difficult not to think of Henrique who needs to be helped. And now, another jack-in-the-box! Banco Universal . . . I should have known. It's not like Henrique to let anyone or anything go. He has to stay involved and pull the puppet strings. So during all those years, he knew my every move.

Now it all makes sense. The opportunity I had couldn't have dropped from heaven. Who else would have trusted a twenty-one-year-old to run an enterprise? On the other hand, Banco Universal did very well with me. It made a good investment. Had I failed, they would have lost nothing more than they would have lost anyway.

But to be fair, maybe Henrique wanted to give me the possibility of being independent . . . also independent from Tom? Could it be that in his mind he thought a free bird could fly away and he would be the one to welcome the bird back into his cage? In the end, the joker in this game was Tom, the rock, so secure that, no matter what, our marriage endured.

How contradictory! Henrique providing my independence when he had not wanted me to exist without him when we were together. He left me. Yet he did not leave my life. And I had no idea! Would he have been there for me if I had failed? He must have trusted me, in his uneven seesaw way.

I suppose his moments of cruelty were when he was most in pain. His loving moments were also full of pain. I wonder if, at any time, he was away from his own anxiety. His joking, laughter, pranks, and games were the child in him, the part of him which was so touching. He gave all of himself. Passionately. He could have been a missionary—a bit perverted—but a missionary. His mission? Anything. No one could resist him. In Henrique's life, hell and paradise walked hand in hand.

I don't want to be tortured with the past we spent together. I wish I could invent a gadget that filters thoughts and lets me breathe—fresh air, fresh thoughts. Oh, Henrique, I can't understand you. Do I have to?

The car draws up in front of the Casa dos Pescadores. Zair opens the door, and I give him instructions to fetch me in an hour. Then to the airport only minutes away.

Henrique is at a small table in the corner. He stands up when he sees me enter, smiles as I approach, and gives me an *abraço*. As I sit down he asks mischievously, "*Cozido*, the Brazilian stew, remember, Oncinha?" I laugh and order a grilled *bacalhao*. He holds my hand. Our knees touch. Of course the table is small.

"You are a master in the art of flirting." I take my hand away. But I don't bother about the knees.

"It's you who is the seductress. Not only with men. You seduce lamps, chairs, your friends, maids-dogs-babies-secretaries, the concierge, the waiter, Silvia, even Carla."

"Do you think it is contagious? I must have caught it from you. The guru. You, the hard-working conquering flirt, irresistible to the masses of people who worship you." I can see he is cheered up by what I say. So I keep the snowball rolling until after coffee.

"Oncinha, I should never have let you go."

At that very moment, the waiter approaches our table to announce that the car is at the door with Zair waiting for me. Perfect timing. I'll give Zair a raise. I am escaping from myself.

"I'll call you tomorrow morning to get your instructions for the day which is all yours. Think about where we should meet. Meanwhile, I want you to know that you can count on me." I give him a peck on his cheek and hurry out before he can say anything.

Though I returned late last night, I am up early. I feel quite well and look forward to seeing Henrique. I told Tom, when he called last night, that I would be spending some time today with Henrique.

"Please, my darling, do not elope without telling me when you will be back," he said. "I plan to be home by Easter which is in another two weeks."

"Carla will be back about that time. Watch out, Tom!" I was a bit surprised at his casualness. "Are you thinking of American suburbia where married couples practice spouse-swapping?"

"I am quite pleased with what we have already and hope that you didn't get any avant-garde ideas from the Leblon Crowd."

At eight, I ring Henrique on his direct line. No answer. So I ring his office. Cosme doesn't know where to find him. I leave a message with Maria Rita, the secretary. By half past nine, Fatima brings me a padded envelope, addressed to me. Written on it, "Please do not open before 5:00 p.m." I think it's Henrique's way of telling me that we are going to meet at five. So I get up and decide to go to the office. I put the envelope in my attaché case and, after a lengthy shower, dress with care so that I can leave straight from the office without having to come home and freshen up. I have some trouble closing the attaché case with Henrique's bulky envelope, probably full of instructions for a treasure hunt. As I leave the house and am about to enter the Mercedes, Zair asks if I received the package delivered this morning by a messenger boy from the Copacabana Palace.

"Are you sure he was from the Copacabana Palace?"

"Yes, he was wearing the uniform of the bell-boys from the apartments at the Annexe."

I decide to open Henrique's envelope right away and not to wait until five. But the car is already at the entrance of my office building. Zair is carrying the attaché case, and while he opens the door to my office for me, I tell him to wait downstairs. I go straight to my desk, full of neatly stacked papers. After a quick glance I turn away, sit back in my chair, and put on the red light at the door. The Do Not Disturb sign. I ring the Leblon house. The butler answers. "Dona Carla is in New York," he tells me. "The children are in Teresopolis until after Easter. Senhor Henrique has not been home since yesterday morning." I am lost. So he has not returned home since I had lunch with him. Strange.

I open the attaché case and take out the envelope. Maybe inside, I'll find a clue to Henrique's sudden disappearance. I try to open the envelope, which is super sealed with powerful adhesive tape and string. I finally have to use scissors and a knife and a gold-rimmed red square leather box falls on the floor. I pick it up and set it on my desk. I press a button on one side and it snaps open. On a black velvet cushion sits a diamond pin. The diamonds are set in gold in the form of a serpentine. Like Brancusi's "Symbol of Joyce" drawing. There are enough diamonds from large to small to cover a fist. I am confused. I can't understand what is on Henrique's mind, and I look for some explanation. There is another red box, similar only much smaller. This one opens in the middle. A chevalier ring with diamonds set in gold. I am not a jewelry expert, but even I can recognize the extraordinary beauty in the design and the quality of the stones.

There must be some other instructions for this game of his. I reach for the opened envelope, and I find a folded white sheet of paper. As I unfold it, I expect a casual lighthearted note. But in his handwriting I read,

"Oncinha, Forgive me. Should something ever happen to me, I would like you to have this ring and pin that go with the earrings. I had this set designed for you years ago for your eighteenth birthday. When I was going to give them to you, I panicked. I was frightened. I was afraid to give you any sort of independence by spoiling you. My anguish reached such a crescendo that my libido made an exit. I hardly slept, and for the little I did it was with a total absence of dreams. I thought I was going mad. I even got to hate you for hurting me. I couldn't bear your wanting anything or anyone besides me.

"I felt threatened by your attachment to Josephine. I had to find Josephine before you arrived in Recife. And I did. I told her that you were dead. I did not spare her the gruesome details of your death.

"I loved you more than life itself. My love for you never died, it only mellowed into something indescribable.

"All this I want you to know and remember. Try to forgive me.

"You are a survivor. I am not."

It's too much, Henrique! Damn You! How could you have deprived me of Aunt Josephine, the only root I had left? I feel angry. I am furious. I look at my watch. It's a quarter to twelve. Suddenly it dawns on me that this is a good-bye letter from life. A confession before the extreme unction. The letter was sent about nine this morning. He didn't expect me to read it before five this afternoon. It would give him plenty of time. His sister Silvia's warnings go through my mind. I wish she were here instead of being in France. I mustn't panic, maybe it's only in my mind. But I read the letter again, and there is no doubt.

I want to call Cosme on my direct line, without going through the office switchboard. Damn it, I can't remember his number. I have to open the safe to find my personal telephone book. There it is. I dial, it rings. After what seems ages, Cosme finally answers.

"It's urgent," I shout. "Try to find a discreet doctor and bring him to the Annexe of the Copacabana. I strongly suspect Henrique is there. Not a word to anyone. Please, no ambulance. I'll be there waiting. Hurry."

I throw Henrique's envelope with its contents into the safe and rush out. Once in the car, I ask Zair if he's sure that the morning delivery boy was from he Annexe. Definitely yes. He knows the boy and his parents. They live next door to where he lives.

I am thinking about how I can get to Henrique, knowing the obstacles which will have to be surmounted once we arrive at the hotel. I see a flower shop. I tell Zair to park in front of it, and I jump out. Red roses. Thirty-six of them. I take them all and ask the florist to make the bouquet as large as possible. Now I hope to have my camouflage and excuse to enter his apartment, provided he is hiding there.

I look at my watch. Twelve-twenty. If only we can reach the Annexe before the boy who knows Zair is replaced by someone on another shift. The Mercedes stops at the entrance on Avenida Copacabana. The bellboy at the door comes to the car.

"Is this the one, Zair?"

"Nao, Senhora."

"Here, take this." I hand Zair a few notes. "Go inside, look around, and find the boy. Ask him if Senhor Henrique is in. Say it's his birthday, and there's a surprise waiting to be delivered in person. Get the number of the apartment. Give him twenty cruzeiros after each answer. I'll wait in the car."

It didn't take long for Zair to accomplish his mission. "Apartment 45," he said, when he came out.

"Zair, please stay in the car in front of the entrance. When you see Cosme with another gentleman, tell him to come upstairs to Senhor Henrique's apartment, without announcing himself. I'll be there to open the door."

I put on more lipstick, grab the bunch of roses, almost bury my face in it and pass the concierge with a wink. In the elevator, I press 4.

In my haste, I pass twice the Do Not Disturb sign on the door to apartment 45. I look for the maid on duty to ask for a vase, and I tell her I want to arrange the flowers in a certain way. Can she help me? I talk and talk while I slide a small note into her hand. How lucky to have found her to open the door for me! My key? "I must have left it on the table inside, when I dashed out to buy the flowers. Don't bother about service. I'd like to rest. I have a big evening ahead. I'll take the vase now. Thank you."

The sitting room is empty. Through the glass doors, the balcony overlooks the swimming pool. To the left, there is a half-open door. Without knocking, I walk in. No one. The bathroom next to it doesn't show any trace of having been used. No toothbrush, no comb. Nothing. I am still holding on to the vase, undecided where to put it.

I turn around, thinking that I panicked for nothing. He might have gone out, and I am stuck with the flowers and with Cosme and the doctor who should be here at any moment. The bastard! He isn't even here! I'm ready to leave. I'll give the flowers to the maid and wait for Cosme downstairs.

I see another door—closed. If it is a closet or a kitchenette, I'll throw the flowers in there. I open the door. It's another bedroom. It's dark. The curtains are drawn. A dim light filters through from the slightly ajar door to the adjoining bathroom. I can't see very well, but then my eyes get accustomed to the darkness. There is someone lying in the bed.

"Henrique, is that you?"

"Hmm."

"Won't you put the light on, please? Or can I open the curtains?"

"No."

I put the flowers on his night table next to a glass and some medicine bottles. Large bottles of pills. I don't want to read what's on the labels. I don't have to. He hasn't shaved. His chest is bare. He is gazing at the ceiling. I look at the bottles. They are full. I don't want him to see what I had feared. I sit next to him on the bed and I take his hand. "Henrique, talk to me please."

"I'm in pain. Such terrible pain."

"What do you feel? Tell me."

"I feel like I'm drowning or suffocating. I am in such anguish. An anguish I can no longer bear." My hand touches his forehead. He talks like a zombie. He seems to be in a trance. "I can't go on anymore. I have no desire to go on living. It's difficult for someone else to understand."

"Henrique, I can." I am not going to tell him that even if he has no desire to go on living it doesn't mean he has to kill himself. "So let's do something about it!"

He turns his head toward me. "But I can't bear the anguish anymore. The hours of intense misery I go through. The total exhaustion I feel. The inability to sleep. The lack of wanting to do anything. The lack of rational thought. I feel so helpless." His eyes water. "I, who was always pulling strings, deciding everyone's life for them. I never thought my judgment could be wrong. I've acted as if I was Zeus when actually I have failed in so many ways."

"How can you say you've failed, after all the incredible things you have done?"

"Look at what I've done to you! You whom I loved and whom I wanted at all costs. I cut your young wings by any means I saw fit, so you couldn't fly away from me to find Josephine! Everything's a mess in my life. I have problems everywhere. At home, in my business, with the children."

I am watching the pain on his tormented face. I feel helpless. I touch his cheek and scoop a tear from the corner of his eye and bring it to my lips. I remember how he used to laugh. But now I watch and hear his cries. The admission of his errors. I see Zeus falling off the mountain.

There is a knock at the entrance door. It must be Cosme with the doctor. I give Henrique a kiss on his forehead. "We have to do something about this. Give me a minute, I'll be back." I leave the room to open the door. Cosme comes in with Doctor Bastian Netto. I put my finger to my lips. "Stay here,

Cosme." I take the doctor to one side and, in short medical terms, I update him. "I can assure you that the patient has not taken anything. He is in need of sleep. Can you take care of the immediate crisis until we find a solution?"

"I agree. An injection to make him sleep would be adequate under the circumstances."

"Can I have your assurance of complete discretion?" I ask.

"Of course."

"And can you prepare the injection before you enter the room?"

"No problem."

I leave the doctor by the door while I approach the bed, "Henrique, you will be able to sleep for a while and feel better. I will stay here with you, in case you need me." I make a sign with my hand to the doctor, I stroke Henrique's head while the doctor empties the contents of the syringe into his arm. Ten minutes later Henrique is fast asleep, a serene look on his face.

Cosme, faithful reliable Cosme. So many years have passed and he is still there when needed. The nanny, full of devotion in emergency. His hair is a little gray at the temples, and he still has that reassuring smile full of humor. That Brazilian gentleness.

I ask the doctor, "How many hours will Henrique sleep?

"I don't know for sure. At least ten and very likely twelve to fourteen hours. I can come back to give the patient another shot if necessary." He gives me his home telephone number as I show him out.

I want Cosme to stay. "Order yourself something to eat here. I am going home to ring Dona Silvia in France to let her know what has happened. She will be able to tell me what to do next. Where to find the best medical care. Who, in the neurological Hospital Henrique built, are in the team she trusts.

I am afraid to ring on the hotel line. The operators usually listen in and gossip."

Before leaving, I check the bathroom next to the room where Henrique is asleep and decide there are too many Gillette blades for someone who uses an electric shaver. I take one of the hotel laundry bags and fill it with any dangerous temptations I can find. Medication, sprays, lotions, blades, and of course the bottles with the pills on the table next to his bed. I even open every closet and every drawer looking for ties and belts. I remove the keys from every door. I give the bag to Cosme and take the key to the apartment with me.

"He's not to be left alone even for a minute. Call your home to let them know you'll be late but don't say where you are. I'll be back as soon as I can." I give Cosme an *abraço* as I close the door behind me.

I step out from the air-conditioned hotel and feel the boiling afternoon heat of the street. What a relief to see Zair, waiting patiently for me. He is a good-looking mulatto with big black eyes and a smiling face. Because he has all his teeth, he smiles a lot. He never removes his tie during service hours, no matter what the thermometer says. He is most professional. Knowing he wouldn't ask, I tell him that all is well and ask him to drive home so that that we can have our late lunch.

I have no problem reaching Silvia by telephone. After the usual "how are Armand and Claudia, and how are you?" I need to hear her laugh so I start with some nonsense, a few jokes that I've heard. Then I pause. I can hear her laughter as she says, "Tell me what's happened? Any problems? *Querida*, you can't fool me." Relieved, I tell her about the latest development with Henrique. I tell her about Carla's trip to New York, about Henrique's letter to me, and my finding him at the Annexe of the Copacabana. I tell her he is very depressed but now is asleep and that Cosme is with him.

"I think he needs to be treated immediately, but I don't know who his doctors are. Henrique gave me the impression he realizes the state he is in. I believe he wants to be away from home and his usual surroundings. Away from responsibilities. He needs to be in a sanctuary where he can find some peace. We must help him. Something has to be done for the storm to pass."

Silvia has stopped laughing. "I'll call you back as soon as I can reach Professor Alter and Doctor Gastel."

"I'll wait for your call at home."

"Where is Henrique now?"

"He's still at the Annexe, in apartment 45, but if you call there at any time, be careful what you say, everybody will be listening in."

One hour goes by. The phone rings. It's Tom, asking how my elopement with Henrique went. "Isn't it too early to be back already?"

"Right you are, Tom, if only you knew. He fell asleep on me." I am very proud of myself for being the greatest liar in the world without lying.

After talking to Tom, I pour myself a gin and tonic from the minibar in my dressing room. The cool drink feels good. While I wait for Silvia to ring, I brood about life's tricks. In my mind I visualize the only sure thing, the big round cake covered with whipped cream. Instead of layers of chocolate, layers of shit. Every day we have to eat one slice of it. This is reality. The whipped cream is what we would like life to be. Illusions and distractions that help to swallow the slices of cake . . . Fate . . . Again, I am involved with Henrique. To see the helpless little boy he has become is heartbreaking. I still remember the Henrique full of rage, telling me, "You are nothing but a little girl, you little animal! You are not even domesticated! I want a real woman." He was the one to teach me, the one I looked up to and depended on. But now, I can see in his eyes how he looks up to me, begging to be helped. He is in such a state that I don't even think of asking where he last saw my Aunt Josephine. Whether he knows if she is still alive. I am so busy and overcome by immediate problems that I don't feel the outrage and anger I should be feeling. I can't see beyond the present moment. I have a vague desire to be alone.

There is a knock at the door. Fatima brings me a tray with cheese, *goiabada* and sliced oranges, "Senhora, you must eat something." The phone rings "Thank you, Fatima, leave it there on the table."

Silvia's voice is excited, "We are lucky. Doctor Gastel arrived in Rio today. I reached her at the hospital. I told her everything you said, and she will call you as soon as she can. We'll make plans after that."

I cut a piece of cheese with *goiabada* to please Fatima. But my anxiety is such that I can't eat anything at this point. The phone rings again. To my relief, it's Doctor Gastel. She mentions our first meeting, at the Leblon house, the night she gave me aspirin for my headache. "It seems now that you have more of a headache." Her voice is soothing. "Tell me everything from the beginning."

When I finish, Doctor Gastel says, "I want to see him with his neurologist and psychiatrist. From what I know, this could be the time for him to have the electric-shock treatment. Silvia told me that he was ready to cooperate on the condition that it be done in your home. It's possible that it will be done right away—therefore, be prepared."

"I'm ready at any time. When shall we meet?"

We agree on seven o'clock the following morning at the Annexe.

I am confronted with making the necessary arrangements as quickly as possible.

I call the office and tell my director that I shall not be available for the next few days, that I'll keep him informed about when I'll return. "Please, handle all you can yourself. Don't call me unless there is an extreme emergency."

Next I check the guest room to see that everything is ready. I remove all the superfluous knickknacks and make sure there are plenty of towels and first-aid items. My heart sinks at the thought of what Henrique will be facing.

I shower and dress in loose attire which I could eventually sleep in. I pick up my small overnight bag, always packed, and am ready to go back to the Annexe. At the door, before leaving, I instruct Fatima that if Senhor Tom telephones, she should tell him I'll be home tomorrow late afternoon. I also tell her she will have her day off, after tomorrow. I mustn't forget to let the staff off when the preparations and the treatment take place.

That evening, it's already nine o'clock when I turn the key in the door of number 45 at the Annexe. Cosme informs me that everything is quiet and that Henrique has slept through all this time without moving. I tell him I'll stay until the morning and call him as soon as I know more after the doctor's visit at seven.

I go out on the balcony. The swimming pool is lit. I recognize many of the people dining at the Pergola. The post-card-view, moon-stars-sea. Waiters moving gracefully among the tables. The contrast between reality and fantasy. Between life in the *favelas* and life in the super-luxurious homes. Between this view of incredible beauty glittering in the evening lights and the inner misery of Henrique in the darkness of his room.

Too much has happened today. I mustn't let myself be contaminated by gloom. I close the glass door to the balcony and, after looking in on Henrique, lie down on the bed in the empty room. The doors are open so that I can hear him if he wakes up. I fall asleep with the lights on. My eyes are closed, and my mind is vaguely awake.

I look in every hour. Sometimes his face quivers. His eyes are closed, and he clenches his teeth. When he opens his eyes he is gentle and gives me an apologetic smile. He wants to know if I managed to get any sleep. Will I lie down next to him? I don't answer and bring him a tall glass of water. I put a straw in it, hold it so he can drink slowly. I coax him on when he stops to doze off. I feed him like a baby, mashed fruit. He smiles. I wait in the room while he goes to the bathroom. I ask him to leave the door open. He takes a shower and puts on clean pajamas. He says he is drowsy. He throws himself on the bed and slips between the sheets. "Don't go," he says. I sit next to him and hold his hand as he falls asleep. An hour later he wakes up. It's almost six o'clock. I order breakfast for us and tell him that shortly we will have visitors who are coming to discuss a course of action to help him out of his melancholia.

We only nibble at the warm croissants, but we drink the orange juice. He lights a cigarette and, after one puff, puts it out. I push the breakfast table into the corridor. In another fifteen minutes they should be here. I empty the ashtray. I call downstairs to let the concierge know that Senhor Henrique expects three guests at seven. To please let them come up without ringing the room.

At seven o'clock, Doctor Gastel and the two medics walk in, and she makes the introductions. They decide to see Henrique separately and consult with one another afterward. Doctor Gastel enters Henrique's room first. After about fifteen minutes, during which I ring room service for *cafezinhos,* she makes a sign to Doctor Leal, the neurologist, to join her. I am left alone with Doctor Luiz, the psychiatrist. I hesitate between taking refuge in the empty room or on the balcony. That's when Doctor Luiz takes my arm, making it impossible for me to escape.

"He is lonely. Horribly lonely," he says, with a scrutinizing look. He stares at me as if he expects me to speak. I don't. A heavy silence follows. I am saved by the waiter who brings the *cafezinhos*, I hand one to the doctor with spoonfuls of sugar, and a relieved smile.

As soon as Doctor Gastel and Doctor Leal come out from Henrique's room, the three of them start to discuss the patient. I take this opportunity to go to the other room, close the door, and turn on the television. I have to clear my mind.

There is a knock at my door. Doctor Gastel asks me to join them. "We have reached the decision to go ahead with the electro-shock treatment," she tells me. "It will happen tomorrow morning. Henrique will get another shot this evening so that he can sleep. He should drink plenty of liquids all day." While we are discussing every detail for the next day's procedure, I see the psychiatrist sneaking back into Henrique's room.

The neurologist takes his leave with the consoling words, "Don't worry, we'll take care of everything." I close the door behind him and turn to Doctor Gastel.

"Do you think Silvia should fly over?" I ask. "Can you please discuss with her what should be done after tomorrow's intervention?"

"I want to think about it and find out what Henrique really wants." She looks at her watch. "I'd better go now. I'll nip in to say good-bye to the two in there. Do you realize they have been together for almost an hour?"

I stay in the sitting room while Doctor Gastel enters the room. Shortly afterward the psychiatrist comes out and tells me that Henrique has asked to see me with Doctor Gastel alone. "Wait for about ten minutes before joining them," he instructs me. Then he leaves.

Ten minutes later, puzzled, I feel a tingle of fear as I walk into his bedroom. The bedside lamp is lit, though the curtains are drawn open and daylight invades the room. Henrique is sitting on the edge of the bed, Doctor Gastel on the chair facing him. I can only see her back. The white hair on the back of her neck. I approach them. He trembles.

"Come here, Oncinha," he whispers, "come and sit next to me." He pats the sheets, indicating where he wants me to be.

I go toward the bed and sit next to him, facing Doctor Gastel. Her face is white. Motionless like white porcelain. She gives me an abstract look.

Henrique takes my hand and places it in Doctor Gastel's hand. She clutches it into hers, brings it to her cheek then kisses it gently and says in an even tone. "Rozalia Bercovici." Shaking her head she says again and again, "Rozalia. My Rozalia."

I am numb. Hypnotized. I don't feel anything in particular. No joy, no happiness. Not even hate or repugnance toward him. My heartbeat must have stopped. I don't hear what Henrique says after "Forgive me, forgive me, can you forgive me?" I don't hear anything. I stop listening. Time must have been performing its healing anesthesia. My feelings have been pulverized by time. Repeatedly, for years, I have embraced Josephine in my mind and in my dreams. But now that I am finally with her, there are no breathless questions, no passionate hugs, no tears, no trumpets playing. This doctor with white hair is not *my* Josephine! I've been waiting for so long for this and now, when it happens, I don't know what to do.

"Can I sit on your lap Doctor Gastel?" I hear myself saying.

We both get up. She opens her arms. We embrace, holding on to each other, and we giggle, giggle, giggle like two schoolgirls.

Even Zeus is smiling. He has done it again.

XLII

According to every statistic, nothing goes as planned. Aunt Josephine, alias Sister Marie Josephe, Doctor M. J. Gastel, or Frau Professor Alter realizes that changes will have to be made. The decisions, so well organized in every detail, must be revised. After consulting with Henrique's psychiatrist, with Professor Alter, with Henrique himself and talking at length with Silvia, it is decided that Henrique should be hospitalized in the clinic in Zurich, Switzerland. It is important for him to be away from familiar surroundings. He needs to be removed from the discord of his life and to be sheltered in an orderly and serene atmosphere in which his only purpose is to get well little by little. Various methods of treatment will be tried, depending on Henrique's reactions and responses.

It is Doctor Luiz, the psychiatrist, who insists on this change of plan. He was the one who encouraged Henrique to face us and finally reveal our true identities. After this, he believes the guilt and regret Henrique feels toward the two people he has hurt could plunge him even more into a downward spiral of despair. The presence of Doctor Gastel and myself would certainly increase his gloom. In the psychiatrist's opinion, I would only be the mirror of his anguished soul.

Doctor Luiz understands the nature and depth of Henrique's torment and convinces him that it would be better to take refuge in a hospital, by far a gentler madhouse than the one he is already in—the tornado in his mind.

The Sanatorium at Kusnacht, in Zurich, is chosen because it has a worldwide reputation for positive results. It was there they discovered that, for certain patients, some antidepressants increase the risk of suicidal behavior. Henrique will be closely monitored as to how each drug he takes affects him.

In no time, arrangements are being made on each side of the Atlantic for Henrique's disappearance from Brazil. Silvia will meet him on his arrival in Zurich. Doctor Gastel, though returning to Zurich in a few days, will not be present during his treatment. Carla who is informed is only too glad to stay away.

Cosme is the one trusted with all the departure arrangements. Passport, ticket, packing, lies, fabrications. Nothing is done through the office. And no one should know where to reach Henrique. The ones who know, including myself, will not disclose the secret under any circumstance, under any torture. We have a cause in common. To save Henrique from himself.

I see him off. At the airport, his last words to me are, "I feel such nostalgia for the euphoria."

Minutes after I return home, Doctor Gastel phones inquiring about the possibility of our meeting before she leaves for Zurich. "Tomorrow for lunch? At the cafeteria of the hospital?"

I have to get used to calling her Josephine or whatever she calls herself now. For "Auntie" makes no sense. It doesn't fit either of us. Marie Josephe? Josephe?

"Let me fetch you when I leave the office and bring you home for a quick lunch," I reply. "At least I'll see you. Then we can plan for later."

"I'll be back next week. We'll have more time to answer the bottomless well of questions since we've been apart."

"I'll pick you up at twelve-thirty tomorrow."

"Whatever you want, my darling. I'll be downstairs. Meet me at the entrance to the hospital."

The next day, I am not even nervous as Zair drives me to pick up Josephine. I ask myself how I can make it a simple lunch when it should stir up a turmoil in me. But somehow, after the tortuous journey full of obstacles, finding each other has been like reaching the destination. It is simple and serene. It's not what I anticipated but I am not disillusioned. I wonder how much I really want to know about what happened.

I meet Josephine on time, and we sit speechless in the car, holding hands. It's comfortable. It's home. Over lunch, we say little and experience much. It is good to be together. If one of us starts a sentence the other one finishes it. An extension of each other's thoughts. A cloud of tenderness floats naturally between us.

We don't ask direct questions, and we don't expect direct answers. Casually, as if twenty-five years have not passed, we discuss our views and thoughts on her profession, my profession, the world, politics. Without ever being personal. The *i*s and *me*s are deleted in our conversation, but it is clear from our opinions who we are and who we have become.

I like talking to Josephine. It removes the last spider webs that linger in my mind. Only she knows how to clear the thick fog which filled the corners of my life. I realize how much I have missed the gymnastics of her mind. I am fascinated by her enthusiasm for new ideas and her intellectual energy. Even when we disagree, it's psychologically healthy and creative.

With all the upheaval that has gone on in the last few days, I have excluded Tom from my thoughts altogether. I am absentminded when he calls. I can't tell him over the phone what's going on. Not about Henrique, not about Josephine. I can't just say, "Aunt Josephine. Remember? I have had lunch with her." It will have to wait for when he returns.

Cosme phones and wants to meet. He has just returned from Zurich. On an impulse, he decided to accompany Henrique on his trip. We make arrangements to meet at the restaurant of the International airport after Josephine's departure to Zurich. By now I think we should have a *pied-à-terre* where planes are taking off. We somehow seem to be at the airport on a daily basis. It's evening, and I have just seen Josephine off. I feel vaguely nostalgic. I go upstairs to meet Cosme. The restaurant is almost empty besides a few flies buzzing on the Ketchup in the center of the table. We order two chicken sandwiches and Coca-Cola. Without any provocation, Cosme talks in his soft voice. He wipes his forehead occasionally with a bandana that he keeps folded in the upper pocket of his linen jacket. He wants to tell me what really happened on that day when Henrique and he (at the time Henrique's pilot) landed the Beechcraft in Recife.

Through Dom Helder Camera, they had gathered all the information they needed. Henrique knew Josephine's whereabouts. He knew everything about her, not only from the stories I had told him while begging him to come with me to find her. He knew every move she made on a daily basis. Everything was planned before this landing. He had organized and supervised every detail.

On that Wednesday morning, as soon as they arrived in Recife, they found their way to the dispensary next to the Igrejinha das Fronteiras. They were told that Josephine had gone to another dispensary at the edge of the jungle. No problem for Henrique. In no time, he organized a helicopter ride. Within an hour, they were there. They waited outside. By ten o'clock, Josephine, in her white smock, opened the door. She carried a medicine bag. A strawhat covered part of her face. The two men, playing Sherlock and Watson, followed her. For the first twenty minutes they found it exciting walking along a trail of knee-high weeds. The adventure of braving the jungle with an ulterior purpose known only to them was thrilling.

But soon, the humidity, the heat and the mosquitoes diminished their enthusiasm. It became increasingly dull. When they saw the first hut with smoke rising above it, actually the only hut, they stopped. A short muscular Indian dressed in bermudas and a tee-shirt greeted the woman in the white smock. He moved aside the bamboo curtain for her to enter. She entered. Then nothing. Suspense. The two men were exhausted. Their starched shirts, now soaked with sweat, stuck to their chests. They leaned against a tree, trying not to fall asleep while waiting. They hoped Josephine wouldn't spend the night there. Meanwhile, in spite of the repellent they had drenched themselves in, they scratched and slapped their flesh with much gusto. When Josephine finally emerged, she didn't hide her surprise. She clapped her hands and laughed. Two white men waiting for her in the jungle. Dressed in white with black boots. Most effective. Barefoot and bare torso or bare all together was more the fashion in those parts! Henrique approached her. He took her hand, introduced Cosme and himself.

While they walked back, Henrique talked about a project of his in Manaus. An emergency clinic specializing in malaria, dengue fever, and other tropical diseases. It was also a place where people with mental problems were occasionally sent. He needed her know-how and experience to organize the nursing and medical department, he told her. How soon could she be available? This project was only a stepping stone to the neurological complex he was setting up in Rio de Janeiro. He wanted her to run the research center. With his enthusiasm and imagination, he inflamed Josephine's inclination for life's perennial adventure.

That same afternoon, the plane landed in Manaus complete with Josephine. Henrique's charisma and what she saw conquered her. Drawn into his *Perpetum Mobile,* she outbid him. Before the evening was over, the two played for the Grand Shlem. Next morning she was in the Beechcraft flying to Rio. All details were being tackled by Henrique's magic machine. The power of imaginative thinking. In this phase, problems didn't exist, only solutions were welcomed.

Josephine was swiftly flown to Zurich. She would assist Professor Alter. During that time she would be taking her doctor's degree. She needed another year to complete her studies. Meanwhile she was in constant touch with Henrique concerning the project he was about to complete, the Neurological Hospital in Rio. Professor Alter's interest in having Josephine assist him was steered by Henrique's ability to tell the story of Sister Marie Josephe. Carl Alter believed that religion was also part of curing the mind. He was seduced by the religious interlude in Josephine's life. Henrique, the *Deus ex Machina,* presented the case so well that, when the year was over and all was going according to his plan, Carl Alter added a codicil to the initial strategy by marrying his assistant. A sure way to keep her invaluable help by his side.

"Did Henrique tell Josephine anything about me?" I ask Cosme.

"Of course not. He never even mentioned you."

"So the story of Josephine being told that I died in a most atrocious way is one of his inventions." I wonder why, when his only purpose was to keep me away from Josephine? While I am at it, I might as well clarify more of the hocus-pocus that went on. "Where did the name Gastel come from?"

"All documents were handled by Angelo."

"Angelo?"

"Yes. The *dispachante.* What would we do in Brazil without them? Angelo is the best. He can obtain any official paper, any document you need in no time. He knows how the system works and how to grease it."

"Come on, Cosme, tell me the story. Why the name of Gastel?"

Poor Cosme, he looks embarrassed. He lights a cigarette, takes a sip of the by now warm Coca-Cola, and submits to my interrogation. With a painful expression, he gives the answer in a telegraphic rhythm. Angelo Dias, Henrique's *dispachante,* was given the task of searching into Josephine's family tree. An appropriate name had to be found for her official papers. The purpose Henrique invoked was that Josephine must have a name that was easy to pronounce by the time she received Brazilian citizenship. Angelo went to work right away. When he had unlimited funds, he could find relatives so distant that some were not even vertebrates. Somewhere in Josephine's family history, he found a great-grandfather on the mother's side, named Gastelanescu. He translated this into Gastel in Esperanto. It sounded fine. Not too Romanian, not too Brazilian, not too Swiss. President Dutra himself signed the document for her citizenship.

I have tortured Cosme enough with my questions. I thank him for what he has done for all of us, and especially for me today. He tilts his head to one side and modestly stares at the ashtray. From his wallet he takes a couple of notes which he leaves on the table. We get up. He walks me to my car and gives me an affectionate *abraço* when we part.

In his unassuming way, he is my historian. He's witnessed my saga with Henrique from the beginning. He knows everything about each player in Henrique's complicated world. Quietly and loyally he stands by his friend in laughter and in pain.

XLIII

"Something has changed," I tell Josephine. She has called to say that she has arrived safely home and to ask how I am feeling. "I feel odd. I go to the office. I fly to Sao Paulo twice a week. I speak to Tom long distance every day. I watch the sun rise and the sun set from my bedroom. But nothing is the same anymore. Maybe I just want to escape the madness of Henrique's world and Cosme's confessions."

"What's happened? What has changed, my darling?"

"I suppose it's me. It's as if I don't exist . . . As if I have become a medium, an interpreter. As if I have forgotten or mislaid myself somewhere along the way. I feel so detached, as if I've become an architect of my thoughts, constructing them as if they are not mine and have nothing to do with me."

"It could be that you want to blur your past, Rozalia. But remember, whatever happened wasn't anybody's fault. You can plan and plan all your life. Then things just happen. There is nothing to pardon or be pardoned for."

"What do you think I should do, Josephine?" It's the little girl speaking to "Aunt Josephine."

"Give it more time, Rozalia. Do nothing."

Somehow I feel better. I've gotten the burden off my chest.

"Thank you, Josephine," I say as I hang up.

*   *   *

When Tom returns for Easter, I can't be bothered to tell him all that has happened during the time he was away. We don't have a wall between us, but there is a hedge growing. Tom is affectionate and patient. He ignores my present mood and tries to stir me into our customary nonsense. I smile but can't get back into our regular way of communication. He tries again. "I really do miss you when we are apart. I need your presence." He takes my hand in both of his. "My true and only love, can you forgive my terrible oversight when I last called? I failed to tell you I love you. I do love you. I really do." He is touching and, after so many years, still doesn't take me for granted. He tries some more. "It occurs to me that for the past few years my life has been divided into segments. It begins and ends with your voice saying 'darling' over the long distance telephone."

"Yes. I know."

"Don't you think we could change our schedule?"

"What do you mean?"

"Spend less time apart. And if it isn't too presumptuous, why don't we redecorate our guest room."

"So you heard about Josephine's reappearance? I think she is too independent to stay with us."

"Have I missed something?"

"Quite a lot . . . Remember Doctor Gastel who we met at a dinner with the Leblon Crowd?"

"Of course, I remember. How can I forget the famous evening that provoked such a memorable honeymoon. You in my arms all night!" Tom draws me closer to him. It's getting dark outside. He takes a long sips from his martini. His eyes have a nostalgic look.

"Darling, please listen. It's important," I say.

"I'm listening." He places his glass on the coffee table in front of him. "Now, tell me what's happened."

"Doctor Maria Gastel is my Aunt Josephine."

"The one you looked for everywhere?"

"Yes. The last link in my family." I recall the comfort I found in Tom's eagerness to replace my loss. How he tried to cheer me up with his performance in the airport restaurant. "Remember, when you went down on your knees making fun of me?" I pause for a minute to bring back the light moments when there was more laughter than sadness. "When you said you knew that marriage was not in my vocabulary but you wondered what I'd answer if you asked me to share my toothpaste with you."

"Please refresh my memory! What did you answer?"

"Let me think, I forgot!" I plant an absentminded kiss near his temple.

Tom smiles. Then shakes his head slightly. "I often ask myself where we'd be if it hadn't been for Josephine's disappearance." He stands up and turns on the record player. It's Johan Strauss, *The Blue Danube*. When he sits down in the armchair facing me he asks, "Do you want to tell me what happened with Josephine?"

"At this point the hows don't matter. What matters was finding her. But why don't *you* tell me, what do you want to do with the guest room?"

"I vaguely thought, or rather attempted to think, that if you are in a creative mood, we could turn around our lives and make it into a nursery."

"And where would we put our guests?"

"It depends on who they are."

Suddenly I realize that the hedge between us has stopped growing. We won't waste any more time on what has happened and what we have done without each other. Our roads meet occasionally, but we each follow our own path. Poor darling Tom, trying everything to bring me out from the miasma of my detachment, but diapers will not be a solution in my case. A child, my child? To love and maybe lose again? I can't. I am not a complete person anymore. Parts of me are gone. The very heart of life with all my hopes is gone. There was nothing I could have done when I loved and lost Odo, Mother, Father. And there is nothing I can do from now on but watch. There is complete silence in my heart. Language no longer exists, and words are no longer necessary to explain because . . . because the ones I desperately loved, are gone.

Carla telephones from New York. I hand the phone to Tom so that I don't have to tell her anything. She tells Tom that she is not coming back as planned but is leaving for Europe. She also tells Tom that Henrique is already there, in Europe. She hopes that we can all get together at some point in the South of France. I know from Vadim, her masseur, whom she has already called to cancel her appointments, that she is meeting Abboudi in London.

Meanwhile, Silvia keeps me informed of Henrique's progress. She will do all she can to keep Carla away, until Henrique has recuperated. Carla is more than willing to oblige. For her, to stay away from the Sanatorium isn't a problem. She tells Tom, whenever she calls, that she's having a good time and is continuing her intensive shopping spree.

After seven weeks at the Sanatorium, where the reactions to each medication he has been given are tested, Henrique is a new person. He has been weaned and is ready to leave. Where to? Silvia suggests her home in the South of France, an idea approved by Professor Alter and Doctor Gastel. We are all invited to join them once Henrique has been there for one week. An interlude, Silvia explains.

I don't want to be sucked into Henrique's world again. I have to live my own life. At this point, my detachment is quite useful. If I'm going to be the architect of my life, Tom and I had better stay away. So we decline the invitation.

From Silvia's occasional reports, we hear that Carla has joined them. That she is adorable with Henrique, she is glowing. She makes everyone laugh, she's loving and amusing. She is "Pucci, Pucci" all over again.

I tell Tom the good news. He winks at me and says, "So Cupid is no longer unemployed."

I don't hear from any of them for a while. I even decide to accompany Tom for a few days to Hong Kong. While I am there, I negotiate the purchase of silk at a very good price. At the same time, Tom and I have a field day, I order suits for him, he orders dresses for me, all delivered almost overnight.

For the next ten months, Silvia and I keep in touch occasionally with postcards from our perennial travels across the continents.

Monday, August 25, 1969. I return from Sao Paolo. I feel tired, and I am changing into something comfortable. Fatima runs in without knocking, "Senhora, Senhora, turn on the television! It's about Senhor Henrique!"

I see a close-up of Henrique's face in that square lit box. My blood freezes in my veins. He is dead! The newscaster announces that he is dead! His words to me at the airport when I last saw him, "I feel such nostalgia for the euphoria," keep repeating themselves. Over a year has gone by since I found him at the Annexe. He called only last week—for nothing, he said. Just to say, "Are you well, Oncinha?" When I asked how he was, he said, "I have problems. At home, with the children and with business." I was in the middle of a meeting. I couldn't talk. Was this his farewell?

Flashbacks of the Henrique I have known rush into my mind. Henrique riding-laughing-crying overlap with the close-ups on television.

I don't know what to do first. I wish Tom were here. Just when I need him to sort things out, his quiet and calm way of handling unexpected events. He has to be somewhere in Timbuktu now! I can't even remember where he is. I panic, I am confused. Shall I call Silvia first? Carla? Tom? Cosme, maybe? Josephine? The direct line to the Leblon house is busy. Cosme's line. Silvia's line. Josephine's. All the lines are busy. Finally, I get through to Silvia who is devastated. She has been asked whether Henrique's body should be embalmed so that she can attend the funeral. In Brazil, by law, due to the hot climate, funerals have to be held within twenty-four hours. No way can she get from the South of France to Rio in time.

"I told them to go ahead without me. I can't face the crowds and all the paraphernalia. I can't face seeing him dead."

"I'll meet you at the airport whenever you arrive. Will you be alone? How about your mother? Claudia? Armand?"

"Claudia doesn't have to know yet, and Mother is on a cruise, somewhere in the middle of the ocean between Genova and Rio. She won't be able to get there for the funeral anyway. They can both be told later. I'm coming alone. Armand will join me in a couple of days." Her voice is shaking.

I am at the airport when the Varig Airlines plane lands in Rio. Silvia, dressed in black, emerges, escorted by an attendant who has her out of the plane and through customs in no time. We embrace. No words seem adequate. Carla has sent the Bentley to meet Silvia. I send Zair away with the Mercedes and join Silvia in the car which drives us to Leblon, her brother's home.

"I'm glad you didn't go to the funeral." I tell Silvia. "There were thousands of people. A huge crowd from all walks of life. Carla only stayed a few minutes."

We arrive at Henrique's home. No one takes Silvia's suitcase out of the car. We pass the tropical plants on the patio. We enter. *Abraços*. Carla. The four children. Ex-in-laws from Argentina. Others we hardly know. I hear voices speaking in a multitude of languages, disconnected words. Talk and talk. No one listens. No one answers my questions. Silvia shivers. A blue vein is showing in her temple. On her otherwise smooth skin I see tears. I dab her tears with my handkerchief. Then I dab mine. Enraged, I feel the frustration of a musician giving a concert for a stone-deaf audience.

Carla takes us to the large bedroom on the main floor. The curtains are drawn. The king-sized bed with only the bottom sheet. A crumpled linen sheet. On the right side of the bed, a patch of blood. His blood. They found him there. A small white enameled basin on the night table with a surgeon's scissors and used gauze. Blood. I see—or maybe I imagine—the imprint of his head on the pillow.

I hope I'll soon awake from this nightmare. I take Silvia's hand in mine. I am about to give Carla a compassionate hug, but I stop. I hear her voice spread with honey, "All the other seven bedrooms in the house are occupied now, but if you'd like to stay here, Silvia, we can prepare this one for you. We have also made a reservation at the hotel Copacabana Palace, just in case."

I squeeze Silvia's hand. Before turning to leave the room, I look again at the pillow.

The imprint of his head.

A dead white butterfly, its wings open, floating on a still pond of blood.

XLIV

Carla is efficiency personified, the *delegado* Ruy Dourado, the boyfriend of Fatima's sister, tells us. Over coffee in the kitchen, he explains how, the day after Henrique died, during the funeral, Carla went to the police in person to retrieve her caliber .32 revolver. The revolver with which Henrique supposedly shot himself twice in the heart. Cesare Reptilbaum, the firm's lawyer, was at her side. He was the one who advised Carla what to say to the police. He was the one to distribute the necessary grease in cash. It was important to avoid an autopsy of the corpse. Carla had to sign the book acknowledging that she was reclaiming her revolver, four unused bullets, two empty cartridges, and only one of the bullets that had gone through the body, ending up in the pillow. The other bullet was left in Henrique's body.

There is something wrong, I think to myself. Yes he died. How? Where? Why? Officially, he committed suicide by shooting himself *twice* in the heart. Is that possible? And why twice—if he missed the first time, the logic doesn't follow. The revolver was in his left hand, but he was right-handed! Carla discovered his body at three o'clock that afternoon. The police were called at nine forty-five that evening. Thirty thousand dollars was paid to the *delegado*, Ruy Dourado, who was not convinced that it was suicide. Finally no autopsy was made. In Henrique's will, Carla and his son Antonio were his sole heirs.

Nobody else. Not Silvia, his sister, nor Claudia, the niece he worshipped. It was impossible that he would have forgotten his niece. His mother, Dona Edithe, received a pittance.

I speak with Cosme, who tells me in detail what happened on that terrible day. Henrique was supposed to lunch at the Copacabana Palace with Mino Levy, Carla's first husband and the father of her three children. Henrique wished to discuss the future of the three young people, who had been living with him and Carla. This time he was determined to separate definitively from Carla, and he was concerned about the way it would affect the children. At about two-thirty Carla telephoned Cosme from the hairdresser to ask where Henrique was. Cosme answered that he was not at the office. She then said she would go home. Once there, she later told Cosme, she tried to enter their bedroom. It was locked. Shortly after three, she tried to ring the intercom from downstairs to speak to Henrique in the upstairs bedroom, as she thought he might be asleep. No answer. She then asked the gardener to bring a ladder and enter the room through the window so he could open the locked door for her. When she entered the room and saw Henrique, she called the office and announced to Cosme and the director, Stelhio, and the secretary, Maria Rita, that Henrique had killed himself. Cosme called the firm's lawyer, Senhor Reptilbaum, who arrived at the house around four and took over. He instructed Carla what to say to the police, who were finally called at nine forty-five.

Over the next few days my mind clicks away at all the questions for which I have no answer. I observe, trying to understand. While Silvia is shattered—quiet, aloof and hesitant, Carla is super active. She seems to be in charge of everything. She runs the house, the children, friends, business, as if she were the undersecretary of state of a great power. Which now, I suppose, she is. At times, she acts sweet and helpless. At other times, she can be sharp and ruthless in her decisions. She manages to get everyone to do something for her. She can be generous, affectionate, and thoughtful, eager to gain devotion and yet hard as nails, with no compassion when the object of her affection becomes useless.

Tom and I are two of the twenty-four guests having lunch in the big dining room at the Leblon House. Carla sits at the head of the impeccably set table—straight out of House and Garden. Fresh flowers, shining silver, crystal glasses, Wedgwood service plates. Serving are two butlers in white uniforms with white gloves and two maids in navy blue with white organdy aprons. An avalanche of perfection prevails as I watch our hostess with a certain admiration. Her smile is genuine. She looks powerful and happy. Gone is the helpless, weak Carla. I am impressed by her composure. Dish after dish is passed around. Exquisitely decorated platters are presented. Still life. Wines. It's a feast. There is no trace of Henrique in the conversation. Silvia is the only one present who is not using her social manners. She talks very little. Fortunately her husband Armand, seated next to her, saves her with adequate small talk, perfect for the occasion.

Some of the guests begin leaving after coffee. I see Tom in a corner with Geraldo, Carla's younger son from her first marriage. Among the four children, he is the one who is grieving Henrique's death most. I join them. Between tears, Geraldo confides in Tom that Henrique was the only person who really understood him. I knew how he worshipped Henrique. Whenever it was possible, he would be close to his mentor. Even when Carla thought he was being a nuisance Geraldo stayed around. He would always be where Henrique was until no one paid attention to him any more.

Stuttering with grief, Geraldo tells us how Carla had decided once again to give Henrique the cocktail of medicines he used to take. So that "Pucci Pucci" should not become too anxious when he realized that he had been tricked into signing over the shares of Mondial to Stelhio, the director of the company. Geraldo had heard Henrique shouting in anger at the obstacles he found whenever he tried to change anything. He was desperate to undo what had been done. Between hiccups, the boy says that all Carla offered as a consolation to Henrique's anguish was a shrug of her shoulders as she asked, "Why don't you kill yourself?" Carla did not even wait for them to be alone. She kept repeating the question wherever they were. She even took the mother of pearl revolver Henrique had given her out of the drawer and left it on the shelf in the passage leading to their bedroom from the study.

Carla approaches us. She seems nervous when she sees us with Geraldo. In a commanding voice, she tells him to go to his room. Then she takes my arm and walks me into the garden. Without any introduction, she goes straight to the point.

"Dear RB, I need your advice." Her voice is soft and uncertain. "I don't know what to do when I have to face Dona Edithe, Henrique's mother. She is due to arrive by ship in a week. Would you mind being there with us? How should I handle my husband's family?" And, she continues, "What should I do with my life?"

I tell her what any psychologist would say. "Do what's best for you. Look at Jackie O. You can do what she did—and better. You certainly have all the attributes." I'll never know whether the words I spoke had anything to do with the way she led her life after that. At the time, I spoke like the Oracle of Delphi.

I hesitate to get involved. Carla wants me to pacify Dona Edith and Silvia. Why me? Yes, I am suspicious about Henrique's death, about his sham marriage. I can't sleep for thinking about what they might have done to him. Do I have to witness all of this? On the other hand, I know Henrique would have wanted me to be there.

The *Giulio Cesare,* is due to dock in the Guanabara Harbor. Dona Edithe, with her maid, is on board the Italian ship on which she cruises every year. After a lot of thought, Silvia and Carla decided that Cosme and Maria Rita, Henrique's faithful secretary, should be the ones entrusted with the difficult task of meeting Dona Edithe on her arrival. Dona Edithe is used to seeing them around during departures and arrivals. They have worked for Henrique for three decades and have taken part in most family events. It is natural for Henrique's relatives to call on those two.

The unanimous decision was that on her arrival Dona Edithe should have a good night's sleep before being told of her son's death. A widow for almost forty years, she worships her son and has a heart problem. The customs and the police onshore, in on the secret, are keen to protect Henrique's mother from the shock. Cosme and Maria Rita fetch her straight from the ship with the fast police *vedetta* boat. She doesn't even go through customs as she is whisked off into Cosme's car. The maid follows with the luggage in Maria Rita's car. Everybody jokes and laughs, and she is so happy to be back. She is surprised that Henrique has not come to meet her, but she is given some excuse and is told that he will be seeing her tomorrow. Meanwhile, he has arranged for the Royal Suite of the Copacabana Palace to be at her disposal with flowers to greet her.

At ten o'clock the next morning, her personal maid has unpacked and tidied the bedroom. Dona Edithe is resting in bed, looking out at the sea and the beach. Two doctors, the general practitioner, and the heart specialist arrive with Silvia and Armand. Carla also joins them. I stand outside the room. We are nervous. We would like to postpone the moment of truth. Another minute, please. Let her be happy for another minute. The doctors don't wait or hesitate, they enter Dona Edithe's bedroom. She does not have to be told anything. She knows. She knows right away when she sees Silvia, Armand,

and Carla. She screams. A long scream. An injection is ready for her. I lean against the door. Paralyzed, I watch her pain. She cries. She wails. They check her heart. Everybody is cajoling, consoling, caressing. But nothing will make her stop. Another injection. She sleeps.

I sense that the fireworks will soon start. Not even two weeks have passed and already there is an orgy of strange events. Cruel characters, the kind to be found in comic strips, enter the stage. But there is nothing comic about these people. First there are plots, treacherous and edgy negotiations. Then events become simple and brutal. Swiftly, Geraldo is shipped to his father in Argentina. He is talking too much. In a moment of rage he accuses his mother of having killed Henrique. The other children, Antonio, Ariana, and Conrado, are sent to London. Paintings are removed from the house. Bank transfers are made. Powers of Attorney are cancelled. Pressure is put on Dona Edithe to sell her shares in the business.

At this point there are three camps: (a) Carla, advised by Reptilbaum and backed by Abboudi plus the rest of her gang; (b) Stelhio, now president of Mondial, in the middle, he possesses the adequate number of shares transferred by Henrique; and (c) Dona Edithe who means trouble for everyone. She still owns a fair amount of shares in the Family Corporation which was the basis of Henrique's empire.

Lawyers are enjoying themselves. By some miracle, Antonio becomes the genetic son, Henrique had out of wedlock with a certain Maria dos Anjos in Corumba, a place very few have heard of. According to the will that Reptilbaum has swiftly registered, Antonio inherits 50 percent of all assets. Everybody is ready to became the minor's guardian. Antonio is the most loved child in the whole universe. Lawsuits are started. Sue, sue everyone.

Meanwhile Carla, in an elegant apartment in Eaton Place, with a white Rolls Royce downstairs and a new leopard fur coat she just bought in Geneva, is enjoying the London scene. While others fight to become Antonio's guardian, she manages to adopt him. The reason in the official papers is "her motherly love for him."

Antonio is already studying at a fashionable boarding school in Scotland. Ariana and Conrado are taking courses at the London School of Economics. Carla keeps in touch with Silvia and, through Reptilbaum, sends a substantial check to Claudia as a legacy from Henrique to his niece.

I am regularly updated by Silvia. She has packed and gone home to the Château du Roque in the South of France. She can't come to Rio anymore, everything reminds her of Henrique. Their childhood together, their youth. It makes her sick to see what is going on. Silvia's attitude regarding the lawsuits is "I don't care one way or another." I remember when she told me that Abboudi and Carla were going to take Henrique to the cleaners. She had seen it all coming. Then, she was desperate to help Henrique. Now that he is gone, what does it matter? She dispassionately watches all the goings on. She is convinced that Dona Edithe will get nowhere in Brazil with any of the legal suits. She tells me that in order to fight savagery, one has to become a savage. The righteous must go outside the law to seek authentic justice, and she isn't willing to take that road. But the batteries of lawyers on all sides get plenty from the loot, while they display their various skills at lying.

I wish I could do something for Silvia. She is the one I feel needs the most support. I never see her cry or scream with pain. But her eyes have lost that mischievous look. On an impulse, I decide to visit her. I will be meeting Tom in Milano for a few days. In less than three hours by car, we could visit

Silvia and Armand for a day or two before returning to Rio. Tom is delighted with the idea. "That much time with my wife! What a treat!"

"Here we come, Silvia, to shake you out of your lethargy!" I tell her on the phone.

I am wearing the ring Henrique sent me. During the day I turn it around so only the gold shows. In the evening when we go out I wear it so that it glitters with my other "decorations for persevering" that Tom has lavishly bestowed on me. Tom never asked anything about the ring, and I never said anything. Not even to Josephine whom I saw only briefly in Rio after the tragedy. Josephine was busier than ever and so was I, torn between work and events connected to Henrique's world. Tom is my diversion from this chaos to simple sane living. Clean air, a hot bath, a diversified but uncomplicated life.

We rent a red convertible Alfa Romeo in Milano and make a vow not to put the top up even if it pours. I wear a red scarf on my head to go with the car. Tom wears one of those caps with a long brim to keep his nose in the shade. The way we feel, we could be on a safari. Away, just the two of us. Tom behind the wheel whistles "tea for two." I laugh and ask him to concentrate on the autoroute. At the French border we show our passports. The *carabinieri*, Italy's military police, take our passports. They call their French counterpart. Now there are five policemen all together turning the pages of our passports. What have we done? I visualize us spending the night in a dingy police station. I brace myself with my best Italian and ask how long it will take us to get to Nice. Then, in French, where can we get a road map. There is no answer to my questions, but to my great relief, we are told that all the *carabinieri* are fans of Pelé, the great Brazilian football player, their hero. My Brazilian passport instigates a long discussion about the football star. There is, however, more to come. In

Tom's passport there are visas, entrance, and exit stamps of countries they haven't heard of. We are a curiosity. Questions and answers go back and forth while all other cars are driving peacefully by, crossing the frontier without being stopped. After a lesson in geography and a thorough discussion of football we are free to continue our route. Two guards offer to escort us on motor bikes, so as to avoid traffic and catch up the lost time. We decline such generosity with thanks. Never again will I ride in a red car.

XLV

It is late afternoon when we drive through the wide open iron gate, the entrance that leads to Silvia and Armand's Château. I am mesmerized by the magnificent isolation of the place. We drive along a large alley through the forest for about five minutes. Thick trees on both sides lean over, their branches almost touching. Rays of light pierce through the foliage where I can see birds flying low, no doubt disturbed by the noise of the motor. We pass a waterfall and, out of nowhere, like an enchantment, appears Claudia, the eighteen-year-old daughter of Baron and Baroness de la Tour du Roque d'Auvergne. She is riding her white horse toward us. She is there to guide us to the main building. Her eyes are like her mother's, and she wears her dark hair in a pony tail. Claudia tells us, as she trots by our side on the trail bordering the alley, that she is training hard for her next horse show.

We pass the valley from where I can see the vineyard on the slopes with grapes almost ripe. When we arrive at the lawn in front of the Château, Armand and Silvia are there to greet us. Both are wearing not-new country clothes in washed-out colors. In haste, I remove my red scarf, but I can't do much about the car that, fortunately, has been toned down by dust and dirt.

Kisses and hugs. We mean it. We are really glad to see them. Silvia and even Armand, usually restrained, share our uncivilized enthusiasm. A tall gray haired *majordome* vanishes with our suitcases through a hidden back entrance door. Silvia is holding my hand. With my free hand, I hold on to the banister when we go up on one side of the double stairwell. Tom and Armand take the other side. We meet on the plateau at the top in front of the large glass entrance door. Tom asks, "Are there regulations and directions about using one staircase to go up, the other to go down?"

I am impressed as we enter each of the large bright rooms. Big French windows let the outdoors come in. It must have been Silvia who modernized the whole interior. It would be appropriate to comment on every detail and gasp in amazement, but it would take up all our time together. However, how can I be casual about the harmony and beauty of each object, the perfect shape of each room? And how can I ignore the little chapel with the stained glass windows by Matisse? I am amazed at how she has managed to add marble bathrooms to the fourteen air-conditioned guest rooms! Finally, I exclaim, "If all this hasn't been synchronized by the great architects Pei or Niemeyer and decorated by Leonardo, it must have been conceived by the hand of the Almighty!"

My idiotic comment seems to please our hosts. I give Silvia our house guest present.

"You can open it later, *querida*. Don't forget to say, It's just what I needed."

I get my thank you hug from Silvia. She seems so fragile now. She has lost weight.

"Is dinner at seven-thirty all right? We won't dress up tonight. Stay as you are."

A maid shows us to our room. Our luggage has been unpacked. The bed has been turned down, nightgown and pajamas laid out. Slippers are on each side at the foot of the bed. Nothing important to decide.

Tom is already under the shower. I open the French windows and bathe in the view. The Château is high enough so that we can see for miles, all the way to the sea. I take a deep breath and inhale the pine scented air. The odor of thyme, lavender, and rosemary under the windows reminds me that I am in the South of France and not on my way to Paradise.

The time on my watch says hurry. I jump into action. After the shortest time ever spent in a bathroom since my most tender age, I am scrubbed and changed. Tom and I look right for the part in clean but understated clothes. We are ready, on the dot, to go downstairs. We meet Silvia and Armand in the study leading to the dining room.

"Are you hungry?" asks Armand.

"We are starved," I admit without any hesitation.

"So there is no aperitif to spoil our appetite and we can dine right away."

Outdoors, in front of the open French window of the dining room, under an awning, a round table is set for five with yellow ceramic plates on crisp yellow linen. The centerpiece is a candlelit bunch of multicolored wild flowers. Camelia bushes and two plane trees, illuminated by hidden spotlights, shelter the enclosure. It's a country dinner for us. All the food, the crisp bread, the creamy yellow butter, the various ingredients besides sugar and salt come from the estate.

The maid and the *majordome* bring one platter after another from the nearby kitchen. After the *crudités*, slices of *saucisson* and a *pate en terrine*, a choice of a roasted *gigot vert pré*, and *lapin a la moutarde*. At dinner, it isn't done to serve an assortment of *fromages* but, for the foreign Barbarians, an exception is made. By the dessert, a *délice du roi* with *fraises des bois,* Tom and I are convinced we'd be crazy to leave tomorrow.

Claudia charms us with tales of her adventures while riding through the forest that shelters wild boar, rabbits, birds, pheasants, and partridges. "I'll go away when the hunting season starts," she says.

Armand explains in detail the production of the different wines we drink. "Each wine has to blend perfectly with the food and the seasonings."

"Armand is in his element," says Silvia. "When he plans a dinner he decides on the wines first, then on the food that goes with them. The cook has strict orders as to what ingredients to use to bring out the bouquet of the wine."

Tom, who is a walking encyclopedia, is in on the conversation. I just listen and sip from my glass quietly. I see the insects and moths goaded by the light, the moon peeking through the foliage of the tree. Nothing, not even the slightest spindle of thought, goes through my mind. Everything I have banked in my head seems to have suddenly slipped away. Everything except for this very moment.

Over brandy and cigars, Tom and Armand make plans for the next day. They discuss a wide range of activities. Shooting, fishing, or combing the estate in the electric cart? Maybe all of it. We'll have to stay until Christmas to do the whole lot. But for tonight, they'll just go for a short walk. There is much to discuss on the various qualities of grapes. Before retiring to bed, Claudia wants to stop at the stables to check on Tiroleza, her white horse.

I am alone with Silvia, who takes my hand into hers. She looks for a long time at the ring on my little finger, then turns it around to where it glitters.

"You'd better put your valuables in the safe while you are here. Recently, there have been a few thefts in the region."

"Whatever you say. But where is your safe?"

"Follow me. I'll take you on a trip to our catacombs."

I follow Silvia into the library. Books cover the wall up to the ceiling.

"Here we go," she says as, with a push, she slides aside the library ladder. Her lips are moving while she concentrates on counting the buttons she presses. A camouflaged door opens.

"Careful, there are two steps" she warns before reaching the bullet proof steel door. She disconnects the alarm, puts the big key into the lower lock, and turns it twice. When she turns the small key in the upper lock, the door opens on a large windowless space. I can feel the air-conditioning and see a thermostat set at the right degree of humidity. Amazed, I look at what Silvia calls their private catacombs. Vertical separations filled with paintings. Silver trays and serving plates wrapped in anti-tarnish cloths. Tables covered by big boxes marked with their contents, described in detail. Various sets of crockery and cutlery for twenty-four or forty-eight. Rolled up carpets and tapestries. Eighteenth-century signed furniture. Ormolu bronze clocks.

"Ali Baba's cave!" I can't believe my eyes.

"When we close the house for a long time we put our valuables in here. Besides, when a member of Armand's family dies, the younger generation moves to smaller quarters. They have no space. So according to the wishes of the deceased, the very large paintings, tapestries, furniture, silver, sculptures, busts end up with Armand, head of the clan. I wouldn't know where to hang all the portraits. Most of them represent severe and unpleasant looking men. So unpleasant, even our dogs could be frightened."

Silvia turns an old and heavily ornate key in the lock of the safe. She then reaches into the pocket of her jacket for a piece of paper covered with hieroglyphs. She frowns while studying it with great attention. It's the code to open the safe. She says she hasn't opened it for over a year. Since the time Henrique, his old self again, went honeymooning with Carla.

They had left her jewels and his important papers in the safe while they went hopping around Europe.

"Don't tell me that Carla's jewels are still in your safe!"

"Of course not," says Silvia, fiddling with the door to the box. "Before their return to Rio they came to recover the bangles. They were both in the best of moods though Carla admitted she had felt naked without her twenty-four carat ring. Her eyes sparkled as she put it back on her finger."

I am about to be catty and say that Carla already has more rings than fingers and probably enough for her toes, when the door to the safe snaps open.

"Good! I was afraid I didn't remember how this infernal machine works. Now that I'm an expert, hurry and put your bangles in."

I take out the little pouch with my valuables which I always wear on a belt under my blouse when I travel. I slide the pouch all the way into the back part of the safe. Silvia closes the door.

"Mission accomplished," she smiles. "The exit is much simpler."

"Oh no! How stupid of me! I'm so sorry, Silvia. I forgot to put my ring away."

"That's what happens to absentminded tycoons when they have to deal with trivial matters." She laughs and starts all the hocus-pocus again, this time without any hesitation. By magic, it opens immediately.

I remove the ring from my finger. I try to reach for the pouch to put the ring in. I can't find it. I fumble around. No pouch but I can feel a lot of papers.

"You'd better try, Silvia. I can't find it. There's a lot of stuff in there. I'm afraid I'll mix up the papers and files."

"What papers and files? There isn't anything in there besides your pouch."

"Have a look."

"To humor my guest, I'll solve the mystery of the disappearing pouch." She puts both hands in the box and removes a bunch of papers.

"Well?"

"You're right." She hands me the pouch that was tucked into a file. She sits down on one of the Louis XV chairs, covered in plastic, and goes through the papers on her lap, one by one.

"I've put the pouch back in the safe. This time with my ring. Shall I keep the door open?"

"Have another look first. Check there is nothing else in there. Then just close it."

I do as I am told. Silvia's voice isn't the same. She seems perturbed.

"Anything wrong?"

"Plenty! These are bank statements. When Henrique came with Carla to pick up the jewels, he must have left the papers behind. I wonder whether he left them on purpose 'just in case,' as he said, or whether he simply forgot them."

"And? What's so important about bank statements?"

"Just a moment, Rozalia! Here, I think there is something for you in this document." She hands me a couple of oversized sheets of paper.

I am speechless as I read the document drawn up by a lawyer, stating that the intent of Banco Universal was not to exercise any power over RB International. It declares that RB International does not belong to Banco Universal, it is irrevocably the sole property of Rozalia Bercovici. I'm astounded. I don't know what to think of this. There is no signature. "It's only a draft. It's not a legal document. What does this mean?" I ask myself. As far as I recall, during the last twenty years there has never been any proprietary interest by Banco Universal, neither have they asked for any accounting. But about a month after the death of Henrique, I received a letter from Banco Universal. It was addressed to me personally as well as to RB International, the Holding Corporation for all the textile mills I own. It was a restraining order preventing RB International from making any transfers, withdrawals or any other transactions relating to the Banco Universal account and any other bank accounts. The letter was signed by the executors of Henrique's estate. At the time, I thought it was just a circular sent to all the Bank's clients. I handed the letter to my firm's lawyer and left for a lecture tour to Tokyo, Osaka, Nagoya.

This document changes everything. Is it possible that the shares that were left with Banco Universal at the time of my takeover, twenty years ago, could have been interpreted as the property of the bank? So to avoid any misunderstanding, Henrique had drawn up this document stating that RB International belonged irrevocably to me? And then did not get around to signing it? Or maybe there is another copy with Banco Universal that Henrique signed. But what if somebody destroyed the signed document and, as a result, my shares are considered the property of the Banco Universal? I only have the unsigned draft. It could well mean that Carla and Abboudi, by taking over Banco Universal, will get hold of everything I own. They are already doing this with the family business by denying Dona Edith and Silvia any participation in Henrique's business interests.

Fate. That dreadful unforeseen fate. I have planned and planned. I have been efficiency personified. I have worked out every detail and made things happen, like on a production line. And then Bingo! Whether I want to or not, now I must get involved in Henrique's world. And who knows, I might even have to deal with Carla! I'll have to find out more.

I show Silvia the unsigned draft and explain its importance. Silvia suggests that Tom and I postpone our departure so I'll have time to examine all her documents. She has many files with copies of the various law suits already initiated by Dona Edithe and others.

Silvia locks up the safe. We carry the bundles of papers under our arms and move upstairs to the library. We help ourselves to a Cordon Bleu Martell, sink into the leather armchairs and are speechless for a while. I sip my drink. Through the open windows I can hear the music of insects, but my mind is in a turmoil. Will I survive this time? I think of Henrique, dressed as Zorro. It's a holdup, he had said. Come with me! Then it was a game, now it's reality. The gun is pointed at me. Then I had laughed. Now I am ready to cry, to scream. Why can't I have a peaceful, boring life? Why must every death I witness be a Nibelungen—a Wagnerian tragedy? Nobody I love waltzes out of life with a contented smile on their face! I am tired! Do I want to go on with this? I'd like to just walk away, to forget everything, to be born again in a place where the air is light, the water is clear . . . Nowhere!

We have to wait for Armand and Tom to return from their walk and, meanwhile, we can torture each other with questions.

"Why are you so excited about the bank statements, Silvia?" I start.

"Here, have a look."

I go through a few pages. I see transfers made in the name of RB International. It doesn't mean anything to me.

"I can't understand, Silvia, do you know anything about this?"

She explains that, during the period Henrique was feeling well again, he opened a joint account with Carla at Abboudi's bank in London in the name of a Panamanian Corporation. He had another account in a Swiss bank in Geneva where Silvia and Armand had Power of Attorney, "just in case of an emergency," Henrique had said. This power of attorney was revoked by Carla on the day of Henrique's death. As the assets held abroad were in the name of a Corporation, Carla and Abboudi's English bank had always denied that Henrique was the legitimate owner. These bank statements proved that the origin of the money was from transfers made out of the Brazilian family business of which Silvia and Dona Edithe had been partners since it was founded.

"Even the account number is Henrique's date of birth!" says Silvia, pointing at the numbers on the top page. "I think it might have been his last joke. I'll end up siding with Dona Edithe."

"What do you mean, Silvia?"

"These bank accounts show undeclared funds which either belonged to the initial partners in the family business, or they are Henrique's English assets. But Carla, as executor of Henrique's will, has not obtained probate. Either way it's fraud. There is also collusion between Abboudi's London Bank and Carla because Abboudi maintains that the owner of the account is the Panamanian Corporation and not Henrique."

"You always said that Carla and Abboudi were a pair!"

"Yes, but Carla and Abboudi deny that there is anything between them but business. The 'impartial' banker is only following the rules." Silvia gets up and puts the papers in the drawer of the desk. "Do you remember when I first met you, I suspected that Abboudi, with the help of Carla, was taking Henrique to the cleaners?"

"Yes, I do. And after Henrique died, still nobody believed you."

"I always said Abboudi was not the impartial banker but the man in Carla's life as well as her partner in business."

"Her partner in B&B, bed & business? But then, I don't understand. Carla married that young man less than two years after Henrique died . . . Ben, whatever his name was, and showed herself off with him in Rio. It doesn't make any sense."

"On the contrary, *querida*. That marriage had a purpose."

"What purpose?"

"To show that Abboudi was only her banker and not the lover who helped her get hold of the loot. It sounds far-fetched, but I know Carla's ways of manipulating people. With this marriage to the young man, she wanted Abboudi to realize that, besides losing her, he was also losing control of the business she had brought along. You'll see, Carla and Abboudi will end up as partners! For life."

"So what are you planning to do?"

"I'll have to think about it."

After my sleepless night, Tom and I are having breakfast alone outdoors. I butter a warm croissant and put it on his plate. "Thank you, my darling," he says while he pours the freshly squeezed orange juice into my glass. I announce that I cannot leave today and that our hosts have invited us to stay on as long as we want. "Can you postpone your trip as well?"

"That's fine with me. Let's stay another day or so. I see you have been overcome by the charm of a relaxed country life!"

Relaxed! I have to tell Tom what I found out last night. How my life and possibly our life together could be affected. By a piece of paper, damn it!

I'll have to talk with him about business. Up to now it's been taboo! I've never done that before. But all this can affect us both. So I tell him about the letter I received from Banco Universal, the unsigned draft I found with Silvia and my fears about what could happen to everything I have worked for all these years.

"Tom, what do you think about all this? What would you do in my place?"

"Rozalia, is RB International that important to you?"

"It is."

"Show me what you've found." I hand him the document. He goes through it carefully, line by line. "You know, my darling, this could very well be just a draft or it could even be the copy of an original which has been signed."

"I've thought about that. But what if the signed document has been destroyed?"

"Then it's possible you'll lose the ownership of the mills. Unless you can prove by other means that you own the majority of the shares." He pours more coffee into my cup before filling his. "You know, Rozalia, the stakes are very high. The people you'll have to deal with use a language of their own. The words 'gentleman's agreement' are not in their vocabulary. They'll try by every means to defeat you. Before you start anything, you have to be prepared for the worst."

"Do you mean that I shouldn't even fight?"

"Your fight could last for years. Is it worth it? Think about it, Rozalia. What is it you really want out of life? You know that, financially, I can provide for everything. We'll have the same standard of living we have today. You never cared much about worldly possessions. Those things never mattered to you. Do we always have to achieve, achieve, achieve? Would it be possible to live a quiet, uncomplicated but fulfilled life?"

Dear Tom, with him, there is no pathos, no hysterics, and no scenes.

"Do you expect me to stand by and let it all happen? To just sit on the fence while I lose my business and watch Silvia and Dona Edithe get cheated?"

"Why do you want to be drawn into other people's affairs? Do you feel an obligation toward Henrique? Or to mankind in general?"

"No, Tom, it's about the way *I* feel. By getting involved in another person's problem, I can identify with them and forget myself."

"I see . . . I hope I've helped you clear your mind on what to do."

"You have. And somehow I feel closer to you than I've ever felt before. I didn't think I could." Stimulated by our loving relationship, I lean forward and kiss his cheek. "What puzzles me, Tom, is the way I can talk to you about anything . . . Even if your universe is so unlike my own!"

"You see, Rozalia, inhabitants of different worlds can live happily together." His voice is full of tenderness. He takes my hand into his. "As long as each of us recognizes that the other's world is different and has just as much right to exist as our own."

A gentle warm breeze scatters a camellia at my feet.

Silvia arrives with her arms full of files. We are sitting at the same table where, the night before, we enjoyed the feast. Silvia puts the files on the table, and Tom draws up another chair for her. I look through the files. Dona Edithe's lawyer did some research on Henrique's death. I read a copy of the report in the police book. It's different from the one I first saw. Nothing is mentioned about the two bullets in the heart. The final conclusion is suicide. The case is closed.

File after file. Document after document. Each one has been falsified. Different signatures for the same name. Henrique's signature is never the same on any of the documents. Four different versions of Antonio's birth certificate. Different mother. No father. Different father. No mother. No parents. A few more combinations in the puzzle. Marriage certificates galore. Carla was super-extra-married to Henrique. Registered in the USA, in Brazil. No two certificates were the same.

XLVI

These are professional crooks! They falsify everything. To them, the law doesn't exist. There are so many of them. Felix Klein, Carla's and Abboudi's eye in Brazil, who warned me more than once to stop digging. He meekly added that harm could come to all I own and even to myself. Stelhio, now president of the Family Business Mondial, negotiating to hand over to the highest bidder the shares which Henrique had put in his custody. An army of them. So the only real chance I have is to play a game of poker with them.

Dona Edithe and Silvia are losing their participation in Banco Universal and many other family interests. As a consequence, my life's work is in danger of falling into the hands of Carla and Abboudi. There is pressure from all sides.

I long to talk to Josephine about my turmoil. The fear of loving and losing again has frozen me emotionally. Even my crutch, my work of all these years, is now threatened to be taken away from me by Carla and Abboudi.

I have to speak to her now. I dial her direct line in Zurich.

"Josephine, I'd like to spend some time with you. Any chance of meeting?"

"Of course, my darling."

"When and where?"

"Let's see . . ." She gives me dates and places where she will be. I in turn give her a list of dates and places.

"Now that we have each other's schedules, let me call you back."

So it goes on for a while, between lectures and board meetings all impossible to cancel, and then one day she is gone forever. Strangely enough the chopper, with Josephine on board, crashed near the Amazon River. I remember when about twenty years ago Our-Indian walked us toward the Xingu River in search of Josephine. When he showed me some bones and a chopper that had crashed and I had believed the bones to be Josephine's, I asked, "Do you know when and how it happened?"

"The spirits must have decided this." I was told. "They have their reasons."

I am convinced that with the Document of Intent for RB International and the bank statements of the Panamanian Corporation, an agreement could be reached with Carla and Abboudi. I tell my firm's lawyer to get in touch with Carla's lawyers to set up a meeting.

It is arrogant of me to think I can handle all these sharks myself. But before Silvia decides whether to sue, it's worth giving it a try. If Silvia sues, it will be only out of a sense of justice, she doesn't care about the outcome. All she wants to prove is that justice can prevail. She is chipping away at corruption by speaking out against it.

Poor Silvia. She will end up fighting not only to avenge innocence but to restore it. If she wins and is able to return to the safety of our civilized existence, it means we have been watching a Hollywood movie, a western where justice is done—truth prevails. The goodies win. The baddies are punished.

My idea of negotiating a settlement with Carla is received with enthusiasm by her lawyers and consultants. They ask if October 5, my birthday, and Geneva Switzerland, the headquarters of Abboudi's banks, are acceptable for a meeting. It's all right with me.

On the agreed date, I check into a suite at the Hotel du Rhone. Carla's bevy of lawyers are staying at the Hotel Richemond. They are coming from everywhere. Brazil, Liechtenstein, USA, France, England. It's fine with them, they all like to travel.

We meet at 9:00 a.m. in my suite. With me are Zezinho in case we have to look through accounts and a local Swiss lawyer in case we have to draw up a legal document. It's all I need. Up to now, everyone seems willing to solve the problem. Anyway, I tell myself, I am on the side of truth and justice!

I have to play hostess at this gathering. I already know most of the people who enter the room for the meeting. I have even met the top Brazilian lawyer socially, he is part of the *granfinos* in Rio de Janeiro society. Dressed in a well-cut navy blue striped suit, Gucci shoes (everybody on Carla's payroll wears Gucci shoes) and a big friendly smile, he hands me twenty four long-stemmed red roses and wishes me a happy birthday. My Swiss lawyer, in his heavy boots and clumsy-looking suit, is ready to collapse. He stutters in a low voice, "I've never seen anything like this before! It must be Brazilian!"

I ask Zezinho to call the housekeeper for a vase and room service for drinks and coffee. I find it difficult to take this jovial atmosphere very seriously. However, we begin our negotiations, and after two tense days we negotiate a satisfactory agreement. I declare, with a poker face, that I know about the document in Henrique's safe at the Banco Universal. I have a copy. If it can't be found, someone must have destroyed it. Should it be necessary, I could name "the someone" at my press conference tomorrow, right here, in

Geneva . . . when I'll announce the usage of a new fiber in the textile industry! I wave in front of them the bank statements Silvia found. The Brazilian lawyer asks to examine them, but I refuse. I mention the Panamanian Company and point at the account number on top of the first page.

"The number is Henrique's date of birth," I say, looking at the lawyer. "I suggest you ask your client to make an offer to Dona Silvia and Dona Edithe before the coming law suit." They make an offer. I laugh. "Try again and double it."

"It will have to be referred to our clients," they say. "We will draw up the terms shortly with our proposal." Visiting cards are exchanged between my Swiss lawyer and the other five. The Swiss was short of cards. He only had one.

During the days and weeks that fallowed, drafts go back and forth. They have to consult with Abboudi and Carla and I with Silvia. It becomes clear that they are not interested in a partial agreement with me alone but want an overall settlement. After months of negotiations, they come up with their final offer. Though RB International would be saved, the amount to be paid to Silvia and Dona Edithe is unacceptable.

Too many months have gone by. Abboudi has been negotiating the sale of his London and Geneva banks to a reputable giant, American Trust. Could it be that he wanted to gain time? A lawsuit could have hindered the outcome of this transaction.

Silvia now consults solicitors in London to see what her course of action should be. She shows the bank statements and documents proving the origin of the money. The solicitors ask if there have been any negotiations and if an offer has been made. She shows the various drafts by which Abboudi and Carla's lawyers offered a settlement and had accepted that Silvia and Donna Edithe had a claim. Without wasting any more time, Silvia instructs her solicitors to issue a writ against Carla and Abboudi's London bank.

XLVII

It is late in the evening when I check in at Claridges. I have arrived a few days ahead of Silvia. Tom and Armand will join us in London after a shoot in Scotland. I unpack the clothes from my suitcase, hang up my dresses in the bathroom, turn on the hot water tap for a minute so that my sartorial outfits will be ready for the next day, a habit I have had for years when on the move. No time to wait for the valet to press my clothes. The other suitcase is my flying office which I never unpack. It's full of papers, documents, and copies of certain files I might need in case of emergency. After so many years, I have no problem running the business from wherever I am.

The phone rings. I look at my watch. I am still on Rio de Janeiro's time.

"Yes?"

"Mrs. Huntington?" asks a man's voice.

"You must have the wrong room," I answer. Nobody has ever called me by my married name.

"Mrs. Thomas Huntington?" asks the voice again.

"Could be. What can I do for you?"

"Can we meet?"

"What about? Forgive me if I didn't catch your name."

"Permit me to introduce myself, Ben Halva."

"Yes?"

"I am calling you at the suggestion of the Baroness de la Tour du Roque. Possibly, I have some useful information to give you."

"Where shall we meet?"

"I am almost across the street from your hotel, at the Tavern of Two Horns. I will be there all evening. You're welcome at any time."

Now I feel hungry and not sleepy, so I go down to the restaurant, but the kitchen is already closed. I might as well have dinner at the tavern. It's dark and crowded when I enter. I look around to see if I can identify Ben Halva. At the bar, a man who looks to be in his late thirties props himself up on a stool. I can't help noticing his Gucci shoes, Brioni suit, T&H shirt, Hermes tie, Cartier watch. Obviously he could have worn the labels on the outside. It must be Ben Halva! He fits perfectly the voice on the telephone.

A pretty young hostess asks me if I'd like to sit at the bar.

"No," I say, "I'd like to sit at a table next to the bar."

"Fine."

I sink into a comfortable banquette, order a beer with . . . I hesitate between a Shepherd's Pie and sausages with mash and settle for fish and chips. And I don't feel the least bit sorry for myself. I look around and do some people-watching. The man who must be Ben Halva orders another of his "usuals" while exchanging pleasantries with the man behind the counter.

"How about the lady, Ben? What will it be?"

"Bring the bottle over here, Mike!"

Ben turns to the woman on the stool next to him and fills her half-empty glass. Strapped into a black dress, her bosoms perilously close to freedom, she smiles, then gets closer, takes his head in her hands and looks him straight in the eye.

"You're talking a lot of nonsense, Ben, I know you too well. You deserted her. Why pretend otherwise?"

"I really tried everything, but nothing worked." He pours himself another drink from the bottle in front of him. "I'm in deep trouble. I don't know what to do." Evidently, they have had too much to drink. She strokes his wavy hair and murmurs, but it is loud enough for me to hear. "Stop worrying and tell me everything. Start with how you met."

"It seems ages ago. I was in Rio de Janeiro." Ben takes a long sip and holds onto his glass. "I was going to have dinner that evening with a friend of mine, a neurologist. On our way to the restaurant, he had to make a call at the clinic. One of his patients had undergone a sleeping cure. He asked if I didn't mind visiting his patient. I laughed, surprised at his request.

"I entered a very 'unhospital' looking room. There was an original Chagall painting hanging on the wall. I was introduced to Carla Moreira Cardoso who was leaning languorously against many lacy pillows. She smiled as she gave me a warm welcome, then introduced me to her ex-sister-in-law and dear friend, Dona Dina. Right away I was informed that both women, when very young, had married and divorced two brothers. Dona Carla asked me to draw up a chair closer to the bed, and we chatted.

"I was ready to leave with my friend shortly afterward, with the usual polite wishes for a speedy recovery. I mentioned that on Sunday I was flying to Sao Paulo on a business trip. The two ladies laughed and said they were scheduled to fly to Sao Paulo on the evening of Tuesday October fifth and how nice it would be if we could meet again there. I said that, unfortunately, my business in Sao Paulo would be concluded by the time they arrived. Dona Carla playfully retorted that if by some miracle I did not leave before their arrival, they expected me to call on them at the Palace Hotel at eight that evening."

Ben leans back in the stool, and the woman leans forward.

"Go on. What happened next?"

"As planned, after two days in Sao Paolo, I was checking out of my hotel. While paying my bill I received a telephone call. It was Dona Carla. She said that she had taken an earlier plane and was already in Sao Paulo with Dona Dina. They very much hoped I could delay my departure until the following day and insisted on seeing me again. I was touched and flattered and I finally gave in. My ego was bursting, and my curiosity took over. So I checked back into the hotel I had just checked out of.

"At eight, as agreed, I called at the Palace Hotel for the two ladies. Only Dona Carla joined me at the bar. 'And Dona Dina?' I asked. 'She preferred to let us be alone for the evening,' was the answer. I was taken aback by such frankness. But I was fascinated. After dinner, we went to a nightclub. Dona Carla switched on her charm, and when I escorted her back to her hotel, she invited me to come up to her suite for a nightcap. Tempting as it was, I managed to refuse. Back at my hotel by one o'clock, I wondered what this lovely, evidently very spoiled and wealthy woman wanted from me. Next day, we ran into each other at Sao Paolo Airport. Carla and Dora were catching a plane to Rio de Janeiro and were then off to New York for a few days before returning home to London. I was flying to Montevideo. Out of the blue, Carla asked me to forget about my trip and accompany her to Rio, then to London via New York. As elegantly as I could, I refused what I considered the whim of a lonely woman. However, I gave her various telephone numbers where I could be reached. She sent me daily letters, post cards, and called the office and my father's home. I couldn't believe I'd stirred such a tornado after a couple of hours of our meeting!" Ben pauses long enough to empty his glass. "On Wednesday, the day Carla returned to London, she telephoned to invite me for dinner for that same evening. She apologized for the short notice and explained she had arrived only minutes ago. As I had a previous engagement that evening, I answered that I'd be delighted to join her for coffee afterward.

"When I arrived at her flat, I met her daughter, Ariana, and a few of her friends who said they had been curious to see the phenomenon that had made such a lasting impression on Carla.

"Boosted and exhilarated after plenty of brandy, I ended up spending the night with Carla. The next morning Dina arrived. Irritated to find me still there, she said that this behavior was unbecoming of a lady living in a house with her young daughter."

"Big deal. Ah, the joy of a quick conquest," says the woman at his side. "There was an easy solution. If you both wanted to go on with each other, why couldn't you meet at your flat?"

Ben's face becomes animated. "Not so simple. At the time I was staying with my father, while my flat was being renovated. So whenever I spent the night at Carla's, I'd leave at dawn before the staff or her daughter were up."

"Quite a woman this Carla to have you get up at the crack of dawn and sneak out like a college boy. What was her secret?"

"Unfortunately, I only found out much later that she had plenty of secrets. But at the time I only knew what she had told me. She had had a first husband, Mino Levy, with whom she had three children. After her divorce from Levy, she lived briefly with Henrique Morera Cardoso, then married him.

"You *mean the* Henrique Cardoso? The owner of the paper factories, Fazendas, and . . ."

"Precisely. The very wealthy Henrique Moreira Cardoso."

I am nervous. I finish eating all the chips on my plate. I am ready to make my move, I must approach Ben. He glances at me, then looks away. I feel the smell of beer and whiskey. I hear snatches of laughter and talk. Ben orders another drink, and the woman at his side murmurs something in his ear that makes him smile.

"Yes," he continues. "I was getting hooked. We found it hard to stay away from each other. The matter of marriage was raised. I loved her and I knew she loved me, but I was conscious of the handicaps which could complicate our life together."

"Come on, you were thirty-five, never married before. So why not take the plunge?"

"Well, there was a vast difference in our financial positions. She had been married twice before. It was a sobering thought that my predecessor, Henrique, had committed suicide. Then she was at least two years older than I am. Also, she had three children, two of whom were young men, as well as a stepson."

"What made you take the plunge?"

"Just before Christmas, I took her to Geneva and then Villars in the mountains to visit her stepson, Antonio, who had broken his leg. We were so happy together in those surroundings . . . we started talking about getting married.

"A long time ago, before meeting her, I had planned to take a trip to the Far East. Still on a cloud, we then decided that if, after this break, we both felt the same, we would get married."

"Did you go on your trip?"

"Oh yes. Carla phoned frequently and in one of her letters mentioned the children she wished us to have."

"How touching. She really must have loved you!"

"Wait. That's not all. In the next letter, she related how her son, Geraldo, had accused her of being responsible for her second husband's death. She was depressed. She asked me, begged me, prayed to be able to join me, and just be with me. I became frantic and phoned her. She was out. I sent her a cable asking her to join me immediately in Hong Kong. I added that her worries had become my worries because I cared so deeply for her. I would do anything to help her recover her stability."

"How romantic! Was she on the next plane?"

With a look of irony, he pours her a drink.

"If only you knew."

"Knew what?"

"Having begged and pleaded to join me, now that I had shown real concern, it seemed she was no longer finding it imperative to join me."

"Were you disappointed?"

"Not really, I was relieved that she felt better. In her letters, full of affection, always signing 'Your Wife,' she assured me that she was well and would wait in London for my return. Then, suddenly, she changed her mind. She'd join me in Acapulco, she had to see me right away. I took the first available plane from Tahiti to meet her in Acapulco. Our reunion was ecstatic. After those few weeks apart I was convinced that our passionate love was there to stay. We decided to marry in a week's time, on January thirty-first."

"Was it magic? Tell me . . ."

"It was wonderful. Every moment together was a delight, a fulfillment I had never experienced before . . . As soon as the ceremony was over, Carla announced that we should have children right away. She went to see the resident doctor at the hotel and had her coil removed. I started to worry at the speed at which events were unfolding."

"Quite understandable. And how was your landing on earth from outer space?"

"Back to reality, we realized we had to prepare her children and my father for the religious ceremony we planned to have upon our return to London."

I wish Tom were here. I feel like laughing. And I laugh best with him. I never heard anyone talk like this before. Ben's voice goes into crescendo as if he were reciting a

Shakespearian play. His language is formal, it doesn't sound like natural speech.

The woman on the stool says something to the barman. He points to the left with the palm of his hand. She gets up and leaves, following the directions. Ben is alone now, his elbows propped on the bar, his head buried in his hands.

What shall I do next? I decide to follow the woman to the ladies' room. I open the door. As I enter, I hear the water flushing. I wait in front of the mirror by the basin. She comes out and opens both faucets. The water splashes me. She smiles and apologizes. She puts her arms around my shoulders. Her breath is pure alcohol. She asks me to join her at the bar. She says she is with a friend who needs cheering up.

I can't believe my luck. I'm getting him handed to me. I introduce myself and ask her name. I quickly learn that Renata is thirty-two years old and met Ben a week ago. I suggest we move to my table. She takes me by the arm, and we walk back toward the bar. When we are next to Ben, she takes his hand, puts it into mine and says that he should meet this old friend of hers. Ben turns toward me.

"Ben Halva," he says.

"I thought so. I am Rozalia Huntington."

Ben smiles and nods his head. I guide them both to my table, and I ask the bartender to bring some sandwiches with the drinks. I foresee a long, long evening.

We exchange a few banal sentences, then I ask, "Mr. Halva, what was it you wanted to talk to me about?"

"I wanted you to know my story. What happened. What they have done to me."

"They? Whom are you talking about?"

"Carla and her gang." He cracks the knuckle of his hand. "I've written it all down. If you find anything useful to you, Mrs. Huntington, feel free to use it."

"But what's it got to do with me, Mr. Halva?"

"I heard about your problems with Carla. Please forgive my intrusion. Maybe my experience can be of help to you." He hands me a bundle of papers. I browse through the first few pages which are letters from Carla to him and which cover what I've already overheard. I read, skipping details. I read about Felix Klein, Carla's supervisor in Brazil, preparing her for the meeting she was to have in London with Stelhio, her 'thief-director' as she called him. All her letters end with how she considers herself and Ben to be just one person, for joy and sadness.

I keep reading, through the pages of notes taken by Ben. So far there is nothing I don't already know. Ben wrote a long letter to his father, an orthodox Jew, announcing his marriage. Carla had to cope with the phone calls to her four children. She had informed Conrado, her eldest son, that she was getting married. After she and Ben gave him the news on the telephone, he congratulated Ben and said, "How does it feel to be part of a mad family?"

Ariana was something else. Her mother had sent her a letter in which she spoke of the happiness she had found with Ben and how she was thinking of marrying him. When Carla telephoned her, Ariana called her mother a liar. She knew that the two were already married at the time she wrote the letter and felt betrayed. After Ben convinced Carla to tell the truth, Ariana wished her mother lots of happiness and affectionately called her Mrs. Ben Halva.

Carla, Ben records, was panic-stricken when it was Antonio's turn to be called. She was afraid of her step-son's reaction, saying she couldn't face a confrontation. Again, Ben had to convince her to face reality and simply tell the truth. When she called, the boy started to laugh and blew kisses over the phone. Next he wrote a letter beginning, "Dear Mum and Dad."

The only one of the four children Ben had not met was Geraldo, who was still in Buenos Aires. For Carla he was "the problem child." She had not seen him for over a year, since the time when he was having hallucinations and was rushed to the hospital. As he calmed down, he told the doctors that the only man who had ever understood him was Henrique and that Carla had killed Henrique. The doctors recommended immediate treatment, but he refused. Carla decided to have Geraldo sedated and flown over to London fast asleep. The result of this was a breakdown in communication between mother and son. However, when informed about the marriage, Geraldo seemed pleased. He said he would fly to Rio de Janeiro to meet Ben and be reunited with his mother.

Now the couple left Acapulco for Brazil. Carla had to attend a meeting and was keen to show off her new husband. In Rio de Janeiro, the social columnists had a field day writing about the rich widow, finding happiness again with the handsome young man by her side. There were many parties, and Ben was greeted warmly. Carla would write Ben touching notes each time she left his side. She only seemed irritated and not herself when she was with Geraldo. But nothing could spoil their happiness in Rio. Even when Carla found out that Stelhio, the director of Henrique's business, had transferred only $1,300,000 instead of $1,500,000 to her account in Switzerland. Stelhio more than once had sent incomplete amounts when making the monthly transfer from Brazil to Abboudi's bank in Switzerland. Carla told Ben that this transaction was a secret and shouldn't be disclosed to anyone, especially not to Henrique's family. There was a lawsuit going on in London against Abboudi's London Bank, Abboudi himself and Carla. They were accused of being in connivance to defraud Henrique's family. The nondeclared English assets that were part of the family business."

Finally, something useful! If Ben testifies, we have additional credibility to any legal cause.

The room is empty. The lights have been dimmed. Renata is still asleep. The bartender asks if there is anything else we want before he closes the cash register. I hand him my credit card, but Ben insists on using his. My eyes are itching with sleep. I want to go to my room. I get up and take my leave. Ben stands, helps me with my coat, and hands me his phone number. I slide the card in the inside pocket of my coat where I have tucked the twenty folded pages of his confession. He offers to walk me to the door of my hotel. I decline and tell him he had better stay with Renata.

I am about to cross the street. There is no one around. A black Cadillac pulls into the driveway. A tower of a man exits the car, walks a few steps, and stops in front of me. He grasps me by the lapels of my overcoat. "Why are you here, RB?" I push him away.

"None of your business!"

"Who says it's none of my business?" Suddenly my head is flung back against the wall. "Who have you been talking to?" His grip has tightened. I am being lifted from the ground.

"Let go!" I shout.

"Do you have anything to do with the trial? Watch out, RB! Leave town! Leave while you still can!" His unwavering gaze warns me not to protest.

When he releases me, my instinct of self-preservation tells me to run across the street as fast as I can and enter the hotel as if nothing had happened. My knees are shaking, my usual calm is gone. First Ben's confession, then this violent warning. I've had enough! I'll give the bastards in Rio something to shake about! I have no doubt about who is behind this warning.

I stop at the concierge's desk and ask for a form to send a cable. I write my message. Then I send the cable to Felix Klein, Carla's spy in Rio. To the office where it can be seen by everyone:

"Please answer urgently if fifteen million dollars transferred from Brazil to Switzerland for Carla Cardoso through the courtesy of Edgar Abboudi all during the year 1972 in monthly installments were the equivalent of the eleven thousand shares held by Stelhio, or nondeclared profits to shareholders and others. Stop. More details are following concerning account in Switzerland. Stop. Love to Lover."

They know who Lover is, Abboudi of course! This telegram will shake the bunch of them. I can just see them. Stelhio, who kept the shares Henrique signed over for him to be a custodian and who is now using them as a power sword in every dealing. Reptilbaum, nervous about all the papers and documents he has been falsifying for years. Felix Klein, the servant of Carla and Abboudi, afraid of losing his job. Carla and Abboudi, afraid of the illegal black market transfers being discovered. None of the bastards will sleep tonight! Nor will I!

My head is ringing, my shoulder is aching but I am satisfied as I take the elevator to the fifth floor.

Once in my room, I throw my coat on a chair, pour myself a drink from the first little bottle I find in the minibar, and sink into an armchair with the twenty pages on my lap. I continue reading Ben's saga.

"By February, it was time for us to return to London. Reluctant to end our honeymoon, instead of flying we booked a passage on an Italian cruise ship leaving Rio for Lisbon and Cannes. After hectic weeks in Rio, we welcomed the peace and quiet on board. One morning, Carla announced she thought she was pregnant but she would not know for sure until the first days of March. Therefore plans had to be made. The previous summer, Carla had rented a house in Vallauris which she told me was now for sale. So we disembarked in Lisbon and flew to Nice to visit the house. Next, we flew to Paris to negotiate the purchase of the house with the proprietor, only to learn that she was in hospital and would not be able to see us until the following week. Again our return would be delayed. Geraldo had flown in from Buenos Aires to await his mother's arrival in London. The only solution was to ask Ariana and Geraldo to join us in Cannes for the weekend.

"Meanwhile, Carla was going ahead full speed with the project of the house. She called Mr. Le Sucre, the attorney connected to Abboudi's bank in Geneva and instructed him to form a Panamanian company. He suggested a Swiss company instead. Le Sucre was in contact with us daily, so that, by Easter, we could spend the holidays in the new house with the children."

I underline with a red pencil the name of Le Sucre. This is something which will delight Silvia. The existence of Le Sucre in any dealings either with Carla or Abboudi's bank had always been strongly denied.

"Ariana and Geraldo arrived in Cannes, and from there on, Carla's attitude changed. She woke up tired and irritable. Confused, I put it down to her probable pregnancy.

"She continued to organize every detail for our Easter holidays. She wanted to add extra rooms to the house and was busily sketching other alterations. She gave the gardener five hundred dollars to buy plants and flowers and told him to clean the pool. On the day we were leaving for London, she even unpacked all our summer clothing, a tape recorder, underwear, camera, books, to be ready for our Vallauris holiday in April."

I stop reading for a moment, to think about Ben's version of the "wonderful love'" he shared with Carla. I wonder at his insistence that he saw no warning of Carla's change of attitude toward him.

I'm back at my homework and turn yet another page, "Within minutes of arriving at our flat in London, Carla showed signs of tension. She inspected every lamp, complaining that the burnt-out bulbs were never changed in her absence. She was convinced that something must be missing although, later, she found this was not the case.

"Next morning, after three days of tension, the fog lifted. Once again, we were laughing and joking. Carla arranged to have the canopy in the guest bedroom removed and stored. She wanted to turn this room into a cozy sitting room for the two of us. The following day, she bought a large bookcase and desk to be delivered within forty-eight hours. Another sofa had to be delivered the same afternoon. When all the furniture was delivered, dissatisfied by the overall effect, she was ready to start again. I was surprised that, even though she was so tired, shopping was still a must.

"Her plan to visit the doctor was postponed. During those days in London, I did not feel the same 'oneness' as in the previous weeks. Yet there were no angry words between us. She was just irritated with the youngsters. Ariana remarked that it was the first time in four years that all the children were together with their mother. Carla snapped back that the last meeting was only two years ago.

"In spite of the friction, our evenings at home were typical of a family reunion.

"Then one morning Carla announced that she had not slept well. Restless, she had paced up and down all night in the sitting room. While I was having my bath, she called out, in a harsh voice, that my coffee was ready. I couldn't understand this abrupt change in her behavior. Every morning since we had met, she used to come into the bathroom and spend a few minutes teasing and talking to me. Something was seriously wrong. I left the bathroom to ask Carla what was the matter. Again, she said that she was just run down. But when I insisted, she finally told me that she was feeling confused about everything, that she was wondering if we had not made a mistake in marrying so hastily and that she was not even sure whether she loved me. I was devastated, not only by what she said but also by her cool attitude.

"I reminded her of how deeply we had loved each other and how I still loved her. But her answer was that she needed to spend a few days alone to sort out her confusion. Afterward, she was sure everything would be as wonderful between us as before. I loved my wife so much that I agreed to do anything she thought might help her. She said, 'I want to be alone but *I do not* want to leave the house.'

"I understood, Carla was asking me to leave our home. She said she knew how uncomfortable it would be for me to be at a hotel or at my father's. Meanwhile, she was already packing some of my clothes into a suitcase. Deeply hurt, I didn't utter a word. I watched her pack my whole life into that suitcase. Overcome with emotion, I asked her to forward my luggage to my father's home, and I left.

"Once in my father's flat, I hoped she would call, but she didn't. I couldn't wait any longer. I phoned and asked if she was feeling better. She said yes, but she was busy, and would call me back 'in a few minutes.'

"Another two hours passed. Again, I telephoned. Carla calmly told me that, after thinking it over, she had decided not to call me back. I begged her to be honest with me, to tell me what had happened. I had to see her, if only for five minutes. After a moment's hesitation, she agreed and suggested that she come over to my father's flat right away.

"For the third time that day, I waited. For hours. For nothing. Finally, I phoned again and was told by Conrado that his mother had 'gone to see Mr. Felix,' who had just arrived from Brazil. After putting down the receiver, I thought that Conrado's voice seemed peculiar. So I rang back. This time one of the maids answered and said that Conrado had just gone out and Madame had 'gone to see Mr. Felix.' The way it was said, it occurred to me that Conrado and the maid were repeating instructions. I decided I had to find out. I took a taxi to my wife's flat. The butler opened the door. I asked if my wife was in and was told that she had 'gone to see Mr. Felix.' Again, those very same words. Ignoring the butler, I strode to our bedroom. Carla was there. She did not seem embarrassed as she led me into the study. Affected by her apparent nonchalance, I reminded her of the promises we had made to each other to always tell the truth. I could not accept the sudden collapse of our relationship without a reason.

"Slowly, her aloofness vanished as she moved into my arms. We kissed and held each other for a while. I felt the horror coming to an end. She said she was confused but still wanted me to be her husband. With the help of her doctor, whom she would visit in the morning, she would overcome her doubts.

"At seven-thirty, that evening, Carla told me she had promised to visit Mr. Felix at the Mayfair Hotel. She said she would be back within an hour and suggested I wait for her so we could have dinner at home, just the two of us. I drove her to the hotel. As I escorted her to the door, she was lighthearted and happy and told me not to run away. She would find me wherever I tried to hide. Elated, I thought my wife was back with me.

"Eight-thirty. Carla was not home. The table was set for two. The maid asked if I wanted to have dinner. I said I would wait. At nine-thirty still no news. Again the maid asked if I was ready to eat. No, I would wait for my wife. I became frantic. I started to phone all the numbers I knew in London, where I thought she might be. First, the Mayfair Hotel for Mr. Felix. There was no reply from his room, nor could he be found in the hotel.

"I then thought that, with the court case coming up in London, Carla must have gone with Felix to see the banker, Abboudi. I knew Abboudi was in London from the twenty-four yellow roses Carla was receiving daily. She had told me that she had had an affair with him and that he was still managing most of her business interests. So I called the Dorchester Hotel to ask Abboudi whether Carla was there. In his soft middle-eastern voice, he expressed his surprise that, after six weeks of marriage, the groom didn't know the whereabouts of his bride. To that remark, I replied how appreciative I was of his very delicate gesture in sending my newly married wife the roses. And I hung up.

"Every fifteen minutes, I phoned the Mayfair Hotel, paging Mr. Felix, to no avail. Finally at midnight, five hours after dropping off my wife at the hotel, I received a visit from Mr. Felix and Mr. Azario, an executive of Abboudi's bank and also a close friend of Carla's. They explained that Carla was very confused and needed a few days on her own. It would be ungentlemanly of me to expect my wife to stay in a hotel, when my father's flat was available for me. Felix said that Carla occasionally behaved irrationally but advised me to respect her wishes, it was the only chance for her recovery and our future together. Dazzled by this continuous seesaw of events, I insisted that, as her husband, I expected the courtesy of her telling me all this personally. Azario answered that our marriage had caused her to be under great pressure and at present she was under sedation, so it was impossible to contact her. I realized that the two men were envoys with instructions and that whatever I said was useless. I walked out. Again, I was in a taxi going to my father's flat.

"A week went by without a word from my wife. On two occasions, I went back to collect some clothes. I telephoned several times a day, spoke to Geraldo, and saw him just as he was leaving for Buenos Aires. I spoke to Ariana several times on the phone and saw her when I went to the flat. I spoke to the maids, the butler and the chauffeur. At length over the phone, I talked to Conrado, to Azario, to Carla's other sister-in-law and closest friend in London. I spoke to Carla's doctor on various occasions, I tried to reach her in hotels in Paris, Geneva, St.

Moritz and again at the Dorchester. I left urgent messages for her to call me, but she never did. Finally, I found out that she had called Conrado from Switzerland.

"Having just had my 'emotional earthquake,' reality started to sink in. Now I was confronted by another problem, financial rather than emotional. I began to understand that I had been trapped. The decorators who were working on my apartment set an immediate deadline for the payment of their account.

"When I had been away, Carla had taken the key to my apartment to oversee the renovation. Without my knowledge, she had called in builders and decorators and approved major works. Knowing that I had an account at Harrods, she ordered two thousand pounds worth of unnecessary decoration, bathroom fittings, carpets, and other items. Upon my return, I received the bills and became aware of this folly but Carla appeased me, saying she had taken care of everything and that there was nothing due to anyone after her shopping spree.

"At the same time, Abboudi's London bank and Carla were being sued by Henrique's mother and sister. The undeclared assets left by Henrique were at the bank in the name of a corporation. The lawsuit had been brought to prove that the assets were Henrique's and therefore part of his estate. The corporation's bank statements clearly showed that Henrique had paid his life insurance from that account as well as the children's schools and personal payments on his credit card, leaving no doubt about who was the real owner of the account.

"It was dangerous for Carla, as executor of the will, to be proven a resident in London, as she had not obtained probate for Henrique's English assets. Mr. Le Sucre had therefore advised her, not to have a bank account in England. This forced Carla to make periodic trips to Switzerland, bringing back ten to twenty thousand pounds in cash each time. Occasionally, these sums were brought to her by friends such as Azario.

She was therefore frequently in need of cash and I made out checks to advance money, which she said she would pay back at a later date. Carla had been reluctant to tell me that most of this money had been for additional expenditures at my apartment. She gave me various other reasons to obtain the extra thousands.

"When we had disembarked from the boat in Lisbon, Carla had telephoned her flat and asked her chauffeur to fly down from London with two suitcases of clothes for her to wear in Cannes and Paris. Before his return to London, Carla told me she had to pay the London staff with a check to be cashed by the chauffeur. Again she suggested my writing a check for a larger amount, in case we were delayed further.

"I didn't have the slightest hesitation in giving her any amount she asked for. I knew she was unable to have an account in England. When Carla inquired about the amount she owed me, I said I could not give her an exact figure. But that we would have plenty of time to discuss the matter when we returned to London. Only after her disappearance did I realize I was ten thousand pounds out of pocket in loans and advances. Now, I had a further nine thousand pound demand from the decorators who would not finish my apartment, which was a shambles and could not even be used. Unless they were paid right away, they threatened to declare me bankrupt.

"Harassed and afraid that there would be more bills for me to pay, it occurred to me that maybe Carla had planned all of this beforehand. I recalled that, when I was about to leave for the Far East, she had asked for the keys to my father's flat. She had said that she wanted to send in her staff to clean it thoroughly while my father was away. Upon my return, I found out that the furniture, carpets, and curtains had all been replaced and the place had been completely redecorated. Yet nothing in my father's flat was more than a year old. Outmaneuvered, I could not make out if my wife was sick or evil.

"A week later, frantic, I received notice from Carla's British lawyer that she was asking for a divorce. In exchange for my cooperation in the immediate dissolution of the marriage, she was willing to pay the decorator's bill and the money she owed me."

Big Ben strikes noon. Finally I have finished "small" Ben's saga. I don't know what to do with all this. How can it help me regain my property? It mostly reflects Carla's need for success, power, money. But now I understand even better Carla's and Abboudi's manipulations. They will stop at nothing. I realize the danger I am in. They will try to take my company away from me.

I look out of the window. It's raining. I put a Do Not Disturb sign outside the door, take a bar of Toblerone chocolate from the minibar, drink a bottle of fizzy water, brush my teeth, kick off my shoes, and, fully dressed, throw myself, exhausted, on the bed.

I wake up the next morning at seven. I've slept for almost eighteen hours. My mind is a blank. Under the door I see a stack of messages which I hesitate to open. Then the call of duty is stronger than my feeling of laziness. I drag myself out of bed. My body aches. I can hardly move my left shoulder. I remember that man. "Leave now, while you still can!" Then the cable I sent. I open one message after the other. Each one says the same. "Urgent. Call Senhor Reptilbaum." Two messages from my office in Sao Paolo, three from the one in Rio, three from the Swiss lawyer. Good! The telegram was effective! I know that whatever I say over the phone will be taped and shown to Abboudi. And, if possible, used against me. I look at my watch. Fifteen minutes past seven. In Rio it will be four hours earlier. Perfect. Three in the morning. I call Reptilbaum at home. I wake him. Dazed, he asks if I can hold on, he wants to find his glasses. I smile to myself, he must have made some notes and wants to turn on the tape recorder. Had I called him at the office, he could have had a witness on an extension. He yawns and fumbles and I apologize for having misunderstood the urgency of returning his call. Then I hang up.

After a long bubble bath, using every little bottle the hotel puts in bathrooms for its guests, I go back to bed and order a big English breakfast. I am reading the news paper when my phone rings. It's Silvia who has just arrived from Paris and has checked into my hotel. "I have plenty of news, *querida*," she says.

"So do I."

"See you soon."

"Not too soon, Silvia. I'm still jet-lagged."

Half an hour later, my doorbell rings.

"Coming!" I shout. Reluctantly, I get out of bed. I slip into a long sleeved robe which covers the black and blue marks on my arms. I run my fingers through my hair as I open the door.

"Sorry to burst in on you like this. I couldn't wait to see you." Silvia puts her arms around me and gives me a Brazilian *abraço*. It hurts my shoulder. I decide to say nothing about the violent warning I was given.

"Come in, Madame. How can anyone resist you? Always full of surprises!" I manage to keep a straight face. I am fascinated by her warmth, her effusive way of talking.

She ignores me as she enters the room, walking past me like a gazelle. Tall, slender, elegantly dressed in a simple Dior light gray suit, she is, as usual, devastatingly attractive.

She looks around the room and comments about the differences between her suite and my miserable room. "Aren't you rich yet?"

"I'm super rich! But not for long."

"Rich enough to own a disposable helicopter?" She bursts out laughing, her white teeth showing through her red, sensual lips. Just like Henrique.

"Are you ready? Your news or mine?"

"I'm older than you, so I go first," says Silvia. "Hold on! Are you free for lunch tomorrow?"

"With you, I'd love to. Is that your great news?"

"Impatient, aren't we?" She gives me a whimsical smile. "We are lunching tomorrow at Mirabeaux invited by a young man I've never met before."

"What? A blind date? The two of us?"

"Two nights ago in Paris, a man called from London. He first apologized for ringing me so late, then said he would like to meet me when I was next in London. I told him I was planning to arrive today and asked him what it was all about. He then introduced himself as Mychkine."

"As in Dostoyevsky's *Idiot*?" By now I am really curious.

"Precisely. He then said, in a mysterious voice, that he would prefer not to talk too much on the phone. I asked if he could give me some indication of the nature of the matter. He whispered that he might have some useful information in connection with my lawsuit in London. If I could meet him for lunch the day after my arrival, he'd tell me more. So we agreed for tomorrow, and I told him there would be two of us. Before he hung up, I gave him your name."

It's my turn now. With a smile, I hand her my twenty pages to read and Ben's visiting card. Benjamin Halva.

I draw the curtains by the sofa and switch on the light. She sinks into the armchair and puts on her reading glasses. She reads. I am silent. I sip my tea and watch her face framed by the curly ash-blonde hair. In bold capital letters I read her delight.

When she has finished, she gets up, gives me a short peck on my forehead.

"Good girl. Thanks. I am duly impressed, Miss Sherlock Holmes . . . I'll pick you up tomorrow for our blind date." She winks at me and takes a grape from the breakfast tray. Then she turns around and smiles, raising an eyebrow. "Ah, I almost forgot to tell you. I've finally got hold of all the documents which prove that, at the time of Henrique's death, his son Antonio was not yet his son—Carla, his wife, was not his wife—Stelhio, the shareholder of the paper factory in Brazil, was not the owner." She paused. "However, a week after Henrique's funeral, Senhor Reptilbaum had fixed most of these 'impediments.' He was compensated for this useful work when he was made president of the firm. Unfortunately, he had to undergo the inconvenience of plastic surgery on the palms of his hands. A great way to remove his fingerprints and cancel any trace on the papers he had falsified. Reptilbaum can now recover his peace of mind!"

"Did you tell him that, when you saw him?"

"Yes. Of course, I did. It's hilarious, isn't it?" and Silvia triumphantly closes the door on her way out.

XLVIII

The room at Mirabeaux is not full. It is still too early for the in-crowd to be there. I suspect that the man who called Silvia in Paris and the one whose confession I heard and read are the same. I look around and can't see anyone who looks like Ben in the bar. I am disappointed not to be able to surprise Silvia.

The head waiter approaches us with the perennial "May I help you? Under what name did you make your reservation?" From the other side of the room, in the far corner, a young man stands up and waves at us. Silvia nods and walks straight toward him. I follow. Ben greets us very politely. Silvia does the introductions. He looks at me, frowns. There is an interrogating look in his eyes.

"We have already met. I listened to your confession!" I say. "Remember, we promised to meet each other again shortly!"

"Of course," he says.

I can't believe my eyes at the change in him, from the helpless victim of the other night to this self-assured man with a deep, very masculine voice.

Silvia, being the eldest and most important woman, is seated on his right. I am on his left, as would be an old acquaintance. I am the only one who is not at ease. I reach for a napkin to twist on my lap and tell Ben that I have updated Silvia on his story. That I hope I have not embarrassed him. "Not at all. On the contrary," he answers and looks at me with his bedroom eyes. I can smell his cologne, which seems fragile among so much free-floating testosterone. "Shall we order?"

After the first course, Silvia asks Ben, "So why did you want to see me?"

"I'd like to be useful to you, if I can."

"Well, what is it you have in mind? And why?"

"Because of the way I've been manipulated and threatened. I was tricked into signing compromising papers, treated as a blackmailer, and threatened to be sent to jail if I set foot in America again."

I say, "You're going too fast now. Let's go back to what happened after you received the notice of divorce from Carla's lawyer?"

He turns to me, "Oh yes. With the decorator's and other bills plus the money she owed me, I found myself under financial pressure. Carla's solicitors, aware of this trump card, used it to force me into cooperating with an immediate divorce. They would pay off the bills and her debt to me, and I would sign the papers. I had no alternative but to accept their ultimatum. They also promised that, after signing the agreement, I would be able to see my wife. I signed, but I did not see Carla.

"Disgusted, I left for the United States and took a trip at random to get away. I was looking for a way to rebuild my emotional equilibrium. I couldn't cope with the idea that I was not given the possibility to see Carla and know from her why she had acted like that. The more I thought about this, the angrier I became. So I decided not to cooperate with Carla anymore unless I could see her, speak with her and get an explanation."

Silvia, with a smile, nods knowingly at me. How could Ben believe that Carla was ever going to meet him? As Ben's tale is unwinding, all signs are pointing to his need of growth hormones for his brain.

"She will never confront you, or be allowed to confront you," ventured Silvia. "Has it ever occurred to you that you were used as a decoy?"

"Decoy of what and for what?"

"Don't you realize how you were used?"

"She might have started with that intention but then she really got involved with me and loved me."

Silvia smiles. "Come on, by showing off with you, she wanted to prove that Abboudi was not involved with her and was not handling the business. Also, she wanted Abboudi to realize that he had lost her and would also lose the business she brought along with her."

"Now that I come to think of it, I remember she did say that she had tried to convince Abboudi to marry her. He resisted the idea saying that, with all the lawsuits going on, it would only complicate matters. But then, when we married, she did tell me that Abboudi was stunned. He couldn't believe she'd go as far as marrying me."

Silvia says, "They were two accomplices in an extremely remunerative scheme! Now they'll have to stick to each other for as long as they live."

"I never thought of it that way, until I had that friendly approach from a Mr. Leon Schnitzel, Carla's new lawyer."

"You mean another lawyer in this free-floating paranoia?" I interrupt. "How did this one come in?"

"Carla's lawyers had decided that we would be divorced in Reno, Nevada. At her expense, they retained two lawyers, one for her and one for me. I was given a form for a Power of Attorney which I was to fill in and deliver to the one who represented me in Reno."

"By then you must have been pretty deranged by all the goings on," I ventured.

"I was furious! So I just told the almighty lawyers that I wouldn't sign the paper until I saw my wife."

"Quite a fixation on wanting to see your wife! I doubt if it helped to soothe the atmosphere," I say.

"By the time I reached Los Angeles, Carla's solicitors in Lodon had become increasingly hostile. They threatened to sue for damages because I was delaying the divorce proceedings. The cheek! Not only did they not keep their promises, but they were going to sue me! Now I'd had enough! I insisted I wouldn't give her a divorce unless I saw her beforehand. No way, was their answer. I could only see her once the decree was passed. At that point, I said, 'Fine, if that's what you want. But then I want a compensation for the emotional, physical and financial damage I have suffered.' I asked for a settlement of two hundred and fifty thousand dollars. I told my Reno lawyer I'd only send him the power of attorney once the financial settlement was agreed to. He said that he would relay my request to Carla and be in touch with me within the next two days."

"Had you asked for a settlement before?"

"No. Not prior to this telephone conversation. I hadn't made any demands besides repeatedly asking to speak to her. I needed to understand what had happened and whether there was any possibility of getting back with my wife. But the lawyers continued to threaten to sue me for 'heavy' damages. So I decided I would fight with whatever means were at my disposal."

"Didn't you realize that you had entered the ring with some real heavyweights?"

"I didn't care anymore. I wanted them to know I'd had enough of being treated like a doormat. The money I was asking was peanuts compared with the enormous amounts Carla and Abboudi had been dealing with in their illegal transfers! I was furious and determined to defend myself. So in a cable to my solicitor in London I mentioned these transactions, the paintings that were smuggled out of Brazil and a few other things I knew about. I added that I was chucking all the divorce procedures and that I was returning to London in two days."

"Was the bomb you planted effective?"

"It must have been, or so I thought at the time. Suddenly, I was informed that Carla wanted me to be in touch again with Mr. Schnitzel in New York, her newly appointed attorney. I telephoned Schnitzel and spoke to him at length. He said he knew nothing about what had happened and asked me to tell him the story of my marriage and its subsequent breakdown. He was most supportive and said he could understand my anguish. He assured me that 'something' could certainly be worked out and that my proposal for a settlement was 'reasonable.' The way he talked gave me the impression that he was trying to protect my interests as well as Carla's. However, before coming to any conclusion, he wanted to go on a 'fact-finding trip' to various places, including Geneva.

"Schnitzel was very punctual in calling me back. In a friendly manner, he told me that seeing Carla was out of question but that my request for a settlement was acceptable to his clients. But the settlement would have to cover the divorce and a waiver of my rights to Carla's assets. Abboudi and Carla wanted a protection against any monetary demands I might make in the future. And that I wouldn't disclose the financial transactions mentioned in the cable to my solicitor. I stated that the contents of that cable had nothing to do with the settlement. It was an answer to the threats I had received to be sued for damages. Schnitzel then told me he would think about the best solution and send me a draft agreement that would protect everyone concerned.

"I returned to London. Convinced that the matter was resolved, I told my solicitor not to take any further steps on my behalf. Finally, Schnitzel assured me that a copy of the draft was being mailed to me. The draft omitted the names of Abboudi and Carla, referring to them only as the 'other people.' The payments were to be made to me in installments over a period of one year.

"Further drafts were sent. I asked why there was no mention of the divorce settlement. Schnitzel assured me this agreement was only to protect his clients from any future demands on my part. Another agreement would have to be drawn up to cover the divorce proceedings. He insisted on a separate document. I objected to the way the document referred to threats and demands on his clients. He said he understood my repugnance but that it was the only legal protection for his clients he could come up with. Though I relied on Schnitzel's goodwill, I continued objecting to this one clause, but he argued there was no way he could eliminate it.

"More drafts went back and forth. I finally drafted my own agreement, adding the names. As I continued to be concerned about the clause, Schnitzel suggested I should come to New York and work it out with him."

Silvia exchanges a conspiratorial look with me and turns toward Ben. "Excuse me for interrupting, but I'd like to ask you just one question."

I hold my breath. I'm familiar with Silvia's reactions, her impatience. Just like Henrique, she has the answer before the question. She already knows the ending of the script. She just can't wait.

"Did you fly to New York? Did you take a lawyer with you to the meeting or at least did you take any legal advice?"

"I just went on my own."

"Like going shopping for satin bed sheets at Bloomingdale's?"

"How did you know? I bought two sets, ivory and light blue."

"I thought you would! I guess you needed some cheering up before the meeting. A kind of relaxation."

Afraid that Silvia would add, "what a fool" to her comments, I quickly interrupt. "When you went to Schnitzel's office, did you take the agreement you had drafted?"

"Yes I did. But when I asked at the reception desk for Schnitzel, I was told that Mr. Schnitzel wasn't there. Mr.

Caponsky, his partner, would see me instead. I was shown into a luxurious, intimidating room. The man behind the desk smiled as he got up. He looked like a casino owner watching me with his vulture eyes. 'You've been highly recommended,' he said. Then we chatted casually for a while until I saw a book of poems on his desk which led to a discussion on our shared love of poetry. Immediately, Caponsky gave me the book and said he hoped I would enjoy it. He added how distressed he was that Schnitzel had had to leave town in a hurry, to see his mother, who was seriously ill. However, Schnitzel had left an agreement with him for me to sign. The agreement would be signed by Schnitzel on behalf of Carla and Abboudi when he returned. There was only one copy of this agreement to be placed in their safe.

"I didn't notice at the time that, on the agreement he handed me, there was only one signature line, with my name beneath it. The prior drafts had contained lines for both signatories. He asked me to sign the agreement.

"I told Caponsky that the clause I had found objectionable had not been removed. I was particularly surprised because Schnitzel had assured me on the telephone that it would be eliminated when we met in New York. Caponsky told me he had no knowledge of any changes and was unable to discuss this with me. He couldn't change a single comma in the agreement. I suggested that I'd wait for Schnitzel's return and work it out with him. Caponsky said that Schnitzel's mother was very ill and he might not be back for weeks. I couldn't extend my stay in New York for more than two days. I told Caponsky that it would have been quite simple for someone to advise me of Schnitzel's absence, before I left London.

"Caponsky agreed that it was unfortunate and suggested that I sign the agreement as it was and work out any modifications directly with Schnitzel, over the phone or by letter. Faced with the alternative of going back to London, returning to New

ROSITA FANTO

York again, fatigued with the unending discussions, drafts and letters, I signed."

"Really?" I glance at Silvia. Obviously she, like me, can't see even a sparkle of dim voltage in his brain's battery.

Ben Halva goes on, unruffled. "Then, Caponsky gave me a check for ten thousand dollars, for the first installment.

"A month later, Schnitzel phoned to tell me that Carla's divorce case against me had to be completed within four weeks. He asked me to travel to Reno as soon as possible where the marriage settlement agreement would be ready to sign. He emphasized that he had added a provision for me to receive an extra twenty five thousand dollars as a result of my cooperation with his clients and the amicable relationship we had developed. There was one more bonus. Carla had finally agreed to have a meeting with me in Reno, prior to the divorce. I could tell her whatever I wanted. I was thrilled with the bait. Schnitzel announced that he had also worked on a new version of the agreement I had signed, excluding the clause that bothered me. Reinforced by his assurances, I flew to Reno."

Ben pursed his lips. He had been speaking without batting an eyelid. Now he caught his breath. "I signed the papers which waived my rights to Carla's estate, delivered my power of attorney to my attorney in Reno and did not contest the divorce proceedings which Carla had started. Schnitzel was in Reno. I reminded him of his promise that I would be able to speak to Carla. He told me she wasn't feeling well that day but would meet with me the next day. The twenty five thousand dollars were paid to me. I never saw Carla, except for a brief glimpse of her in the court room.

"During this time in Reno, Schnitzel repeated that it would be better to treat the two hundred fifteen thousand dollars, the balance owed to me, as a business transaction. Ready to cooperate, I was unconcerned how Abboudi and Carla were treating the payment. While Schnitzel was considering the best way to conclude the financial part of the marriage settlement, he told me it was necessary to validate the Reno decree in England.

"I therefore instructed my solicitors to cooperate with Carla's to speed up the proceedings. Meanwhile, Schnitzel asked for more information which he apparently needed to decide on the form of the commercial transaction which would be part of the famous agreement. Weeks went by. During this period, he phoned to assure me that all was going well regarding the commercial form of my marriage settlement. He asked me to name the companies in which I had an interest. Officially, Abboudi and Carla could then be purchasing one of these companies. Though I wrote to Schnitzel furnishing him this information, I added my preference for a straightforward divorce settlement. Another month went by and Schnitzel sent me the letter from the Brazilian attorney who insisted upon the commercial transaction.

"Cables, letters, and calls continued until I received confirmation from my solicitors that the English validation of the Reno divorce was completed.

"Shortly afterward, I got a cable from Schnitzel saying that the financial settlement was imminent.

"I flew to New York on the agreed date. Schnitzel's office had made my hotel reservations. Next day, I went to his office to sign the final agreement. That day, I was received by Schnitzel and Caponsky in their big conference room. I was first asked whether I'd ever been represented by a lawyer. Then abruptly, with a short laugh, Schnitzel informed me that it wasn't their, nor their client's intention, to pay me anything above the thirty-five thousand dollars I'd already received. Caponsky added that the agreement I had signed at their office could be used as evidence of my blackmailing and extortion attempts, if I ever told anyone about what was in the signed agreement. Through their powerful connections, they'd have me extradited from England to America where I'd be put in jail. The same would happen to me if I disclosed to anyone the circumstances under which the agreement had been signed. Caponsky said he would see to it personally that I would end up in prison.

"It came as a shock to hear the meanness in their voices when they described prison life. I'd be lucky to come out alive or, at best, sane. In closing, Schnitzel told me that Abboudi and Carla would do nothing further provided I remain silent."

"The back and forth cables, all the complications, all of this, only to get Carla a divorce?" I ask.

"Yes, Mrs. Huntington. Incredible! Their only purpose was to stall for time and get the divorce proceedings through. I was appalled that attorneys could resort to this sort of gutter tactics and blackmail!"

"Carla has achieved everything she wanted from you." With a touch of admiration in my voice I can't disguise, I say, "Abboudi has quite a team!"

Silvia isn't surprised. She had worked it out before the end of Ben's story.

"I know what these people are capable of." She pauses, as if she's thinking it over, "Would you be willing to sign an affidavit on everything you've told us?"

"Yes. With pleasure."

"Are you sure?"

"Oh yes! I have nothing more to lose."

"Then I'll have a solicitor call you and take down all the points you have raised. I hope you don't mind if he asks a few questions." She reaches into her pocket book and removes a note. "Do you remember, Mr. Halva, the address Carla had in her passport?"

"Yes. An address in Geneva."

"Do you remember what it was?"

"Yes, I even have a copy of her passport with me, showing her address."

"May I see it?"

From a black crocodile wallet Ben takes out two neatly folded sheets of paper and hands them to Silvia.

There is a long pause before Silvia smiles and says, "Of course, the address is the same as Abboudi's."

*   *   *

"Leave while you can!" The words keeps ringing in my head. I am having nightmares now. Sinuous ropes, serpentines, harpoons thrown at me. I find it hard to concentrate on my work. Leave! Get out! But how can I? All this disrupts my routine. It turns my life upside down.

I never utter a word about the warning I had. To no one. It would be far too unbelievable even to Tom who, with Armand, is back from the shoot. Just for the weekend. Then he'll be off again. The four of us are inseparable during this time in London. Saturday we lunch at San Lorenzo. The place to be seen and to see who's in town and be kissed at the entrance by Mara, the owner. Sunday we brunch in the Grill at the Connaught. The conversation is mostly about quails and pheasants. Silvia joins the chatter while the mantra in my head keeps repeating, "Leave, while you can." I'd only spoil their fun, their joie de vivre, if I told them what happened.

I look at Silvia. I am so close to her, she could be my alter ego. I understand her every thought. Strange how Henrique managed to have my fate depend on hers. If she loses, I lose. His way never to let me go. To be in my life no matter what. I must cut myself off from all this. Determined, I slice a piece of the venison on my plate and take an angry bite.

XLIX

Silvia wears a new hat in court that Friday. Her elegance is certainly noticed. The judge, in his wig and robe, sits high upon a podium facing us. We are seated on the rows of benches, like in an amphitheatre.

Ben's affidavit is even more detailed than we had expected. It clearly points to Abboudi and his bank. It points to the bank employees who were instrumental in helping transfer Henrique's fortune into Carla's and Abboudi's laps.

Abboudi's council asks the judge to retire to the chambers to take notice of the new discovery. They are afraid of the press because of the nature of the affidavit, detailing the intimate relationship between Abboudi and Carla.

The way everything has gone, there seems to be no doubt about where justice lies. The sentence has to be favorable to Silvia.

On Monday, however, the mood changes. Even Silvia's pompous barrister, Mr. A. C. Robin, in a moment of amnesia, forgets who his client is and attacks her case with ironic nastiness. I never liked him from the start, but now I despise him. The judge makes a 360-degree turn after the payoff he must have received over the weekend. However, the bank's motion to strike out the proceedings is dismissed. I can't believe this is possible in England.

*   *   *

We are going to meet our respective husbands at the Cadogan Hotel where Silvia and I are planning to have tea. In the lounge is the exhibition of drawings by R. Fanto for the Oscar Wilde Playing Cards, which we all want to see.

As I am about to enter the hotel from Sloane Street, a black Cadillac slows down. The tinted back window is lowered, and a hand waves a black handkerchief. Then the car takes off. Again I say nothing to Silvia besides, "I wish the policeman who arrested Oscar Wilde here would arrest the bastards we are fighting."

Silvia displays a bitter smile as we enter the hotel and sink into the puffed up armchairs. In the cozy lounge where people whisper rather than talk, we order their five o'clock high tea. Orange Pekoe, scones, heavy cream, three different kinds of jam, and small watercress, cucumber and egg sandwiches—a ceremony not to be neglected. After a few minutes of the ritual, I look Silvia straight in the eye.

"Silvia, I hope you don't feel any responsibility toward me."

"What are you trying to say, Rozalia?"

"Perfect strangers are getting hold of what belongs to us. If we go on fighting, they'll win. They'll get hold not only of our possessions but of our lives."

"Yes, *querida,* I know."

"Enormous amounts of money have already been spent. Trips, lawyers, long-distance calls. We've had our fun in the name of principles and justice. The obvious result is, it leads nowhere. Now, let's be practical and constructive."

"What's on your mind?"

"Silvia, do you want to devote the whole of your life to fighting for justice in the courts of law? There is no way you'll ever win. There is no hope of succeeding. Every verdict to

every lawsuit will be bought. Corruption is their strategy . . .
You can go on and on, until nothing is left. Yet, there is a way
to change this, and then wait for life and time to do the rest."

"I suppose you're right. Even Felix Klein once told me they
are on the inside and I am on the outside. They can use my
money to buy off anyone they want for as long as they want.
Felix said they have ways to deal with any situation. They have
friends. In *their* world, anyone can be bought." Silvia now
has the smile of someone starved beyond hunger. "*Querida*
Rozalia, what is it you want me to do?"

"Chuck it all!"

"I don't get it, *querida.*"

"Chuck it and let them choke on it with time."

"How do we do that?"

"We hand over to the Brazilian Government all documents
proving the illegal transactions made by Carla and her crew,
to Abboudi . . . Let the government deal with it! They'll fine
the . . . out of them. At least someone will get something out
of all this!"

"You're serious?

"Yes. If you knew that part of what you give up would be
going to build schools, roads, and orphanages, would that
make you happy?"

"Of course, Rozalia, I'd like that!"

"Do you want to think it over and talk to Armand and Dona
Edithe about it?"

"No, Armand doesn't want to hear about this. And Dona
Edithe is so emotional, no one can talk to her."

"So it's a deal?"

"Yes, without any hesitation. It's all right with me. How
about you, Rozalia? No regrets?"

"None. Just let me have the bank statements you carry in
your bag, before the two hunters return."

"There you are." Silvia slides the envelope into my bag as the two husbands come through the door. They look healthy and happy from their hunting trip while we look pale and harassed even with all our makeup.

*   *   *

I have no trouble making an appointment the next day with Dr. Andrea Silva Ramos, the lawyer in the legal department of the Brazilian Consulate. He is ready to see me right away. I explain. I show. We meet again and again. He wants to thinks about this. He is young enough to still have ideals. He wants to check that everything will be going into the right hands. All the way to the president. He wants this bomb to come as a surprise. Without warning, without bribes.

"It's strange going through all the papers again," I tell Dr. Andrea Silva Ramos. "It almost feels dirty." He listens with interest to my story. He knows all about Henrique, about Mondial, about Banco Universal, even about RB International. He is appalled to learn of the injustice that is going on.

He flashes a smile. His eyes narrow. He gets up from his chair, moves to the nearest window, then turns around and looks at me. "Do you know what you are asking me to do?" I nod. "Don't you want to keep even a part of this money, Dona Rozalia?"

"No. Nothing."

How about Dona Silvia?"

"The same. Nothing!"

"The fine charged to Carla and Abboudi for illegally transferring money out of Brazil will be enormous! Also Carla, as the executor of Henrique's testament, will be fined for not declaring most of the assets. Let alone the English and Swiss Bank accounts!"

"I know. As long as it will be used for building roads, hospitals, orphanages, and schools."

"In the name of my government I thank you." He points to the bottom of the letter. "Please sign here."

I sign the letter that will be sent to the Ministerio da Fazenda, and the one to the president of Brazil. I attach the pile of documents and bank statements. Included is a list explaining each transaction and proving the origin of the funds. I join, as a reminder, the copy of the cable I sent to Felix Klein.

Dr. Andrea Silva Ramos says I have given him a treat, the likes of which he has never encountered before! He then asks if I am doing this out of anger. I shake my head. The only reaction I have is one of relief.

Months later, Dr. Andrea Silva Ramos tells me the successful result of what I had initiated. I know that Aunt Josephine, not necessarily Doctor Gastel, would have been proud of me. She would have said, "You came with nothing, you leave with nothing." I remember her making tea in a samovar, putting the silver spoon in a glass with a silver handle, pouring the boiling tea. Two lumps of sugar, a slice of lemon. The home-baked cake on a plate with tiny hand-painted flowers. She told me then, "There are many roads to choose from. You'll have to decide which one to take. There is no suitcase to carry when your mind and heart are filled with treasures. All the rest is ephemeral."

*   *   *

Silvia's pain, though fiercely felt, is controlled. There is no self-pity in her grief. Having lost her brother, she feels no despair at her financial loss.

Abboudi's and Carla's lawyers receive a well-deserved Oscar nomination for their work. One of the lawyers is made President of Abboudi's bank in New York, another is named

President of the Brazilian conglomerate. A couple of them pass away, leaving substantial assets to their heirs. After Carla's divorce from Ben, she and Abboudi have to tie the knot "until death do us part."

But one day, years later, everything Carla learned with Abboudi is being used to take care of him. Edgar Abboudi departs life dramatically. Choking. Does crime pay? The answer is: Crime Pays. There is no justice in the courts of law.

Carla enters a new life, from shades of gray into blinking neon lights. In her social whirls, and in her unrelenting quest for social status and respectability, she donates gifts to charity. I understand Carla's determination to get all she can.

Oh! There is more. Carla makes it into the places that really matters to her. FORBES Special Issue. Billionaires. The World's Richest People. She moves from one home to another with a battery of lawyers, and an army of bodyguards.

*   *   *

I stand under the shower. The cold water runs down my skin. I scrub and scrub myself hard. So hard that, had I been tattooed, the marks would have faded. I watch the water run down the drain. Everything else is going down the drain. Is there nothing I can do besides watch? Emotionally I feel naked and vulnerable. I am a powder keg in search of a match. I must get away! I would like to go home if only I knew where home was. The wanderer in me has found in Tom a strong and sheltered harbor. But now, I want to cut myself free to recuperate. Only by leaving everything behind, do I feel I can go forward. Survive, with humor with irony. At sixteen, I boarded the Bahia leaving for Brazil, leaving behind the Johan in me. Freeing myself from fear, from all constraint. I'll have to start all over again. From nothing. I'll keep flying, flying, flying never to come back . . . flying from nowhere to NOWHERE.

I arrive at the airport. I don't want to be rushed. As a frequent flyer I can turn up at the last minute and be taken straight through. But then I'll miss the airport feeling, which I find soothing. There will be nothing more to decide for the duration of the journey. Nothing else to do besides inhale the special airport odor which is something like mashed rubber tires mixed with a dash of fuel and puree of cactus.

When I am at the counter and hand in the ticket with my passport, the girl at the check-in asks if I have any hand luggage. I stare at her. She points at the three pieces of elegant brown luggage with the engraved initials R. B. I shake my head and explain that I am not the owner of the monogrammed luggage. I am curious to see the passenger on my flight with the same initials as mine. I look around but see nobody who suits the luggage. I check in my own two elegant brown but unmonogrammed suitcases.

In the first class waiting lounge, between biscuits and tea, I wonder which of the passengers fits the initials. Nobody looks like someone connected to the mysterious luggage. I am about to pursue my search in the ladies' room when my flight is called and I am escorted to the plane. Minutes later I am seated comfortably. I am the only passenger in the cabin. The stewardess hands me a pillow, a blanket, a package with socks, and all the necessary tools in case we end up on a desert island and I need to brush my teeth and file my nails. There are many other first aid gadgets to discover. Though by now I should know what is in these packets, I always open them with the enchantment children experience under the Christmas tree.

I fasten my seat belt, take a deep breath of the airplane odor, plug my ears with the gadgets, draw the curtain by the window, and doze off.

When I open my eyes the plane is above the clouds. The stewardess passes with the trolley. Plenty of caviar, champagne, and other basics for first class passengers. In as low a voice as possible I whisper, "Please can I have hot water with a slice of lemon." I am glad the elegant elderly lady with gray hair seated in the opposite aisle doesn't hear me. She must have boarded after I dozed off. I can see her profile, with the turned up nose and dark glasses, as she nibbles at the miniature blini with caviar. After a while, she gets up and heads toward the bar. She looks slim in a striped gray pants suit. A bluish silk sweater blends perfectly with the color of her hair. Three rows of pearls cover part of the wrinkles on her throat. On her wrist, she wears a man's watch next to a twisted gold chain. A signet ring and a thin gold wedding band on her pinky are the only ornaments on her long fingers. Her hand, covered with liver spots, holds on to a brown leather beauty case engraved with the initials R. B. So this is the person belonging to the luggage!

My eyes are glued to the elderly R. B. I see the mirror of myself reshaped by the passage of time. I hear through my earplugs the monotonous sound of the engine. In delineated perspective, I visualize an immense emptiness that is both terrifying and seductive, infinite and precise. Even the twisted gold chain on her wrist and her signet ring are like mine! I begin to imagine her naked body under her impeccable appearance, the sagging breasts, the wrinkled flabby skin pale, and cold . . .

I close my eyes, bemused by the feeling of suddenly knowing everything before it happens. I find myself trying to piece together my own experiences. I want to understand my life, to await old age with serenity and be prepared to erase the past. Distorted by time, past events can't be the same in the light of present circumstances. My trepidations as a young girl were not the same as my trepidations today. I was one person then, now I am another. Everything can be rearranged piece by piece into endless patterns. I can wait to be in my nineties to sit in front of a window and think about life's meaning. But by then, my thoughts and preoccupations will be for immediate problems. Incontinence. Arthritic pains. Senility. My medicine chest, like the Bible in every hotel room, will be in a drawer by my bedside.

Have I survived because I was Jewish, Catholic, Christian, Agnostic—a God-fearing Agnostic? The eclectic part of me was the board I floated on, toward survival in any society at any level. Saved by humor, irony, objectivity. There was nothing heroic about my life's journey, I did what an accountant would do. I had no choice, sink or survive. I chose to survive. I'll never know why. I swam because I didn't know any better at such an early age.

There is no special pathology to my attitude. I will never forget the injustice I have suffered and the crimes that have gone unpunished, but I believe that forgiveness restores human dignity. It is not out of altruism, but forgiveness is the best way of avoiding the dehumanization that hatred brings. Hatred is too much of a one-way street. It leads nowhere except to self-destruction. I am still too busy trying to live the rest of my life. So I keep walking, even if at times I drift off, until again I am on a road that leads to a beam of light.

Nothing can ever compensate for the lost years, the suffering, the dislocation. My grief has never died. It only has relented a little after a long time. Some things have lost their importance. What was, is not what is. What is, is not what will be. Changes continue. I see the small snowball rolling in the snow on the landscape of life. Particles are added. The ball rolls on. It grows in volume. Then, it vanishes in time and space, corroded. It becomes powder, then water, then disappears into earth, into NOWHERE.

We will land shortly. Will Tom meet me in a yellow sweater with an armful of yellow flowers as he always does?

"Are you comfortable?" I open my eyes. "Please fasten your seat belt. We are about to land," says the stewardess with a smile.

Acknowledgments

I began writing this book ten years ago, when I saw photographs and documents on what had happened in Romania to Jews in the late nineteen thirties and early nineteen forties. I was outraged by the silence kept by those who knew about the barbarities of the Légionaires and the Iron Guard. About their use of the "train of death" in which Jews of all ages were packed alive in train cars with no windows, no doors, no air, no food, no water, on top of each other in heat of 130 degrees, until they were asphyxiated, and died. This and other inhuman acts had been practiced by organized groups not known by the world.

When I was in Brazil, I saw documents, and forgeries by a powerful group of shady international bankers who got hold of a family conglomerate after the death of its Founder. In exchange for a hefty sum of money, the local police declared that his death had occurred by suicide, with two bullets in his heart. Again I witnessed total silence to a known crime. I then decided that Injustice had to be revealed. In telling my story, I started in my own way on a quest for Justice.

During my research in Bucharest and Jassi I was helped by Sonia Seinberg Cerbu and Guta Bogdan. Brigita Forssius offered a source of valuable data on the role of Swedes during this period. For the Marseille episode Andre Dimanche has been most valuable. Jean Pierre Lacroix described Monaco during the war on the telephone from Paris. Gianluca Tramontana told me about the traveling folk poets in the interior of Brazil. Harold Shiff and other lawyers furnished the legal documents for last part of the story. Elisabeth Scharlatt gave the title.

I am especially grateful to Clinton Smullyan, Ellen Carol Jones, Morris Beja who courageously read the draft and suggested many improvements. With thanks to Nikki Mannering, Carmen Firan and to Sally Arteseros for editing help.

About Rosita Fanto

Multi-lingual, multi-cultural, multi-exiled, and multi-assimilated, R.Fanto has gone from Romania to Brazil, the United States, Switzerland, Italy, England, France and Monaco. She has undergone one transformation after another: teacher to author, artist-publisher to film producer. Her manifold credits span the range from a documentary on Henry Moore for French television to "Presage," a unique visual and tactile publication that grew to 300 volumes and is exhibited in major museums including the New York Metropolitan, Kent State University, the Victoria and Albert and the Louvre.

She has been the originator of countless unusual and offbeat ventures. Collaborating with Richard Ellmann on "The Oscar Wilde Playing Cards Book," she produced a new form of literary criticism. On her own, she created "Ulysses a Vaudeville, The James Joyce Cards," which has also been acclaimed for its successful stage decor on the set of Bloomsday On Broadway at Symphony Space in New York. A jubilant, free-style sequel in book form, *Joker's Joy*, snatches clips and snips from the press to the delight of Jokers and joyful Joyceans alike. Two earlier Mood Strips *Hope* and *Escape* are illustrated emotions in five languages. This is non-traditional storytelling where the word integrates the picture. *Lady of the Cards and the Biographer* tells the story of an affectionate friendship between two elderly people.

Ever-ready to debunk a serious literary or pictorial subject, R.Fanto believes that strong light can enlighten or can blind, and that High Culture should be accessible to Low Brows. For her, the impossible does not exist. Nor are there any problems; only solutions. Above all, she finds the temptation to make something out of nothing irresistible.

Get Published, Inc!
Thorofare, NJ 08086
25 February, 2010
BA2010056